CARLY FELDMAN

The Eosiaid

BOOK ONE OF THE SKY QUEEN TRILOGY

For my grandmother, Carolyn Kimball
September 2nd, 1930 - March 11th, 2024

Whose grand adventures in life,
Whether on a bike, a plane, or horseback,
inspire me to create my own adventures.

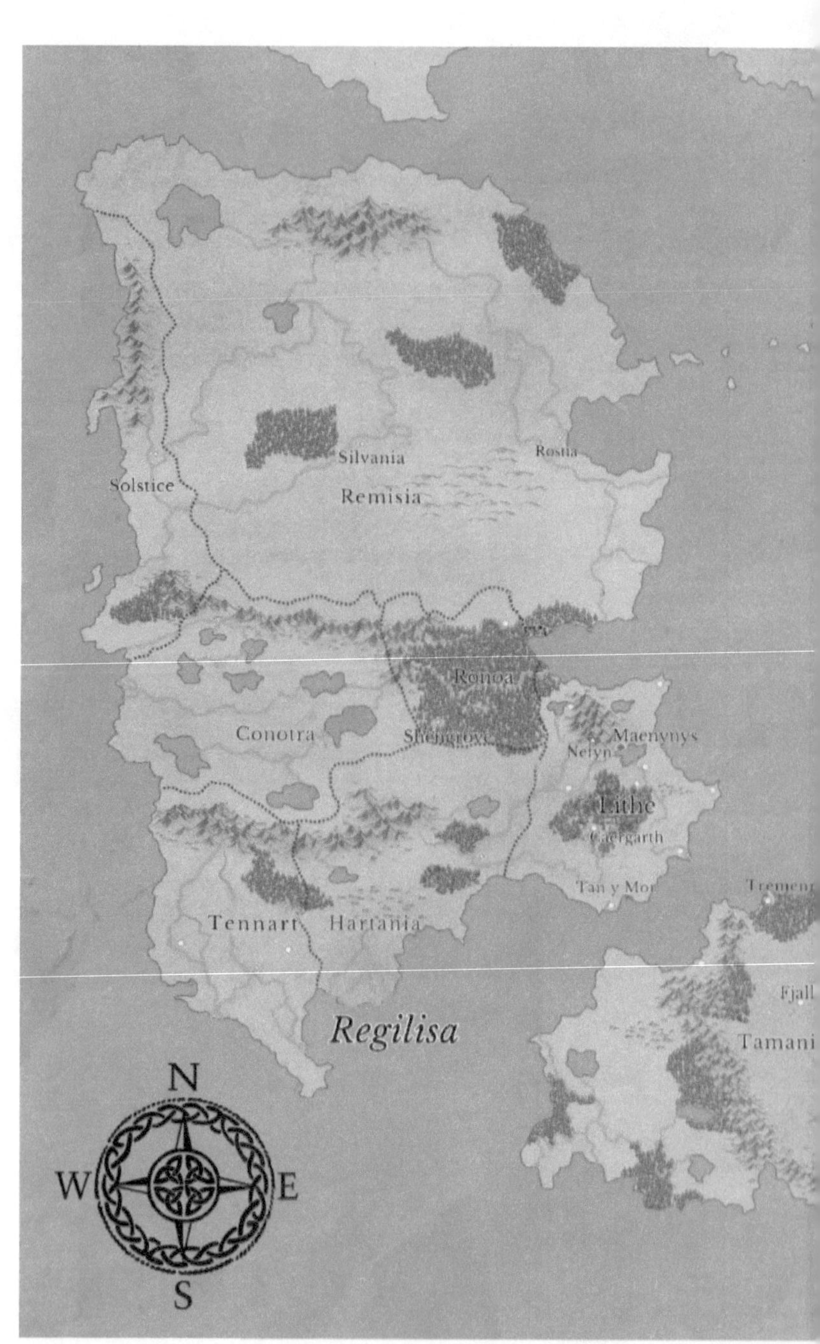

Solstice
Silvania
Remisia
Rostia
Ronoa
Conotra
Shengrove
Maenynys
Nefyn
Lithe
Caergarth
Tan y Mor
Tremen
Tennart
Hartania
Regilisa
Fjall
Tamani
N
W
E
S

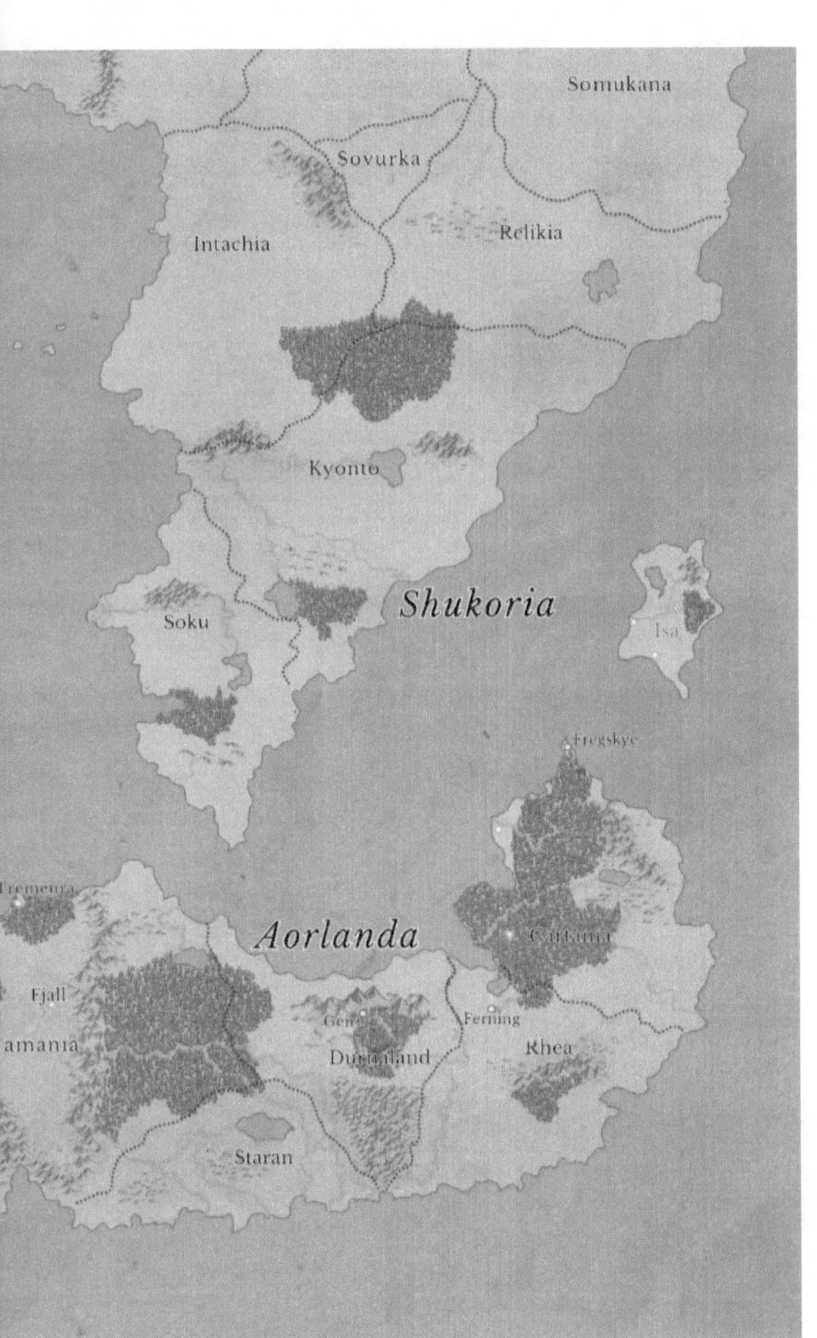

Somukana
Sovurka
Intachia
Relikia
Kyonto
Shukoria
Soku
Isa
Fregskye
Tremenra
Aorlanda
Carunia
Fjall
amania
Gen
Ferning
Durmland
Rhea
Staran

Contents

Preface

You say you want to know the moment I knew everything had changed. But the problem is, there wasn't only one moment. There were thousands, millions—shards of memories, seconds, and heartbeats, where the past was suddenly the past and the future was suddenly the truth. I can't parse these apart or find the one with the heaviest weight—the biggest piece of glass from all of these shattered memories. Too many are equal in size and shape to hold value over the others.

No, they all rely on each other. They build together to form this stained-glass history of my life, and this kingdom, and this world. If you want to know the moment, you must know all of the moments. And the first moment was when the priestess spoke in her low, clear voice on my twenty-second birthday, the words echoing through the cavernous temple and its towering golden dome.

1

The Inauguration

"You will be much more than our Benadur, Aneira Elfyn."

I looked up at the priestess from where I knelt on the cold marble tiles, as she stood in her white flowing robes trimmed with gold, the altar of the Sky Queen rising behind her. Head Priestess Gywenn smiled down at me with her softly curved lips and secretive brown eyes, her long black hair falling in waves around her shoulders.

Flecks of snow-white ash fell from my forehead, where she had just anointed me with the Fire of the Sun, the ashen residue left after a certain kind of tree was burned at a certain time of day. I couldn't remember all of the details. A purely ceremonial event, I had to be marked with the ash by the head priestess before my public inauguration, to ensure that the Sky Queen herself knew of my ascension.

I felt anxiety flutter through my stomach as I made eye contact with her and heard her words fall away around me. There was no one else in the Nefyn Temple of the Sky Queen. Witnesses were not permitted at this ceremony. As a result, I felt less hesitant in asking for clarification, as I knew my father wouldn't find out and, therefore, wouldn't berate me for doing so.

"More than a Benadur?" I asked her, too timid to form a longer, more coherent question. Her smile grew yet maintained its simple kindness as she bid me to stand before her, and I did so as she spoke.

"Some Benadurs are remembered throughout history for their deeds. And you shall be one of them."

I resisted the urge to frown and managed to keep my composed expression. "Why…why do you think this?" It didn't sound likely, and I had always been wary of the priestess's predictions.

"I am attuned to the movement of the stars, as you are attuned to the power provided from them," she said, and the cryptic answer was all I needed to disregard her prediction. I smiled as pleasantly as I could and nodded, knowing that any further questioning would lead to equally unsatisfying answers.

"It is time for the inauguration," Gywenn said, looking at me with an intent smile. "Are you ready?"

I hesitated as she stepped down from the dais, my eyes sliding past her and onto the statue beyond.

The Sky Queen was always depicted the same way: Her hair was said to be made of sunlight, so the locks of the statue were covered with shimmering gold leaf. Her irises were gold as well, and she was always donned in layered robes of varying shades of blue, representing the skies. The statue before me, raised on a carved marble altar that looked out over the temple, was slightly larger than life size, if we were to believe that the Sky Queen truly took the form of a human. I wasn't so sure—especially now, I was more in disbelief of her than I ever had been in my life. Because it simply didn't make sense that I was standing there, with ash on my face, about to become a ruler of a province. Even as part of me was stunned by the beauty of the icon, hair and eyes glowing in beams of sunlight filtering through the many skylights in the golden dome above, I was wracked with doubt.

It was a small province, the province of Nefyn, and the capital city in which I lived was a proportionately small city, with only about a thousand residents. Yes, I would become a ruler, a Benadur, but with limited power. And still that power terrified me.

All of these thoughts would be viewed as heretical in the eyes of the priestess standing beside me, as they directly conflicted with the teachings of Awyrcred, our system of belief, our way of connecting to the Sky Queen. I tore my eyes away from the statue. Only a couple of seconds had passed since Gywenn had asked me the question, but she was already looking at me with an open, curious face. The kind of face I wanted to be honest to.

But I lied. "Yes. I'm ready," I said as I forced a smile.

She nodded with a calm smile, gesturing for me to make my way across the rotunda, and I paused for only a moment before beginning the walk across the white tiles, every footstep echoing with intention. It was like the room was made to amplify every sound, and I felt like I could hear my heartbeat every time the echo of my steps reverberated back to me. The wooden benches that were usually placed in rows through the center of the room for the monthly sermons had been removed, and it made the temple feel uncomfortably large and imposing, the air still and cold around me. Gywenn followed behind me after a moment, but I knew she would remain inside the temple, as her part of the ceremony was over. Large double doors made of solid gold stood out against the marble walls on the other side of the room, and I knew I was to open them without touching them—once again, a part of the ceremony.

When I neared them, I reached out with my mind and felt them clearly there—their massive weight and cool, smooth surface, and exactly how much pressure needed to be exerted for them to open. And then my mind pressed out against the doors, and light spilled from between them as they obeyed my force.

At first, it was too bright for me to see what was beyond, but then I discerned the deep blue of the sky, and the white stone of the courtyard, and the road beyond that led away from the temple, and the vibrant shimmery green of the trees that lined both sides of the road. As I passed through the golden glow of the doors on either side of me, I saw Calliten waiting outside, a tight smile on his face, along with a troop of twenty-two stoic guards, all in full regalia and plate armor. He would be leading the procession, this ceremonial march from the temple to the city square, fulfilling his role as the elder Benadur, leading the younger one to power.

I felt some hope I hadn't been aware that I was holding onto falling away. He would not be warm today. He would not act like my father, though he was. He would act like my superior only, expect only the best from me, and be kind to me only if I met his expectations. It was a weak consolation for the last few years of irritated, biting criticisms and passive aggressive comments. Though he stood before me, I knew that my father wasn't really there.

Calliten was wearing his finest clothes, a maroon coat and dark trousers, and everything was embroidered with gold and silver in intricate designs. His long golden-blond hair was tied back in a low ponytail with a matching maroon ribbon, and his green eyes were as cold and calculating as usual. A few wrinkles around his eyes and mouth showed his years, but overall he appeared quite youthful.

The company turned to face away from me as I came down the few steps that led to the courtyard, and Calliten turned a moment after them and indicated that the march would commence with a single hand signal. I knew that I would follow him, and I knew not to speak a word—once again, a part of the ceremony. I turned back to look at the temple as we walked away, and saw the priestess standing in the doorway, her calm smile persisting.

We joined the road, paved with the ubiquitous white stone bricks that made up most of Nefyn, and the city was dead silent around us save for our own footsteps and the metallic stomping of the guards that flanked us. I tried to get control of my nerves, knowing that the ordeal was far from over.

The wide road cut straight through the heart of Nefyn to the city square, a massive, rounded courtyard where the stones were laid in intricate swirling patterns. These patterns led the eye to a stage, made of the same white stones, that was built up against the side of the Benadur's office on the northern edge of the square. The other sides were bordered with various establishments, offices, and a garrison for the city guards. The white stones reflected the early morning sun over the square, making everything and everyone standing in it appear unusually bright. The sun-warmed breeze was a slightly comforting contrast after the cold air of the temple.

Usually the patterns of the gray and white stones beneath our feet would have been very noticeable, intertwining knots and circles, but on this day they were impossible to see. The city square was filled to the brim with people, the entire population of Nefyn. Over a thousand people.

All waiting for me to appear.

I only realized that the square had been filled with the noise of chatter once it had died down at the arrival of my party, and an unnatural hush fell upon the people. I became more aware of the blood rushing through my ears, my heart pounding, but I forced myself to concentrate on moving forward. A walkway had already been cleared for us to pass through, and I kept my eyes looking straight ahead, as it was incredibly unnerving to be subjected to so many people staring at me.

We finally reached the white-stone stage, and Calliten indicated for me to climb the steps first. I ascended the stairs with heavy, definitive footsteps, now allowing my eyes to flash from face to face in the crowd, never lingering on anyone in particular. My heart nearly beat out my chest, but I ignored it. The people stared back at me, some smiling and some not, all with open, captivated expressions. Then Calliten joined me, coming to stand a few feet to my left, and the guards moved to surround the base of the platform.

Calliten smiled at me but I saw the iciness behind it, and my face remained blank. I didn't have the capacity that I normally had to behave civilly towards him. He didn't hesitate in commencing the ceremony as he stepped to the edge of the stage, and fully assumed his public persona.

"Aneira Seren Elfyn," he said in a clear voice. "Eosiaid the Younger, of the year 314, fifth age."

Some cheers and clapping emanated from the crowd, but most remained silent with rapt attention.

Calliten turned to me, and I saw how the smile didn't reach his eyes. "People of Nefyn. Your Younger Eosiaid has served you well these past twenty-two years, and now has completed her training. In my eyes, in the eyes of the Sky Queen, and in the eyes of you, our citizens." More cheers this time, and Calliten paused strategically, knowing exactly when the crowd would react to his words. "She has one final test, one last example of her power. The Eos will heal now," Calliten said, with a performative, sweeping gesture of his left arm.

I cleared my throat impulsively as two guards carried a podium up the stairs, and set it gently in front of me. Staring down, I saw exactly what I expected, what I had been dreading.

The small bird lay on its side, unmoving. It was past trying, too tired to even try to fly away. Its bright colors made me pause for a moment in surprise, with its vibrant purple wings and yellow chest—I had expected some sort of common bird, like a sparrow. But I recognized this as the rare and coveted Myneth nightingale. I cradled it in my hands, careful to avoid the broken wing, and held it up for the crowd to see as I had been instructed to do. It was as light as air, and simultaneously downy soft and rigid with beak and talons. The people were silent, expecting.

The silence was numbing, and my hands began to tremble, the bird shaking slightly as a result. I took a deep but shaky breath, keenly aware of Calliten's eyes on me. If this went wrong, it wouldn't just be his disappointment I would have to deal with. If I was unable to heal the bird, if it were to die, I would be seen as unfit to ascend to the title of Benadur by all who witnessed this. Officially, I would have to return to training for another two years, but after witnessing my failure, it would be difficult for the people of Nefyn to trust me again. It would be a rough two years of proving my worth to them, over and over again.

I had been healing for almost my entire life. It was the most important aspect of my role as an Eosiaid and a future Benadur. As we had healing abilities, it was our duty to help the people we served with their illnesses and injuries. But now, as I looked down at the bird and the prospect of losing my reputation and wasting my next two years, I felt like I had never healed before.

My pause was too long for Calliten, and I heard him quietly clear his throat behind me. I blinked, knowing that sound of displeasure, and steeled myself. I closed my eyes, looked inward and found my power, and began to trust myself again.

My power flowed from me to the bird, a healing energy that felt gold in my mind, but was invisible to the eye. I did not touch the bird besides how I held it in my now-still hands, but felt the broken bones with my mind, and pieced them back together. The bird opened its eyes slowly as strength began to flow back into its muscles. The shards of bones and torn muscles moved under the feathers and skin, and I looked away quickly, disturbed by the sight.

When the bird stood in my hands and began a song, I stopped the mental reorganization of its body parts. I set it back down on the podium, where it gave a few hops before jumping into the air and flying away above the crowd.

This was met with loud cheers and calls, a celebration of the inauguration of a new Benadur, a new leader, a new healer. I was all of these things, born into it as so few were. I had been training my whole life to fulfill my duties, and that day, on my twenty-second birthday, I was officially a Benadur of the Province of Nefyn, Kingdom of Lithe.

And the worst part of it all was that I never wanted any of it in the first place. The excitement around me was something I could not access, something I could not feel. Why would I want power when I had no power over my own life? Why would I want adoration when there was nothing to adore?

A smile hid these questions from the crowd as I stepped down the stairs, my destiny trailing behind me like a cloak.

>«

A horse was brought for me, and as the people still celebrated throughout the courtyard, causing my ears to ring with the sounds of their whoops and cheers, I was eager to get out of the city and back to my home. I mounted the horse as quickly as I could despite the elaborate dress I had been forced to wear for the inauguration and was led away along with Calliten, while the guards marched on either side of us once again. This time I rode before Calliten, and the sea of people parted again as we passed through. No one attempted to get close to us—the guards would have prevented it, and though the citizens of Nefyn were elated and energized by the events of the day, I sensed that they respected us far too much to even want to approach us. We weren't simply leaders to them. That was our main role, certainly, but we were also blessed by Sky Queen. We were Eosiaids.

Still, some people elected to follow us on our path out of the city, only falling back when we passed through the large gates and over the bridge that opened up onto the Nefyn plains. The green expanse was bright and glittery in the morning sunlight, and I felt relief course through me at the sight of my home, the Benaty, less than a mile away. It was made of the same white stones, rising above the sea of grass like a castle made of snow, and the white road led directly to it. As the city gates closed with an echoing thump that I felt in my chest, finally cutting off the sounds of hundreds of raucous people, I let out a deep sigh that I hadn't known I had been holding onto.

But only a few moments later, Calliten urged his horse forward to ride alongside me, and I looked at him with trepidation. There was never any way to know if he was pleased or not, until he was criticizing me.

"Your celebration dinner will be nearly as important as the ceremony," he said without looking at me, his eyes fixed forward as he maintained a regal posture in his saddle.

"Prominent citizens will be in attendance, as well as Benadur Hanien from Mynyddpen."

"Why?" I said without thinking, the mention of Hanien souring my tone. I regretted letting my emotions color my voice, as Calliten turned to look at me sharply, displeasure in his stern expression.

"Because I invited him," he said, before looking away from me dismissively. His voice was curt and tense, indicating that there was no point in asking more questions about the issue. I relaxed slightly, as I was relieved Calliten hadn't decided to lecture me for using a rude tone. Still, I felt quite a bit of disappointment at the realization that I would have to socialize with Hanien, a very pompous Benadur from a neighboring province. I hadn't known that he would make the journey to Nefyn for my inauguration, and I suspected that Calliten had forgotten to inform me on purpose. The more I knew in advance, the more I could interfere with whatever he wanted—or so he thought.

"Alright," I said blandly, knowing that nothing good could come out of complaining. The best course forward would be to just get the meal over with.

Once we arrived at the bailey of the Benaty, we dismounted and our horses were led away to the stables. Calliten glanced at me as we walked up the wide steps that led to the main doors of the Benaty, and something about his expression let me know that he was displeased.

"Go wash up. You still have ash on your face," he said.

A cutting reply came to mind, but I held my tongue. "Fine," I sighed as I approached the door, but apparently my worn tone was enough to upset him.

"No attitude in front of Benadur Hanien or any of our guests this evening, do you understand?" he said, his voice low and calm, contrasting with the angry glint in his eyes. I felt my lips press tightly together, my own anger growing inside of me, but I simply nodded. Without another word he turned back towards the heavy wooden doors and opened them with his own magic, the anger and force of which caused them to bang against the walls.

Once inside the doors, I turned away from Calliten immediately, climbing up the massive stone staircase in the center of the grand foyer, all the way to the third floor. I liked living on the third floor. Calliten's chambers were on the second, which meant I rarely had to see him on most days.

My room was perfectly mine, one of the only parts of my life that Calliten wasn't able to control. A large window complete with a cushioned bench looked down on the bailey, and the city of Nefyn in the distance. As I walked in, the curtains were opened and light streamed in, warming up the space after the chilly night had brought the temperature down. To the left of the doorway was my desk, currently covered in loose pieces of parchment and books and quills and bottles of ink. On the other side of the desk was a large, ornate bookshelf, and each shelf was nearly overflowing with books of all sizes, some with the binding nearly falling apart, they were so old. My bed was against the far left wall, piled high with pillows and blankets. There was little I loved more than a good night of sleep.

I walked over to my vanity and wash bowl against the right wall of my bedroom, which castle attendants kept filled with fresh water. I washed my face as Calliten had asked, the last of the white ash falling from my forehead with the water. I dried my face on a towel, also set out by an attendant, and tried not to study myself in the mirror. There was something uncomfortable about knowing exactly what I looked like before a meeting with Hanien. Something I didn't like about knowing what he was seeing.

Still, I couldn't help but take in my flushed, freshly washed cheeks, unusually ruddy against my pale skin and contrasting with the deep green of my eyes. I had always liked my eye color, but sometimes I wished it was less flashy, less noticeable. Sometimes I wanted to be able to blend into my surroundings, until I disappeared entirely.

>«

As I had a few hours to myself, I left the castle and searched the guards' quarters for my archery instructor, Triana. I found her sparring in the training yard, a sizable grassy enclosure on the southern side of the Benaty, and I watched for a few minutes as she and her opponent exchanged swings with their wooden training swords, the rods cracking against each other with every strike. I recognized the other guard as Rhys Llewellyn, who happened to be the brother of one of my favorite people in the world, Mariwen Llewellyn. Both Rhys and Triana were wearing light leather armor, and both were breathing heavily; I suspected they had been sparring for a while. Rhys was much taller than Triana, but I knew she was a more experienced fighter than he was, as she had begun her training a few years before him. Even I could tell how precise and agile her movements were, though I knew next to nothing about sword fighting. Rhys was holding up against her out of sheer force of will— or so it seemed to me. They were like opposing forces: Triana, small with long black hair tied into a braid, a narrow and determined face; Rhys, tall and broad with dirty-blond hair that shone brightly in the sun, his features calm and composed.

Triana turned suddenly and paused in surprise as she saw me standing a few yards away on the edge of the yard near the wooden fencing, and Rhys hit her with a solid rap on her sword arm, forcing her to drop her weapon.

"Ow!" she exclaimed, glaring at him for a moment as she rubbed her forearm. Rhys simply stared at her in surprise.

"Are you okay?" I asked, already feeling guilty for distracting her, and stepping towards her slightly. To my surprise, her pained expression fell away and she laughed.

"Of course, milady. Rhys just caught me by surprise," she replied easily.

"I'm sorry," Rhys said, stepping towards Triana as well, visibly uncomfortable.

"Wasn't the goal to hit me?" she asked him with a raised eyebrow.

"It was the goal…but I didn't expect to do it," he replied, eyebrows deeply furrowed.

"I'm sorry for distracting you, Triana," I said. She shook her head, her long black braid falling over her shoulder.

"The both of you need to stop fretting. It's just sparring, and it's my own fault for allowing myself to be distracted." Her left hand fell away from her right forearm, and she picked up the training sword from the grass at her feet. "How may we help you, milady?" Triana asked, smiling at me again. "I don't suppose you came to inquire about an archery lesson?"

I grinned back. "Only if you have the time. I'd like to do something fun today, at some point."

"Of course. Rhys and I were almost done anyway, so now is a good time."

The three of us walked to the armory, on the western edge of the training ground. It was a small wooden building, nondescript and the kind of building the eye just slid over, especially when viewed next to the large and imposing Benaty. The sun was just past its highest point, burning brightly in the clear azure sky above us, the air filled with the smell of warm grass and dirt. I was pleased to take a moment to just appreciate the day, despite the stress of the morning, and the coming stress of the evening.

"Did you hear the report from the border scouts?" Triana asked Rhys as they walked a yard or two before me. "Sawel said the Hartanians are mobilizing soldiers again."

Rhys sighed. "They're never organized enough to be an issue. Not to us, at least," he said quietly.

"Sounded different this time," Triana said with a small shrug.

"Why?"

"From what they saw, anyway. The encampments were bigger. And it sounds like Llanwenyth have had more trouble lately maintaining their borders."

I frowned hearing this, and noticed Rhys's shoulders tense. Llanwenyth was the province to our south that also shared a border with Hartania. Border disputes with Hartania were as old as time, but the kingdom had never posed a real threat to any of Lithe's provinces. Llanwenyth was slightly smaller than Nefyn, so perhaps that was why...

"If that's really how it is, then Maenynys will get involved," Rhys replied, releasing the tension in his shoulders with a shrug. I frowned at his words as well. Were these skirmishes enough to get the capital city of Lithe, Maenynys, and thus the power of the king, involved? I considered asking Rhys and Triana what they thought, but we arrived at the armory, and our attention turned to picking our bows and arrows for archery practice. Rhys was only there to deposit his training sword and bid us farewell as we strapped quivers to our hips and filled them with arrows.

"Are you sure you have time to be giving me a lesson today?" I asked Triana. She looked at me with a small frown as she handed me more arrows.

"Of course, milady. Don't worry about me. I need archery practice just as much as you do," she replied easily.

"Well, I doubt that," I said with a small, derisive laugh, and she smiled at me.

"Ready then?" she asked. I gripped the smooth recurve bow I had picked out and nodded with an answering smile, and we left the small building and set off across the training yard, where a small shooting range was set up on the other side. We passed a few sets of sparring guards, but most of them seemed to be elsewhere.

The range consisted of five bales of hay with burlap targets hung over them, and staged at increasingly greater distances from the shooting line. A wooden fence bordered one side, with the rolling green hills of the plains stretching into the distance beyond. Behind us was one of the outer walls of the Benaty. Triana and I were the only people at the range at that moment, and all was quiet. We did some simple arm stretches to warm up, and then Triana spent a few minutes simply watching me shoot and offering tips on my form. Though I had been shooting with her for over two years, and was now quite proficient with the weapon, she continued to critique me and offer me all of her insights as to where I had room to grow. Triana was well-trained in archery; she was likely the best archer at the Benaty. Calliten had allowed her to give me lessons, and I was still unsure as to what his reasons were. He never allowed me to do anything if it didn't serve some sort of purpose. Usually, he wanted to make sure I was well-loved by the townsfolk. I didn't see how archery would affect that at all, but I didn't want to jeopardize my lessons by questioning it.

"You're not expanding completely, milady," Triana said with a small, frustrated sigh at one point. I glanced over at her and lowered the bow slightly.

"I don't feel like I could possibly expand anymore," I protested, frowning down at the weapon.

Triana glared thoughtfully at the ground, her mouth pressed into a tight line. I knew she wasn't upset with me, only with her own teaching abilities. "Just…push more," she said finally. "There's always a little more you can do. You have to push yourself."

I had to stop myself from telling her that I was already pushing myself. "Okay," I said after a moment and turned back towards the target. Triana watched me for a bit longer, and after commenting that I was doing better, began shooting the target beside me. For a long time we simply released arrow after arrow, until our quivers were empty. We walked together to the targets to pull the arrows, and Triana began speaking. We had been quiet while shooting, so her voice surprised me a bit.

"I saw your ceremony today, milady," she said, her voice light and relaxed, and I thought she sounded pleased. "It seems that you did very well."

"Thank you," I said, although I was a bit tired from all of the congratulations. I had only done what I had been training to do for my entire life and healed a living creature. But I supposed it looked different to those without magic. And, I had to admit, for a moment the stress of the event had nearly overwhelmed me.

"I would imagine it was very stressful, though," she continued as we reached the bale, as though she could read my mind, and we began to pull our respective arrows out of the dense hay. "With all those people watching and everything."

"Yes, I don't really enjoy having so many eyes on me at once," I agreed.

"Well, I'm glad it's over then." Triana grinned easily as she turned back towards the shooting line, having retrieved all of her arrows. I followed soon after, smiling to myself.

I took a short break to ensure I didn't overexert myself, while Triana continued her shooting, her face set in concentration.

"Are you concerned about Hartania?" I asked her suddenly, right after she released an arrow. She watched it fly, hit the target, and then turned to look at me with questioning eyes.

"Oh. What the scouts saw?" she asked as she drew another arrow from her quiver and nocked it. She held her bow low as she considered the target and my words, her fingers light on the string. "I wouldn't say I'm concerned. I'm sure we can handle whatever they come up with."

I let her complete her shot before responding, the string twanging as she released her fingers, the arrow hissing through the air, and the thump of finality as it embedded into the bale.

"But if it's true about Llanwenyth…" I persisted. She turned to me with a smile.

"Still. We don't know how well trained Llanwenyth's soldiers are. We don't know exactly what's happening. But Nefyn has never had issues with Hartania, and I don't expect that to change."

I nodded slowly, and Triana picked another arrow from her quiver, then looked at me curiously. "Don't worry, milady," she said with another smile. "We have some of the best soldiers in Remisia here." I repressed a sigh, and agreed with her that I shouldn't be worried. I knew that I was just sensitive to change, always searching for any sign of danger.

"I know," I said, nodding. Triana returned to her shot and I ended my break, picking up my bow once again.

We continued for a while longer, until the sun was beginning to grow low in the sky and the afternoon breeze began to pick up. Triana huffed out a sigh after releasing an arrow, and turned to me with a slight frown. "My free time is over soon, milady. If you don't mind, I'm going to make that my last shot."

I nodded and set my bow down on a wooden bench behind us. "I should head back inside too. I'm sure Benadur Calliten is wondering where I am. And, unfortunately, I have to get ready for dinner."

After pulling the arrows from the bales one last time, we returned the equipment to the armory, and I dragged myself up to my room, where I began to prepare myself for the dull evening ahead of me.

»«

Dinner proved to be an odd affair. Though I had to dress up once again, I refused to put myself back into the elaborate dress I had worn all morning, and instead opted for a lighter, simpler lavender dress, but still ornate enough for such an important dinner. When I entered the dining room, the heavy blue curtains closed against the black night outside and lit with candles suspended on two chandeliers above and five candelabras that lined the table, I was a little surprised to see who exactly Calliten had invited to the event, as he had never deigned to tell me the specifics.

Besides Hanien, who sat just to Calliten's left, there were a few wealthy people from Nefyn and their family members present. There was Dylan Sayer, the elderly and old-fashioned wine merchant; Nia Evans, the serious and humor-lacking instrument maker; and Owain Llewellyn, the quiet and slightly eccentric owner of the most successful general store in the city; among a few other people that I didn't know quite as well. At the sight of Owain, I searched the seats near him for the flash of bright red hair, and felt a wave of happiness when I found it glowing in the light of the hundreds of candles that filled the room. The owner of the hair turned soon after I entered the room, and her wide smile mirrored mine.

"Mari," I exclaimed as I approached her, and she leaned on the back of her chair to face me.

"Congratulations, Eira! You looked amazing today," she said earnestly, her bright blue eyes wide and shining.

"Thanks. I'm so glad you're here," I said, as I finally glanced around at the people with her. Of course, there was her father, Owain, as well as her mother Deryn, on her other side. And next to Deryn was Rhys, Mari's brother, whom I had seen sparring with Triana earlier in the day. Owain was smiling at me pleasantly, and I blushed, realizing it was rude of me to go straight to Mari, when Owain was the reason she was there in the first place.

"Thank you for coming, Mr. Llewellyn," I said, a bit formally, but I reasoned it was better to err on the side of caution.

"Thank you for hosting us," he replied easily, and there was something so honest and genuine about his manner that I felt my anxiety melt away. Mari got her red hair from him, though it was turning gray on his temples, and he had kind and wise eyes with little wrinkles around the edges. For a moment, I felt a bit of envy—towards Mari, I realized with a wave of shame. Though I never would have said it aloud, I wished so much that I had had a kind father.

"Benadur Aneira," my father called from the end of the table, only a few seats away, the tight and displeased smile that I was so used to seeing already fixed on his face. Without another word I made my way to my seat on the other side of Owain, already knowing what Calliten's demand was. I sat down quietly, and as I did, the chatter around the table ceased. Everyone was aware that with my arrival, dinner was finally beginning. Calliten stood with a more pleasant smile on his face, and addressed the guests.

"Friends," he began, "we thank you deeply for your presence here tonight. Benadur Aneira and I feel blessed to have such a beautiful, wonderful, and prosperous city to live in—with much thanks to you and your families." Around the table people smiled at the compliments, though I knew Calliten didn't care about them personally. He was only buttering them up, so that he could maintain his good reputation around Nefyn. If only people had known what he was really like and what he really thought about them.

"Today marks the momentous occasion where my daughter, Aneira, has come of age. I hope you will welcome her with open arms as your new Benadur, an equal to me by all rights. She has worked hard to prepare for this day, and I know she will not let you down."

I blinked, stopping myself from openly rolling my eyes; there was no way Calliten actually believed that.

"Though I am truly filled with pride on this day," he continued, "it would be wrong of me to say that that is the only emotion I feel today. I can't help but miss my lovely wife Lara, Aneira's mother who loved her so dearly." He looked at me then, and I stared at him, caught off guard by this whole commentary. Calliten rarely brought up Lara, who had died of a rare disease, a fearfully deadly one called the Wood Death, when I was only four years old. Truth be told, I had so few memories of Lara, I thought about her even less often than Calliten mentioned her. "She would have been very proud of you," Calliten said directly to me, and there was something genuine in his eyes, something that I didn't want to comprehend.

He paused, regained his composure, and put his performer persona back on. "To you, Aneira. May your time serving this city and province be successful and auspicious," he said as he raised his glass of wine towards the chandelier above us. Around the table, everyone grabbed their glasses and mimicked him, the many glasses twinkling in the candlelight.

"To Benadur Aneira," Hanien said as he lifted his glass, and smiled at me from across the table.

"To Benadur Aneira," came the echo, and I blushed as everyone ceremoniously took a sip of their wine after the toast. As they did so, Calliten leaned towards me and whispered, "Now you must say some words. Stand up."

I glanced at him, fighting back a glare, and nodded curtly as I stood. Somehow this was almost as intimidating as healing the bird in front of a thousand people, but I knew I had no choice. It was a dinner in my honor, after all. Everyone's eyes fell on me once I was standing tall, and

Calliten sat down, allowing me to be the sole center of attention.

"I would just like to thank you all myself for being here this evening, and enjoying this meal with me," I said, putting all of my energy into sounding calm, kind, composed, and grateful. It was a complicated mixture to perfect. "It means so much to me to have your support, and I promise to be a just and attentive Benadur to you, and to all of Nefyn. Now, I…I think we've been waiting long enough. Let's bring out the food, shall we?"

This was met with a light smattering of applause and happy murmurs in agreement, and I took my seat, knowing that the worst was over. I glanced at Calliten, and was surprised to see an odd look in his eyes, one that I had almost never seen.

"Good job," he said brusquely as a server set down the first course in front of him, and I realized then what it was. It was approval.

2

The Discovery

The dinner went by quickly afterwards, and I was overjoyed when, at one point, Owain kindly switched seats with Mari so that I could speak with her at length. I had befriended Mari when we were children, at a Benaty dinner much like the one we were at that night. Her carefree nature and fathomless sense of humor entertained me to no end, and she seemed to enjoy my personality just as much. Whenever we got together, it usually ended up with us both laughing until we couldn't breathe.

I couldn't allow that to happen at my inauguration dinner, however, and I could already tell that Calliten was displeased the moment Owain and Mari switched seats—but I hadn't been the direct cause of that, as it had been Owain's idea, so I couldn't see how Calliten could get angry with me for it. Mari and I were so invested in our silly conversation, that neither Calliten nor Hanien could even break in, which I was perfectly fine with. So it was that I avoided speaking directly with Hanien that night, and had yet to be chastised for such an accomplishment. I went to bed happy and full of good food, thankful that Mari had been at the dinner, which had made it all the more pleasant.

The next day, however, I knew I would be unable to avoid him any longer. Putting off this meeting would only serve to hurt me in the long run.

I was awoken by a castle messenger knocking on my door, and I answered with bleary eyes. Through the cloud of fatigue, I was informed that Calliten had called for me to attend an early lunch with himself and Hanien. I made some noise of understanding, shut the door, and fell back into bed. But I knew there was no possibility of returning to sleep, now that I knew how my day would progress.

Within an hour I was up and dressed, making my way to the dining room. The dark wooden doors, carved with intricate patterns of leaves, were even more imposing now than they had been the night before. Now I knew exactly who was on the other side of them, and there was very little chance of this meal being pleasant. I took one last deep breath before gripping the cool bronze handle and pulling the door open.

Hanien and Calliten sat at one end of the long table, the tall windows behind them illuminating the room with bright sunlight, the dark blue curtains pulled aside to let in the natural light. They both looked up as I entered, pausing in their conversation, and both stood to welcome me, as was customary whenever someone arrived for a meal.

"Congratulations, Benadur Aneira," Hanien said, his smile wide and warm, and almost convincing. I crossed the room to stand on the other side of the table from him, and returned his smile, as both men studied my reaction.

"Thank you, Benadur Hanien," I said.

"Sit across from the Benadur, Aneira," Calliten said, a little bit of impatience coming through his voice as he took his seat at the head of the table. Hanien and I sat near him, on opposite sides of the table, making it difficult for me to avoid eye contact with our guest.

"Your ceremony was wonderful yesterday. From where I stood, it was quite an impressive performance," Hanien remarked, that warm smile remaining on his face. "Although I apologize that we were not able to speak last night." I knew very well what sort of charm he possessed. Kind brown eyes implored me to provide a heartfelt response, his handsome face deceptively open and compelling. I knew he was handsome, with clear olive skin, well-groomed facial hair, and long dirty-blond hair tied back at the nape of his neck into a braid. He wore expensive clothes too, his royal blue coat embroidered with gold thread, just like the dress I was wearing.

I didn't have much experience with men in a romantic sense, but I had developed a healthy amount of skepticism towards people in general, mostly thanks to Calliten's twofaced nature. He, too, could be quite charming when he needed to be, and I was terrified of being manipulated by such people.

"I hadn't known you planned to attend," I said, just as a servant set down a glass of honey wine in front of me. I took it quickly and sipped, using it as an excuse to not elaborate and to not comment on the fact that I had obviously been too busy the night before talking to Mari, and that was the reason he had been unable to speak to me.

"Of course. Little would have kept me from seeing such an important moment in your life. After all, Mynyddpen and Nefyn are deeply connected and have been allies for hundreds of years." My eyes flicked to Calliten's face, which was unusually blank as he held his glass in his hand, periodically drinking from it, while looking at Hanien.

"That's...that is true," I managed to say. "Well, I thank you for coming to show your support. It is greatly appreciated."

"No need to thank me. You must be quite relieved that it's over," Hanien said, before taking a small sip of his own wine. "To no longer be considered an apprentice—I remember how wonderful I felt on my own inauguration day."

I nodded and cleared my throat, though I didn't need to. He was only a couple of years older than me, but spoke with such a patronizing tone. "Well, yes, it is nice to not be an apprentice. I…I hope the people trust me."

"Did you see them?" Calliten broke in, a slightly mocking smile on his face. "They absolutely love you."

"Love and trust are two different things," I blurted out, and an awkward silence followed. My mind raced with ways to fill the silence as Calliten stared at me with displeasure, and Hanien's smile fell just a bit. But thankfully, I was saved by the servants, as they set down small bowls of soup in front of us, our first course. I began to shovel the soup into my mouth, not pausing to consider the temperature or even what kind of soup it was. I just wanted this lunch to be over.

Calliten and Hanien followed my lead, although at a much more polite speed, and conversation naturally ceased as we ate. But soon the small amount of soup was gone for each of us, and our bowls were quickly cleared as we waited for the next course in the meal.

"May I ask what your plans are for your second appearance?" Hanien asked, sounding genuinely curious. Calliten looked at me expectantly, bidding me to provide a decent answer.

"Ah yes. I believe I will be healing a guard who somehow broke their leg," I replied, my hands fidgeting underneath the tablecloth.

"That will be quite visual, I expect. I'm sure many people will come out to see it," Hanien replied, sounding impressed. "When will that occur?"

"One week from today," Calliten broke in, not trusting me to give the correct answer, even though I had certainly known it. I hid my scowl as best as I could, but also hoped that

Calliten entering the conversation would take some of the pressure off of me.

"I wish I could attend, but I will have returned home by then," Hanien said, with the perfect amount of remorse in his voice, his brows furrowed and eyes downcast. I was surprised, and though I certainly wasn't disappointed by his words, something about the way he phrased the sentence made me uneasy.

"When…when do you plan to return to Mynyddpen?" I asked.

"Tomorrow morning," he said, and his easy smile returned as he looked at me intently.

"I will be accompanying him back to Toryth," Calliten said, and I turned to him, even more surprised.

"Before my appearance?" I asked, confused. It didn't seem like something Calliten would want to miss.

"I'll be back by then. I'll only stay in Toryth for a day," Calliten said, his tone dismissive as a small frown appeared on his face.

"Benadur Calliten is going to help me with a small project." Hanien grinned, excited, and clearly wanted me to ask what sort of project. I opened my mouth to force the question out, but didn't have to follow through, as the next part of our meal arrived: roasted chicken along with an assortment of seasonal vegetables.

While we ate, Hanien and Calliten periodically commented on some political news they had heard from nearby provinces, eventually talking at length about some odd upset happening in Hartania, the neighboring kingdom to the southwest. They had often antagonized the provinces on their borders, one of which was Nefyn, but none of the little territorial skirmishes had ever led to larger battles. I managed to stay out of the conversation, listening to their dry and distanced takes with feigned interest. Triana had managed to convince me not to be concerned about these matters, but Hanien and Calliten were downright casual.

While we waited for the third and final course, Hanien forced me back into the conversation. "I was wondering, Aneira, if after this meal you would like to go for a walk with me around the gardens? I haven't been able to explore them very well, and would love your guidance."

I gaped at him for a moment, my proximity to freedom ripped away from me. I didn't have to look at Calliten to know that he was staring at me with a stern expression.

"Of course," I agreed, the fake smile I had to put on nearly breaking my face. Hanien looked relieved as his smile grew.

»«

Walking with Hanien around the garden was as unpleasant as I had expected. Though the garden itself was lovely with winding paths and blossoming trees, and a rainbow of spring flowers grew along the flagstones we walked on, and the day was perfectly warm and sunny with a light breeze—this man was intolerable.

"Just the other day, I was able to heal a woman's broken wrist," he said with a wide smile.

"Oh," I replied, not having any idea what he wanted me to say to that. Did he expect congratulations?

"Yes, it was quite complicated. I'm sure you're aware of how many bones are in a wrist," he said, now with a serious, thoughtful frown. "Obviously, with the Eos it all just goes right back where it's supposed to, but the feeling of so many bones can be quite overwhelming, wouldn't you agree?"

"Absolutely," I said with a small nod, and though I couldn't put any real effort into it, it seemed to please him as his smile returned.

"I feel very fortunate that I was able to be here today, Aneira," he said. If I had had any interest in him, I would have asked for him to call me Eira. But I didn't care enough about him, and being called Aneira was only a mild irritation when compared to just being in his presence.

Then I noticed his tone, and how soft his voice had gotten, and how quietly he was speaking. He paused in our stroll, forcing me to as well, and I stared at him, frozen in anxiety. He took a small step towards me, and I glanced around, hoping no one saw just how close he was getting to me. I fought off a sense of repulsion, and met his warm expression with a blank stare.

"I hope you were pleased to see me today," he said, masterfully adding a touch of trepidation to his voice. I felt my eyes narrow. It was all so fake to me, and I couldn't help but be offended that he thought something like this would work.

Still, I didn't want to upset Calliten, whom I had to live with, and who controlled most aspects of my life. And if he heard that I had been dismissive while Hanien was pouring his heart out to me, I would have to answer for that.

"Yes, it has been pleasant," I said, practically monotone.

"I was…I was hoping to discuss something with you," he said, continuing on as if I hadn't replied at all. I braced myself for whatever he said next, already sure that I wasn't going to like it. I hated the expression in his eyes, that shallow warmth, the calculating gaze underneath. The feeling that all of this was entirely outside of my control.

"I'll be turning twenty-five soon," he said, and the statement surprised me. I relaxed slightly, wondering if this was simply an invitation to his birthday celebrations.

"And so I am in search of a spouse."

I felt the air still around me, or I was numb to it; I wasn't sure which. Whatever sense of security I had felt moments before evaporated in an instant, and I internally begged for the ground to open up beneath my feet. No words came to my lips, and I had no way of telling what my expression conveyed. I hoped he couldn't tell how utterly appalled I was.

"Calliten agrees with me that we would be a good match," Hanien said after a moment, and I noticed uncertainty enter his voice and his eyes, some of the warmth there leached away. I thought it seemed genuine. He really was unsure of my reaction. I shook my head without thinking.

"I-I am honored. However…" I paused, waiting for the words, the perfect words to get me out of this situation to come to my lips, but nothing happened.

"I understand that this is an important decision," Hanien said. I looked at the ground between us, thankful that he was still two feet away from me; he had not tried to come any closer. "But I cannot wait any longer. I thought it was time for me to express my intentions to you."

I nodded, still numb to the entire situation. Part of me acknowledged that he was being unusually honest, but that didn't make me any more comfortable. The idea of forming any sort of partnership with him was intolerable to me. I lost track of how long the silence stretched between us, and then

I heard Hanien sigh. Perhaps he was growing frustrated with me.

"Perhaps the three of us could talk further over dinner," he suggested, and I looked up at him. His features were tense, his jaw clenched and brows furrowed. I had never seen him so openly perturbed. "I thought it best I speak to you in private about this first, though."

I nodded slowly. "I appreciate that."

Hanien looked at me intently for a moment, and just for that moment, I considered that, perhaps, we were quite similar. Both younger Benadurs, forced into this mess just because of how we were born and who we were born to.

"Let's return inside, then," Hanien said, brushing past me along the path, surprising me with his abruptness. He turned after a few paces, and then I saw a coldness in his eyes that he normally managed to conceal. "We can speak more at dinner."

»«

I did not intend to be found for dinner.

As Hanien made his way back inside the Benaty, I went to the stables. I had the stable hand saddle my favorite horse, a bay mare with white socks and a small star on her forehead, Nimue.

I considered my plan as I waited, and acknowledged that it wasn't much of a plan. As Calliten had not told me himself that I needed to attend the meal, I figured it wouldn't be a terrible thing if I happened to be in town visiting Mari that evening. Hanien would likely tell Calliten that he had planned to speak with me further about our hypothetical nuptials, but they would be forced to leave the following morning anyway, and I wouldn't have to deal with Calliten's anger until he returned a couple days later.

I was only putting off the inevitable, but I decided that was better than dealing with it that night.

Soon, I found myself riding down the road towards Nefyn, the plains around me warm and glowing in the afternoon sun. Despite the warmth, a chill wind cut through the cloak I was wearing, and I was thankful to make it inside the city walls, passing through the gates with relief. I left Nimue at the stables in the bailey there, and continued on through the city on foot, the white stones reflecting bright light all around me. I strolled through the network of bustling streets, navigating the sprawling merchant district, a large variety of shops and vendors lining both sides of the street. I continued on as shoppers entered and exited doors, bells ringing each time they were opened.

I arrived at Llewellyn's Goods, the eclectic general store owned by Mari's father. A two-story stone building with an especially steep roof, it sat at the end of one of the main streets in the merchant district. It wasn't a typical general store by any means, and Owain prided himself on stocking it with oddities from around the Empire. Upon arriving at its doors, I peered inside through the window and saw Mari with her head down on the counter in the back, perhaps taking a nap. I smiled and reached for the door, throwing it open with enthusiasm so as to wake her up.

The bells chimed with aggression overhead as I stepped inside, and Mari sat up straight, a lock of her hair sticking to her cheek. Her eyes widened as she saw me, and she stood up suddenly. "Eira! What are you doing here?" she asked. She had definitely been napping, as she immediately rubbed one of her eyes.

"I need refuge from Hanien," I said, cringing slightly as I shut the door behind me and walked across the store, coming to stand on the other side of the counter. She seemed to wake up at my words, and as she blinked a glint of mischievous curiosity entered her eyes.

"Tell me everything," she insisted, coming from behind the wooden counter and walking across the room. She took a small wooden sign down from where it hung on the wall next to the front window, and I saw that it had the word CLOSED painted on it in large white letters. She opened the door, hung it on the outer doorknob, and turned back to give me a grin. I raised an eyebrow.

"Are you sure that's a good idea?" I asked.

"I need to eat my lunch sometime," she said with a small shrug. "Are you hungry?"

I shook my head. "I was forced to take an early lunch," I sighed. She nodded absently, now heading past me, to a small door behind the counter that led into a back room.

"Hold on, I'll be right back," she said as she disappeared through the doorway, and I took the chance to look around the store and see what Owain had decided to stock as of late. Besides the typical requirements of general stores—sugar, flour, building materials, tools, and so on—I noticed a large shelf on one side of the room filled with wooden carvings of the strangest color I had ever seen. I walked over to them and studied them more closely. The carvings were of all types of things, horses and houses and birds and swords. But the wood itself almost seemed to glow, especially the further back it sat on the shelf. As I studied it, mystified by the intriguing silver tones, I heard Mari open the back door again and walk over to come stand next to me.

"Shenwood," she sighed, sounding impossibly bored by the items. I turned to look at her, and it seemed she had just finished rolling her eyes. She was holding a small green-cloth pouch in one hand, which I assumed held her lunch. "Da bought all of this, and expects people to buy it. Either we have to lower the prices, or we'll never sell a single piece. Honestly, I think the only people wealthy enough to justify purchasing these sorts of things are you and Calliten," she said, glaring at the items in question. I looked at one of the price tags and saw that it was indeed quite extravagant.

"I'll buy one," I said with a small shrug.

"Oh no," Mari said quickly, frowning at me. "That wasn't what I meant—"

"I know," I laughed. "I just really like them. I've always loved the myths of the shenwood forest and the Soul Tree. I used to dream of adventuring to Ronoa just to find it." I smiled while thinking of those childish aspirations, grown from the rumors and stories surrounding the mystical trees of the neighboring kingdom of Ronoa.

"The Soul Tree?" Mari frowned at me.

"Yes. You've heard the story, I'm sure. The largest tree in the world grows somewhere in the Ronoan forest, and it's said that only those of pure souls can find it."

Mari pursed her lips, looking doubtful. "And what do you get if you find it? Your deepest wish granted?"

I laughed. "I'm not sure. It always seemed like proving you were of a pure soul was the most important reason to try to find it," I said. "Anyway, it's just a myth—no reason to set out just to get lost in a foreign kingdom." Mari nodded in agreement.

"So," I said, looking back at the carvings, "do these really glow?"

"Yes. Here, grab one you like, and we'll take it to the back room," Mari suggested, and I grabbed one of the carvings of a horse that reminded me of Nimue, and Mari led me to the back room. It was extremely dark as all of the curtains were closed, and below the covered window was a small table and dilapidated leather armchair. Besides that, the room was filled with excess stock—bags of ingredients and crates of various items like rope and nails. The room was so dark I was barely able to discern these things, but when I looked down at the horse in my hands I could see it clearly.

"Wow," I murmured as I stared at the glowing piece of wood in my hands. The silvery light emanated from it to form a hazy halo in my palms, and the horse itself, though inanimate, seemed imbued with mysterious power.

"It is impressive," Mari admitted with a small sigh. "It wasn't a wise investment, in my opinion, but Da was too taken with it to pass it up. And I can understand that."

"I'm definitely buying this horse," I said, still gazing down at it with growing appreciation.

"That'll make Da very happy," Mari said, before throwing the dusty curtains open and allowing the afternoon sun to light up the room. We both blinked in the sudden brightness, and then Mari pulled out a wooden stool from behind a crate and set it next to the window. "So," Mari perched herself atop it and opened her lunch bag, "hiding from Hanien, then?"

I nodded, and she gestured for me to take a seat in the old armchair beside her. "Just until tomorrow. He and Calliten are leaving in the morning." I sunk into the worn cushions, taking a moment to get situated.

"Won't Calliten be displeased that you're hiding, though? He's been trying to get you and Hanien together for years," she said as she pulled out a hand pie and immediately took a massive bite.

I grimaced slightly, not knowing where to start. "There's not much he can do about it. He didn't tell me that I had to be at the Benaty this evening, and he's leaving with Hanien tomorrow. So he won't be able to yell at me until he gets back. And anyway, however mad he gets at me, it will be much more tolerable than spending another moment with Hanien."

Mari huffed out a derisive laugh, pausing in her eating to look at me intently. "It's been that bad?" she asked.

I nodded, and took a deep breath. "It seems Calliten has accomplished his goal. Earlier today, Hanien told me he is looking for a spouse and thinks we would be a good match."

Mari had just taken a bite, but froze at my words, staring at me blankly with her mouth obviously full. "What?" she mumbled through the food, and I barely stopped myself from laughing. She swallowed hastily. "Really? I didn't expect for it to ever actually happen."

"Well, it did."

"Are you alright? You must feel sick," she said, her eyebrows turned upward in concern.

"I don't feel great," I admitted. Then I leaned back in the chair with a groan. "What am I going to do?"

"It's not a sure thing, is it?" Mari asked, uncertain.

I looked over at her. She was genuinely concerned, her lips in a tight line and the pie forgotten in her hand. I sighed and looked at the dark wooden boards of the ceiling, noticing a few cobwebs in one of the corners.

"I don't know," I said honestly. "I don't see how I can get out of this, if it's something Calliten really wants."

"You can refuse," Mari said, her voice angry and determined. I looked at her again with a small smile, and saw her glaring at me.

"We'll see," I said. "Maybe Calliten will listen to me on this."

Mari nodded emphatically. "He has to. This is an important decision that you should be able to make for yourself." She remembered her pie then and took another bite, while looking out the window with a thoughtful expression. I turned and looked out at the view beyond as well, the bright colors of the day pleasing to me. The window faced away from the street that the general store marked the end of, and behind there was a small grassy slope, and then the back walls of buildings from a neighboring street not too far away. But the slope continued, and I could see nearly the whole expanse of the merchant district, the white stone walls and blue-slate roofing, undulating into the distance. White clouds rolled slowly across the blue expanse of the sky, casting intermittent shadows over the city, which just served to make the parts shining in the sun seem brighter.

It was a beautiful sight to me—a beautiful city.

Mari continued to eat silently, and I enjoyed her quiet company, until we heard the bells of the front door chime. She immediately sat up with a groan.

"I put the sign out," she muttered to herself as she wrapped her second pie back up in the bag and set it on the table beside me. "I'll be back soon," she said, her voice exhausted once again as she walked to the front room. But she paused in the doorway, and I saw her glare at whoever stood in the shop. "Oh," she said, her voice echoing with some surprise. "It's you."

"Good afternoon," a man responded, with a bit of a snarky tone. The voice was familiar, and on a hunch, I stood from the window seat and glanced around Mari's shoulder to see her brother Rhys standing near the front door. He was dressed in casual clothes, a light blue tunic and dark trousers. I almost always saw him in Benaty armor or formal wear like he had been wearing at dinner the night before. His hair was tied back, which was also unusual, and he was currently wearing a dismissive expression as he eyed his sister.

Then he saw my face appear behind Mari's shoulder, and the expression fell away instantly. "Oh," he said, eyes widening in surprise, and perhaps a bit of discomfort. "Good afternoon, milady," he said with much less snark, and much more politeness.

"Good afternoon," I said.

"I, uh," Rhys stumbled, looking back and forth from my face to Mari's. "Da sent me to make sure you remembered to set out the new spices he had shipped from Conotra."

"Ah, I forgot," Mari said, before sprinting to one of the cupboards on the side of the room and throwing the doors open. She pulled out a small crate and began to shove the tiny glass bottles of spices on a spice rack near the bags of flour and sugar, and sent Rhys a withering glare. "Don't tell Da about this," she warned, not pausing in her work as she spoke.

Rhys snorted. "Why shouldn't I?" he teased. "This is why he sent me. He knew he couldn't trust you."

"It's not like the one of the three customers I've had so far was going to buy spices."

"They might have, if they'd seen them," Rhys argued.

"Oh, do you think so?" Mari snapped as she worked.

"You can't say for sure—" Rhys replied as he crossed his arms defensively, but Mari cut him off.

"You really can't help yourself, can you?" Mari said as she thrust another bottle on the rack, causing the whole thing to clatter loudly. "If you don't like how I do things here, why don't you run the shop?"

"Because I have a real job," Rhys replied.

"That's rich—" Mari said, before stopping abruptly as I let out a short laugh, even catching myself off guard. Mari turned to me, her mouth open in surprise, and Rhys looked at me as well, as his face turned red in embarrassment. He uncrossed his arms before putting them behind his back, assuming an at-attention position.

"I'm sorry," I said quickly, before either one of them could comment on my outburst. "It's just—you're very entertaining," I mumbled, still quieting my laughs.

"My apologies, milady," Rhys said, suddenly formal again. "Mari and I will be more respectful in your presence from now on." Mari rolled her eyes dramatically as she put the empty crate back in the cupboard, the spice rack now full of the important spices.

"For Sky Queen's sake, Rhys, you don't have to talk to her like that. Eira is just a normal person," Mari insisted, crossing her arms just like Rhys had done a few moments earlier.

Rhys glared at her but remained silent. Mari sighed deeply. "Fine, do whatever you want. Now, if you don't mind, I'm running the shop today and Eira is providing me with her company."

"Milady," Rhys said, turning to me with serious eyes. I blinked, surprised at his intensity. "Please know that you don't have to stay here on behalf of my sister. I'm sure you have much more important things to attend to—"

"Rhys…" Mari groaned.

"Oh no," I said quickly, shaking my head. "I came here myself, without Mari even knowing I was planning to. After the events of yesterday, I would quite like to simply sit and chat, especially with someone so entertaining and friendly as your sister."

"Oh, then… My apologies once again," he said with a slight, unnecessary bow.

"Wonderful, Rhys," Mari sighed, and she grabbed his arm, and attempted to push him towards the door. "Thanks for stopping by, then."

"Da wanted me to be here today," Rhys said with a frown as he remained solidly where he stood, looking down at his much shorter sister. She stopped pushing on him, and looked up to glare at him.

"What?" she demanded.

"He says he thinks you might need help. He expects more foot traffic today, and—"

"He…he said that? I can't believe it," she exclaimed, stepping away from him to glare at him more directly. "He doesn't trust me at all, does he?"

Rhys's lips pressed together and his eyes narrowed in irritation. "Of course he does. He hired you to run the shop. He just thought you might need some extra hands."

"Sure, that's what he says, so it's less of a blow," she sniffed and crossed her arms once again. "And clearly you agree with him, seeing as you're here and constantly criticizing me."

"To be fair," Rhys said, sounding a bit hesitant, "you did forget to put out the spices."

"Do you know what, Rhys?" Mari said, angling her chin up, drawing herself up to her full height, which was still about a foot shorter than Rhys. Nonetheless, there was something intimidating about her, and Rhys didn't reply, but simply stared at her, waiting for her to continue. "Why don't you run the shop by yourself today? See how that works out for you."

His eyes narrowed again, hearing the challenge in her voice. I knew these two were competitive. Though I hadn't had too many interactions with Rhys directly, I knew from the way Mari spoke about him that they were always comparing their achievements to each other's. He considered her words for a moment, before a wide smile broke out on his face.

"I would love to," he said, his smile strained and not reaching anywhere near his eyes. "Why don't you go out and enjoy the rest of your day?"

"Lovely. I appreciate it very much," Mari said, her smile quite similar to her brother's, before she turned to me. "Come on, Eira. Bring the horse. You can pay us back later," she said, before walking around the counter to grab her shoulder bag.

"Oh, I..." I began, looking into the back room at the carving in question, sitting on the windowsill.

"Get the horse," she repeated, her voice low and serious, and I decided it would be best not to argue with her. I grabbed the horse and put it in one of the large pockets of my cloak, and we escaped into the bright white street, Rhys waving us goodbye.

Together, Mari and I wandered around the city, avoiding the busiest areas, and making each other laugh hysterically with our very different senses of humor—hers being loud and ridiculous, and mine being more dry and sneaky.

Just before sunset I voiced that I was hungry, so we decided to stop by a street food vendor where I bought a couple of pies. Mari bought only one, not quite hungry after her late lunch, but not wanting to miss out on the delicious treats that Nefyn's street vendors had to offer. We found a grassy lawn to eat on at the top of a hill that overlooked the city, and we ate in silence for a while as we enjoyed the view. The sun was setting behind us, making the buildings begin to appear gold and glowing, windows reflecting fiery light back at us. For a moment, I was able to feel content.

"So, how does it feel?" she asked, looking over at me as she leaned back, her hands planted in the lush grass behind her. I frowned at her, not knowing what she meant.

"Eating?" I asked, gesturing at the last few bites of my pie still in my hand. She laughed, a short, surprised, cackle.

"No. Being a Benadur. Officially," she elaborated.

"Oh," I said, setting the last bit of pie down on my lap, a bit caught off guard by the question. "I don't know. I think the same. I'm just glad yesterday is over. I hate events like that."

"Do you mean the ceremony or meals with Hanien in attendance?" she asked with her trademark mischievous smile, and I laughed.

"Both," I said after a moment, and she nodded knowingly as I finished my pie.

"It's unfortunate that he's so handsome," she mused, and I looked at her in surprise, my mouth still full. "I just mean," she said, raising a hand when she saw my expression, "you must have considered—"

"No," I insisted with my mouth still full, the word coming out muffled. I swallowed hastily and continued before she could respond. "I understand that he's attractive, but…that does nothing for me. Honestly." I shook my head, my repulsion towards Hanien something deep and innate. He was, very simply, deeply unlikable in my opinion.

"Nothing?" Mari said, raising an eyebrow. I glared at her, not enjoying being questioned in such a way.

"You know well enough that I've never been attracted to anyone," I said, looking away from her, out over the city. My frown persisted. I didn't like talking about these sorts of things, even with Mari. She was the only person I would even consider having these discussions with, and only because I knew she wasn't really judging me.

"I know," Mari said, softening her voice, knowing that she had put me on edge. "I guess, I just wonder sometimes. Even if you don't like him, maybe it wouldn't be so…bad."

I let out a deep sigh and leaned back on my hands, my fingers threading through the cool grass. "It would be simple, I suppose. Partnering with him," I murmured. "But I don't want to hate the person I have to spend most of my time with. And I certainly don't want to be forced into something like this by Calliten." I paused, thinking it through, and feeling a wave of repulsion once again. All I had to think about was his bragging and his unsettling smile, and it all became clear to me once again. I could never be with a person that made me feel so awful. "I don't just not like him," I added. "I find him repulsive. On a level that would be quite hard to change."

Mari leaned back like me, nodding slowly. "Then you have to convince Calliten that it can't happen. That you won't go through with it," she said, like her mind was made up, like I could stop this union just like that.

"I'll refuse as long as I can," I said. "But I don't know what will happen."

Mari was silent at this, perhaps sensing that I didn't really want to talk about it anymore. The sun sank lower towards the roofs in the distance, and beyond that, the Great Plains of Nefyn stretched into the golden haze.

"If you could go anywhere else," Mari said, voice hushed and distant, "where would you want to go?"

I glanced at her, saw how her eyes studied the plains and the hazy far-off lands, and knew she wanted adventure even though she rarely said it aloud. "Maenynys, maybe," I said, thinking about the capital of Lithe. "I don't remember what it looked like. But I know it's beautiful and grand."

"What would you do there?" Mari asked, turning to smile at me. I shrugged.

"I don't know," I frowned. "I suppose it would be nice to study. Spend time at the library, or even enroll at the university."

"Ah. An academic," Mari said, grinning.

"Well, what would you do?" I asked.

"I want to go to Silvania," Mari said, sitting up straight at the thought of the capital of the entire Remisian Empire. "It's a massive city, you know, ten times the size of Maenynys. Think of all the food they have there—"

I snorted. "It's always about food with you, isn't it?"

"And the canals. You can take boats around the city. Can you imagine?" She looked at me, eyes sparkling, and I couldn't help but feel her excitement rub off on me.

"Perhaps we can leave someday," I said. "We can go to Maenynys, and then journey across the Great Bay, following the rivers and roads until we reach Silvania. And then we'll explore the city and eat as much as we want."

Mari let out a giggle, and then I found myself laughing as well. It was nice to laugh. It was a distraction from the glaring fact that everything I had said would never happen.

I would likely travel to Maenynys again, and maybe Mari could go to Silvania. But I knew that I would never leave Lithe so long as I was a Benadur. It was my duty to stay and protect my province, and leaving would be an abject abandonment of my people.

I would fulfill my duties, whether I wanted to or not.

》《

When I woke up the next day, I was in a good mood. Bright sun was streaming in through my window already, indicating that it was late in the morning, and I was sure Calliten and Hanien would have set off for Mynyddpen already. Everything had gone to plan, and I would enjoy my days without Calliten—the calm before the storm. I had managed to sneak into the castle long after dinner time, having spent the day with Mari and even having dinner with her and her parents, Owain and Deryn. They had been very welcoming, and apologized for Rhys's absence—he had an evening shift at the Benaty after closing up the general store, and was forced to eat dinner with the other guards. I didn't really mind. Although his arguments with Mari were fun to listen to, I found his ever-formal manner towards me tiresome.

My spirits were high as I climbed out of bed and dressed in comfortable, simple clothing, knowing that there was no one in the Benaty that I had to impress. A comfy, cotton tunic and sensible leggings with soft boots were what I elected to wear when nice dresses weren't required. I didn't mind the dresses, and most of mine were quite gorgeous, but I liked to wear other styles of clothing when I could, especially for the sake of comfort.

I started my day with a trek down to the kitchens, where Mrs. Bowen insisted on giving me a plate heaped with eggs, bread, sausages, and pastries.

She hefted the plate into her arms, and it was so full I was worried one of the sausages was about to roll off. "Where would you like to eat, milady? I'll get a nice table setting ready for you."

"Oh, that's quite alright, Mrs. Bowen. You've done too much for me already. I'll just take this to my room. I'd like a quiet morning to myself," I smiled, and held out my hands for her to pass the large plate to me.

"Are you sure, milady?" she asked, dubious of my request.

"Absolutely. This all looks so delicious, and I'm very excited to dig in," I said earnestly. "But I mean it; you've done enough."

"Alright, then," Mrs. Bowen said with a small smile as she set the plate in my hands. It was even heavier than I thought it was. "Just let me know if you require anything else," she said as I turned back towards the door, moving carefully so as not to disturb the mountain of food. I smiled at her and nodded.

"Thank you," I said before slipping out into the hallway, up a couple of flights of stairs, and back to the comfort of my room. I sat in the window seat and set the plate on the bench in front of me, eating absentmindedly as I watched the guards do exercises and chores in the bailey below. A sense of freedom fell over me as the possibilities for the day lay out before me, endless. I looked over at my desk and smiled at the silvery-gray shenwood horse, reminding myself to pay Mari for it next time I saw her.

A knock on my door interrupted my meal, and I got up to answer it, curious as to who would be coming to see me. Opening the door, I was surprised to see Dafyd, one of the scribes of the Benaty. "Good morning, milady," he said with a small bow. He was an older man with gray hair and a large nose, and who was always polite and formal, but whom I enjoyed speaking to anyway. There was just something nice about his manner.

"Good morning, Dafyd," I said with a small nod. "How can I help you?"

"Benadur Calliten bid me to give you this note," he said, before procuring a small piece of parchment from a pocket and handing it to me. I felt my spirits fall slightly at this, hoping that the note wouldn't be too scathing.

"Thank you," I said, smiling at Dafyd.

"Of course, milady," he said with a small bow, before turning down the corridor, having completed his task. I sighed and shut my bedroom door, and unfolded the note with a sinking feeling as I returned to the window seat.

Aneira. Fill out tax forms on my desk. Will discuss your absence when I return. Calliten.

I sighed again upon reading this, not at all pleased that he had given me a task to do while he was away. Still, I knew it could have been worse, and I didn't think the tax documents would take too long to fill out. I had been doing that sort of paperwork for years. I returned to my breakfast, and tried to not dwell on how angry Calliten would be when he returned from Mynyddpen in a couple of days.

After eating as much of the breakfast as I could and resolving to eat the rest for my midday meal, I left my room with the intention to start my day with some fun, light reading. I walked to Calliten's wing of the Benaty, intent on infiltrating his private library. I knew he kept all the most interesting books there, the most thought-provoking ones. There was one that I had started that described the countries of Aorlanda, the snow-swept continent to the southeast of Regilisia. It was said that civilization began there, at the top of an icy mountain, the tallest mountain in the Four Lands.

Arriving at Calliten's library, I shut the door behind me as I entered the room, the silence of which was pressingly loud. Calliten had left the heavy red curtains shut, and very little light reached inside the room. I walked over to them first, tied them back, and opened the windows. Sunlight and fresh air rushed in, and I took a moment to look out over the Nefyn plains. The distant mountains extended above the horizon as a gray mass, and a darker shadow blurred their base and the plains slightly further to the south, and I recognized it as Gwanwynn Forest. I had passed through those trees once, on the way to the capital city of Maenynys, but I hardly remembered the trip. When I was three, Calliten had brought me to the meeting of all Lithe's Eosiaids over the age of two. It only happened once every twenty-two years, and just a few years from then I would have to make my first trip as an adult.

Turning away from the vibrant green view, I made my way around the expensive chairs and couches with which Calliten had decorated all of his rooms, to the shelves overflowing with books that lined the walls. Some were old, some had never been read. They stuck out at odd angles and lay across one another. Calliten didn't actually come in here to read very often, and I knew the book I was looking for would be right where I had left it.

Once I had located it and pulled it from its dusty resting place, I flopped down on one of the plush couches and flipped to where I had left off. Durnaland: the country of the Beginning.

It is in this realm that Mount Aornadur stands, the tallest mountain in the world. At the highest point on its peak live the monks of the Himinnir. They are said to be the purest worshipers of the Sky Queen, and so live as close to Her as possible. They are also most knowledgeable about the Eosiaid, as they all have the power of the Eos themselves, as a requirement. According to the few sources that have ever made it to the peak and back, they know of the origins of the Eosiaid; they know the truth, buried under the myths and legends.

I put the book down on a low reading table, and lay back on the couch, considering the passage. It was food for thought. What was the truth? How could I be certain what I believed to be true really wasn't one of those myths? I couldn't. It was rather unsettling, but I knew the only way to know anything for sure was to visit these monks, who lived halfway around the world.

Or, perhaps, the person who wrote the book knew nearly as much as them. Frowning, I picked up the book once again and flipped to the last page, where I found a short note about the author.

Catrin Morgan lives in southern Lithe, where she studies ancient texts. Though her passion is historical texts and interpreting them, she also enjoys knitting, gazing over the Fethwen Mountains, and avoiding human contact.

I suppressed a laugh at the odd summary, then shut the book once again, as I wondered just what sort of person this Catrin was.

After a few minutes of idle thinking, I decided to distract myself by doing the work Calliten had asked me to do. I got up, tripped over the couch leg, and regained my balance as I neared the door to his study.

The inside of the study was decorated in the same way as the library—garishly. But there were fewer books, and it was slightly smaller. In the corner sat the ornately carved dark wood desk, covered in papers—official documents, bills, letters, and so on. He wasn't the most organized person, I knew, and as I looked at the mess I wondered how I was even supposed to find those tax documents he had told me to look over. Halfheartedly, I started shuffling through the papers.

I was a bit lost in thought as I flipped through the pages, thoughts of the curious nature of taxes and political power wandering through my head; the taxes that were due to him by the villages and cities of Nefyn, and the taxes that he owed the king. And then of course, I thought, the king had taxes due to the emperor, a man named Laurentius that lived to the north in the capital city of Remisia, Silvania.

After a few minutes of looking through the piles of papers on top of the desk, I decided to open the drawers and look in there. The first two I opened were practically empty, but the last one held a box. I would have ignored this if not for my initials, A.S.E. written in large letters on the lid. Curious, I opened it to find more papers, but these papers were all about me—my birth certificate, my inauguration notice from the king, official Eosiaid registry documents, and so on. I looked at each page, allowing myself a break from the search for the elusive paper I had been looking for.

Aneira Seren Elfyn
Birth: The Twenty-Eighth of April, Two Hundred Ninety-Two,
Fifth Age
Registered Eosiaid & Common Magic User
Benadur in April, Three Hundred Fourteen
Mentors: Calliten and Lara Elfyn
Province: Nefyn, Lithe

. . .

Almost all of the papers were in this fashion, and I was really having quite a bit of fun reading all these important facts about myself.

Then, written on the paper at the very bottom of the pile, something caught my eye. "Aneira Seren Perry." The first two were my given names, but the last was a name I didn't recognize. I read the paragraph above it, and felt my body tense in disorienting confusion, a sickness filling my stomach.

With regards to Benadurs Calliten and Lara Elfyn;
The child has been obtained from the city Nefyn. She was born April the 28th, of the year 292, Fifth Age, in the hour of the Eosiaid. She is in good health. The remains of the parents were removed from the house. She will be in your care within three days.

"This isn't about me," I thought. "It can't be. It can't—"

Their papers indicate that her name is Aneira Seren Perry.

For a long time, I simply stood in shock. Then, at some point, I must have sat down. The sun sank below the roof's overhang, and made the room blindingly bright. The sun moved lower, and the room grew warmer, and I started to sweat. Even my bare feet perspired a little, the carpet becoming slippery beneath them. It could have been hours, or days, before I looked down at the paper. Yes, it still read the same way. It still implied a great deal. It still meant everything was a lie.

I read it again. And again. I tore the words apart in my head; did they have to mean what I thought they meant?

It was addressed to Calliten. It regarded a child…obtained from Nefyn. This child shared my exact same birthday. This child's parents' remains were removed… That meant they were dead, didn't it? And then it said the child would be brought to Calliten…and then—*Aneira Seren Perry.*

I was not Calliten's daughter.

My parents were dead.

3

The Investigation

I made it to my room, somehow, and there I stayed for the rest of the day. Servants brought me food at some point, and I ate it only because I knew I needed to. I spoke to no one and considered my swirling thoughts and questions in the silence and privacy of my room, but I wasn't sure what I was going to do until well into the night.

In the morning, before the sun had even risen, I dressed and rode into the city. I was there before most people were awake, once again moving like a wraith through the mist, but this time with a different destination in mind. I could only think of one place that might give me answers, only one place that might know what the truth was.

The temple loomed in the mist, its golden dome dull and one-dimensional in the poor light. I opened the heavy door using the Eos out of instinct, and then questioned the action… I had to question everything now.

Inside the rotunda, the dim light from the tall windows was cold and grayscale, the colorful icon of the Sky Queen, arms outstretched and reaching towards the sun above her was lifeless and unimpressive. My footsteps echoed around the empty, rounded room as I crossed the floor to stand before the altar, staring up at her with a defiant glare.

"Benadur Aneira," someone spoke softly, and I turned to face the voice, coming from my left. I saw Gywenn, looking mildly surprised, which was a strange expression for her as she always seemed perfectly composed. Today she was wearing light blue robes with silver embroidery. I realized the white ones were ceremonial, and not to be worn every day. Her black hair was tied back in a single braid today, falling halfway down her back.

"Priestess," I said with a small bow—everyone, even Eosiaids, had to show respect to the priestesses.

"Can I help you, Benadur?" she said, now with her usual soft smile appearing on her face.

"I'm not sure," I said honestly. "I just…I needed to speak with someone. Someone who probably knows more than me."

"Knows more about what, may I ask?" she replied as she came to stand beside me, glancing at the icon that I had just been staring at. Now I only looked at Gywenn, wondering if this was a terrible idea, if I should just leave.

I shuffled through my myriad of questions filling my mind, trying to find the most tactful one to start with. "Did you… How long have you been a priestess for?" I asked her, frowning at her slightly. She looked surprised, and I supposed it wasn't something she was often asked.

"I've been trained since a young age, as a child," she said, regaining her composure. "I've officially been a priestess for twenty years, since I was fifteen, and the head priestess for the last seven years."

I nodded, looking back at the Sky Queen as I vaguely remembered the ceremony where Gywenn became the head of our temple.

"Back then…maybe a couple of years before you became a priestess, do you…do you remember a couple living somewhere in the city? Their last name was Perry," I said quietly, my voice barely above a whisper. Any louder and I was worried it would start trembling.

"Perry?" she repeated thoughtfully, and then her eyes widened slightly with recognition. "Oh yes. The woman, Ffion I believe—she was quite pregnant when I heard they moved back to Maenynys to be closer to family."

A chill seeped through to my bones at her words. So it was true, then. They were real.

"Maenynys," I repeated. That was the story that had been spread to explain their disappearance.

"They couldn't raise their baby in their cottage anyway," Gywenn continued on, nodding slightly as she remembered. "The condemned one, on the other side of the graveyard— it's haunted. That's the other reason they moved, or so I heard."

"You…you remember so much," I said quietly.

She smiled. "It is part of my job—to know the people I have sworn to help. And I remember talking to Ffion frequently, especially during her pregnancy. She was worried about the baby, but couldn't explain why."

I stared at her, and wondered why she couldn't have helped them, even though it was clear that Gywenn had no idea what had really happened. She had no idea that I was the baby Ffion had been carrying.

"Thank you, Priestess," I said, turning back to the Sky Queen. I felt Gywenn's eyes remain on me, but didn't have the energy to look back at her.

"Benadur…are you alright?" she asked softly. I felt the heat of tears threatening to leave my eyes, and I sniffled.

"No," I said. "But I can't talk about it. Not right now."

"Whatever has happened, you can safely speak to me. I will speak of this to no one," she said, and I turned to her just as a tear escaped down my cheek. In all of the emotions I felt, so chaotic and new that I felt physically ill, I wanted nothing more than to say the truth out loud. But the words wouldn't come. I smiled thankfully to her, but shook my head.

"I truly appreciate it. But right now I just have to…have to be with this by myself."

Gywenn nodded, still composed but with a bit of worry in her eyes, and for a while neither of us said anything. "Would you like me to leave you, then, Benadur?" she asked softly. I cleared my throat and blinked, finally looking away from the icon.

"I have to leave, actually. Thank you, Priestess, for spending this time with me," I said. She smiled in her soft, kind way.

"I will be here if you find that you need to discuss anything. I'm always happy to listen," she said.

I attempted a smile, nodded, and left the temple without speaking another word.

»«

My feet led me towards the condemned cottage, and I stood at the base of a green hill, blinking up at it in surprise. No one ever talked about it, and I realized that should have struck me as strange. I had heard a rumor that it was haunted, just as the priestess had said. I hadn't ever really believed it was true, but I had also never had a reason to investigate it. Now it stood before me with a whole new meaning, haunted only to me in a very real way.

The sun had burned away the morning fog already, and the bright light illuminated the dilapidated shack, making the old, cracked windows glitter with multiple suns. It was surrounded by overgrown grasses and weeds, and some ivy had made most of the building's walls its home. The leaves shone green and glittery, still covered in dew. I stared at it, wondering if I really wanted to get any closer. But my legs gave me the answer as I found myself ascending the hill, staring up at the little house as I climbed.

There was only a narrow stone walkway, overgrown and mostly hidden in the tall grass, and I felt the dewy blades brush my ankles beneath my dress as I passed over them. All too soon and after an unusually long expanse of time where I climbed the endless hill, I arrived at the door to the cottage and found it to be half-rotten and nearly falling from its hinges. I pressed on it gently, hands shaking, and wasn't surprised when it gave out and fell inwards on the dusty floor with a loud groan. I hesitated for a moment before stepping around the crumbling door, and coughed as the smells of wood rot, dust, and mold met my nose. I covered my face with a hand, and went inside fully, compelled to investigate further.

From the sunlight that managed to make its way through the ivy and dirty windows, I could see I was in a sitting room. The simple wooden chairs were broken and still deteriorating, as was the table that only had two legs and was lying on its side. There was a disgusting old rug covering the wooden floor, its colors obscured by a thick layer of dust. On one wall was a small bookshelf, void of any books. Ivy sprang through every crack in the walls and ceiling, and tendrils hung like decorations. I walked around the broken chairs and bits of splintered wood in a daze.

There was one other door on the other side of the room and I felt the need to go through it—to see the whole house, to see everything that had belonged to these people. I reached out and grabbed the doorknob, and discovered that the door wasn't even fully shut as it opened with barely any effort from me. Inside was a sparsely furnished bedroom, with just an ancient double bed and a single table inside. I realized, numbly, this was probably where my parents had slept, and maybe even where they had died.

The little table, positioned next to the head of the bed, had a single item on it—a book. I blinked, caught off guard, as I believed the house to have been stripped. But for some reason this book must not have been considered valuable. I picked it up, unsure if I should disturb it from its resting place, but too curious not to. I carefully wiped the leather cover to see that it was a very dark red color. There was no title on the cover, no design. I inhaled deeply and opened it.

It was a journal. It belonged to Ffion Perry, according to the inside cover. I flipped to the first entry, and felt my breathing turn shallow as I began reading her words.

Oct. 17 291 5E

I decided I would start writing in a book about my life once I got pregnant. I found out not two weeks ago, and although it's been quite the rush since, I've finally found time to purchase this book and start the chronicling. Emrys would likely think it's silly, but it's always made sense to me.

My parents want us to move back to Maenynys right away. We refused. That city is just too loud and dirty, and Nefyn is so peaceful and sweet. I think it must be the perfect place to raise a child. Of course, my parents don't understand this at all. They've never been all that understanding, have they? Never took to Emrys that much. Their loss, really. He's probably the most wonderful person I've ever met.

But oh, what a pointless bunch of things to talk about. I'm writing this to remember the good, not how much my parents don't like my husband.

We've been living in Nefyn for about a year now. Emrys has planted a little farm on top of the hill our house is near, and oh, we've just got the sweetest house. It's small, but so cozy, and the fireplace warms up the whole thing when it gets cold. We mostly stick to each other, still a bit wary of everyone. Nefyn doesn't get a lot of newcomers and we're regarded quite nicely, but still as if we were some strange creatures the townsfolk have never seen before. It's a bit unnerving.

Anyway, I'm due in April. Isn't that exciting? I'm not allowed to do much until then, being pregnant and all. Seems a bit silly, I mean, I can still walk and everything. But something about not stressing the baby…

I flipped through the pages. A name caught my eye. I stopped.

Jan. 23 292 5E

I'm probably only crazy (well, I definitely am), but Benadur Elfyn has been regarding me quite strangely. It's always as if he knows something about me, but he doesn't want me to know he knows. He sort of stares at me and frowns, even if I'm smiling quite nicely. And then I feel like he's watching me as we pass in the street, or when I leave one of his appearances with the rest of the town. I hope it's not about the baby. I hope I'm crazy. I haven't even talked to Emrys about it, it sounds so silly. Why would the Benadur have any interest in me? I'm just one of the recluses that live in the cottage on the hill. Oh, it's probably only my imagination. I hear it can get quite creative when you're pregnant.

I felt nauseous. He had known I was coming. He had known somehow, before I was born. I couldn't accept it, though, that their deaths had somehow been at Calliten's order. There must have been some explanation, and my mind raced to try and piece the puzzle together, but the pieces wouldn't fit. I forced the thoughts from my mind, the implications too painful for me to confront at that moment. I flipped to the last entry, and my throat was suddenly dry when I realized it was written only two days before my birth.

Apr. 26 292 5E

I've been getting the worst feelings. Sudden bouts of panic, panic that something is wrong with the baby, something will go wrong in labor… Nothing can stop them, and worse yet, Emrys has been getting them too. That's really the most unsettling part. I can only conclude that it's because he sees how stricken I am, but sometimes I swear these panics come on both of us at the same time.

I just want to welcome a healthy baby to the world. Preferably a girl (I've just thought of her name—Aneira Seren. I must tell Emrys), but I can't be picky I guess. Please, just let them be healthy.

I stood there for a while and simply tried to breathe, but the smell and air were suffocating, and I didn't know what else to do but grab the book and leave, to get far away from that place. I crept out of the house, not wanting to disturb anything else, and almost wished I'd never come in the first place.

It was sun high outside, and I took a few moments to blink in the sudden brightness. The smell of fresh bread wafted over the small field that lay between the cottage and the town, and the warm, homely scent could not have been more at odds with the thoughts and feelings warring inside of me. I felt numb through to my bones, images and phrases bouncing uselessly in my mind. I walked through the city blindly, winding through the streets with no real understanding of where I was. I considered going back to the temple in a vague sort of way, but was repulsed by the idea of telling Gywenn all that had happened, even if I could trust her. The thoughts were better kept inside of me, where they lacked logic and sense. Once they came out, I would be forced to make them real.

"Eira?"

I blinked, and was brought back to my surroundings as the noise of the city crashed down around me—birds singing and trees rustling and the distant chatter of humans. It took me a few minutes to recognize where I was, but then I saw the stairs to the clock tower, and the clock tower itself, rising above me. I looked at it for a moment, surprised by its proximity, and then turned to find the thing that had awoken me.

Mari stood in the road a few feet away from me, the city of Nefyn laid out behind her. We were nearly at the top of the city with it falling away below us, gently sloping down towards the plains and the Benaty beyond. I almost fell into another reverie as I stared at the view, but a sudden harsh wind brought me back to the present, and I focused on Mari's concerned face as I tightened my cloak around me against the chill.

"Mari," I said, and the odd note in my voice surprised even me. Mari stepped towards me, hesitantly, her expression only growing more grim.

"Has something happened, Eira?" she asked, her voice slow and cautious.

"Yes," I replied as she laid a gentle hand on my arm.

"Come, let's get you inside somewhere. We're not too far from my house—"

I shook my head. "No, I can't…I can't impose," I said, my breathing once again shallow and quick. I couldn't look at Mari anymore, and instead I stared at the toes of my shoes peeking out from beneath my dress.

Something kept Mari from arguing as she said, "Okay. Do you want to go home?" she asked me.

I hesitated; the question was so confusing to me. Home was the Benaty. Did I want to be there? Calliten wouldn't be there. That was a good thing. But the servants were there, and what would they say about me? I argued with myself for a moment, before finally accepting that I had nowhere else to go. I nodded slowly, and Mari's hand tightened around my arm.

"Come on, then. Is your horse in the bailey?" she asked me, and I nodded as she led me down the hill, back through the city. She put my hood up for me, and I was thankful as I felt the heavy wool cover my hair and obscure my face from most angles. I kept my head down, knowing that it would not be good for the citizens of Nefyn to see me in such a state. If only I understood what sort of state I was in, and how I could be free of it.

A few minutes later we were riding back to the Benaty. Mari's family had their own horse kept in the courtyard stables, and she was able to borrow him for the evening. The white bricks rose out of the grassy plains, same as always, but there was a new tint to it for me. It had a veil of secrecy laced over it. It was a place I had grown up, where I was taught things about myself that were untrue, by a man I could no longer trust. Memories echoed through my mind, memories of playing with Calliten on the grounds, him chasing me through the grass that was taller than me; of when he used to give my school lessons and not the various tutors he ended up hiring over the years; of my childhood, as I wasn't fond of remembering it.

Mari helped me dismount once we reached the Benaty's bailey, and led me kindly through the castle, all the way to my room, where she knew I preferred to be at all times, but especially at that moment. She called for a servant and asked them to bring us tea and pastries, and then had me sit on my own bed, while she turned my desk chair around to face me.

"Alright," she said with a sigh. I looked at her, finding the strength to focus on her face. It was still concerned, but determined. "You must talk, Eira. Whatever it is, you have to get it out."

"I don't know how," I said honestly. "I can't understand... I don't know what happened."

"Were you injured?" she asked, glancing over me for a moment, but I shook my head. "Alright. Has Calliten or Hanien said something?"

"Maybe," I whispered. "I don't know. I can't...I can't accuse him... He's my father... I thought..."

"Eira," Mari said, reaching forward and grabbing my hand where it rested on my knee. I realized I was no longer looking at her, but the wall behind her, and the movement caused me to refocus on her face again. "You're not making sense. Can you...can you start at the beginning?"

I took a deep breath, keeping her warm, freckled face clear in my mind as I nodded.

"Okay," I said. "The beginning." She nodded and gave me a small, encouraging smile, still holding onto my hand. "I found an old letter," I began. "In Calliten's study. It was addressed to him and my mum. And…and it was about obtaining…me."

"Obtaining you?" Mari repeated when I paused.

I nodded, took a deep breath, and continued on. "It said that they had obtained a child with my name, from a couple living in the condemned cottage in Nefyn. The couple… The letter said they were dead and…and removed from the house. And that Calliten would…receive me soon."

A heavy silence hung between us, and I shut my eyes tightly, wishing so much that I hadn't said those words out loud. Still, I found myself continuing. "So this morning I went to the temple and asked the priestess. I told her their name— their surname. She remembered them and said that they had decided to move back to Maenynys because… because the cottage was haunted. So then I went to the cottage…and I found this." I produced the journal from beneath my cloak, which I had been holding onto so tightly my knuckles had turned white. I handed it to Mari, and she flipped through it, her face completely blank.

After a few moments of dense silence, she looked up at me with a resolute expression. "There must be some kind of misunderstanding," she said swiftly, handing the journal back to me. "Where is the letter you spoke of?" she asked, standing abruptly.

"It's… I left it in his study," I said, managing a small frown. A small light of hope lit up inside of me. Mari was right. I must have misunderstood something.

"I'll be right back," Mari said, turning towards the door. "If the servant comes, make sure to eat," she said as she opened the door and disappeared out into the corridor, not waiting for my response. I sighed as the door shut behind her, hoping that she could tell me where I had gotten it wrong, but a nagging voice rang through my head: my own. Logic was not my weakness. In fact, I tended to rely too heavily on logic, omitting room for human emotions and fallacies. I knew what I had read in that letter. I knew exactly what it said, each and every word.

I knew what it meant, and even Mari didn't have the power to undo that meaning.

A servant arrived with a tray of tea and a plate of assorted pastries, and I thanked her as she set them down on my desk, doing my best to put forth a normal and kind expression. Whatever sort of face I made, the servant did not find it worth commenting on, and she soon left me in peace. I grabbed a pastry, knowing that I was hungry even though I couldn't feel it, and began eating while I waited for Mari to return.

When my door opened without a knock, I looked up to see Mari entering my room with the letter in hand. Her expression was inscrutable as she shut the door behind her and sat once again in the chair, facing me. I stared at her, forgetting about the pastry in my hand, and waited for her to speak.

She took a deep breath as she looked at me, her brows furrowed deeply. "Let's…let's read over this together," she said finally, and her tone made that light of hope extinguish in an instant.

"There's no point," I said, that numb feeling I had felt in the city covering me again like a blanket. "It's clear you read it the same way I did."

"But there must be an explanation, Eira," Mari said, raising her voice slightly. I shook my head and studied the pattern of the stones that made up the wall behind Mari, knowing that we would not be able to find an explanation—not one that I wanted to hear.

"Then you must speak with Calliten about it," she said firmly, putting the letter on the desk beside the plate of pastries, and crossing her arms while glaring at me.

"He won't return until tomorrow," I said with a small shrug.

"Then you must confront him tomorrow. If you show him this letter, then he'll be forced to explain it to you."

"What if I don't want him to?" I said, my voice suddenly harsh and pained. I felt the tears prick at my eyes again, but I fought them back as I met Mari's eyes. Hers were wide, surprised by my outburst.

"What?"

"If he's just going to tell me…tell me he's not my father… that my parents are dead…that he might have even…" But I couldn't finish the sentence, the air stopping in my lungs. Shallow, so shallow, I felt like my lungs had shrunk, or my ribs had formed a tiny prison around them. I heard the little puffs of air as they left and the little gasps as I tried desperately to breathe.

"Okay, it's okay," Mari said softly, but I couldn't focus on her, or anything, my room a vague blur around me. I felt her sit beside me on my bed, and her arm wrapped around my shoulders. "Breathe, it's okay." She repeated calm words like that until the air came a bit more easily, until I could sit up straight and look at her. She smiled softly as she sat back, a bit further away from me, so that she could look at me levelly.

"You don't have to do anything, Eira," she said. I blinked, not understanding what she meant. "You don't have to talk to Calliten about this. But you won't get answers if you don't. Is that something you can live with?"

I felt my face tense into a deep frown, knowing what she said made sense, but not feeling the sensibility of it. "I...I can't think right now. I can't think about this anymore," I said after a few moments of silence, rubbing my face in exhaustion.

"Let's do something, then," Mari said, standing up quickly, smiling down at me. "Let's finish our tea first, and then get out for a bit. Does that sound alright?" I nodded slowly, realizing that I craved distraction. "Alright. Here, I'll pour your tea," Mari said, still smiling as she turned around and busied herself with preparing our drinks.

»«

I was able to enjoy my day with Mari, the letter forgotten for the time being on my desk. We finished our tea and went out into the gardens, wandering along the paths, and had much more pleasant conversations than the one I had had with Hanien only a couple of days prior. Mari could chat forever about anything, and I listened to her stories with gratitude, knowing that the shock brought on by the letter was still there inside of me, underneath layers of careful obstruction. Mari was the best distraction of all, and I even found myself laughing at times, of stories about how she bested Rhys once in a play sword fight, and about the time they fought over who the family cat liked more.

Eventually, we returned to the Benaty for dinner, and Mrs. Bowen gave us massive bowls of stew when we stopped by the kitchens. We carried them up to my room where we ate on the window seat and watched the sunset, and I devoured the soup in numb, contented silence.

"Would you like to come stay at my house?" Mari asked as she neared the end of her bowl. I looked at her in surprise, pulling my eyes away from the fading hues of magenta and violet.

"Oh," I said, thinking it over. "I...I don't think so. I appreciate it, but...I really don't want to impose on your family."

"They wouldn't mind at all," she said, a slight frown on her face. "And you know it."

I sighed. "Yes. You're right, I know. I just...I'm not ready to be around people right now."

"I'm people," she observed correctly, and I smiled.

"Yes, but I know you. I'm comfortable around you... But I'm worried I would act strange around anyone else, and make them concerned. Just look at how your brother treats me," I argued. "If he sensed that something was wrong, which he surely would given my behavior today, he would be all too concerned about me."

Mari shrugged and had another spoonful of the stew as she thought over my words. "I guess you're right," she said finally. "But if you change your mind, you could show up in the middle of the night and we would ready a room for you right away."

I smiled, touched by her generosity. "Thank you. I really do appreciate the offer. I want to be alone, though, at least for tonight anyway. I have to figure out what I'll do tomorrow..." I trailed off, not wanting to explain any further.

Mari nodded, but didn't respond with words. We sat in silence for a while longer, until the stars were twinkling above the city, mirroring the lanterns and torches that were being lit throughout the streets and windows. I stood to light some candles as my room was growing increasingly darker, and as I had just finished lighting the last wall-mounted candle, I heard Mari sigh. Turning to look at her, I saw she had stood as well from the window seat, and was stretching and yawning.

"I should probably head home," she said regretfully. "Are you sure you're okay?"

"I'll be fine," I said, setting down the candle I was holding on my desk. "Thank you for spending the day with me."

"You don't have to thank me," Mari said, smiling softly. I decided not to argue with her, as I knew it would go nowhere.

"Come," I said instead, gesturing towards the door. "I'll walk with you to the bailey, and send a couple of guards with you for safety."

"Oh, you don't have to—" Mari said, waving a hand, but I cut her off and linked my arm with hers, leading her out of my room and into the hallway.

"I insist," I said with a smile. She grinned back and didn't argue with me as we walked down to the bailey, and I watched her ride away through the gates with two guards, one on either side of her, thankful for the time she had spent with me, the patience she had shown me. But a fear grew inside of me, the fear that I would have to face what she had helped me avoid for most of the day.

I returned to my room where I sat on my bed and stared at the letter still folded on my desk. I had memorized the words, anyway, and didn't have the mental strength to read it again. It was their meaning that gave me pause, their meaning that instilled that fear in me. It seemed impossible for Calliten to be able to offer me any sort of explanation as to its meaning, so I wasn't sure there was any point in bringing it up with him.

But what was I supposed to do with it, then? Mari had asked if I would be able to live with these questions, with these implications. Suspecting Calliten of something but never confirming it. Could I go on as I had been doing before reading this letter?

I knew the answer. I stood from my bed and dressed in sleep clothes as I felt resolve grow alongside the fear. I blew out the candles and got into bed, wrapping myself tightly in the warm blankets, feeling calmer than I had all day. There was only one course of action I could live with, only one that I could see myself doing, though it was the one that scared me the most.

When Calliten arrived the next day, I would show him the letter. And I would demand answers.

4

The Strange Intruders

Not knowing what time Calliten would return, I went through the motions of my day without much investment in my actions. I conversed with Mrs. Bowen, ate breakfast, and even returned to Calliten's study to finally find the tax forms and complete them. All the while I was listening for some sign of Calliten's return—the sound of a carriage rolling into the bailey, or a servant announcing the event to me. The day seemed to pass in a slow haze, and I was simultaneously bored and on edge, knowing that a difficult conversation would be taking place very soon.

I was in my room reading an old book at my desk, when I heard the gates being lifted in the bailey outside and heavy wheels rattling over the cobblestone pavement. I stood from my desk and walked to the window, and was unsurprised to see Calliten's small but garishly decorated white carriage coming to a stop in the grounds below. An odd feeling came over me as I saw him emerge and cross the bailey to the main doors with long strides, looking as he always did—critical and irritated. I hesitated for a moment, unsure what this feeling was, and it took me a moment for me to realize it was sadness. Deep, regretful sadness.

I stood and grabbed the letter, telling myself that I could not put the confrontation off. It had to be done, the sooner the better.

I knew he would go straight to his study; he always did after returning from a trip. I walked to his quarters and every step felt like I was walking through sand, the effort constantly making me want to stop and turn back to the safety of my room. I pressed on, though, the need for answers stronger than any other force within me.

I knocked on the door to his study, and bristled despite myself when I heard his voice. "Come in," he said, his tone already tired. I entered and he looked up at me from where he stood by his desk, the tax forms I just completed that morning in his hand.

"I'm surprised you did as I asked, seeing as it's usually such a difficult task for you," he said dryly, waving the forms slightly, and sending a cutting glare my way. The words and expression rolled off of me. Nothing he could say or do would have any effect on me until I heard from his own mouth what the truth was.

"What is this?" I asked, crossing the room and handing him the letter.

"I don't know, but it can wait," he snapped, ignoring the paper that I proffered him. "We need to discuss your behavior earlier this week—"

"No," I said. "We need to discuss this."

"Aneira," Calliten said while closing his eyes with deep displeasure. "You disappeared for a whole day while Benadur Hanien was your guest. Have you any idea how rude that was?"

Some of those words finally sank in for me, and my hand holding the letter dropped to my side as I glared at him. "My guest? I don't remember inviting him."

"He was visiting for your inauguration," Calliten replied, raising his voice slightly. "Have you no respect for your fellow Benadurs?"

"I have respect for those who deserve it, and Benadur Hanien has never proven to me that he is one of those people."

Calliten sighed heavily. Apparently, I had crossed some sort of line for him. "Are you so socially inept that you had no idea of Hanien's intentions?" he asked quietly, pinching the bridge of his nose. "Or were you perfectly aware and that's why you disappeared the other day?"

I paused, and decided to play dumb. "I have no idea what you're talking about. If you would please answer my question—"

"Aneira," Calliten said loudly, almost yelling. "This is not a game. You are a Benadur now, and with that comes certain responsibilities."

"And those responsibilities include listening to a boring man brag about his mediocre accomplishments?" I replied, feeling my face contort into a deep glare.

"Can you look past yourself for just one moment, and realize being a Benadur isn't just about you? It's about all of Lithe," Calliten insisted, leaning on the table in front of him.

"Allies are necessary. Partnerships are required—"

"No," I said, the word cutting through his like a slashing knife. He stared at me, eyes wide in disbelief. "I refuse to form any sort of partnership with him."

"You don't get to refuse," Calliten gritted out, the last glimmer of his patience quickly ebbing away. "It's required of all Benadur, all Eosiaids in the Empire. You must be married by the age of twenty-five."

I blinked. "You're lying," I said, but my tone was weak, reflecting my confusion.

"I'm not. And I've told you of this before," he replied, now slightly confused as well, but still filled with rage.

"I thought…I thought it was a suggestion," I said, still not quite believing him. Why would the Empire compel all Eosiaids to be married by a certain age? What could be gained from that?

"It is not. And Hanien is a wonderful match for you," Calliten continued, tone now slightly beseeching. "Surely, you can see—"

But I was shaking my head, and even as he spoke I felt my attention shift back to the letter in my hand. It had so much more value, weighed so much more heavily, than thoughts of marriage and Hanien and the Empire. Before Calliten could finish his defense of my pairing with Hanien, I once again held the letter up, this time shoving it right in front of his face.

"I don't have time for this. Tell me what this letter is," I said, my voice unusually low. Something in my tone gave him pause, and he snatched the paper from my hand, glancing over it. His eyes immediately widened as he recognized the text, and he looked up at me, mouth open slightly. To my surprise, his voice was heavy with rage once again. "Where did you find this?"

"In there." I pointed to the drawer that I had opened, where he had stored a box of documents, labeled with my initials. He turned and looked at the drawer in question, then whirled around to stare at me with a deadly glare, crumpling the letter in his hand.

"You had no right to go through my private drawers," he said, his voice contrastingly calm compared to his expression. I would have been unnerved if I had cared enough.

"I couldn't find the tax documents. You're disorganized," I explained.

He gaped at me, and then threw the letter on the ground near his feet, out of my sight on the other side of the desk. Then he rested his hands heavily on the reddish surface of the desk, hanging his head slightly.

"I didn't want to explain—not yet," he said quietly. The words shot straight through the armor I had built up around me, and I felt my composure begin to crumble.

"So it's true then?" I asked, my voice wavering. He looked up at me, and still his green eyes were set into an angry glare.

"Did you…did you kill them?" I whispered.

"Who?" he asked, standing up straight. "The people in this letter?"

"My parents," I said.

"Lara and I are your parents," he hissed. "We raised you, not these people."

"Did you have them killed?" I asked again.

He was silent for a moment as he regarded me. "No," he said finally, before looking away from me. "I should have told you this a long time ago, but…but I liked the way things were," he said, and now his voice was unusually quiet. All of my muscles were tense, waiting, knowing the answers weren't too far away, and scared of what they were. Already, one answer had been made clear: Ffion and Emrys Perry were my biological parents, and they were dead.

"Tell me what?" I said, my voice still caught in a whisper. I was captivated as Calliten looked at me with something I had never seen in his eyes before, something that took me a few moments to recognize. Regret.

He opened his mouth to speak and I waited for the words. But then heavy footsteps echoed in the corridor outside, and a guard burst through the door. I blinked, recognizing Mari's brother, Rhys. He was breathing heavily, and his eyes locked on Calliten, hazed with fear as he began speaking.

"Under attack," he breathed out. "Foreign forces from the south."

"Has the garrison been alerted?" Calliten asked, and Rhys nodded. Calliten turned to me, a familiar expression of anger back on his face. "Go to your quarters. Stay there," he said.

I glared at him. "I have every right to fight along with you and the soldiers," I replied.

"I haven't trained you to fight. If they have Eosiaids, you would be killed," he said as he came from around his desk and approached Rhys, who still stood in the doorway.

"What do you care?" I yelled at him, and he paused, turning to look at me with an incredulous expression. But he mastered it so quickly, and turned away from me to look at Rhys.

"Take Benadur Aneira to her quarters, and ensure she stays there, away from the danger," he told him. Rhys hesitated, and Calliten narrowed his eyes at him. "You take issue with this, soldier?" he asked.

"No, sir," Rhys said quickly. "I only feel that my skills may be best used on the battlefield."

"I have no doubt of that. But it is equally important to protect the Benadur," Calliten said brusquely. "Is that clear?" Rhys nodded, whatever hesitation he felt repressed.

"Go with the soldier, Aneira," Calliten said, turning back to look at me.

"I don't need protection," I practically yelled, exasperated. "I'm an Eosiaid."

"An Eosiaid who doesn't know how to fight," Calliten yelled back. "Do as I say!"

An odd sensation came over me, and I felt myself being pushed towards the door. I gasped as I realized Calliten was pushing me with the Eos, using his power against me. I flailed with my magic, but couldn't figure out how to push back. I stumbled towards the door, nearly falling into Rhys. I turned to look at Calliten as he released me from his force, aghast that he had done such a thing.

"I can do that all the way to your room if need be," he said calmly.

"Our conversation isn't over," I warned, and he paused remembering what we had been talking about before Rhys had interrupted.

He nodded once. "Fine. Now get out. And don't let her leave your sight," he added to Rhys, who nodded in response.

I fled the room, not wanting to be in Calliten's presence for a moment longer. I ran to my room, Rhys's loud footsteps echoing off of the stone walls of the corridors behind me. I reached my room and slammed the door behind me, not even considering allowing Rhys inside. The entire situation was ridiculous.

I walked to my window to try and see the battle, but Rhys had said they had come from the south, and my window faced west. I watched as soldiers sprinted across the bailey with desperate, intense expressions. All were in full armor and laden with weapons, and many were leading horses from the stables, where they mounted their steeds and then rode out beyond the gates. I watched, numb and confused for a long time, until the bailey was empty and quiet. All of the guards had left, having ridden out to meet the enemy on the plains.

The view now as uninteresting as it was on any other normal day, I flopped down onto my bed, the numbness wearing off and the confusion growing. Calliten and Lara were not my parents—he had confirmed that. He had confirmed that they were dead, but he denied having them murdered. I believed him, I thought the way he had said it had seemed so honest. And he had been just about to tell me something, something he had hidden from me my whole life. Something he was supposed to have told me a long time ago. My heart beat harshly as I wondered what it could be, my mind running in circles. The only thing that pulled me away from these endless thoughts was the sound of hoofbeats pounding through the gates below, before slowing in the bailey. Curious to see who had returned already, I went to the window and blinked in confusion at what I saw below.

Two people were dismounting their horses, and I blinked in surprise at their appearance. They were both young women, one of which looked Remisian with curly dark hair and dark eyes. She wore leather armor and trousers, and her sword glinted in her hand as she surveyed the bailey with a relaxed and disinterested expression.

The other woman was smaller, but similarly dressed and armed. She had straight silver-blond hair and bright blue eyes, which darted around her surroundings, clearly on edge.

They turned suddenly towards the gates, raising their swords as they did so, and a moment later five guards rode into the bailey; even from inside I could hear their yells as they charged the Remisians. Their swords glinted in the bright afternoon sunlight, flashing like tiny flames. Then, in an instant, they were all thrown from their horses as if caught on a violent gust of wind. They fell to the ground, and the Remisians watched them, as though waiting to see if they got up. The horses cried in fear, and ran off through the gate and into the grassy fields beyond, thankfully not trampling any of their riders. When none of the guards stirred, the two women turned back towards the main entrance, and began to climb the steps that led to the large double doors, two floors below my bedroom.

As they drew nearer, I felt a growing sense of foreboding within me, as though my body was warning me to run. They were clearly enemies, and they had just attacked my guards. I knew not what they were interested in within the Benaty, but I knew that as a Benadur I was at risk. Where was Calliten? Had he gone to the battlefield already? I stood frozen, staring at the attackers as they neared the doors below me, willing myself to go to my bedroom door and tell Rhys what was happening. But the feeling that arose when I saw the strangers kept me in place, with a sickly sort of captivation.

Just as they were almost out of sight, at too steep an angle for me to see, two of the guards that had been thrown from their horses rose and ran quietly at the attackers, attempting a stealthier attack this time. I held my breath as they approached the two women, just as the smaller woman was reaching for the door handle. I craned my neck to watch in disbelief as she turned at the last second, took in the sight of the guards who immediately froze, and then—

I blinked, and blinked again, not believing my eyes. She had disappeared, vanished from my sight. The brown-haired woman raised a hand and one of the guards immediately fell backward, tumbling down the stairs with a series of clangs, coming to a stop in a heap of limbs and armor, unmoving. I gasped in disbelief then, as the blond appeared as though from nowhere, right behind the second guard. Before the shock of her sudden teleportation could really sink in, she had dragged her blade across his neck, and he fell on the stairs, already dead. His head was almost completely separated from his body, lolling oddly against the stone now painted red with his pulsing blood. The shock seeped through all the way to my bones locking me in place, as I felt a rising sense of nausea fill my abdomen. I wanted to move, to rush to my door and tell Rhys what I had just seen, but my brain was refusing to accept the truth. And then the blond woman looked up at me from where she stood below my window, and a smile of malicious humor spread over her face as our eyes met.

In an instant I threw myself away from the window, raced across the room, and opened my door with aggression, nearly running into Rhys as I passed through the doorway, not realizing he would be standing right outside. He jumped back slightly to avoid me as I struggled to come to a stop, and stared at me with a bewildered expression as I began babbling.

"Intruders—" I said, searching for the right words. "I just saw…in the bailey…some guards were attacked, killed, they came in through the main doors—"

"What?" he said, in a tone that told me he understood perfectly well what I had said.

"They've gotten through to the Benaty. They're inside now," I said, my tone desperate.

His expression told me that he doubted my words, as he pressed his lips into a thin line before responding. "You're sure that's what you saw, milady?" he said, too polite to openly contradict me.

I nodded, the matter too urgent for me to take offense. "Yes. They're clearly Eos. They were able to take out five guards at once easily. They…" I trailed off, not knowing how to describe the intensity of the attacks that had taken place on the steps, especially what I thought I had seen the blond woman do. I felt Rhys staring at me, but couldn't bring myself to say another word, and I knew that he wouldn't push me. At that moment, the racket of a fight reached our ears from beyond the hallway, and I saw Rhys tense and reach for his sword. I couldn't help but find this incredibly stupid.

"I just told you—they took out five guards with no effort. Your sword will do nothing against them," I said, glancing up and down the corridor, waiting for enemies to appear at any moment. Rhys was visibly torn on what he thought he was supposed to do. "We have to run—now. I don't think I would be able to fight them either, even with the Eos… I don't know how to fight with it—"

"Milady, if you would just stay hidden in your room—"

"They won't stop until they find me and Calliten, don't you understand?" The fighting was growing louder, echoing off of the stone walls in ominous ricochets. "They might kill you in the process, so we need to run—"

The noises were coming from the stairwell at that point, and Rhys made his decision. "Follow me, milady," he said, before turning in the opposite direction from the sounds of battle, leaving me to scramble after him. We ran down the hall, towards Calliten's wing.

"Where are we going?" I asked as the tapestries blurred passed me, their gold threads sparkling as the afternoon sunlight streamed in through the windows on the opposite wall. The rest of the details were lost, though, as we kept our pace quick.

Before Rhys could reply, he suddenly skidded to a halt. I caught up with him then and looked over his shoulder to see the brunette Remisian woman emerge from the central staircase. She smiled, and it would have seemed genuine if she hadn't been holding a bloody sword in one hand. She stood thirty feet away, and I felt like I could somehow feel her power emanating from her in waves. It was a disorienting feeling, one that I couldn't fully understand.

"You're one of them," she said in a thick Remisian accent, her voice light and curious, staring straight past Rhys, at me. Still caught off guard by the power I felt from this stranger, it took me a few moments to understand her words. "One of the leaders here." She took a few steps towards us.

Rhys drew his sword before I could warn him not to, the scraping sound of metal echoing off of the stones around us. A warm beam of sunlight hit the blade and starbursts appeared on the stones on the far wall above the staircase. Our attacker stood there, and wore a disconcerting smile as Rhys planted his feet in a fighting stance.

"Do you not know who we are?" she said, almost laughing. At that moment, I sensed someone moving in the hall behind us, and I turned just as the smaller woman appeared from nowhere, as though appearing from another dimension. She collided with Rhys before I could make a sound. While I watched in shock as Rhys hit the ground, his sword knocked out of his grasp before hitting the wall with a loud clang, the first woman rushed at me. I turned towards her as though I was moving through water, just too slow, and felt terror grip me as I felt the force of her charge before she was even near me. My feet left the ground from the powerful push, and my body went limp as I waited for the painful crash back to the ground.

All of the air in my lungs was knocked out of me as I landed flat on my back some ten feet away from where I had been standing. In an instant, the Remisian woman was standing over me. I felt my teeth grind against each other as my instincts took over, and I pushed out with the Eos, trying anything to fight back. For a second, she seemed to be bracing herself against my unseen force, then I felt force meet mine, just a bit stronger, overpowering me. I released the magic, breathing heavily with the effort and the failure. She smiled again and watched as I tried to stand up.

"So poorly trained," she murmured, before grabbing both my arms, pulling them behind my back, and then forcing me to stand.

I tried to push her away but already felt her power pushing back at mine, and decided to save my energy. Once I was on my feet, I looked to where Rhys had fallen and saw he was still lying there. The other woman looked at the one who was restraining me and said something in a language I couldn't understand, I assumed so that I would be kept in the dark about what they planned to do with us.

The woman behind me laughed lightly, then replied in the same language. I searched for anything that could get me out of the situation I was in, but it was clear that they would easily overpower me again if I tried anything. I focused on my breathing, attempting to remain calm, the rhythmic movement of my lungs somewhat comforting.

Then the smaller woman was beside me, and taking my arms from the other. They were efficient, leaving me no chance of escape while they transferred control. The vicelike grip on my forearms never left, only changed positions slightly as the blond took the place of the brunette Remisian. I watched as she walked over to Rhys, raised her hands before her, and smiled as Rhys's form began to levitate, as though laid out on an invisible stretcher. I felt my breathing increase again, despite my efforts. Was Rhys…?

Rhys groaned as he shifted in the air. It was clear he was quite restrained by the woman's magic, and was not able to move much at all. I exhaled audibly. He said no more, and then he was floating past me, and I saw his eyes were closed, and his nose was bleeding. He had hit his head rather hard on the stone floor, it seemed, when the blond had collided with him.

That woman was now pushing me down the stairs, following the Remisian and Rhys's floating body closely.

"Where are we going?" I demanded, my voice hoarse and uncertain.

The woman behind me laughed. "Somewhere better for us to talk," she said lightly.

"You…you must let me go," I said, tugging feebly in an attempt to release my arms. But the woman's grip was strong, and she was unfazed. I looked ahead at Rhys, his head lolling with each step, his armor creaking as he shifted every now and then in the air.

"I really think you want to talk to us," the woman behind me said. We had already started on the next flight, passing the second floor without a glance, and I felt certain that we would run into someone—a guard, a servant, even Calliten— once we reached the ground floor. The staircase opened up into the ballroom, which was eerily empty. It just didn't seem right.

"Help!" I yelled, and was immediately silenced with a hand over my mouth, the small blond woman easily placing both of my wrists into one of her hands, and maintaining the steadfast grip. Besides the physical force of her fingers around me, I also felt a sense of magic twisting around my wrists, keeping them together. A part of me marveled at such magic, the precision required for it indicating that the woman was incredibly well-trained with the Eosiaid.

"If anyone were here to help you," she said quietly beside my ear, "they wouldn't be able to. You saw what we are capable of. Do you really want to put more people in danger?"

Slowly, feeling numbness overtake me, I shook my head. The hand over my mouth retreated, then returned to my arms, where I was sure I would have bruises for days to come.

We passed through the ballroom, through the large double doors that led to the Great Room, and once again was met with oppressive silence. Turning down one of the many side passages, I was eventually pulled into a small windowless room where servants and other staff completed paperwork and expense reports. It was empty save for a small wooden desk, and we filed in, the woman behind me pushing me to the opposite corner. I turned around just as the magic holding up Rhys's body was released, and he fell the two feet to the stone floor with a thud. The brunette woman turned to me, her expression oddly blank, and I allowed myself to study her features in the silence that followed. All I could hear was my own breathing.

She was tall and slender, but clearly muscular under her leather armor. She wore knee high boots and a short cloak, and her curls were pulled up into a high ponytail. She had an olive complexion, common for people of Remisia, wide brown eyes, an oval face. She also gave off a sense of power that I had never felt before, and I felt my fear grow even greater as I studied her. She stared back at me, her expression remaining neutral, and I braced myself when she opened her mouth to speak.

"What's your name?" she asked, and I didn't respond. The blond woman, still holding onto one of my wrists, jerked my arm roughly.

"Answer her," she said. I didn't look at her, but could hear the venom in her voice. I took a deep breath. Perhaps complying would help me out of the situation.

"Aneira," I said as I looked up, doing my best to make level eye contact with the woman who had asked me. "And yours?" I said, attempting to sound bold.

She smiled, somehow both warm and cold at the same time. "Cassia," she said. "And this is Varina." She nodded toward the blond that stood slightly behind me. I resisted the urge to glance at her.

"And what are you doing here?" I asked, still maintaining stability in my voice, somehow. Cassia's smile remained.

"We're here to help you," she said. I frowned, and she continued without prompting. "Maybe you saw that Varina is no ordinary Eosiaid. I'm not either. We have been blessed twice over by the Sky Queen, you see. There are many of us, throughout Linra, and now… now we are finding each other. And change is upon us all."

"What does… Why bother us?" I asked, somewhat stupidly, as I was beginning to lose the calm demeanor I had carefully crafted over the last few minutes. "We have nothing to do with this."

"Everyone does, now," Cassia said cryptically, before addressing Varina. "Go and help Naani and Dennu in the other room. The older one is stronger."

"I'm not so sure," Varina said, monotone, with a slight edge in her voice. I sensed a strange energy running between the two women as they stared at each other, a current deep and complicated.

"Need I remind you that Riki gave me the authority on this mission?" Cassia asked, her smile growing thin.

"Riki rewarded you for something I did," Varina said.

Cassia's smile fell away instantly, her eyes narrowing.

"We will not discuss this now," she said firmly. "You must do as I say. I have this." She gripped the gold hilt of a dagger that was strapped to her hip, and pulled it slightly from its sheath, revealing a bright silver blade. I felt Varina shift to my left, and the frustration rolling off of her in waves. I glanced at her from the corner of my eye, and saw that she was grinding her teeth while staring at the dagger as Cassia slid it back into the sheath. Her eyes held a challenge for Varina, and the two stared at each other. After a moment Varina finally nodded, releasing her grip on my arm without a word, and left the room, the door shutting soundly behind her. I stared at Cassia, wondering if I could get her to speak openly with me. I doubted it.

Rhys groaned again on the ground, and I kneeled beside him without thinking. His brows were furrowed, the blood drying over his lips and cheek. Some had dripped into his long golden hair while he was being carried, and glued the strands together in the dark liquid. He lay on his back, and I noticed he was beginning to move, just his head at first, and only slightly, but I thought he might have been waking up. This idiotic guard had nearly gotten killed for me, and more than that, he was Mari's brother. I would never be able to live with myself if he really did die because of me.

"Rhys," I whispered, conscious of Cassia staring at us, still standing behind the desk. He murmured incoherently, as his eyelids began to flutter open. Eventually, he was able to focus on my face, and his look of confusion only grew.

"Milady?" he questioned.

"Don't try to fight, okay?" I whispered. He began to look around the sparse room, angling his head in different directions, and quickly found Cassia, where he paused, and I thought he was about to question her as his mouth opened. Then it shut, and he looked back at me. He tried to sit up, and was able to prop himself up on one elbow, while the other hand went to his head. He groaned, then felt his broken nose gingerly.

"What happened?" he said hoarsely, barely above a whisper.

"Don't worry, just rest," I said gently.

"Where are we?" he pressed, looking over at Cassia again, who remained still and silent, observing us.

"We're still in the Benaty, on the first floor. I don't know what they want, exactly—"

"I told you," Cassia said, sounding impatient. "We're here to help you. To liberate you. This is the beginning of a new era for the Remisian Empire."

I stood up to face her, not liking how she towered over us. Below, I heard Rhys shuffling, trying to get to his feet as I had. "Aren't you Remisian?" I demanded. She smiled in that disconcerting way again.

"Yes, and I know better than you do all the ways the Empire is failing, all of the space for improvement," she said.

"Just tell me…tell me what's going on," I demanded, raising my voice. "You're holding me hostage, you've attacked my home and my city—I deserve to know!"

To my outrage, she laughed. "I promise you, Aneira, you won't be so upset once we explain everything to you. But we need a bit more time. Our leaders haven't yet arrived, and it's best to hear it from them."

I stared at her. I had assumed she was the leader of this operation. "You're not…? Who are your leaders?" I asked, confusion clear in my voice.

"You'll learn in time," she said, then came out from behind the desk to stand in front of me. I stood my ground, though I wanted to run away. She was a couple of inches taller than me, and I stared up slightly into her warm brown eyes, which shone with an odd energy I couldn't quite define— somewhere between malicious and mischievous. She stood only a couple of feet away from me, and I could sense the power from her as I had the others. It made me tremble slightly, though I tried to conceal it. Rhys got to his feet, finally, just behind me, and knew well enough now to not engage. Still, I could tell he was tense even though I wasn't looking at him. I heard him take a few steps towards the door, but Cassia paid him no mind, knowing full well that he wouldn't be able to escape.

Cassia appraised me for a moment, before saying, "A new day is coming, Aneira. And there is nothing you can do to stop it." Her hand reached out to grasp my shoulder, and I felt my breathing accelerate. When I felt the pressure of her hand grip my shoulder through my tunic, I felt as though all the air from the room had gone. Dimly, I was aware that I was in a deep state of panic, but knew no more and no less. I saw her face contort into a frown at my reaction, before my vision went black, and the terrifying sensation of falling into nothingness overcame me.

When my vision returned, it was as though I was seeing through a fog, but the details I was able to see only served to confuse me more. I was in a room, but not the one I had just been in; it was no room in the Benaty. It was larger, with plush rugs on the wooden floors and elaborate paintings on the walls, and a large, ornate, four-poster bed was situated in the center of it. Cassia sat on the edge of the bed, looking alertly at the door behind me, like she was waiting.

I blinked, beginning to panic even more, not wanting to speak, yet wanting to scream at the same time, and demand to know what was happening. But she never looked at me, and before I knew what was happening, the fog covered the room and obscured everything from my sight with complete darkness. Then I fell again, and when I opened my eyes I was once again looking at the clear, lantern-lit room that I had been in. I was flat on my back on the floor just as Rhys had been a few moments prior. He was leaning over me, and attempting to pull me into a sitting position.

"Milady," he said urgently. "Are you alright? Please, we have to leave—quickly."

I looked up at him. He was holding me awkwardly now, and I almost blushed at the realization, before I found the strength to pull myself out of his grasp and stand up on my own. I gasped at what I saw on the floor before me. Cassia's unconscious form.

"What…?" I began, looking at Rhys, my head still swimming from the strange episode. He held up a wine bottle, now shattered and jagged on one end, and then I noticed the blood matting down Cassia's curls. "What did you do?" I asked, slightly horrified. Rhys looked affronted.

"What I had to do," he said, his tone lacking the politeness he normally used when speaking to me. He was indignant. "She was distracted when you fell. It was the only chance we were going to get. Now let's go. The other one could come back at any moment."

I nodded numbly, and though I shouldn't have cared at all, I hoped her accomplices would heal her. We left the room, Rhys still carrying the bottle, holding it like a weapon. We emerged into the hallway, and when I glanced outside the large windows on the opposite walls, I saw the green fields of Nefyn stretch into the distance, and upon them a battle raged. Rhys and I both paused at the sight. The sun was lower in the sky, and shining from the opposite side of the Benaty, so the armor and weapons glittered like distant silvery jewels. It was too far to see any details, but it was clear nearly all of the Nefyn guards were out there, and the force they were fighting was formidable in their numbers.

"Come on," Rhys insisted after a moment, and we raced down the hall; I realized belatedly, away from the main doors.

"Where are we going?" I hissed. "We need to escape."

"We need to at least locate Benadur Calliten," Rhys said, voice resolute.

"What?" I demanded, entirely offended by the idea. "What are we going to do when we find him? There's no way we can take them!"

"We will wait for the guards to return," Rhys said, insistent. We slowed our pace as we neared more servants quarters, listening for voices. Still, I thought this was an idiotic plan, and continued to voice my opinion.

"What if the guards don't return?" I whispered. "What if we lose?" Rhys didn't respond as he quietly approached door after door in the long hallway, listening intently.

"Llewellyn!" I said as loud as I dared. He turned away from a door to stare at me, appalled. "I am leaving this place at once, and I demand that you escape as well. Calliten is on his own."

He appraised me for a moment, and it was then that I noticed once again that his nose was bleeding. It continued to run down his face, escaping down his neck and under his chest plate. I felt a tinge of guilt at the sight and I took a step toward him, unconsciously. He stared at me as I neared, still in shock from my outburst.

"May I...?" I said, beginning to reach up slightly though I hadn't finished my question. "May I heal this?" He seemed frozen in place, and I knew that I should wait until we were outside, or somewhere safe, but I couldn't bear to see him bleed a moment longer, knowing that it was blood shed for me.

He nodded, not responding out loud, but his expression was somber. Faintly, I wondered why. I closed my eyes and lowered my hand without thinking, reaching out instead with the Eosiaid. I felt the break in my mind, held it, and put the bone back into place as gently as I could. I patched up the broken blood vessels quickly, and felt as the bleeding ceased. When I opened my eyes, his were shut tightly, as though he was willing himself to disappear.

"All done," I said softly, and his eyes opened again. The hand that wasn't holding the broken bottle went to his nose, and he felt it with trepidation. When he felt no pain there, he smiled slightly.

"I thank you, milady," he said with a small bow. I smiled a bit at his returned formalities.

"Thank me by escaping with me," I said.

His smile fell away instantly. "I have a duty to the Elder Benadur," he said quietly, frowning at the ground.

"And to me as well. And you can help me—now," I said, voice becoming desperate. "But you can't help Calliten. I heard Cassia. They have him in another room. There are three of them there, and I don't know how to fight. And they are so powerful." I stopped abruptly, beginning to breathe quickly again.

Rhys nodded, still with a hint of trepidation. "You are right, milady," he said quietly. "Though it is hard for me to admit, I cannot help Benadur Calliten as it is right now. But...where will we go?" he asked, eyebrows furrowed.

I thought quickly. "We will check on the city's garrison. If they've been lost, then we..." I stopped talking again, the thought of the city falling overwhelming me. Concern for Mari filled me to the point I couldn't think of anything else. I stared at the pale stones of the floor, barely aware of where I was. I heard Rhys speaking, and it brought me back to the moment.

"Then we will do what we have to do," he said simply, then set off down the hall towards the main doors, and I ran to keep up with his quick pace.

5

The Road to Maenynys

I stopped for only a second in a room where I was certain money was stored, and was also able to secure a bag from the small storeroom as well. Rhys kept watch outside the door, constantly glancing up and down the hallway as I shoved a pile of coins into the leather pouch.

Once the money was acquired, we ran as quickly as we could down the hallway, through the Great Room, and finally through the large main doors that the attackers had left open.

"Weapons," I huffed, and Rhys nodded in agreement. We both were in desperate need of something to fight with. I knew I was better with a bow than I was with the Eosiaid in terms of fighting, and I wanted a good sword as well, though I hadn't had much training with one.

As we ran down the wide white-stone steps, I noticed that the guards that had been attacked were gone. There was still a pool of blood staining a couple of the steps, but I didn't look closely. I pushed all thoughts out of my mind and focused on running to the armory on the left side of the bailey.

It was a narrow, wooden room, the walls lined with shelves and racks of weapons: spears, swords, and bows, for the most part. We spent very little time in there, as we chose weapons quickly, and I opted for some light leather armor. It was sure to offer a bit more protection than the linen tunic and trousers I was wearing. I struggled with one of the buckles that had to fasten just above my shoulder blade, grunting in frustration as the seconds passed, and my fingers only continued to slip.

"Could I…?" Rhys began hesitantly, speaking from behind me, where he had just finished buckling a greatsword scabbard around his waist. I turned to look at him over my shoulder for a moment, before shaking my head quickly.

"No, I've got it," I said stiffly as I finally grasped the buckle, securing the strap. I grabbed a decent bow, as many arrows as I could fit in a quiver, and a suitable twohanded greatsword, as Rhys busied himself with similar tasks. Then, with almost a frenzied pace, knowing that the other attackers could discover that Cassia was unconscious at any moment and begin searching for us, we sprinted across the bailey to the stables.

The stables were large, and had about a hundred stalls, with five different rows stretched along the room, away from the doorway. Windows lined the walls, and filled the large room with warm evening light. Only a few horses remained, and Rhys silently approached one, a large black horse with white markings on its face, and began to saddle it. I remembered this horse's name was Cai, though I had rarely interacted with him myself. I quickly found my favorite, a mare named Nimue. She grew excited when she saw me. I supposed she had felt left out when all of the other horses had been taken from their stalls. She pawed at the ground impatiently as I opened the gate to her stall, and followed me eagerly as I led her back towards the doorway to saddle her. My hands were shaking as I cinched the saddle, and I forced myself to remain calm. Rhys had already finished, and was waiting in tense silence in the doorway. Once my saddle and reins were properly in place, I swung myself into the saddle, and we rode out without a word.

The wind rushed by my face with unending howls as we broke into a gallop and emerged from the gate, the stone road to Nefyn stretching before us, with the tall green grass expanding out forever on both sides. It was a warm day, the low evening sun heating the stones of the road and reflecting back at us. Nefyn glittered less than a mile away, and we raced towards it, but I became aware of an uneasy feeling inside of me. Looking out towards where we had seen the battle from inside the Benaty, I felt my anxiety grow to see it was over. Metal shone through the grass, hundreds of yards away, too far to see exactly what the source was. But there were only a few people moving, both on foot and horseback, stepping slowly through the battlefield, as though searching for something in the remnants. From so far away, I couldn't tell if they were our attackers or the Benaty guards, but it didn't actually matter that much. The real question was, where had everyone gone? Surely there were more survivors than just the few who still stood on the field.

I set my sights on the gates of Nefyn, which grew nearer and nearer as we maintained our swift pace. Rhys and I still hadn't spoken since leaving the Benaty, but there wasn't much yet to say. We found ourselves in an odd and frightening situation, and I could barely breathe through the constant panic I was feeling, let alone speak.

Soon I was able to make out four guards who stood outside the city gates, and I squinted at them, as once again, something felt off.

"Turn back," Rhys called suddenly, before pulling on his reins and turning Cai around. I was still studying the soldiers at the gates, and now saw they weren't wearing Benaty armor. Though it was still hard to tell, it actually looked like a style commonly worn in the neighboring kingdom of Hartania.

My reflexes kicked in just as I saw them react to Rhys's abrupt change in direction; distantly I heard them calling to us, before two mounted their own horses and began to gallop towards us. I turned Nimue around as quickly as I could and caught up to Rhys after a few moments.

"Where are we going?" I yelled over the sound of pounding hoofbeats on the stones below us, and the wind roaring in my ears. "We can't return to the Benaty. They'll have discovered that we're gone by now."

"I don't know, milady," Rhys yelled back.

I thought quickly, weighing our options. "We need to get help," I called to him. "We…we'll go to the king. To Maenynys." It was risky. It wasn't for certain that the king would provide help, but if ever there was a time for the capital to send help to one of Lithe's provinces, this was it. The province of Nefyn had been overthrown in a matter of hours, and this was no ordinary force. These Eosiaids, with their strange, unheard-of powers, were like nothing Lithe had seen before.

Rhys looked over at me at my words, wide-eyed, and didn't respond immediately. He glanced behind us, then leaned forward over his horse's neck even farther, attempting to gain a bit more speed. I looked back as well, and thought that the people following us looked a bit closer. The Benaty loomed before us, growing larger, but I knew that we shouldn't get anywhere near it.

We turned off of the road and headed slightly south, galloping straight into the tall grass. The beating of the hooves was muffled now, the grass lush and soil soft. Still, the noise filled my ears along with the wind, as we skirted around the Benaty in a wide arc. Looking back periodically, it seemed like the soldiers chasing us were falling farther and farther behind, though they showed no indication of giving up yet. We slowly turned east, the sun setting behind us, behind the northern mountains. The grass was illuminated and glowing in the golden hour, and the sight of the rolling hills and plains extending into the darkening distance would have given me pause in its beauty in any other situation. As it was, my mind was focused on only one thing—reaching that distant horizon as quickly as possible.

We rode hard, in complete silence for nearly fifteen minutes. I could tell the horses wouldn't be able to maintain the pace for much longer. The golden hour faded behind us as we raced headfirst into the night. As we ran up and down the languid hills, different views were revealed to us at each crest. Soon, when on the higher ground, we could see a darker section of land growing on the horizon, and I recognized it as Gwanwynn Forest. It took up a large section of central Lithe, and we would be spending the majority of our trip to Maenynys within its boughs.

"The horses need to rest," Rhys called to me as we reached one of the crests of the hills. We slowed our pace, and both of us turned to look back at the shadowy landscape behind us. It was still bright enough to see, but the color was leached from everything, appearing gray and lacking depth. We squinted at the hills, the black shape of the Benaty nestled within them over three miles away at this point, and the city of Nefyn was visible just behind it, as it was illuminated with twinkling lights dotting the shadowed hillside. Above the city, the stars began to blink into view, as night officially fell over Nefyn.

Though we scanned the hills between us and the Benaty for some time, no shapes moved through the grass or appeared at the tops of the hills.

"They must have turned back with the sunset," Rhys murmured. Everything was strangely quiet to my ears, after the extended amount of time being buffeted by wind and hearing the horses' hooves pound over the ground with rhythmic booming. Now all I could hear was the grass whispering in a light breeze and evening birds chirping in the occasional shrub that dotted the plains. But behind it all, I felt like I could hear the silence of the land and of the encroaching night.

"They must not have known who we are," I said, still growing accustomed to the odd feeling of quietness. Rhys looked away from the plains, to frown slightly at me.

"Who *you* are, milady. They care nothing for me."

I opened my mouth to reply, but couldn't think of a decent response. My nerves were frayed, my mind stretched to its limit, and the events of the day were finally catching up to me. I leaned forward slightly, feeling my breathing increase. Now, in this moment of rest, my body finally had time to shut down in the complete panic I felt.

Rhys grew concerned immediately. "Milady? Are you alright? Your breathing is—"

I gasped slightly, finding the air thin and thick at the same time—too light inside my lungs, and too heavy on my chest. "I'm—" I tried to say I was alright, and not to worry, but all I was able to do was sharply inhale and exhale, over and over again. My breathing was shallow, squeaky, and not enough. I shut my eyes and gripped the horn of my saddle resolutely, as I felt myself swimming through the air, and I was worried I would fall from the saddle before I knew what was happening.

"Aneira, you're…you're hyperventilating," Rhys said from somewhere to my right. I kept my eyes shut tightly, willing myself to get control over my body, but the panic and fear I had been suppressing for the last couple of hours had taken hold, and I barely knew where I was. All I knew was fear. My lungs convulsed with each tiny breath, never getting enough air, never able to expand.

I heard sounds from where I knew Rhys had been when I had shut my eyes. He had been astride his horse, just as I was, I thought distantly. But then I felt warm hands cover mine on the horn, and they were pulling mine away from the saddle, holding them gently in the loose air, my only connection to something solid. My eyes remained shut.

"Let's get your feet on the ground, milady," Rhys said calmly from somewhere beside my right hip. "It's easier to breathe down here."

I tried to reply, but only squeaks came out. One hand left mine, and then an arm wrapped around my waist. "I'll help you dismount, milady, if you allow it." With my violent breathing still in control, all I could do was nod. Before I could register it, I was pulled gently from the saddle, where I collapsed into Rhys's side, before he lowered me to the ground. My eyes opened then, the pale slate sky curving above me. Rhys's face appeared in my field of vision soon after my eyes were opened, though I didn't focus on him; I wasn't sure if I could.

"Let's…let's think about some grounding things," Rhys said, his words distant to my ears though he was only a couple feet away from my face. "What's your name?"

"Eira," I gasped, frowning. How could this help?

"Your full name?"

"Aneira…Seren…Elfyn…" That surname slipped out without much thought, as it was the one I had known for nearly all my life. The name Perry echoed in my head, but I pushed it aside. I couldn't deal with thoughts of that in addition to a panic attack, which in that moment felt like a massive hand squeezing my heart and lungs.

"And how old are you?"

"Twenty…two…" I noticed now that the monstrous hand on my lungs had loosened its grip slightly. My breaths were able to go a bit deeper, a bit longer.

"Where are you from?"

"Nefyn." A bird passed overhead, scores of feet above us, and if it sang, its song did not reach my ears.

"Who am I?" I looked at his face, pale in the gray light of first night, and focused on it for just a moment. His expression was nearly blank, but like a mask, and I wondered if he was hiding something. I had no energy to dwell on it.

"Rhys Llewellyn," I said after a moment, and then looked away from his face, fixing my gaze once again on the endless sky.

"What is my job?"

"A…guard." It was then that I was able to take a full, tension-relieving breath, and the monster's claw fell away entirely. But the marks remained, the indentations, the reminder of what had happened. I continued to breathe in deeply, thankful, but fatigued.

"Can you sit up, milady?" Rhys asked after a moment. I nodded and pushed myself up first to my elbows, and then to my palms, my hands planted behind me in the cold, dewy soil, the wide blades of grass laced through my fingers. I looked over at Rhys, who kneeled next to me. That mask was falling away, and visible worry was etched on his face.

"I'm sorry," I said quietly, finding that I was still catching my breath, my quiet huffs echoing in my own ears. I wondered how it sounded to Rhys. He frowned at me as he continued to kneel beside me.

"No need to apologize," he said firmly, then pushed himself from the ground to stand up. Immediately, he extended a hand towards me. "I think it's best if we keep moving though—if you feel able enough, milady."

I nodded mutely, and put my hand in his, the warmth of his once again surprising me. He hoisted me forward and onto my feet easily, then dropped my hand a second later, once he was sure my feet were planted firmly on the ground. I stared at him, still in shock from the entire day, and this situation.

"I'm sorry," I said again, somewhat dumbly.

"Milady—" Rhys said with a sigh, but I interrupted him.

"I'm sorry you're here with me," I said, and he looked taken aback—and possibly hurt. I blushed, and tried to backtrack. "No, I mean, I'm glad you're here, really. I'm thankful to have someone with me. But…I'm sorry that you've been forced out of Nefyn…I guess, by me." I looked at the ground, at the dew-covered blades of grass that reached toward my knees in the places where it hadn't been pressed into the earth by our feet. Nearby the horses nickered as they nibbled on the green blades, filling a short silence where Rhys didn't immediately reply.

"What other options would I have had?" he said, the sadness evident in his tone. I looked up at him then. He was looking off, back towards Nefyn, where the lights were shining in brighter contrast against the deep darkness of night. The hills were pitch black against the starry sky, and the lights of the city looked like an extension of that, like stars fallen to the earth. He stared at them with the same mask as before, trying so hard to hide whatever emotion he was truly feeling—the emotion he was ashamed of. "Nefyn is lost," he continued after a moment, and turned to look at me then, his expression set and determined. "The city is under their control—whoever they are. Their leaders will have arrived by now, and if the ones they had sent were that powerful…how powerful must the leaders be? If I hadn't been killed in the battle, I would be at their mercy. Just like everyone else."

I felt tears prick at my eyes. I couldn't think of anything to say. I knew everything he said was true.

Rhys turned away from me, and swung himself into Cai's saddle without hesitation. "Let's ride to Gwanwynn Forest, at least, this night. It will be easier to hide our tracks once in the forest. It seems they've stopped pursuing us, but still, it's best to be safe."

I nodded and mounted Nimue. And then we were off into the dark of night, the amorphous shape of the forest looming ahead.

»«

We stopped a couple of hours later, having gone a mile or so into the forest. The trees were old and tall, their trunks many feet thick, with gnarled roots protruding from the ground. Our horses were well trained, though, and they stepped over any obstacle with ease, even if we couldn't see the roots ourselves.

The forest felt crowded and dense though the trees were far apart, and the understory sparse. It was full dark by the time we were immersed within it, and the odd shifting of dark gray shapes and shadows would have spooked me away, but I had nowhere else to go. We were nowhere near the main road that ran from Nefyn, through the center of Lithe, and over to Maenynys, which lay closer to the eastern side of the country; but planned to make our way towards it the following day. I guessed that we were only a couple miles north of it, and I hoped it wouldn't take too long to find it. It would be impossible to traverse the forest without the road.

We stopped in a large glen, and an awkward silence persisted as we made a little campsite. We deemed it safe enough to build a small fire, and as I laid out my cloak to at least have some protection from the hard ground, I realized I was incredibly hungry. I racked my brain, trying to remember if there was a town somewhere in the forest along the road. I thought there was one called Fynnonbach, but I couldn't quite remember where it was. I thought about this, trying not to panic over our lack of food, and glanced around the glen. I hoped that the more I stared out into the trees, the less nervous I would be about spending the night in the forest, but the flickering shadows extending out into the darkness did not serve this purpose well. Pushing the odd shapes and shadows out of my mind, not to mention the odd sounds of crackling twigs under little paws or hooves, or the deep echoing hoots of birds that sent shivers down my spine with every reverberation, I focused on the flickering flames before me. Small but just a couple feet away, branches popped and crackled as they burned and I hugged my knees to my chest, relishing the feeling of breathing deeply despite the situation I was in. Rhys arranged his cloak on the ground on the other side of the fire, his movements slow and measured, as though he was relaxed. We were silent as we both settled near the fireplace, but the thoughts in my mind were loud enough to distract me from the quiet, now no longer awkward to me.

"We'll need to buy food tomorrow, at the first town we come across," he said, nearly making me jump in surprise after such a long silence.

I nodded. "I think, once we get on the road, the first town is Fynnonbach."

"We'll reach it tomorrow, won't we?" he asked.

I nodded, a bit hesitantly. "I'm almost certain."

Rhys nodded absent-mindedly. "Well…we'd best get some sleep," he said, looking at me with some hesitation. I supposed he didn't like having to dictate our actions, but I didn't mind. If he hadn't said anything, I was likely to just sit there in a stupor all night. I nodded, agreeing with him immediately. We allowed the fire to begin to die and lay down on our cloaks. I rolled mine around me like a cocoon, and felt sleep take me much more quickly than I had anticipated.

»«

We awoke as the sun rose, seemingly at the same time. Barely acknowledging each other, we didn't hesitate in getting back in the saddle and continuing on through the forest. Though strange sounds still echoed around us, the bright light of the sun filtering through the leaves above us gave me a sense of security.

We were riding only for a few minutes before Rhys broke the silence. "I hope you slept well, milady," he said, his voice startling even though he spoke softly, as it cut through the still morning air of the forest.

"As well as I could," I responded, keeping my gaze ahead, studying the trees before us and scanning for any potential dangers. I was thankful that the trees were growing far apart, and the land was relatively flat.

"Perhaps we can buy some bedrolls when we reach Fynnonbach," Rhys suggested. Without thinking, I looked over at him with a small frown.

"I'm not sure it would be worth the investment. It should only take three days to reach Maenynys," I said. "I can suffer for those few nights."

"Decent sleep is necessary for keeping strength, milady," Rhys replied, glancing at me with uncertainty.

"That's true," I said with a small frown, thinking it over. "Well, if you insist. I was able to grab a large sum of money before we left, so it isn't really an issue."

Rhys raised an eyebrow. "How much money?" he asked.

"I didn't count, but it weighs quite a bit," I said with a small shrug. "Don't worry yourself about money, though. I'll handle it."

"Are you sure?" he asked, suddenly concerned with furrowed eyebrows. I frowned at him, confused.

"Am I sure about what?"

"That you want to handle it? I could carry the money for you," he said.

"That's not necessary," I replied, unsure why he would even offer. "I would prefer to keep it, as long as that's okay with you."

"Of course, milady. I only wanted to ensure that that's what you wanted," he said, looking back towards the trees before us, suddenly stoic. The sunlight shone through the leaves above us and cast everything in a green glow, and I fell silent as we continued on through the calm morning. Leaves crunched under the hooves of our horses, and birds sang in the winding branches above, their tweets and trills loud and cutting in the stillness.

"Milady," Rhys said suddenly, after an immeasurable amount of time riding in silence. I nearly jumped at the sudden sound of his voice, but managed to hang onto my composure. "I don't want to upset you, but there are events we should discuss from yesterday."

I nodded slowly, but didn't look in his direction. "You're probably right," I agreed.

"May I ask what happened while I was unconscious?" he said, and I felt his eyes on me from where he rode a few feet away. I looked over at him for a moment, and nodded again.

"Cassia—the curly-haired one—she used the Eos to levitate you to the room you woke up in, while Varina held on to me, and forced me into the room after you. I tried fighting with the Eos but they overpowered me so easily… Calliten never trained me for combat like that." I paused, but Rhys remained silent so I continued. "Cassia… She said that they were there to change the Empire."

"The whole Remisian Empire?" Rhys cut in, surprising me. I nodded. "Well, that isn't possible. It has the most powerful military in Linra."

"You saw what they could do, though," I said.

"I saw them do things with magic I hadn't seen before, but I have rarely seen examples of magic, milady. Only whatever you and Benadur Calliten have accomplished. So I don't think that I fully understand the capabilities of the Eos."

"I had never seen anything like that," I said firmly. "It was…abnormal. Cassia put out this energy I had never felt before, even from another Eos. And Varina…could become invisible. Or teleport or… Well, I don't know. That's how it looked to me."

"People can't teleport," Rhys said quietly, clearly questioning my statement but not wanting to call me a liar outright.

"I don't know what it was," I said, a bit frustrated. "But she disappeared and reappeared in another spot just moments later. That's what I saw."

Rhys was silent for a few moments. "Regardless, they have taken Nefyn so easily. They clearly have powers that I have never heard of—and it sounds like you haven't, either."

I nodded my agreement. "But Calliten hid many things from me," I said, unable to hide the bitterness from my voice. There was an awkward pause, and I looked at Rhys to see him frowning at the trees before us.

"I interrupted a serious conversation between you two," he stated.

I wasn't sure if he was looking for a reply, but I offered one anyway. "That is true," I said. "I discovered…something. And I needed answers from him, but…" I paused, looking over at Rhys. He looked at me, and I searched his eyes for something, something that I needed to see there for me to tell him the truth. "I want to be honest with you, Rhys," I said.

He nodded once. "Of course, milady. If it is a sensitive matter, I promise to keep whatever it is to myself."

I took a deep breath. "Calliten is not my father. Benadur Lara was not my mother," I said, allowing the words to hang between us.

Rhys stared at me as the words sunk in. "What?" he said after a few long, silent moments.

"My parents were killed near the time of my birth," I continued, my eyes moving back and forth from Rhys's shocked face to the forest before us. "Calliten ensured their deaths were concealed, and Benadur Lara's pregnancy was faked. They adopted me, and hid the truth from me. A couple of days ago, I discovered an old letter that disclosed the true nature of my birth. When you came into his study, I had just asked him what it meant."

"I-I'm not sure what to say," Rhys said after another long pause. The tone in his voice surprised me, suddenly full of sadness.

"I…I thought, for a moment…" I began, unsure if I should say the rest of the sentence. But there was something about the way Rhys was looking at me, like he was truly concerned, with deep and understanding eyes, like maybe if he knew then it wouldn't hurt me as much. "I thought he might have had them killed. But he said that wasn't true…"

"Calliten?" he asked in a hushed voice, though we were alone. I nodded, avoiding looking at him even though I knew he was looking at me. "But…why would he…?" He trailed off, shaking his head slightly.

"Because somehow he knew I was an Eosiaid." A beam of sunlight filtered through the leaves above and hit my face, causing me to squint momentarily, before I was brought back to the darkness.

Rhys suddenly let out a huff-like laugh, and I turned to stare at him, surprised to see a glint of humor in his eyes and playing on the corners of his mouth. He saw my expression and immediately the humor fell away, back to that stoic gaze from before. "I'm sorry, milady. I don't know why…why I laughed," he said.

"You can be honest with me, Rhys," I said evenly. "And you don't have to call me milady."

"What should I call you then?" he said, already sounding uneasy at the thought.

"Eira," I replied without hesitation.

"That seems rather informal."

"Would you prefer for me to call you Second Lieutenant Llewellyn?" I questioned.

"Of course not."

"So why be so polite to me?" I argued.

"Because I'm sworn to serve you, not the other way around. You are my superior," he said with a deep frown.

"I think, given the circumstances, we should drop the formalities," I said with a firm voice.

Rhys was silent for a moment as he rode facing forward, scanning the wild forest before us. "Alright," he said finally. "If you insist."

"You'll call me Eira?" I said, a bit dubious. He looked over at me with a warm smile, and something about it nearly made my heart skip a beat.

"Yes. Eira," he said, that smile and my name leaving me dumbfounded. The smile fell slightly when I didn't respond. "Are you alright?" he said.

I blinked and looked away from him quickly. "Yes, sorry. I was…I was just surprised you agreed to use my name."

His smile returned at this, but there was also a hint of confusion in his eyes. "Well, it was an order from my superior, so I had to," he said, and I frowned at him for a moment, before realizing he was attempting a joke. I relaxed and felt a smile come to my face. Until I remembered what we had been talking about before all of this talk about how he should refer to me.

"So…why did you laugh?" I asked, and I saw his hands tense on the reins.

"I'm not sure," he said after a short pause. "I guess…it all hit me at once."

I stared at him, hoping that he would elaborate without me having to ask, and he sighed as he looked over at me. "What happened yesterday—those people, the battle… There were Hartanians, did you notice? And now what you say about Calliten and your real parents… How…how could that happen? And why did all of this happen at the same time?" He continued to look over at me, his eyebrows furrowed in dark uncertainty. I knew exactly what he was saying, what he was getting at, but I knew that if I let it all hit me at once I would be thrown into another panic attack.

"I don't know," I said, trying to sound calm as best as I could, keeping my voice measured and level. "I don't know what's happening or why it's all happening now. All I know is that we have to go to the capital before it's too late. If they take the capital, then all of Lithe will be lost, won't it?"

"They could have already taken it," Rhys said quietly.

I was silent for a while, considering this grim thought. "Let's hope not," I said, just as quiet as Rhys.

6

The Foreign Soldiers

A short while later, I noticed a gap in the trees ahead. Squinting, I felt relief rush through me as I realized it was the road, dappled in wavering beams of sunlight. I pointed it out to Rhys and we hastened on through the last few dozen yards of wild forest, excited as the appearance of the road meant Fynnonbach would not be far off. My stomach had long since passed the typical feeling of hunger, and now bordered on pain. From the quality of the sunlight, it seemed to be about noon when we finally joined the road, the empty river of stone, dirt, and gravel extending through the trees, in one direction towards Nefyn and in the other direction, Maenynys. The massive tree branches arched over the path and cast deep, contrasting shadows that repeated into the distance.

"We must be close to Fynnonbach," Rhys said, and I knew he must have been just as hungry as I was.

"Yes," I agreed, attempting to sound positive despite the growing desperation I felt. With the level ground laid out before us, we were able to maintain a quick pace. We were silent for the next couple of hours, looking out for any sign of Fynnonbach, anticipation growing within me, with just the songs of birds and the crunching of leaves to meet our ears.

After crossing a river via an impressive stone bridge, we arrived on the edges of the small town. The first area that we passed by was lined with small farms, the produce growing abundantly from plants of all shapes and sizes: fruit trees and corn and potatoes.

The homesteads themselves were small and simple wooden structures, formed from the same gray-ish wood as the surrounding forest. The forest seemed far away here, though, as so much of it had been cleared for the farmland and the town. Beyond the farms and houses was an expanse of rolling green hills dotted with grazing cattle and sheep, and the darkened edge of the forest was at least a mile away both to the left and right.

We continued on along the main street in silence, as buildings became more frequent and farmland fell behind us, and I was a little surprised to see that there were very few people out and about. We only passed a couple other riders heading past us on their way out of town, and both simply glanced at us with tension, before looking away. Having rarely left Nefyn before, I wondered if this was typical behavior.

Closer to the center of Fynnonbach, we found a small marketplace and a stable where we could tie our horses while we ate and shopped for supplies. Rhys let out a deep sigh as he dismounted, then turned to me after tying his horse's reins to a wooden post just inside the stable. "Meal first?" he said, raising his eyebrows.

I nodded as I went through the same motions with Nimue, ensuring she was secure despite my need for food. We exited the stable and looked up and down the street, trying to spot some sort of inn beyond the multi-colored tents of the marketplace and the few people that loitered around the area.

"Ah, there it is," Rhys said, pointing slightly back towards the way we had come, and I saw a tavern a few buildings down, on the other side of the street. Knowing that they would have warm meals and not caring at that point about the quality, I nodded again mutely and began to cross the empty road without looking back at Rhys, my stomach clenching in pain.

We entered the tavern and found it to be quiet inside. There would usually be musicians of some sort playing at the taverns in Nefyn, but it was dead silent in this establishment, with only two patrons already sitting inside, both elderly men. They didn't look up from their bowls as we shut the door behind us. The barkeep stood behind the bar on the opposite side of the room, a middle-aged woman who already wore an irritated scowl as we walked through the door.

"Sit where you like," she said to us as she waved a hand dismissively, before disappearing through a door behind the counter. I glanced at Rhys who shrugged. I decided that sitting down quickly could only help speed things along, so I sat down at the edge of one of the long tables that spanned the width of the room, and Rhys sat on the bench across from me.

Before I could ask Rhys what he thought would be best to do next, the barkeep appeared beside us, seemingly from thin air.

"We've got beef soup, if it's food you're after," she said, her tone bored and dull. "Some bread too."

"We'll each have both," I said quickly.

"You want mead or ale with that?" she continued in the same tone.

"Mead," I said.

At the same time, Rhys said, "Ale." She looked back and forth between us for a moment, before sighing heavily and leaving our area.

We waited in silence for her to return with our food and drink, and even through the pain of hunger, I felt that there was something awkward about that lapse in conversation, unlike the many silent hours we had already spent together. I glanced at Rhys, who was staring out the window with a blank expression. It bothered me that I barely knew this person and that I was essentially stuck with him for an undefined amount of time. It would have been easier for me to travel on my own in some ways, but I knew in other ways it would be much harder. And I supposed we were bound to talk more on the way to the capital, which was still two days away.

Our food and drink soon appeared, and we began eating with voracious intensity. The feeling of finally easing my hunger was nearly a spiritual experience, and before I could really even comprehend the fact that I was eating, the soup and bread were gone. I looked up, slightly surprised, and saw that Rhys had finished eating as well.

He sighed heavily, then took a sip of his ale. He looked at me as he set the tankard back down on the table.

"I'm guessing you don't want to stay here for long," he said.

I shook my head. "No, we should just buy supplies for the rest of the ride and get on our way. We can reach Maenynys in two days if we travel fast and only rest for a few hours at night."

He nodded in agreement, and if there was anything about this plan that he didn't like, he declined to voice it. I didn't have the energy to press him on it, and went to the counter to pay and tip the barkeep.

We then went out to the marketplace, blinking in the bright afternoon sun, and bought enough food for two days for both of us. Rhys still insisted on buying bedrolls, so I inquired with a shopkeeper about where we would be able to purchase them, and he directed us to a general store on the other side of Fynnonbach. We also needed packs to carry the food and waterskins, so the general store proved to be a necessary stop anyway.

Within an hour we had everything we could think of that would make the rest of the journey bearable, and without any further hesitation we loaded our new packs onto the backs of our saddles, and left Fynnonbach behind us in the golden light of the descending sun.

»«

The next day passed in a blur as we rode through Gwanwynn Forest, the shock of the events in Nefyn from two days prior finally beginning to wear off. For me, the shock was replaced with resolve. We had nowhere to go but the capital, and only the capital would help. Rhys and I spoke to each other rarely. I found that I simply didn't have anything to say to him, and apparently he felt similarly towards me.

That night, I was relieved to have a bedroll to sleep on, and slept much better than I had rolled up in my cloak. Still, I didn't allow for us to sleep for long, as I wanted to reach Maenynys as quickly as possible. I refused to think of what was happening in Nefyn while we were traveling, assuming that the invaders were not the most just or merciful people, and worrying deeply about my own people.

I was especially worried about Mari, but could not bring myself to voice these concerns out loud, as I was sure Rhys was even more distraught than I was. I couldn't imagine the fear he felt for the safety of his sister, parents, and friends. I wanted to ask him, to extend that same kindness that he had offered me when I had opened up about Calliten and the things I had discovered, but I feared that I would be crossing the line. It was impossible to tell with Rhys where the line with him even was, though. We had only been traveling for two days together, and while he had finally begun to call me Eira rather than milady, I could tell from his tone and general manner that he was still acting overly respectful towards me.

So it was rather surprising to me, as we sat around a little fire on our third night of traveling, just a few hours' ride outside of Maenynys, when Rhys brought up all of these things himself.

"I apologize, Eira," he said after clearing his throat. I looked up at him from where I had been staring blankly at the fire, a half-chewed bite of bread in my mouth. I frowned at him in confusion. "For…well, I feel like I may have made you uncomfortable. Or been a less than pleasant travel companion."

I swallowed the bread quickly, feeling the frown deepen on my face. "Have I done something to make you think that?" I asked. "I-I think you've been perfectly pleasant, actually."

"I haven't spoken much," he said in a slow voice, still a bit hesitant. I watched as the firelight flickered over his face, solemn and serious.

"Neither have I," I countered. "I believe we both have had a lot to think about."

Rhys nodded, but didn't seem convinced as his face remained serious, his eyes downcast towards the fire, studying it like I had been moments earlier. "I just wanted to be truthful. There have been many moments these last few days where I've wanted to say something, but…but I'm still not used to…" He trailed off, but my brain filled in the rest.

"You're not used to treating me like a regular person," I finished, perhaps a bit bluntly. He looked at me sharply, opening his mouth to protest my wording, but I continued. "It's fine, Rhys. It is hard to change habits and ways of thinking so quickly. I assure you, though, I am a regular person, despite the Eos. I believe we've always been equals, but especially right now."

"But you're…" He gestured vaguely at me, a confused and self-conscious frown covering his face. I found his discomfort slightly funny, but refrained from expressing any humor at his expense. "You're an Eosiaid. You're holy."

I couldn't help it—a short laugh escaped my throat. "I'm sorry," I said, even while a grin broke out on my face at the sight of his affronted expression. "It's just that… No, I'm really not."

"But Eosiaids are blessed by Sky Queen," he argued.

I shrugged. "I don't feel very blessed right now," I said.

"You have the power to heal," he pressed on.

"And to hurt and destroy. There is balance in everything that I can do," I said. "Which makes me just like every other person."

Rhys looked at me with doubtful eyes, but didn't comment on that claim. Instead he sighed. "I have had a lot to think about," he agreed with my previous statement, obviously realizing that arguing with me about my level of holiness was pointless. "I'm…I'm terrified."

"About your family," I said quietly, looking back at the fire instead of his face.

"Yes," he said in an equally subdued tone. "My parents and Mari…and the other guards. I'm scared of what has happened to them."

"To be honest," I said, still avoiding his eyes, "I'm scared too."

I sensed he stared at me then, and I was compelled to look up. There was emotion I had rarely seen in a person in his face, his eyes shimmering, flashing with fire, like his feelings were ready to jump out of his soul and manifest before us as flames. His lips were in a tight line, his jaw tense, and not for the first time I was struck by how much he could convey just with a look. I knew so much then—how he felt about his family, how he felt about Nefyn. And there was something else, something that was harder to define…

"Whatever happens…" he said in a tone I hadn't heard him use before, dark and heavy and pure with honesty. "Whatever happens, I'll be right beside you, and we will do everything we can, together."

"For Nefyn," I said, mirroring his tone, captivated by his promise. A small smile appeared at the edges of his mouth, nearly unnoticeable.

"For Nefyn," he echoed.

»«

By late morning the next day, I could sense that we were drawing closer to Maenynys. The dirt road became wide and paved with large flagstones, and we passed wagons laden with goods for trade every hour or so. There was an odd air around every person we saw, as they were wrapped in tense silence, ignoring us with intent. I was fine with this, but the tension they gave off was disconcerting. I didn't speak of it with Rhys. If he noticed, he didn't say anything, and I didn't see any benefit in bringing it up. Maenynys was in reach, and hopefully with it, our journey would come to an end.

The trees grew small and sparse as we reached the eastern edge of Gwanwynn Forest. The sky stretched above us, clear and blue, a warm spring breeze blowing directly against us. "The breeze from the lake," I said aloud, mostly to myself.

Rhys's eyes met mine as he rode a few feet to my left in the now-desolate road, brows slightly furrowed at my words.

"The lake? The one Maenynys is built on?" he clarified.

I nodded, pulling my eyes back to the road before us, a little embarrassed that I had spoken out loud without thinking.

"Yes, Maenynys is built on an island in the center of a lake."

"Have you been before?" he asked, his tone suddenly curious, and when I looked at him, his expression was open and thoughtful.

"When I was very young. Every twenty-two years there is a grand assembly of all of Nefyn's Benadurs. I went when I was three—which means the next one is in three years," I said.

"Hopefully," Rhys muttered, ducking under the low-growing branch of one of the last trees of Gwanwynn Forest. I frowned at him, displeased by the implication of his comment.

"Everything is going to be fine," I said firmly.

"I apologize for offending you," Rhys said immediately, and I heard the polite tone he used to speak to me as a Benadur returned to his voice. This also displeased me, as the last couple of days had proved he had the ability to treat me as an equal. Now he was taking a step back, and though it bothered me, I also had to admit that it didn't matter. If everything was going to be fine, was going to go back to normal, then my relationship with Rhys would return to that of a superior and an inferior, whether I wanted it to or not.

I did not reply to his apology, and we fell into a disconcerting silence as we rode the last couple of miles to Maenynys. The road began to climb up a steady hill, flanked on both sides by wide expanses of bright green grass, practically glowing in the midday sun. As we reached the crest of the hill, the city of Maenynys came into view, and I heard Rhys take in a sharp breath.

Maenynys sparkled with white stone and glittering glass on its island, rising from the crystal waters of the lake like a grand monument. Even from so far away, still three miles, I could see the Brenty towering above it all, the residence of the king. Its many white spires reached for the sky, tipped with gold and large jewels that sparkled and nearly blinded me and Rhys as they reflected the sun back towards us. Massive silver-stone bridges cut across the lake in three different locations, connecting Maenynys to the rest of the country.

I looked over at Rhys, curious to see his expression, and wasn't disappointed. His mouth was slightly open and his eyes wide as he took in the city, his eyes darting from bridge to lake to the Brenty.

I couldn't help but smile at his awed reaction. "What do you think?" I asked him. He looked at me, and it seemed as though he literally had to tear his eyes away from the view. He saw my grin and attempted to master his expression, shutting his mouth quickly and lowering his eyebrows, but still there remained a glint of shock in his eyes.

"It's very impressive," he said, then allowed a small smile to appear on his face as well. "It is certainly more than I expected."

"Of course the capital of Lithe is this grand," I said, gesturing at the city, my arm swinging above Nimue's neck. "You shouldn't have expected anything less," I teased. His smile grew, knowing that it was only a joke.

"Well, there's no time to waste, is there?" Rhys said as he gripped his reins, looking once again at the city, and the road that led to it. "It will still take some time to reach it."

I nodded and we began the ride down the slope, which continued for the next mile before finally flattening out slightly. Wildflowers of yellow, red, and white began to appear the closer we got to the lake, the dots of vibrant color beautiful and contrasting with the sea of green that surrounded us.

Still, the closer we got to the city, the more anxious I became. I questioned everything—how we would gain approval to speak with the king, if he would be sympathetic with our cause, if he would believe us at all... There were too many questions cycling through my mind, and all the while I knew that the only thing that I could do was continue onward, and do my best with whatever came our way.

"It will be alright, Eira," Rhys said quietly, his voice cutting through the silent warm air around us. I glanced at him, surprised that he had noticed my anxiety. "Your knuckles are white," he explained, gesturing at where my hands were holding onto the reins. I loosened them immediately.

"Sorry," I said without thinking.

"Why are you sorry?" he questioned.

I shook my head. "I'm just...I'm just worried."

Rhys nodded as though he felt the exact same way, though he seemed so much more relaxed than me. "We're almost there. It will all become clear soon." And somehow I found it comforting, and I felt some more of the tension leave my body.

A mile away from the bridge, though, something began to feel off again. I squinted and saw that three people stood at the entrance to the bridge, standing completely still and facing the road. Two were on horseback, one on foot.

"Guards?" I questioned. Rhys studied the forms as well, and nodded.

"It makes sense for the city to post guards at the bridge entrances," Rhys said with a small shrug.

"That's true," I said, but couldn't shake the feeling that something was wrong. We continued riding in silence, as I tried to hide the unease that I felt.

We approached the guards, and I frowned when I now only saw two, mounted on tall black horses. I was sure I had counted three figures only a few minutes before. The two guards positioned their horses to fully block the silver-stone opening to the bridge, and used a spear each to close the space between them.

"Halt, travelers," one said. He had a deep voice, and his face was hidden beneath his helmet, shining in the sunlight. "State your business in the city."

"Visiting family," I lied quickly. Rhys didn't even glance at me, but kept his gaze fixed calmly on the soldiers in front of us.

There was a pause where I held my breath, and then the guards lowered their spears and urged their horses to the side of the road. "You may pass," he said.

"Thank you," I said with a curt nod, and then urged Nimue forward, Rhys just behind me. As I passed the guards, I noticed the one that had spoken to us was smiling oddly, his eyes hidden beneath his helmet. I attempted to ignore this unsettling expression as I looked forward, taking in the bridge extending out before us.

It was long, and the stone that it was made of glittered slightly in the sunlight. The water extended below us in either direction, and the city rose above the horizon of the bridge in front of us, the turrets and spires of the Brenty reaching towards the few clouds that dotted the blue sky. The water lapped and splashed against the stones a few yards below us as gentle waves met the immovable posts of the bridge. A misty breeze blew at us from the side, and for a moment I was pleased that nature was sometimes so kind.

Though the guards had let us pass, though the weather was beautiful, though we were only a few minutes from the city gates, a panic rose in my chest, and all at once, with one blink of my eyes, I understood why.

In the span of a blink, she was standing there, only a few yards in front of us. Her teeth were barred in something akin to a smile, and she looked just as road weary as us. She held a sword in one hand and the gold-hilted dagger in the other, both glinting with sunspots. Her blond-silver hair was escaping from the braid she had put it in, and strands blew around her face in the wind.

Nimue and Cai were understandably frightened by her sudden appearance, and both horses reared with distressed whinnying as they began to back away.

"You're easier to find than I thought you would be," Varina said, her voice rough but triumphant. I looked at Rhys, fear in his wide eyes, and we both looked back at the entrance to the bridge to see that the guards were halfway between us and land, facing us with spears pointed in our direction.

I looked back to Varina. She was now a few yards closer and she slowly approached us, and I could tell from how she smiled at us just how pleased she was that she had trapped us.

"What do we do?" I whispered to Rhys, unable to hide the desperation from my voice. He glanced at me, then dismounted in a smooth movement, drawing his sword and assuming a fighting stance right in front of me and Nimue. She pawed at the stones beneath us, tossing her head in anxiety.

"Rhys," I yelled at him.

Varina grinned even more from where she stood a few yards before us, her blue eyes flashing. "Haven't we done this before?" she asked him.

"Not properly," he replied. "You resort to your illusions—not a fair fight, is it?"

Her smile was still all teeth. "A great warrior uses all their skills to their advantage."

"But only a coward disappears entirely," Rhys countered.

She laughed, a cold, huffing sound. "You pretend to understand just what I can do," Varina hissed. I noticed her knuckles turn white around the hilts of her weapons as she gripped them with all her strength. Her eyes met mine and I felt a chill at the sneering humor in her expression when she looked at me. "How sad," she said, mocking me. "You're so weak that a commoner has to protect you. You're a disgrace to Eos everywhere."

"Don't speak to her," Rhys said, raising his voice just slightly, but still maintaining his composure. But Varina kept her eyes locked on mine, ignoring him.

"And yet you escaped. They think you're worth something, but I know you've just been blessed with good luck," she said. I tried to make sense of her words but simply couldn't.

"She has nothing to do with you—" Rhys began, but Varina looked at him suddenly and quickly interrupted him.

"One way or another, she is returning with me to Nefyn," she said to him, her menacing grin falling away. She pointed the dagger at him and tilted her head slightly. "No one cares if you die in the process."

"Rhys, stop." I managed to find the words, but he ignored me, and before I knew what was happening the two began running at each other, quickly closing the distance between them. A second after Varina had begun running, she disappeared entirely, like a wraith in a shroud of fog, and the sight triggered something in me I had never felt before.

I was acting before I knew what I was doing. I dismounted from Nimue's saddle and jumped the few feet to stand in front of Rhys, no concrete thought in my mind, only the need to stop what was about to happen. Magic energy exploded out from me in an innate, intuitive form, both natural and incredibly jarring to my senses. I pushed the energy outward from Rhys and I, towards where Varina had been, using it as a wall to separate her from us. Though she was invisible, Varina ran into my wall of energy, and I sensed it as she was knocked off her feet and the sword and dagger left her grip. They became visible once again as they arched through the air towards Rhys and I, and again, the magic emerged from my body like a reflex, and pushed the weapons down from their arc, so they landed right in front of us. The dagger glittered brightly as it clanged against the stone, and without thinking I picked it up. I looked down at it for a moment, before a sudden movement distracted me and I looked up.

Varina lay in the middle of the bridge just a couple yards before us, limp with her eyes closed. Unconscious, she was unable to maintain her invisibility.

"Let's go," Rhys said without hesitation, turning and swinging himself into the saddle with his sword still drawn. Even as I followed his lead and got back in my saddle, I felt confusion at his words.

"Where?" I asked. He turned Cai's reins toward the city and then turned to frown at me, pulling back slightly on the leather in his hand.

"Into the city, before she wakes up," he said. I felt like he was yelling but I couldn't be sure.

"But she'll find us in there," I argued. "We need to get far away from here." The city only had three exits. Once we were within its walls, it would be nearly impossible to get out if Varina kept looking for us…and something told me that she would.

"The guards are blocking the exit," Rhys said, openly glaring at me, and this time I was sure he was yelling. Nimue stepped and pawed restlessly, and I struggled to rein her in and keep her still, while still holding onto the dagger.

"And those guards clearly work for her. Who do you think controls Maenynys now?" I yelled back.

I watched as doubt entered Rhys's eyes, and took my chance. I turned Nimue back the way we had come, towards the guards who hadn't moved from their post halfway between us and the end of the bridge. I assumed Varina had told them not to move. I got Nimue to break into a gallop, and accessed that innate part of me, so motivated by fear. Their spears were pointed to me and Nimue snorted in protest but I pressed my calves into her sides, and I let the energy burst from me, another violent wave mimicking the ones below the stones we stood on.

The guards were thrown backwards just like Varina had been, and I rushed past them only moments later, their armor still clanging against the stones beneath them. I wasn't sure if they were conscious or not, but I didn't want to stay and find out. Just as I reached the edge of the land, and the grass swept away from me in both directions, curving up the wide hill, I turned around and saw Rhys was right behind me. He nodded once, his expression set and grim, and I looked forward once again, with only the thought of putting distance between us and Varina on my mind.

We both slowed our pace once we were deep in the forest, the trees towering above us with gnarled, groaning branches. We were both breathing heavily, from the ride and from the adrenaline, and I avoided his gaze even as we slowed to a stop, my eyes fixed on the road behind us.

"We need to keep moving," I said, looking for any sign of pursuers.

"Yes," Rhys agreed, his voice solemn. The sadness in his tone surprised me, and I turned to stare at him. He was already staring at me, once again with too much emotion in his eyes for me to understand.

"Are you…?" I began, unsure of what to say.

"Thank you," he said, voice quiet and subdued. I blinked, surprised.

"What?" I asked. My mind simply couldn't understand the events of the past few minutes, and this expression of gratitude was yet another strange moment.

"For what you did. For stopping her…and the soldiers," he said.

I felt my stomach drop as his words set in. "I don't even know what I did," I said quietly, looking down at Nimue's neck.

"That was the power of the Eos," he said slowly, as though he was uncertain of what he was saying. I looked up at him, unable to stop a glare from spreading over my face.

"It wasn't what I was taught to do. It was… uncontrollable."

"And you can't stand the feeling of being out of control," he said, so level and calm. I opened my mouth to reply, then shut it tightly. He sighed and shook his head before continuing. "You saved my life, and your own freedom. And…I understand this might be hard for you to hear, but you may have to use the Eos like that many more times before this is all over."

"But I don't even know what I did," I argued. "I know that it existed in that way, but I've only ever healed. Eos aren't supposed to hurt people."

Rhys sighed, and looked back towards Maenynys, thinking over his response as his frown deepened. "Thinking like that isn't useful, especially now. Something we've never experienced has happened, and…we're going to have to be able to do things that we haven't done before."

I hesitated for only a moment, before nodding in agreement. My stomach sank as I recognized the truth in his words, and the fear that lived in me as a result.

»«

We rode at a swift pace further into the forest, until the sun was low beyond the thick branches that separated us from the sky. Evening birds trilled and sang high above us, loud and echoing through the trees, and I listened to them intently, as they distracted me from the situation we were in.

"Let's stop for a moment," Rhys suggested, and I nodded numbly without looking at him, pulling on Nimue's reins until we came to a stop. The road had returned to dirt, and the dust settled slowly behind us, glowing here and there in a patch of the dying sunlight breaking through the tree canopy.

"So," Rhys said with a deep sigh, and I sensed that he was looking at me as I looked at the settling dust. "What now?" I turned to face him, astride his black horse and looking at me like I was his commander. Somewhere in my mind, I was able to acknowledge that I was, even though I didn't want to be.

"What now?" I repeated, as I felt a small frown grow on my face. I tried to smooth my features, to not give away how distraught I was, but it was no use. "I don't know what now, Rhys. I have no idea what to do."

"Alright," Rhys said easily, his voice level and relaxed despite the situation we were in. It only served to frustrate me further, though I hoped this wasn't evident to him. "Well, we aren't being followed, that seems to be clear. It's getting dark. Why don't we head off the road a ways and set up a camp?" he suggested.

I paused, thinking over his words slowly, and then nodded, agreeing it was a good idea. It had been a long day, and rest sounded nice.

We rode half a mile directly through the trees, until we found a nice clearing just as the last bit of golden sunlight disappeared beyond the trees, casting the forest into pale shadows. We set up a camp in silence, but decided not to light a fire, just in case guards had been sent after us or Varina herself was on our tail. Rhys passed me some bread and other snacks, and I ate mindlessly, staring into the trees as if the answers lay somewhere among them. The thought of Varina stalking us through the woods sent a shiver of fear up my spine, but Rhys didn't seem to notice.

"Have some more," he said quietly beside me, and offered me another chunk of bread. I considered declining, but also knew that it would bring me a small amount of comfort. I took it from him, this time my fingers accidentally glancing over his.

A feeling raced through me, powerful and frightening, and before I could react, the sight of the shadowed forest disappeared, and instead I saw Rhys. Only Rhys. But he was different, younger, a bit smaller. Clad in armor, but not the set he was wearing currently. Not in a forest but a grand parlor of a rich household. His expression was determined, if a bit wary, as he adjusted one of the straps on his shoulder. And before I could say or do anything, the parlor faded away, and the forest returned. For a moment I felt nothing but my body vibrating in abject fear, and then I heard Rhys's voice above the sound of blood rushing in my ear.

"Eira? Eira? What happened?" He sounded frantic so I turned to look at him, vaguely noting the piece of bread still clutched tightly in my hand. Even in the low light of the evening, I could see his eyes were wide in fright, and I blinked.

"What happened?" I asked.

"You…you seized up, for a few seconds, it was like you went unconscious and tense at the same time," he tried to explain, but I just frowned at the bread in my hand, slowly uncurling my fingers.

"I saw you," I whispered, and he only looked at me silently. I refused to look at him, still disoriented. "But you were younger."

"What…?" Rhys tried to come up with a response, but failed to finish his question. I blinked a few times, shook my head, and breathed deeply.

"It must be the stress. And exhaustion," I said with finality, turning to look at him and hoping my expression was determined. If I didn't get a hold of myself, he would be frightened to no end. And we both had to be in control.

"Are you sure?" he asked me. He was still tense, my explanation bringing him no comfort. I nodded.

"We need a plan, and we need rest," I said firmly. I had to direct the conversation away from what had just happened, and towards what we would do next. "Maenynys is out of the question."

Rhys nodded slowly. "Yes, Maenynys is under their control. So…all of Lithe is under their control or soon will be," he said, frowning at the ground like he was solving some kind of logic problem.

"Yes," I agreed. "And Varina has been following us, and laid that trap. We don't know if she'll continue the pursuit…but we should assume that she will. Especially since I have this," I said, picking up the dagger from the ground beside me.

Rhys frowned at it, then looked back at my face. "Why did you take that?" he asked.

"I don't know." I frowned back at him, not because I was upset by the question, but because I was as confused as he was. "It fell in front of me…and I know it's important to them."

"How do you know that?"

"When we were in that room with Cassia—you were still unconscious—Cassia held this up to Varina to justify telling her what to do. It shows…who is in charge," I said, now looking down at the blade in my hand with a confusing collection of thoughts swirling through my mind.

After a few silent moments I heard Rhys let out a sigh. "We're off track again," he muttered, and I looked up at him, his brows now furrowed in frustration. "We have to find help," Rhys said, looking up at me as the deep frown remained on his face.

"There's nowhere else to go," I said, shrugging my shoulders slightly, before placing the dagger back on the ground.

"The Empire," Rhys said with force, and I blinked at him in surprise. "We are subjects of the Empire, and the emperor will not sit idly by while one of his kingdoms falls."

It was my turn to sigh. "Rhys…the Empire has eyes and ears and spies everywhere. They knew what was going on before we did, I assure you. Either the Empire will interfere in this or it won't. We will have no effect on their decision."

"Well, then what are we to do?" Rhys demanded, now speaking swiftly and at a higher volume. I bristled. "We can't go back to Nefyn. We will surely be captured. We can't go to Maenynys. It seems nowhere will be safe for us. So what are you suggesting we do?"

As he demanded answers, I felt myself begin to relax. Someone had to be in control, and being asked these questions in such a raw way made me feel compelled to answer.

"There are too many unknowns," I said without thinking. Thinking was my downfall—for this moment, all I could do was speak on instinct. "The people that captured us in the Benaty were Remisian, but the guards they controlled were

Hartanian. Hartanians aren't the ones in control. They're simply the armed forces being used to capture areas of Lithe."

"Alright," Rhys said in a slow, dubious voice. "That doesn't help us though—"

"Well, who are these people controlling the Hartanians?" I continued, picking up a dried, fallen leaf and tearing at it absentmindedly. "We know they have unseen powers, things that I'm sure are unusual for an Eosiaid to be capable of. Just look at what Varina was capable of doing. And Cassia said that she and the others were blessed twice by the Sky Queen… And that there are people superior to her, that she wanted me to meet…"

Rhys waited impatiently while I let the thoughts rush through my mind, my fingers shredding the leaf in my hand until it was in tatters on the dirt in front of me. Then I looked up at Rhys, the only answer having come to me at last.

"We have to learn about who these people are before we can even think of saving Lithe," I said as I looked him dead in the eye. He stared at me, either taken aback by this suggestion, or the force that went behind it.

But he regained his composure and gave me a curt nod. "Alright," Rhys said, glaring at the ground. His tone told me that he wasn't entirely on board, but he wasn't offering any other suggestions. "How do we learn more about these people, then?"

"There's a book I read," I replied, the cover of the book clear in my mind, the texture of the pages like a ghost on my fingertips. Though it wasn't with me, I remembered the words that had caught my attention. *According to the few sources that have ever made it to the peak and back, they know of the origins of the Eosiaid; they know the truth, buried under the myths and legends…* "This book says that there are myths and legends surrounding the truth of the Eosiaid, and the only people who know the whole truth live at the top of Aornadur in Aorlanda—"

"You are not suggesting that we—" Rhys broke in, suddenly tense at my words.

"No, no. The author lives in southern Lithe somewhere—I think in Caergarth."

He raised an eyebrow at this. "You think?" he repeated.

I sighed, exasperated. "It's my best guess. Her author description simply states that she lives near the Fethwen Mountains, and I know there's a large library in Caergarth—the biggest in the kingdom outside of Maenynys. Any scholar would want to live near it."

"And you think she might have some answers about these Eosiaids?" I nodded.

"She's the only person who has ever even implied that there are secrets about the Eosiaid…that I've heard of, anyway. I-I've read a lot of books, and I've never seen anyone speak of the Eosiaid in the same way she has. Like there's more to it than we know. Than even I know," I said, and the more I spoke about it, the more I was sure this was the right thing to do. Rhys was silent for a long time, staring off into the trees as he considered my words.

"I…I can't think of any alternatives," Rhys said, finally, with a shrug. I let out the breath I was holding in relief. "To Caergarth, then."

I grinned. "To Caergarth."

7

The Search for Catrin Morgan

The road to Caergarth was a straight shot south from Maenynys, and I estimated that it would take us at least five days to reach the academic city. We had to follow the road we were on back to Fynnonbach, and then continue on the eastern road that diverged from there, until we reached the Grand Road that led from Maenynys to one of Lithe's largest ports, Tan y Mor, situated on a southern bay. It only took us a day of riding to reach the Grand Road, and as we traveled, I began to notice something that made me deeply uncomfortable.

"When was the last time we passed someone?" I asked Rhys as we set up a small camp, after traveling about a mile down the Grand Road. Twilight was nearly over, and I could barely see as Rhys frowned at my question while chewing on his bread. We sat in the tall grass between the trees of the forest, still opting to not have a fire.

Rhys shrugged after taking a few moments to think. "I don't know. Probably since Fynnonbach this morning."

"Isn't that odd?" I continued, unable to keep the anxiety out of my voice. "I mean, we're on the Grand Road now and we haven't seen anyone. I would have thought it would be packed."

"Things are different now, aren't they?" Rhys said, voice suddenly subdued and quiet.

I nodded slowly, feeling my lips press into a tight line. Stars began to appear in the endless dark dome above us, and I looked up to study them and the crescent moon, trying not to think too much about what sort of country we lived in now.

"Perhaps we shouldn't take the Grand Road, then," I said, looking back down at Rhys's shadowy form. "Surely they'll have guards stationed at various crossroads and checkpoints, ensuring that only verified travelers are passing through. And it would be easier for Varina to catch us on this road."

"She'll probably spend a couple days searching Maenynys for us," Rhys said.

I frowned, unsure if that was true. "I'm sure she'll ask the guards which way we went," I replied, hesitant to disagree with him outright.

He looked thoughtful at my words, frowning into the distance. "Maybe, but perhaps she'll still assume we went back into the city after attacking them. After all, where else would we have to go?"

I shrugged. "Maybe you're right. No matter what, she'll likely have a hard time finding our trail, but at most she'll be delayed for a couple days—if she does choose to pursue us. It may be worth it to diverge from the road, simply to make it more difficult for her to catch up with us."

"If we leave the road, it will take us well over a week to reach Caergarth," Rhys said, with a warning tone in his voice. Though I couldn't see his features clearly in the low, ghostly light, I could tell just from his voice how doubtful he felt.

I sighed. "Fine," I said after a moment. "We'll stay on the road. But keep your eyes out for any sign of danger. This…this isn't the Lithe that we're used to anymore. And someone might be hunting us."

"We'll ride as fast as we can," Rhys said. "Get there in just a few days. And hope that Caergarth itself isn't under their control yet."

"Now that they have Maenynys, it's only a matter of time before all of Lithe is gone," I said quietly.

"That's why we'll travel fast," Rhys replied without hesitation, and the resolution in his voice surprised me to no end.

»«

We woke up early the next morning and began the swift ride to Caergarth. We took care to not overwork the horses, and allowed them water breaks whenever we happened to pass a stream. Though we were silent for the first few hours of riding, with the sunlight streaming through the porous canopy to our left, Rhys surprised me when he suddenly began speaking.

"There's something I feel the need to ask you, Eira," he said, and I glanced over at him, curious. He continued looking straight ahead, his jaw and shoulders tense.

"Okay," I replied, already curious.

"What happened to you when that woman touched you? And the other day? It was like you went unconscious, but only for a few seconds. I thought maybe she had harmed you, but it seems to have happened again, and I can't determine the cause." He finally looked over at me, the concern bright in his eyes, along with some amount of trepidation.

"I'm not really sure," I said quietly, hoping to hide my own fear from him. I had thought nearly endlessly over what these episodes could mean, and all I could conclude was that I was deeply, concerningly ill. Still, I felt I owed Rhys some honesty—an explanation. "For a second it felt like I was somewhere else, and all I could see was Cassia, sitting on a bed. But she didn't say anything to me, and I...I came back to the real room so quickly. I didn't even have time to wonder what was happening." I paused to see if he would respond to this, but he remained silent. "And then...with you, I saw you standing in a rich parlor in a suit of armor. You looked younger—perhaps a teenager."

There was a heavy silence between us, until Rhys broke it. "Strange," Rhys murmured, staring down the road once again, as it cut straight through the forest, the land in this area exceptionally flat. His manner was rather casual for such a topic, one which certainly brought my sanity into question.

"Yes," I agreed, looking away from him. I figured that was the end of the conversation, or at least hoped that it was, and he surprised me when he started speaking again.

"I was...I was very concerned. In both of those moments," he said, eyes fixed forward. "I didn't know what to do to help you."

I paused, unsure how to respond, especially when he spoke with that tone, his voice low and holding back meaning from me.

"I...I don't think there was anything you could do," I said, deciding to ignore whatever strange emotion he was concealing. "And in any case, I'm sure both visions were stress induced."

"Most likely. You have been through a lot these past few days," Rhys said, glancing over at me, and I saw the remnants of his concern in his eyes as I nodded mutely. I didn't want to comment on that either, and soon we fell back into a comfortable silence.

》《

A couple of days passed, and the only people we saw on the road were haggard-looking traders, their carts laden with bricks forged in Tan y Mor. I could only assume that the invading forces hadn't properly spread to the southern reaches of Lithe yet, as we didn't see any Hartanians or soldiers of any kind. Still, we were wary as we traveled along the Grand Road, constantly scanning the road in front of and behind us, listening for the pounding of hoofbeats.

The road left Gwanwynn Forest on our second day of traveling along it, and the world opened up to reveal the central plains of Lithe, a wide expanse of rolling green hills, which, at this time of year, were dotted with orange and yellow wildflowers. They swayed and danced in the pleasant spring breeze, and if I hadn't been so desperate to reach Caergarth, I would have found the scene stunningly beautiful, and allowed it to sink in.

As it was, I was incredibly stressed, and didn't have any emotional room for appreciating natural beauty. I had only one goal—to get to Caergarth and find Catrin Morgan. And even as we got closer, I grew more and more worried that it would be difficult to find her. I didn't even know for certain that she still lived there. But deep down I also knew that these worries didn't matter. We could only do what we thought was best to do, nothing more and nothing less.

The road passed beneath us with no incidents, but even that put me on edge. Where were the soldiers, the Hartanians? Why were they not patrolling one of the largest roads in the kingdom? Perhaps, I thought, they had somewhere more important to be. But where? Surely the capital was important, and that's why they had been guarding the bridges there. But why had they so quickly claimed the gates of Nefyn after the battle? It must have just been momentary, to leave no question as to the outcome of the battle.

Thoughts like these spiraled through my mind as we made our way along the Grand Road, over hill after rolling green hill, the flowers growing more and more bright and numerous as the days passed.

Every now and then, a monument from the old folks could be seen on rising hills, giant gray-blue way stones and old crumbling stone watchtowers. The old folks intrigued me and I had studied them as much as I could, even going so far as to become fluent in the Old Tongue. The language of my ancestors, before a Remisian had ever set foot on this land. Even my current state of deep thought and fretting couldn't entirely stop me from having fanciful wonderings about that ancient way of life, under the eyes of the many native gods.

One day, though, I was so lost in my anxious, tumultuous worries about Caergarth, our objective, and the general state of our kingdom, that even Rhys noticed my pensive state, probably because I hadn't spoken since we had woken and started riding at dawn. It was now past noon.

"Are you alright, Eira?" Rhys asked, his curious voice cutting through the still air and making me jump slightly. I looked over at him, eyes still wide in surprise.

"What?"

"You're very quiet. And you've had an odd glare on your face for over an hour now," he explained.

I cleared my throat, shaking my head slightly. "I'm fine. Just…just worried. As usual."

I was surprised even further, but in a much different way, when he smiled over at me in a warm sort of way. Like somehow just his face could comfort me. "It's alright to be worried," he said, voice so gentle. "I don't know how you wouldn't be worried in this situation."

I nodded slowly, the words actually giving me strength— worry wasn't something I could fight. It was innate to this situation.

"Just…try to remember that I'm here with you. If…if that's something you want to remember," he said, looking away from me suddenly, and focusing on the road ahead. I thought I saw a hint of pink light his cheeks, but I wasn't sure, and I would have ignored it either way.

"I'm very thankful you're here, Rhys," I said, grinning despite myself. "I appreciate your kind words."

He didn't say anything in response, so the ride continued in silence, albeit a much more relaxed silence for me.

»«

Caergarth loomed above us, built atop a wide, flattened hill. The gray city wall curved around it, and all we could really see of it were some spires from the temple, and the roofs of a few other exceptionally tall buildings. Behind the hill, the Fethwen Mountains stretched their jagged snowy peaks towards the sky. We simply stared in awe for a few moments, having just crested a hill that had revealed this view to us. Between us and the city was a dense forest, one that I was surprised hadn't been cleared.

"Shall we?" Rhys asked after we had enjoyed the view for a few minutes. I nodded and urged Nimue forward, and we began to descend the hill. Soon enough we were among the trees, and this forest was dark and odd and echoey, even compared to Gwanwynn Forest. As far as I knew, this forest was named Caergarth Forest, but I hadn't heard much about it as it was, all things considered, very small. The strange noises of creatures in the branches and snapping twigs on the forest floor around us put me on edge in a way I couldn't quite understand. Barely any sun reached through the low, thick branches, and the air around us felt like perpetual twilight. I barely felt like I was breathing as we traversed the forest, waiting to see beams of light through the trees, and feeling deep relief when that light finally met my eyes. Rhys was equally as tense and silent the entire time we were in the forest, and I was oddly thankful that he was feeling the same things as I was.

When the road finally emerged from the trees, we found ourselves blinking in the forgotten sunlight, looking up the steep hill to the city. The road switched back a couple of times up the hill, before arriving at the city gates. We hastened on, the end of our journey so near, and I was excited to get off the road even if we couldn't find Catrin Morgan. My main goal was just sleeping in a bed for the first time in over a week.

The road up the hill was well maintained and smooth, and large rocks bordered each side, denoting the edge of the cliff. This side of the hill was in the shade at this point, the afternoon sun low enough in the sky that we couldn't see or feel it for the city and hill between us.

The guards at the gate were wearing the armor of the Caergarth garrison, and I breathed out a sigh of relief at the sight. They halted us and demanded our business, and I told the same lie as before, and told them that we were visiting family. They didn't have an issue with that, and allowed us entrance, the gates opening just wide enough for our horses to pass through.

The next hour or so passed in a blur as we both wanted nothing more than to get to an inn and rest. We found one fairly close to the city gates, left our horses at the stables there, and rented two rooms with no issues.

"I'm going to take a nap, I think," I told Rhys through a large yawn as the innkeeper, a young woman with brown hair tied up into a tight bun, led us to our rooms.

I saw Rhys stifle a yawn in response to mine, and simply nodded in response. He gestured at me to take the first room we were led to, and I did without arguing. Inside, I let my pack fall to the wooden floor with a heavy thump, and took in the small room for just a moment: a bed, a small table, a single candle. The pale light of the afternoon was filtering through a small window, so the room was delightfully dim. I collapsed on the bed and let sleep take me, ignoring the slightly lumpy mattress. It was significantly more comfortable than the bare ground that I had been sleeping on for days.

»«

When I awoke, the hearty smell of stew was filling my room, and beckoning me out into the common room, the prospect of hot food too enticing to ignore. Wearily, I climbed out of the bed and opened my door, still blinking the sleep from my eyes. I was slightly surprised to see Rhys sitting at a table by a large stone fireplace, a bowl of the stew in his hands. I obtained my own bowl without further hesitation, from a large vat on one side of the room, and joined him at the small table. He looked up from his bowl in surprise as I sat down across from him, but then smiled when he saw it was me.

"How did you sleep?" he asked me, setting down his spoon. His hair was a bit mussed on one side, I assumed from how he had been sleeping, and I surprised myself with the sudden urge to smooth it out for him. Ignoring that, I ran my hands through my own hair, a bit self-conscious, as I replied.

"Well. How about you?" I said simply, finding the occasional tangle with my fingers. I gave up on smoothing my hair, and picked up my spoon instead, having put off eating for far too long.

"Quite well. I hadn't realized how exhausting traveling has been," he said, then let out a yawn.

"A bed with blankets and a pillow was quite nice," I commented, and he nodded in agreement.

"So," he said after a moment of silence where I simply enjoyed the hot food in front of me. "How do we find Catrin?"

I swallowed the stew I had in my mouth, and then frowned. "I think the best place to start—the only place I can think of, really—is the library."

Rhys nodded. "You think she still frequents it?"

"I don't know," I said with a shrug. "I don't even know if she still lives here. I know the book I saw her name in was written recently, in the last ten years or so, but that doesn't mean she still lives here. Or that she's even alive."

Rhys sighed. "Still. The library sounds like a good start. We can go first thing tomorrow."

I agreed, knowing that we both deserved a bit more rest before going on our next adventure, even if it wasn't going to be quite as exhausting as the last week.

>«

The next morning, Rhys and I ate breakfast in silence in the small, low-ceilinged dining room of the inn. We both knew what our objective was, and were both still tired despite the hours of sleep we had both gotten. I supposed he had his own worries that he had been battling with. Once we were done eating, Rhys cleared his throat.

"Do you know which way the library is?" he asked, his voice still gravelly with sleep. I ignored a strange feeling that arose inside of me at the sound, and focused on answering his question.

"Um…no. But I can go ask the innkeeper," I said, then stood quickly, not wanting to wait for a response. I felt like my face was warm—what was wrong with me?

The innkeeper, a young woman that looked to be barely out of her teenage years, informed me that the famous library was in the center of the town, next to the Benaty. I thanked her, and soon Rhys and I emerged onto the stone paved street, breathing in the refreshing spring air, slowly warming in the bright sunlight.

Caergarth wasn't very large, and we only had to walk about half a mile through the winding stone streets, passing the locals who didn't send us a second glance. "Everything is…normal here," I said in a quiet murmur as we passed two women chatting happily.

"I wonder why," Rhys said, frowning slightly. "Why haven't the troops come here? Caergarth is a provincial capital."

"We've only seen them in Nefyn and Maenynys," I said, mirroring his frown as we made our way to the side of the road to avoid a large horse-drawn cart laden with fresh fruits. On either side of the road were charming stone houses, all some varying shade of gray or blue.

"It's like they aren't interested in the rest of the kingdom," Rhys continued. Then he sighed heavily. "Let's just be grateful," he said with a small shrug, looking over at me as we turned around a bend in the road and saw the tall, spired Benaty before us at the end of a wide lane, and the imposing library beside it. Even from where we stood, a few hundred feet away, the tall stained-glass windows were blinding with glittering sunlight.

We passed the Benaty, and I admired the elaborate architecture that put my own Benaty to shame. Nefyn's Benaty didn't have those spires, or tall windows with the largest single panes I had ever seen, or the artistry with which the stones of its walls had been laid. I realized I was feeling a bit of envy at the sight and was thoroughly annoyed by this. I had much larger problems at hand than who had a nicer castle than me.

We arrived at the massive, ornately carved wooden doors of the library, and I hesitantly grabbed the handle and pulled, wondering vaguely if we were allowed to enter such a prestigious building. Rhys grabbed the door from behind me and helped me pull, and the nostalgic smell of old books and dusty pages met my nose, beckoning me in further.

We found ourselves in a foyer of sorts, and I heard Rhys let the door shut gently behind us. To one side in the foyer there was a low wooden table, and on the other side of the table sat an old man dressed in robes. He looked up at us as we entered and approached the table, and smiled at us with serene patience.

"Good day," he said in a low, calm voice. "May I inquire as to your business at Caergarth Library?"

"Um…yes," I said. "We…wanted to explore your stacks as we are only in Caergarth for a couple of days," I answered quickly. "And we are both hoping to study next year at the university in Maenynys—and this is the grandest library besides that of the King's collection." The lies had come so easily, I wondered if there was something wrong with me.

The man smiled, approving of my answer. "Very good. It is always wonderful to meet fellow academics. Please sign in here"—he gestured to a roll of parchment, which already had a few names scrawled on it— "and remember that no book can leave the library. We will search your bags and pockets upon exiting."

"Of course." Rhys and I both nodded, and signed our names as quickly as we could.

"Please enjoy your time in the library, and consider offering a donation so that we can maintain our collection," the old man said, and then pointed to a large wooden box on the other side of the foyer. The top had a hole cut into it, the perfect size to slip a coin into.

"Thank you," I said, debating whether or not it would be wise for me to use our money on something as frivolous as a donation. I had been able to pack quite a lot of money into the pouch…

Before I could decide, however, Rhys had already passed through the entryway into the main room of the library, where I could already see shelves and shelves of books, their beautiful bindings calling out to me. I followed him, and remembered that we weren't there to read. We were there to find Catrin Morgan.

Still, the grandeur of all of those books even gave Rhys pause, and we stood next to each other, staring at the towering stacks in awe. Each one must have been twenty feet high, and each one was equipped with a ladder, to make it possible to reach the highest shelf. They were arranged in concentric circles, and we stood outside of the largest one. We were in a massive round room, like the rotunda of the temple in Nefyn, except this one must have been three times the size. Above us, a domed ceiling stretched towards the sky, and glass skylights dotted it, letting light stream down on various points around the library floor, making the books the light touched glow with warmth.

I continued to look up and noticed that there were floors above us as well, denoted by balconies lining the rounded walls. I counted four of them and saw the shelves lining the walls beyond them.

"Okay," Rhys whispered, "how do we find her?"

"We have to ask people," I said.

"Why couldn't we ask the old man?" Rhys asked, frowning down at me.

"It's his job to keep out people who might cause trouble," I said.

"Why is looking for someone causing trouble?"

"It's not what the library is for. It would be a misuse of it."

"But why would he care?"

"I don't know, Rhys," I hissed. "I'm just being careful. If we get banned from the library, we have to come up with a new plan. It would be a huge setback. I'm not risking anything."

Rhys sighed and ran a hand through his hair. "Alright," he said. "So who should we ask?"

We both looked around, not seeing anyone in sight anyway.

"Should we split up?" I wondered aloud.

"No," Rhys said, tone resolute, and I looked back up at him in surprise. "We'll never find each other again. Look at how many stacks there are."

I nodded, knowing he was absolutely right, but also feeling a bit disappointed that he hadn't meant—something else. "Come on, then," I said, stepping between two of the stacks in front of us, entering the first circle. "Let's find someone."

We soon came to the conclusion that we should not ask people who were obviously engrossed in a book. They wouldn't take kindly to being interrupted, surely. We passed a few such people bent over the small desks that were scattered between the stacks. When we rounded a stack and emerged into one of the smaller circles, close to the center of the room, I saw a young woman who was putting books back and wearing long blue robes, and I knew she was an employee of the library. I gestured at her, and Rhys nodded, then motioned for me to approach. I did so, fighting off nerves at the prospect of talking to a complete stranger.

"Excuse me," I whispered as I came to stand beside her, she turned to me quickly, clearly surprised, midway through setting a thick book back on the shelf in front of her. She had bright blue eyes and auburn hair pulled into a low ponytail that trailed down her back. Her face was dotted with freckles, and I thought she was one of the loveliest ladies I had ever seen.

"Yes?" she asked hesitantly. "Can I help you find something?" She was frowning at me slightly.

"I-I'm looking for a person, actually. I think she might frequent this library, and I'm not sure how else to find her," I said honestly. The girl narrowed her eyes.

"A person?" she repeated, and I nodded.

"Yes, an author. Her name is Catrin Morgan."

The girl looked away swiftly, and I sensed an odd energy coming from her. "I can help you find books, not people. Good day," she said dismissively.

"My apologies," I sighed, before turning back to Rhys, shaking my head. He sighed as I led us away from the girl, feeling embarrassed by the encounter.

We continued to approach library workers and inquire about Catrin, but no one seemed to recognize her name. We asked anyone who wasn't in a deep reading session, but no one had ever heard of her or her books. Hours passed, and soon we were hungry. Not wanting my stomach to growl in such a quiet building where any small sound seemed to echo, I asked Rhys if he would like to find some food, and he agreed. On our way out, I dropped a few coins into the donation box, and Rhys frowned at me.

"Why did you do that?" he asked once we were outside. The fresh air was nice, even if I did enjoy the smell of dusty books.

"What? Donate?" I asked as I descended the steps that led to the road.

"Yes," Rhys said from a couple of feet behind me.

"It's the least I can do," I replied curtly, not liking his tone. Why was he upset? It was my money, after all.

"We only have so much, though," Rhys said, taking a few long strides to walk beside me. I knew he was looking at me, studying my expression, but I refused to look at him and kept my eyes on the road ahead of me, scanning the buildings for any sign of a tavern or a street food vendor.

"We have enough to spare a couple for a library," I said dismissively, but Rhys didn't accept that.

"We don't know how long we'll be away from Nefyn. If we run out of money—"

"We're not going to run out, Rhys," I said, raising my voice slightly.

"You can't know that for sure," he said, openly glaring at me now. I stopped walking and looked up at him with defiance.

"It is my money, Rhys," I said. "I'm not worried, and I will ask you to cease your fretting as well."

"It may be your money," Rhys said, looking down at me with some masking of his expressions that I had never seen him use before, "but I am reliant on it just as much as you are. Please consider that before you throw away coins again." He walked away then, continuing along the road without a backwards glance towards me. I frowned in frustration, trailing along behind him, completely annoyed by his behavior. I knew how to manage my money. I didn't need his criticism.

I decided to let the conversation die. There was no point in pushing back against his behavior, especially as I was going to continue using the money however I liked. I understood his concerns on a basic level, but I wished he had more trust in me.

We found a street pie vendor, purchased a few, and found a low brick wall bordering a garden to sit on as we ate. We remained silent, the small argument having formed a rift between us that neither of us seemed willing to rectify.

The sun was high in the sky, but slowly falling towards the western horizon, and I sighed, wondering if it was even worth continuing our search within the library. As I mulled this over, Rhys stood suddenly, before turning and looking down at me with a curious expression.

"Well?" he said, "Shall we continue?" The tension that had been in his form during our argument was gone, and he seemed as though nothing was wrong. I frowned slightly, wondering if he was acting.

"Sure," I said, and stood swiftly, brushing a few crumbs from my tunic.

Back in the library, we continued on in much the same way that we had in the morning, with no success. After another hour of these frustrating whisperings with strangers, Rhys and I sat down at a table near the center of the circles of books, the tightly curving stacks giving me the feeling of deep insulation.

"No one knows her," I sighed, still whispering, and still very frustrated. Rhys didn't look much happier as he ran a hand through his hair and mimicked my sigh.

"Maybe it's a pen name," he suggested.

I frowned. "Maybe," I conceded. "But if that is the case, there's nothing we can do. This is the only name we have to go off of."

Suddenly, the beautiful scribe that had been so dismissive to me earlier in the day appeared from behind one of the stacks, her eyebrows deeply furrowed and pensive. I stared at her, wondering if she would chastise us for our conversation, though I hadn't thought we had been talking loudly.

"You really want to meet this Catrin?" she said to us quietly as she came to stand at the end of the table between us.

"Um…yes," I said hesitantly.

"Why?" Her tone was low and serious as she continued to glare down at us, her fingers tense around the large book she held in her hands.

I glanced at Rhys, and he nodded slightly. We both thought it best to be honest.

"We need her help," I said. "We think she has information that could help us—help us fight back the invading forces from Hartania."

"Invading forces?" the woman said, her voice dripping with skepticism as she eyed both me and Rhys with suspicion.

"They took our home, in the north. The province of Nefyn. And the capital. They have soldiers stationed at the bridges of Maenynys."

"I don't believe you," she said, her frown relaxing into a blank stare.

I grew frustrated. "It's true whether you believe us or not. We were forced to abandon our home, and went to Maenynys to get help from the king. But we were forced to flee at the bridges. I had read one of Catrin's books, about the kingdoms of Aorlanda, and in it she mentions— implies—that there is more to the Eos power than we know. The people that took Nefyn—they have powers we've never seen before, and—"

"What sorts of powers?" she asked. Her eyes narrowed at me, and I realized she was challenging me.

"One could appear and reappear in another place," I said. "Another—she said their leaders all had something about them that made them powerful."

"I have no reason to believe this account," she said dismissively.

"Please," I said, and she stared at me, something in my voice giving her pause. "Our family and friends—they're all in danger. We have no one else to go to. Catrin is the only person I've ever heard reference something hidden about the Eos. That there's more to it. We need to understand that, now more than ever."

The woman was frozen for a few seconds, evaluating me, and then Rhys. He looked back at her levelly, and after a moment she sighed deeply, then walked around the table behind Rhys and took a seat a few feet down the table from him. She set the book down on the table with a hefty thump, and for a few seconds that was the only noise I heard, echoing in my ears.

"I have no reason to believe you," the scribe said, looking between us.

"I understand that, but—" I said, the frustration I felt now obvious in my voice.

"But," she said, interrupting me, "I know Catrin would appreciate the chance to hear you herself."

My suspicions were confirmed. "You know of her," I stated.

"Indeed," she agreed with a nod, then sighed. "My name is Aerona. I am Catrin's apprentice."

"What?" Rhys hissed, the surprised anger in his voice made it obvious that he hadn't expected that response. "Why have you been interrogating us then?"

Aerona glared at him, her blue eyes piercing and violent. Rhys didn't back down. "Because I need to protect her. Her identity is a secret carefully kept by all who know her."

"Why did you tell us then?" I questioned, asking the opposite of what Rhys had just asked.

Aerona raised her eyebrows at me. "Because your tenacity is impressive, and though I don't quite believe your account, your voice is honest and open. And I know Catrin will want to hear what you have to say, as I just pointed out."

"How can we meet her?" I asked quickly, wanting to get to the point.

"Meet me at the edge of the forest below the city at sundown," Aerona said quietly, her voice deadly serious. "I will take you to her."

Rhys and I nodded in agreement, and Aerona stood without another word, disappearing with her book, and the hushed rustling of her robes as she rounded a bookshelf.

Rhys and I stared at each other, and I wondered if he was feeling what I was feeling: surprise, determination, relief, trepidation, and perhaps a bit of fear.

"Well," he said after a moment. "We found her."

$$8$$

The Cottage in the Woods

At the bottom of the hill, as twilight fell upon the lush green leaves of the trees, we waited on horseback for Aerona to appear.

"I'm sorry," Rhys said into the hushed chilled air, surprising me.

"Why?" I asked, looking over at him. He was looking at me with some conflict in his eyes, with his eyebrows furrowed and lips in a tight line.

"About earlier. About the money. I hope you don't think that I don't trust your judgment."

I paused, as that was exactly what I thought, and considered if I should be honest, or simply laugh it off. "Well, that is how you acted," I conceded after a moment.

"I shouldn't have responded like that," he said levelly, not at all upset by the admission. "I was frustrated with how the day had been going and was in a sour mood. I shouldn't have questioned your decision like that."

"I just need to know... We have to trust each other, don't we? And that made me feel like you don't trust me," I said honestly. I realized I was being much more open with him than I had anticipated, as if I somehow knew that my words would be well-received by him, whether he wanted to hear them or not. There was a promise of calmness and civility in our discourse, and this was something I was not used to experiencing.

Again, in the low light of the forest, the sun having already set beyond the hill of Caergarth, and the Fethwen mountain range that it was a part of, Rhys's expression was conflicted.

"I do trust you, Eira," he said, his voice still so level and heavy, I didn't know what to say in response.

I stared at him for a moment, until the sound of approaching hoofbeats from the direction of the city pulled my attention away from him.

Aerona appeared on the road from behind a particularly large and gnarled tree, her face barely visible in the low light. It was set and serious, as though she had reason to be displeased at the sight of us.

"You're here," she said, her tone somewhat disappointed as she approached us, her chestnut horse uncommonly large. It stood a few hands taller than Nimue. Aerona looked down at me, then Rhys, and then sighed. "Alright. Follow me," she said, turning to continue on deeper into the forest. Rhys and I glanced at each other, before I urged Nimue after her, and Rhys followed behind me.

We were dead silent as we passed underneath the swiftly darkening boughs. It was becoming difficult to see, complete nighttime only minutes away, and I hoped we would arrive at Catrin's home—or wherever we were meeting her—before too long. Aerona diverged from the main road without warning, her steed crunching through the dried leaves and twigs and shrubs that covered the forest floor. I turned Nimue to follow her with much hesitation, and quickly discovered that, despite the forest debris that became mulched underneath Nimue's hooves, Aerona was leading us down a very narrow, and very poorly kept path. Shrubs and trees crowded in from either side, scratching against my legs unpleasantly, but the path we were on was void of any such vegetation. It was so dark at that point that I could only see the vague twisted shapes of branches arching into the trail, and Aerona's form a few yards ahead of me, hazy and shifting in gray tones, continuing on without ever glancing back to see if Rhys and I were alright.

It seemed we followed this winding trail through the forest for some time. At one point it forked, and Aerona led us to the left. The darkened forest was beginning to give me chills, and not just from the cold air. The sounds and echoes of creatures seemed particularly malevolent in this unknown forest, on this mysterious path, on our way to meet a stranger.

Then a light appeared from behind a large tree trunk— an orange, flickering light. A candle, I thought. I looked at Aerona, but she gave nothing away. We drew closer to this light, and soon I could see the form of a house from between the trees. I let out a breath I hadn't known I had been holding, but remained quite tense.

Soon we were in a small yard, and I could see the house more clearly. It was a quaint cottage made of stone and wooden beams, and the light I had seen was indeed a candle, burning in one of the small windows beside the front door.

"You can tie your horses here," Aerona said as she dismounted, her feet sinking slightly into the moist earth. She looked at us expectantly, before tying her reins to a wooden post stuck into the ground a few yards away from the cottage. Rhys and I followed suit without a word. I was eager to have my feet back on the ground, and felt my heart rate accelerate at the thought of meeting Catrin Morgan within minutes. When we were done, I turned and saw Aerona waiting for us by the front door, glaring at us openly.

"You can tell Catrin your story," she said as we came to stand before her, "but that doesn't mean she'll have any interest in helping you. I brought you here because I think she might. But be prepared to leave." It was a warning, and I narrowed my eyes slightly. Not only a warning, I realized, but a hope as well. Aerona hoped that Catrin would be sending us on our way.

"We understand," I said, impatient to be allowed inside.

Aerona's lips tightened, but she nodded. "Wait here," she said as her hand came to rest on the doorknob. "I want to give Catrin some warning."

"Alright," I said, a bit annoyed. I sensed Rhys nodding next to me. Aerona turned the knob and entered without another word, the door creaking loudly as it opened, and then shut with a decisive thump.

I sighed audibly without thinking. "It'll be alright," Rhys said, trying to comfort me. I turned to look at him, his hair glowing silver in the light of the moon, his eyes reflecting the stars. Everything else was in shadow. "Catrin will want to help us."

"You can't know that," I said, my instinct to be dismissive taking over.

"I can feel it," Rhys insisted. I looked away, back towards the old wooden door, willing for it to open, for Aerona to finally invite us inside.

"She has no reason to want to speak with us," I murmured. Somewhere in the forest an owl hooted loudly, more loudly than I spoke. Still, Rhys heard me and ignored the bird.

"Of course she does," Rhys said, and I could tell from his tone that he was frowning at me.

"And what is that?" I said, crossing my arms and turning to look at him, this challenge a nice distraction from the waiting.

"We have an interesting story to tell. At the very least." He smiled, a hesitant smile where his eyes looked down at me with an almost apologetic emotion in them. I couldn't help but smile back. He was trying to keep me calm, and I appreciated that, even if it was folly.

"You're right," I sighed, and a comfortable silence fell over us. It only lasted for a few moments before a strange feeling washed over me, the feeling of anticipation, like dread but better, like anxiety but calmer…like fate promising an appearance. Then the door was thrown open, the orange light of the candles inside casting us and the yard beyond in a warm glow, and a middle-aged woman stood before us, a toothy grin on her face. We froze in shock at her sudden appearance, and I noted Aerona standing awkwardly behind the woman. The strange feeling still coursed through my body, strongest in my heart, and I knew intuitively that this woman was the cause. Catrin.

Her eyes fixed directly on my face, and her warm and welcoming smile grew with recognition. "Hello, Eosiaid," she said with cheer, her eyes twinkling with some hidden humor. I gaped at her. And then I understood.

"You're…you're an Eosiaid," I stammered.

She laughed and rolled her eyes. "Why don't you two come in? I can barely see you out there in the dark. Come in, come in," she insisted, moving away from the doorway and beckoning us into the little cottage. I stumbled forward through the doorway, and heard Rhys behind me. Aerona pointed at some cushy chairs, the upholstery old and faded to gray from what I guessed used to be a bright blue, situated in front of a small fireplace on the wall opposite from the door. I did feel a bit chilled from the cold nighttime air, so I took a seat without hesitation, sinking into the old cushion immediately. Rhys sat in the chair beside me, and Catrin and Aerona took the seats facing us.

In the bright light of the fire, I was able to see Catrin much better. She was older, but still strong and able-bodied. Her long brown and gray hair was intricately braided behind her head, and she wore a very simple tunic dress of deep plum purple. Her eyes were bright and inquisitive, and the few wrinkles on her face concentrated around her mouth and eyes, indicating years of laughing and smiling. She had a distinctly kind and welcoming feeling to her, and I felt myself become a bit more relaxed at her pleasant expression, even as that strange feeling continued on inside of me.

"Aerona tells me you have a story for me," Catrin said after only a few seconds of awkward silence with just the fire crackling and popping between us. She leaned forward slightly, her eyes still full of humor, and I paused, too many thoughts racing to be spoken at the same time.

"Yes," Rhys began when I didn't immediately respond.

"How did you know I'm an Eosiaid?" I blurted out. Catrin and Aerona had been looking at Rhys, but now both turned to me. Aerona frowned at me, likely wondering why that was the first thing out of my mouth, while Catrin appeared bemused.

"What do you mean?" she asked, patience in her voice.

"You…you said, 'Hello, Eosiaid,' to me. But I hadn't told you, or Aerona…" I tried to explain.

"All Eosiaids can sense Eosiaids." Catrin smiled at me. "But you know this." She tilted her head as she appraised me, and I felt embarrassment and confusion wash over me at her words.

"I…I hadn't…I hadn't felt that…before. That feeling. Is that what you mean?" I asked, piecing the puzzle pieces together, not at all sure that I had found the correct configuration.

"Oh, child," she murmured, still kindly. "You've had a very strange life then, indeed. Have you not met another Eosiaid before? Besides your mentors?" she questioned, her emotive eyes now expressing a bit of pity. I froze for a moment, caught off guard by the question.

"Yes," I said, thinking of Hanien, as well as the strangers who had invaded my home. "A few."

"And you remember the first time you met them?" she asked, now clearly curious. Aerona let out a quiet sigh of annoyance. I glanced at Rhys, backlit by the fire, but he simply nodded at me curtly, encouraging me to answer Catrin.

"Yes," I said quietly. "But…but I definitely didn't feel anything like that," I insisted. "What do you mean, we can sense each other?"

Catrin pursed her lips, and turned her head to look at the fire, the orange flames dancing in her eyes. "It's odd that I'm the one to tell you this," she said, frowning slightly while still looking away, as though she was thinking very carefully about each word. "I don't know how it's possible for you to have met another Eosiaid without having felt the sensation that accompanies such an event. It seems you have had a very sheltered upbringing." She looked me over then, now appraising me, and I could tell she was hiding some emotion from me, with the careful, neutral expression she maintained. "Yes, we can sense each other upon our first meeting. It is slightly different for each Eosiaid, what that feeling entails. For me, it is pure joy—excitement," she explained. She continued to stare at me as I absorbed this. I wouldn't have believed her if not for the fact that I had just experienced exactly what she was talking about. I had the evidence; she provided the explanation.

"Um," Rhys said hesitantly, looking between me and Catrin with concern. "Eira, are you—"

"I'm fine," I said quickly, shaking my head slightly, as if that action could rid me of my confusion. "I apologize for my tangent. That subject isn't why we came here."

Catrin smiled again. The fire crackled. Aerona continued to sit stiffly, staring at me with an untrusting, tight-lipped glare, her hands folded neatly in her lap. Catrin leaned forward again, just slightly. "No, it isn't. I'm very interested in the few details Aerona was able to convey to me."

"I…I have read your book, about Aorlanda," I began, unsure how far back I needed to go. "In it, you imply that there are powers of the Eosiaid that we don't even know about. That only the monks on Aornadur know everything there is to know."

Catrin nodded, and though her smile remained, the curious glint in her eyes shined brighter. "Haven't you seen some evidence tonight that even you don't know everything there is to know?" she pointed out.

For some reason, I felt myself tense in response. "I have never believed that I know everything," I replied immediately.

Catrin laughed. "I didn't mean to offend you, child," she said with abject humor.

"My name is Eira," I said, softening a bit. "And this is Rhys."

"Eira, and Rhys," Catrin nodded. "Well, continue, Eira."

"Rhys and I are from the province of Nefyn," I began, now coming to the heart of the story. "But our home was recently attacked—by Eosiaids with powers I had never seen before."

"What sorts of powers?" Catrin asked.

"Invisibility was the only one I saw with certainty, though the other I met was extremely powerful…in other ways that I don't fully understand," I summarized, knowing that that explanation didn't come close to the truth. But no matter how well I tried to explain it, I would never be able to translate the awe I had felt witnessing their feats.

"Extreme, you say," Catrin said thoughtfully. "And with these abilities, they were able to take your home?"

"Along with the army they had summoned from Hartania," Rhys added, unable to hide his emotions about that fact.

"Hartania?" Catrin said, finally sounding a bit surprised, as she looked at him sharply. "This is the work of Hartanians?"

I shook my head. "No. The woman in charge that we… spoke with… She was Remisian. I think from near the capital. But there were others with her, with foreign names," I explained quickly, remembering the unfamiliar names she had mentioned to Varina, the ones who had been holding Calliten in another room.

Catrin blinked at me. "A global attack," she muttered, momentarily looking at the fire. She seemed lost in thought for a moment, before looking back at me, much of the humor gone from her voice. "This is quite an operation they've managed to organize."

"It's worse than that," Rhys said, his voice low. "We went to Maenynys to get help. But were attacked by Hartanians guarding the bridge. It seems the capital has been taken as well… And it's only a matter of time before the Hartanian forces are spread through the kingdom."

"That's absurd," Aerona broke in, her tone as withering as her expression. "You're saying the only parts of the kingdom that are in control of these Hartanians, and some foreigners, and this one Remisian"—she said the list with a mocking tone—"are the capital and your home?"

"You don't have to believe us," I said, growing angered by her dismissive attitude. Rhys held up a hand, asking me to stop. I inhaled deeply and tried to calm down.

"I know how it sounds," Rhys said, his voice smooth and pleading, warm. He spoke directly to Aerona, and I saw as she froze, frowning at his careful tone. "But it is the truth. We haven't come here to fool you or use you in any way. We are simply pleading for help. Any information you or Catrin can give us about unknown Eosiaid powers could help us win back our home. We just need to know what we're up against, what we have to defeat. Because right now, we don't have a home. We don't have anywhere to go. And we need someone's help."

A heavy silence fell over us as Rhys ceased speaking, but continued to look at Aerona, and then Catrin, hoping to sway one of them.

"Of course," Catrin said suddenly, her wide smile firmly back on her face. Aerona nearly jumped at the cheerful sound of Catrin's voice. "I certainly believe you, and despite her behavior, Aerona doesn't actually get to make decisions around here. We have a guest room you two can stay in. But first, would you like dinner?"

The sudden change in topic—and our acceptance—was so surprising that neither Rhys nor I knew what to say.

Aerona sighed and stood. "I'm making roast vegetables to go with the chicken I killed yesterday," she said in a dull, defeated tone as she passed through a doorway and into what I assumed was a kitchen. "Eat some if you like. It'll be ready in an hour." The kitchen door shut behind her with a solid bang.

Catrin sighed. "She'll come around," she said, her warm smile slowly thawing away my surprise.

"Uh…thank you very much, Catrin," Rhys said, apparently having found his wits.

She waved a hand and frowned. "Don't thank me yet. I don't know if I can be of any help, but I can think of a few old texts to start with. This will require some research, you know."

"Of course," I agreed, even though I wasn't completely sure what she was talking about. I was so taken aback by the events of the last half hour or so that I had no energy to ask for an explanation.

"I also want to know more about you, Eira," she said, now looking at me thoughtfully.

"Me?" I repeated with a frown.

"Yes. I don't think you fully understand. Sensing other Eos—that feeling you got when you met me—that is one of the most basic qualities of being an Eosiaid. Yet you felt it for the first time today. That is incredibly odd to me, and I can't help but wonder what other aberrations you may have experienced," she explained. I frowned and felt anxiety rise in my stomach.

"I'm…I'm not an experiment," I said, trying not to glare at her. Her smile remained, already soothing me.

"No, you're not. You're an Eosiaid, and you deserve to know all that you are capable of," she said, her voice calm, low, and caring. I froze, not used to such an expression being directed at me. "Wouldn't you agree?"

I hesitated for a moment. And then I nodded, the beginning of a smile forming on my face.

»«

Dinner was quiet, Aerona's stormy attitude clouding the small kitchen. We each sat on one side of a small, square wooden table, a few candles in the center of it lighting the dim room. I allowed my eyes to settle on the small flickering flames as I processed the conversations that had just taken place with Catrin. How could I not have experienced something so integral to the Eosiaid until now? What else could I be missing? The vegetables and chicken passed through my mouth without much notice. I ate mindlessly.

Eventually my food was gone, and Catrin was already standing and carrying her plate to a wash bin, readied with soapy water. "You can leave your dishes in here," she said as she dropped hers into the bin.

Rhys stood quickly, his own plate in his hand. "I'll do the washing up," he said, moving to stand beside Catrin.

"No," Aerona began to argue as she stood up as well, but Rhys was already grabbing a dish rag and scrubbing at the remains of our dinner. Aerona sighed, defeated once again, and dropped her dish into the tub with a hefty splash, leaning carefully around Rhys's large form. Then she disappeared from the kitchen without a word.

"My, how polite," Catrin enthused, a humored smile on her face as she watched Rhys doggedly clean the first dish, and I realized that she wasn't talking about Aerona's displeased behavior. Hesitantly, I stood as well, handing my dish to Rhys, who took it from me with an odd smile. He almost seemed embarrassed, although I couldn't figure out why.

Catrin let out a loud yawn just as Rhys took my plate. "Since Aerona seems to have abandoned us, I will show you to the guest room, Eira," she said, grabbing one of the candles from the table and beckoning me to follow her from the room. I glanced at Rhys, who smiled at me more naturally.

"Go," he encouraged. "I'm almost done anyway." I nodded, and followed Catrin back into the sitting room. We crossed over the large Conotrian rug that covered much of the hardwood floors, wound around some worn, ancient sofas that I hadn't noticed upon our first entry, to the opposite wall where a door was slightly ajar. Catrin pushed it open and entered the dark room, and set the candle on a dresser situated beside the door just inside.

What I saw inside the room instantly put me on edge. A single bed, large though it was, sat centered against the far wall. Across from the door was a window, and a rectangle of moonlight was cast on the floor in front of the bed making the floorboards glow. Under the window were my and Rhys's bags—Aerona must have moved them in after dinner. I paused as Catrin turned to me and smiled, apparently not seeing the problem.

"Sleep well. Let Aerona know if you need anything," she said as she turned away, back towards the sitting room.

"Um," I said, my voice attempting to catch up with my thoughts. Catrin turned to look at me curiously.

"We will have a longer talk tomorrow. I have many questions for you, as I'm sure you have many for me as well," she said as she looked at me slightly over her shoulder, and all I could do was nod. Calling attention to the problem would only make it more embarrassing.

"Thank you for your hospitality, Catrin," I managed. "I…I look forward to speaking with you tomorrow."

"Sleep well," she said with a small wave and tired grin, before finally shutting the door with a quiet, decisive click.

I heard my breathing, loud and jarring in the dead quiet of the guest room. I grabbed the candle and turned back to look at the bed. It was big, but not big enough for two people who did not want to be in a bed together. I stopped myself from groaning in irritation, and instead forced myself to think of a plan—an alternative to this deadly embarrassment. The only thing I could think of was the sofa. Yes, before Rhys was done in the kitchen, I would be fast asleep on the sofa, and that would save me from a conversation with him about this predicament.

I grabbed the extra woolen blanket that was folded at the end of the bed, set the candle on the nightstand, and then snatched a pillow. As quietly as I could, I turned the doorknob, opened the door, and slipped back in the sitting room. I flopped onto a sofa and was still arranging the pillow and blanket when I heard the kitchen door open. I sighed, knowing my plan was foiled, and already felt my face heating up at the sight of Rhys crossing the room slowly towards me, looking at me curiously.

"Isn't there a guest room?" he asked in a low whisper, frowning down at me. I stood up quickly, untangling myself from the blanket.

"Um," I said, not knowing what was best to say. I hoped he couldn't see how red my face was sure to be, with the fire dying and the only light in the room being that of the dying embers. He himself was hard to see, his expression inscrutable in the dimness. "So…you can use it."

Now I could see his frown clearly, his brows furrowed in confusion. Then understanding seemed to dawn. Of course, why would a guest room have more than one bed?

"It's alright," he said immediately. "You can sleep in the guest room, and I'll take the sofa."

"No, I—" I began, but he held up a hand and smiled. I paused, caught off guard by the expression. Why? He had smiled at me hundreds of times.

"I don't mind, Eira. I'm used to sleeping in the guards' sleeping quarters. This sofa is luxurious in comparison."

"But—" I still attempted to argue, floundering for some reason to justify my sleeping on the sofa instead of him.

"Eira, please. Can I ask you something?" he said, his voice low. His eyes fire. I was captivated.

I nodded.

"Don't argue with me just this once," he said, with the air of a sigh, and I nearly laughed in surprise. I wanted to laugh at myself. "We're both tired," he continued, "and the sooner we get this sorted, the sooner we can get to sleep."

"I… Fine," I said after a moment, and I looked away from him, towards the darkness of the floor. I turned back to the guest room and walked around the sofa. When I got to the door of the room, I turned and frowned at him. He was still standing there, waiting for me to enter. "But we should switch. Tomorrow you get the room." He smiled.

"We can talk about it tomorrow," he said with a small nod, and I paused again for a moment, wondering, quite simply, what was so incredibly wrong with me.

I shut the door behind me and heard the blood rushing through my ears, overwhelming me for a moment. The flickering light of the candle cast the room in a faint glow, and I let out a deep breath, attempting to release the tension I felt. I was safe, in a room with a bed, and was losing myself in trivial worries. I crossed the room and sat heavily on the bed, looking for a moment at the candle and how it danced in the darkness. Then, in my peripheral vision, I saw something sparkle on the ground to my right.

I turned and looked closer, seeing the hilt of the dagger I had taken from Varina sparkling faintly in the light of the candle. Just the golden end protruded from my bag, and without much thought I stood and took it out. I had used a spare bit of leather to wrap around the blade, but now I unwrapped it as I sat down once again, this time cross-legged and facing the foot of the bed, undeniably curious about the weapon. I knew it was important to the people in charge of taking over Lithe and that Varina certainly coveted it. But now, holding it in my hands and looking at it closely for the first time, I saw nothing particularly impressive about it. The blade was silver, the hilt was gold, and vines were inlaid into the gold, giving it a delicate appearance. It was lightweight and well-balanced, but there was nothing about it that seemed especially magical.

I gripped the hilt and held it properly in front of me, blade up, frowning at it. And there was no way for me to expect what happened next; the way my hand seized around it with painful pressure, the tremor that went up my arm, or how quickly my vision darkened.

Another vision appeared just after the world went dark, and I saw the faint, wavering image of Cassia and Varina standing in the main entrance hall to the Benaty—my Benaty. Cassia's lips were pursed; she looked upset. She held the dagger in a carved sheath covered in the same design of vines, offering it to Varina. Varina's face was blank, but in a forced sort of way, even as she took the dagger from Cassia's outstretched hands.

"You can't fail," Cassia said, the words echoing around my mind, like a whisper in a cave. Then the entire scene was gone from my sight, before Varina could even open her mouth to respond.

The dagger fell from my hand as the room I was actually in returned to my senses, and luckily fell flat on the wool blanket covering the mattress. I was gasping for air, but quickly mastered my distraught breathing, hoping that Rhys hadn't heard anything. I stared at the dagger, now resting on the bed in front of me, bewildered and frightened. My hand still spasmed lightly and I let it drop to my knee, willing the twitching to stop.

Exhaustion overtook me as my mind replayed the scene I had just seen over and over again, and I wanted it to stop. I grabbed the band of leather and carefully wrapped the blade once again, climbed off the bed with slightly shaking limbs, and placed it under the bed. Then I crawled under the blankets, blew out the candle, and attempted to pretend that I hadn't just had another vision. Whether or not I was successful, sleep soon overtook me. And though dreams are just another type of vision, these were ones that I welcomed.

9

The Ancient Texts

The next morning I awoke in the guest room, with bright clear light streaming in through the window. I glared at it for multiple reasons, before standing with some regret. I remembered my episode with the dagger from the night before, but resolved to not think about it. I had enough to worry about, and I couldn't even be sure what had happened. I was concerned, certainly, but there were only so many things I could actively worry about. Rhys especially didn't need to know about it. He had no reason to be more concerned than he already was.

I walked to the window, somewhat curious about the view outside, and saw the edge of the clearing only a few yards away. Tall trees packed in close to each other, making the house nearly impossible to see unless you were just outside the clearing. So secluded. I wondered why Catrin had chosen this place. I wondered many things about her.

The sounds of shuffling in the sitting room pulled me back to the matters at hand, and I took a deep breath before making my way to the door, and entering the sitting room.

It was chilly, the fire having died hours before in the night, with only the ashy remnants of the logs remaining on the grate. Cold, indirect light coming from the small windows by the front door illuminated the stone walls of the room. I had been so overwhelmed the night before when meeting Catrin that I hadn't noticed the many paintings that covered the

174

walls—mostly portraits of people I didn't recognize, their severe faces staring out at me.

Rhys was already up from the sofa, where the gray blanket and small pillow still lay. The door to the kitchen was open on the other side of the room, and the clatter of dishes could be heard from within, so I entered, assuming I would find Rhys inside. Instead I saw Catrin, who was just sitting down at the table with a plate piled with slices of bread. A small bowl of butter was already on the table in front of her.

She smiled at me as I entered, and began talking before I could even open my mouth. "Good morning! I hope you slept well. I would invite you to eat bread with me, but I think you might like to wait for Aerona and Rhys to return with the eggs."

I blinked at her. "Um…eggs?" I said, realizing I was still shaking the sleep off.

"Well, yes. It's always nice to start the day with some fried eggs, don't you think?" She looked down at her plate of bread and frowned slightly. "I'm too impatient to wait, though, and to be completely honest, the best part of breakfast for me is the bread. Or, well, if I'm being really, truly, completely honest, the butter." She grinned as she picked up a tiny silver butter knife and slid it through the butter on the dish in the center of the table, and then began slathering her first slice of bread.

"Rhys went to get the eggs too?" I asked as I took the seat across from her, watching with mild interest as she built up the layer of butter until it was nearly as thick as the actual bread.

"Yes," Catrin said as she set the knife down on the butter dish. "He insisted on helping her. She seemed quite irritated by him," she laughed, before taking a large bite of the fatty breakfast.

I nodded, understanding how Aerona felt to some extent. Rhys had some undying need to be useful to people. "He's just trying to be polite," I offered, not wanting to get into the complex inner workings of Rhys's brain.

Catrin was still chewing when the back door of the kitchen was thrown open, and Aerona stormed into the room, a small basket hanging on one arm. Rhys came in behind her, a sheepish smile on his face. I turned in my seat to watch them enter, curious how Aerona could be so cross so early in the morning. Surely Rhys wasn't that annoying.

Aerona lit the fire under the stove that was situated beneath the window behind me, then whirled around to fix me and Rhys with a stern glare. Her auburn hair was tied back in a long braid, and it whipped through the air as she turned, the epitome of drama. "Fried eggs, then?" she said, her tone accusatory. Rhys slowly sat down in the seat to my left, as I searched for my voice.

"Um…you don't have to—" I started with hesitation.

"Aerona," Catrin said, pausing in her breakfast to glare at the girl in question. "Be kind, please. Cook the eggs and don't gripe." Aerona stared at Catrin with defiance for a couple of still, silent moments, then huffed out a sigh, and grabbed a pan. Catrin shrugged, and began buttering another slice.

"So, Catrin," I said as I heard Aerona begin cracking eggs into the pan behind me. "I was wondering when we could continue our conversation from last night."

"Anytime, dear," she said with a small frown. "I don't do much in a day, you know."

I heard Aerona mumble something behind me, but none of us commented on it.

"We can start right now, if you like."

"Oh, but I don't want to be a—" but I was cut off again.

"There's no point in wasting time, eh?" Catrin said, pointing a corner of her bread at me, a small grin on her face. "Now, the question is where to begin." She stared out the window behind me with a contemplative expression as she took another large bite.

"Well, last night you said that you would have to go through some texts. I was wondering what sorts of texts you were talking about."

She swallowed, nodding slightly. "Old ones," she said with a dry laugh. "The primary sources I've referenced for many of my books."

"Are they at the library in Caergarth?" Rhys asked curiously, leaning forward with his elbows on the table.

"Some," Catrin said with a small shrug. "But the most important ones I've managed to keep for myself." I thought she sent a wink my way, but my sight was obscured suddenly by Aerona's arm setting down a plate with two perfectly fried eggs on it in front of me.

"Thank you," I said, turning to look at her, but she was just setting down Rhys's plate in front of him. Then she turned without a glance in either of our directions, and exited through the back door in a rush.

"Will she not eat?" Rhys asked, concern showing in his furrowed brow as he turned to look at the door she had just disappeared through.

"She eats," Catrin said, not exactly answering his question. "She likes to take a morning walk, though. Now," she said, turning back towards me, "what were we talking about?"

I took a moment to think as I buttered a piece of bread. "You've kept the most important sources for yourself," I said.

"Yes. Well, the ones most important to me. The ones I find most interesting. Today we can look through some together. We'll look for any mention of Eosiaids with enhanced or special abilities."

"Have you heard of anything like that before?" Rhys asked.

Catrin looked at him thoughtfully. "There's always been legends, but most assume those to be exaggerations. Like the legend of Ceridwen."

"The Flamebringer," Rhys said, smiling slightly. "I like that story, but I never assumed it was real."

"All stories have a core of truth," Catrin said, her eyes twinkling.

"So you believe us, then?" I asked without thinking. Catrin stared at me for a moment, before blinking in surprise.

"Of course. Do you think I would insist on Aerona cooking your eggs if I thought you two were liars?" she asked. I was unsure how to answer that question, and was relieved when Rhys spoke up.

"It's just…I think we're both surprised that you agreed to help us so quickly," Rhys said.

"When you get to be my age, you learn to judge people quickly." Catrin smiled at us. "You two are uncommonly authentic."

"Well…thank you," I said slowly.

"Now," Catrin said as she stood, "I'll gather some books we can start our search in, and will bring them to the sitting room while you two finish your meal. And when Aerona returns from her walk she'll be attending her position at the library in the city. I'll have her bring some books back with her that might offer some information as well."

"Thank you," Rhys and I both said, but she was already out the door and disappearing into the sitting room, apparently eager to begin her research.

Rhys and I continued our breakfast in silence, and I wondered if he felt awkward from our conversation the night before or if it was just me.

I beat Rhys to washing the dishes once we were finished eating, and was surprised when he didn't argue with me for too long about it. Perhaps he could see that it was useless, and perhaps the sounds of Catrin setting down heavy tomes on the long, low table in the sitting room was too enticing for him. He left to begin helping with the search, and it only took me a couple more minutes to finish the washing before I joined them.

Catrin had moved aside some curtains on the opposite wall to allow more light in, and as it was a bright, clear day outside, the room was much brighter than when I had previously passed through it. She had also lit a fire, and the logs were just beginning to catch from the smoldering kindling. She and Rhys sat on the two sofas facing each other, with the low table in between them. As I had guessed, it was covered in books, the types of books I had only seen in stately libraries like that of Caergarth. They were old, their ages unfathomable to me, some with leather covers, and some wooden, and some cloth. Most were incredibly dense, but a few were small and thin.

"Come, sit," Catrin said impatiently, and I quickly sat down on the sofa beside Rhys. Catrin smiled once I was seated, and then sighed as she looked down at the books between us. "I've selected these as they are the texts I own that speak most on the Eosiaid. Of course, the things these books say have not been worked into any of my books. If the Empire knew these were in existence, they would be seized, burned… And I would be put to death." She picked up a smaller one in a casual manner, as though she hadn't just said something incredibly grim, and Rhys and I exchanged an uncomfortable look.

"What? Why?" I asked, unable to hide my confused frown. She looked up from the book and blinked at me.

"Why? Well, they tell the truth. Of course," she said, looking at me with that same odd smile she had worn when she found out that I had never sensed another Eosiaid before, her head tilted slightly to the side in a questioning way.

"The truth?" I repeated.

Her smile fell slowly. "Tell me you're joking," she said, letting out a dry, hopeless laugh. "Dear Sky Queen above, tell me you know…"

"Know what?" I demanded, growing agitated. Rhys laid a hand on my shoulder, attempting to calm me.

Catrin sighed, held her head in her hands for a moment, then looked back up at me, her expression conflicted. Then her eyes slid over to Rhys beside me.

"I think I should speak to Eira in private," she said. Rhys nodded, and made to stand up, but I grabbed his forearm to stop him. He looked over at me in surprise.

"Whatever you tell me, I'm going to tell him later," I said, glaring at Catrin.

She huffed and pursed her lips. "You put him at risk with this knowledge," she warned, and that made me hesitate.

"If it's alright with both of you," Rhys said, his voice calm, his manner collected, "I would prefer to know what this truth is. Whether or not I'm supposed to know is irrelevant at this point."

Catrin nodded slowly, and I relaxed, as did Rhys. Catrin took a deep breath, and then looked at me dead in the eyes, now eerily calm.

"What do you know of your parents?" she asked me, and I felt every muscle in my body tense at those words.

"Do you know what happened to them?" I burst out, nearly yelling. "How do you—"

"Calm yourself," Catrin said, closing her eyes and holding up a hand. I stopped speaking, but felt my breathing come harder and faster. "This is the truth. The truth all Eosiaids share. We are blessed—and we are cursed. All of us—you, me, your mentor—were all born into this world utterly alone."

A heavy silence hung over the table between us, the books and this truth a massive chasm between us. Catrin stared at me, something in her eyes pleading with me to understand. To accept.

"Alone?" I whispered. She nodded.

"No Eosiaid has ever met their parents. For us to have this extraordinary life…they must give us theirs."

I couldn't tell how long the silence lasted this time. I was aware of Rhys beside me, as unmoving as I was. The air felt thick and time felt slow, meaningless. The truth settled in around me like a cloak I would forever wear.

"How?" Rhys spoke first.

Catrin looked at him, something like sympathy on her face. "How has it been kept from you all this time?" she asked, and he nodded, apparently not finding the words to respond out loud. "It's a great choreography that the Empire mastered centuries ago. Eos are born very rarely. Before they are born, living Eosiaid can sense them developing, that kernel of power growing within another human. The parents have no idea—of course they don't. Benadurs have the task of meeting with their people often, don't they? They're healers. They attend to the pregnant often, which means they'll certainly know when an Eos child is about to arrive. If that Benadur is unable to adopt the child— perhaps they have yet to find a spouse, or they already have too many heirs, or there isn't enough time to set up a false pregnancy—they will alert the proper authority. In most of the kingdoms of the Empire, this is the king's court. The king will send out Eos soldiers who will retrieve the child when it is time, dispose of the remains, and cover up the deaths of the parents as some sort of accident. A house fire is a typical story." She paused, as though she was expecting us to have questions. "Would you like some time alone?" Catrin asked as she looked at me, her voice soft. I shook my head.

"No. I just need a moment. Are you…are you really telling the truth?" I said, shutting my eyes tightly.

"You don't have to believe me, if you find it too difficult," Catrin said. My eyes opened, and focused on her, sitting on the couch across from me.

"It is difficult, yet I do believe you," I whispered. Rhys sighed beside me, and somehow I knew from that sound that he believed her too. I glanced over at him, and his expression was grave, marked with lines of consternation.

"Why?" Catrin asked, looking at me with an open, curious face. I blinked at her, wondering why she would ask me that.

"I don't know," I said honestly. "It makes more sense than the other options."

"Which are?"

"That—" I stopped suddenly, still not wanting to say the words. I pushed on, forcing myself to hear them out loud. "That my father killed my parents and stole me. That magic is passed through blood, even though my parents were obviously commoners. None of those things could be true."

Catrin nodded. "Logic. How it can hurt us. But then… your mentor has committed other great wrongs against you. You can't ignore that."

I frowned at her. "I haven't discussed his treatment of me with you."

"In a way, you have. He has hidden so many things from you, Eira. These are lies in their own way, and they have been of great detriment to you."

"I agree that this is quite an offense. But not sensing Eos…" I began, and Catrin could tell my tone was argumentative.

"Is one of your most basic and primary senses. And somehow he was able to hide it from you. Imagine if he had taken your sight or your hearing."

"How did he do this?" Rhys asked, almost demanded.

Catrin shook her head. "I have no idea. I've never heard of such an ability," she said, now frustrated. "Perhaps we'll also find the answer to that question in one of these books." She picked up one of the bigger books, whose brown leather binding was nearly falling off.

At that moment the back door to the kitchen opened and shut, and a heavy silence fell over us as Aerona passed through the doorway into the sitting room. She came to stand between the low table and the fireplace, frowning down at the three of us in turn, as we glanced up at her with hesitation. Or at least Rhys and I did. Catrin continued to flip through the stained pages, acting as though she was oblivious to Aerona's presence.

Aerona huffed. "What's this aura? It's like someone died in here."

Catrin looked up at her then. "We've been discussing some heavy topics." Aerona sat on the sofa next to Catrin, across from Rhys, and looked at the book in Catrin's hands.

"Which were?" she asked curiously. Catrin glanced at me, and I knew what she was wondering. And I knew that Aerona would know if we were keeping things from her, and it wouldn't help to gain her trust to do so.

"I hadn't known the truth," I said slowly. She frowned at me. "About my birth. As an Eosiaid." Her eyes widened. She glanced at Rhys, and then Catrin.

"How is this possible?" she asked, looking back at me. Her tone was causational again, and it set me on edge. Could she possibly be blaming me?

"My father—mentor never told me."

"And no one else did? I know I'm one of the only commoners in the Empire to know the truth, but for an Eos—"

"That's enough, Aerona," Catrin snapped, and she shut the tome in her hands decisively. "She didn't know. Now she does. No more questions."

Aerona glared at Catrin, but didn't respond. Once again I found myself wondering what sort of relationship they had. And that moment seemed as good a time as ever to change the subject.

"How did you two…?" I started, but couldn't manage to finish the sentence. Still, Catrin understood, while Aerona glared openly at me.

"Aerona ran away from home, and I took her in. She's quite interested in books, you see," Catrin said, now smiling slightly.

Aerona rolled her eyes. "Why do you care?" she asked me.

"I'm curious how a commoner and a recluse Eosiaid came to live together," I said, attempting to stare her down. Catrin laughed at my explanation. Rhys, apparently not interested in this line of discussion, picked up one of the smaller books from the table, one with a faded blue cloth cover, and began to skim through it.

Catrin directed her smile at Aerona. "We are an odd pair," she said, and Aerona sighed.

"It's true," Aerona admitted. "And what Catrin said is true. My parents died when I was young, in an accident. I was taken in by an aunt and uncle, but they were…neglectful. I was twelve or so at the time. I ran away, and made it all the way to the Grand Road, a few miles from my village. No one paid me any mind, not to harm or help, though I passed scores of travelers and I was in quite a state. No one helped until Catrin saw me. She came up to me and asked me where I was from, and where I was going. And I told her I was from Gwythllan and that I didn't know where I was going. She asked me if I liked books, and I did, of course, and I told her so. And she asked me if I wanted to help her write and study, and do all the things that pages do."

She stopped talking then, then looked down at her hands, perhaps embarrassed from opening herself up to us.

"And she's been helping me ever since," Catrin said, with an obvious note of pride. "I could tell the moment I saw her that she was a good, helpful, studious child. Perhaps with some trust issues—"

"Catrin," Aerona hissed, turning red.

"But a good friend," Catrin finished, and Aerona became so red it was like her face was a small sun.

"And you two?" Aerona asked suddenly, looking between Rhys and me. "How have you two come on this journey together?"

Rhys responded before I even opened my mouth. "I was stationed to defend Eira during the battle that ended in our province's defeat. She insisted that we escape together, and we did."

For some reason, it seemed like Aerona relaxed at his explanation. Her expression turned softer, and I thought I saw the hints of a smile at the corners of her mouth.

"You're a dedicated guard then," she said, and Rhys frowned at her.

"Hardly. I abandoned my city in a time of war," he said. I glared at him, wondering if he regretted coming with me.

"We already talked about this—" I started, but he turned and smiled at me in a comforting way.

"I'm glad I'm alive, Eira, and I'm glad I escaped with you. But leaving during a battle is not what guards do. And should we ever return, and save Nefyn, I will refuse to resume my position."

"That's idiotic," I said, and he blinked in surprise. "You're here to get information and weapons to help us take back our home. If we succeed, you deserve to be Captain of the Guards."

Rhys laughed lightly and ran a hand through his hair, a sign that he felt uncomfortable. Aerona watched this exchange with interest, while Catrin went back to flipping through the book in her lap. "Well, I'm not sure I deserve that honor, but…the day is wearing on, isn't it? And we have a lot of books to get through. Aerona, will you help us search?" Rhys asked her, looking at her directly. She took a moment to respond.

"Ah…no, I can't. I have to return to the library. And I'm sure Catrin has a list of books for me to return with…" She trailed off, as Catrin produced a piece of parchment from underneath one of the tomes on the table, with a long list of titles scrawled on it. Aerona frowned at it as she took it from Catrin's hand, and stood.

"Why don't you accompany her, Rhys?" Catrin said, looking at him as he stared at her in surprise.

"I'm sure she wouldn't want—" he began, frowning at Aerona, who was also staring at Catrin.

"She'll have a lot of books to carry back, and I'm sure she would appreciate the help," Catrin said.

Aerona looked down at the list of books in her hand, and sighed. "It will be a lot to carry," she muttered, before looking at Rhys. Her expression was apologetic, a small, awkward smile appearing. "I wouldn't mind the help, if you could spare it."

Rhys smiled naturally, and it made me feel oddly angry. "Of course. Let me retrieve my cloak."

A few minutes later they were out the door, and oppressive silence fell over me and Catrin. The only sounds I could hear was the wind in the trees outside, howling and filled with power, and the popping of the logs in the fireplace. It was a chilly day outside, and the fire was necessary to keep the stone house from uncomfortably chill temperatures. I grabbed a book soon after the door had shut, wanting to distract myself from the uncomfortable emotions I felt growing inside of me unfettered. But my eyes slid over the words without comprehension, the image of Rhys and Aerona riding together through the woods grating me to no end, like a tiny thorn, one I was unable to find and remove.

"Are you alright, dear?" Catrin asked after an immeasurable amount of time, bringing me back to reality. I felt how my face was creased in a frown, and tried to smooth it quickly as I looked up at her. She was smiling at me, and there was something knowing in that smile.

"Perfectly fine," I answered. "Just…not exactly sure what to look for, to be honest."

"Skim for keywords—anything about the Eosiaid, power, gift, and so on."

I looked down at the book in my hand: *The Meaning of Eosiaid,* and looked back up at Catrin to frown at her. "That would be this entire book," I said, showing her the cover.

"Better read the whole book, then," she grinned. "In any case. Would you like to tell me the truth now?"

"What?"

"Something else is bothering you—not just that you aren't sure what to look for," she said. She was leaning back into the sofa, relaxed and warm, and I felt myself give up. Maybe she could help me.

"I think it would have been better for Rhys to stay here." There. That was the truth, wasn't it?

"Aerona needed help with the books," Catrin reminded me.

"Yes, well," I said, clearing my throat. I frowned down at the book in my hands. Then I sighed. "I suppose, perhaps, I'm uncomfortable being separated from him after all this time."

"You two have been traveling together for some time now," she said with a small nod.

"Yes. Two weeks or so," I said. "And we went through the battle together. I-I don't know what I would have done…if he hadn't been there." I reminded myself that it was due to him that we had been able to escape from the room where Cassia had been keeping us.

"No matter how much time you may have to spend apart, I am sure you two will always have a bond," Catrin said. I smiled at her, the words only making me feel slightly awkward.

"I appreciate you saying that, Catrin," I replied, before sighing down at the book in my hands. "I apologize for letting my emotions get the best of me."

"Don't apologize. You'll find that those who smother their emotions often go insane."

I smiled weakly at this, not exactly finding it comforting, and opened my book back up without another word, intent on moving on from this topic. There were a lot of books to get through, and I didn't want to waste any more time.

>«

Aerona and Rhys returned a few hours later, sometime in the late afternoon. At the sound of the hooves stomping down the wet earth in the clearing outside, I jumped up from where I was still reading on the sofa, across from Catrin, and strode to look out the window beside the door. Golden light filtered through the tops of the trees to the west and fell on Rhys and Aerona's faces. Both were smiling with warmth, which was a new and somewhat disconcerting expression to see on Aerona's stoic face. It made my stomach clench in a sensation I didn't totally understand, that smile and the way she looked at Rhys and laughed at something he said.

"They've returned," I said quietly as I walked back to the sofa, sat down and picked up the book I had abandoned. Catrin raised an eyebrow at me, but gave no other response. A moment later, Rhys and Aerona opened the front door, bright smiles on their faces and the dying lilt of laughter falling from their lips. Their eyes fell on Catrin and me as they entered the door and closed it behind them, and Aerona's expression immediately returned to her usual stony glare. I felt nauseated suddenly, but forced myself to ignore the sensation and continue reading the book in my hands.

"You haven't moved at all," Rhys commented with a grin, setting down a large canvas bag on the floor beside the sofa. I nodded, feeling as though attempting to speak to him would lead to some awful sound coming out of my mouth. I listened as Aerona moved around the back of the sofa on nearly silent feet, and made her way down the hall to the right of the kitchen.

Rhys sat on the sofa beside me, and I could so easily tell that he was concerned by my behavior. I risked a glance at him, and he was looking at me with that concern open on his face. I could also sense Catrin's stare as she observed this interaction, but that didn't surprise me.

"It's just been a long day," I said, offering him a smile as I raised the book in my hands.

He grinned in response. "Well, there's still a bit of daylight outside. Why don't you take a break? We can go for a walk."

I balked at this idea, and I hoped that response didn't show on my face. "Well, I—"

"Yes, you should," Catrin said, nodding with sagely wisdom. I glared at her, feeling that she understood all too well what I was upset about. "This sort of work requires frequent breaks."

"Why didn't you tell me to take a break hours ago, then?" I smiled at her.

She smiled back, then shrugged. "I didn't think about it. But now that Rhys mentions it, I agree that a break for you is in order."

It was no use to argue with them, and within minutes I was following Rhys out the door and into the golden light beyond. We were silent as we walked along the path into the shadowed forest. The tops of the trees were glowing in the last rays of the sun, but down on the ground, it was quite gray and leached of color, twilight having already settled there.

"So," Rhys said after we had gone a few yards along the path. "I'm guessing neither of you were able to find anything about the special powers."

I shook my head, even though he couldn't see since he was walking ahead of me. "No. It's hard to come by books that tell us anything other than…than what we already know." I didn't want to bring up the horrifying truth that Catrin had just explained to us that morning, but Rhys sensed it in the undertone of my words. He turned suddenly to face me, his face shadowy and serious, and that concern in his eyes had returned and was all the more serious now. I stared at him, surprised and overwhelmed.

"Are you alright?" he asked softly. I nodded, my mouth open slightly, as I felt myself pulled to him. I fought the urge and stayed in place, mystified by this strange feeling. "Because I'm still shaken by this morning, and I can't...I can't imagine how you feel," he continued. His open warm eyes imploring me to be honest with him. I wanted nothing more, and yet found it incredibly difficult to do so. The evening birds sang in the branches above us, and I listened for a moment, finding the strength to respond.

"I—" I cleared my throat impulsively. "I'm shaken too. It makes some things make more sense, though. Calliten had never been honest with me, and I always knew that. Even when I didn't know what he was hiding from me."

"I had no idea your relationship was so...strained," Rhys said, his voice still comforting and soft. I looked at the ground between our feet, somehow feeling embarrassed by his words.

"Calliten is very good at presenting a certain image," I replied.

"Eira," Rhys said, prompting me to look at him. "I'm sorry." I blinked at him, surprised by the rawness in his voice and his expression. How honest. How open.

"It's not your fault," I managed.

"I'm not saying it is," he replied with a small, sad smile. "But I want you to know...you're not alone with this. You can always talk to me." My heart ached at his words with a sensation I had never experienced before, but then the sight of him and Aerona walking through the door and laughing together crossed my mind, and the feeling immediately soiled into sickness. Again, I gave him a weak smile, and nodded.

"Thank you. I…I know that," I said. And I wished I meant it.

10

The Sacreds and the Inherents

The next day passed in much the same fashion as the first, except Rhys stayed and helped Catrin and me search the books. Occasionally, one of us would find a word or phrase that seemed strange or important in some way: Sacred power, the Inherents, the prophecy… But no explanation was ever given, and we could never derive context around these words from the rest of the text. This frustrated me to no end, while Rhys and Catrin were able to remain calm and simply continue their reading.

On the third day, I dropped a book down on the table in anger, which garnered a glare from Catrin. "Respect the book," she warned, but refrained from chastising me any further. I huffed, and Rhys looked at me from where he sat beside me, a sympathetic smile on his face.

"Let's spar," he said. I turned to stare at him, forgetting about the new book I had just picked up.

"What?"

"You've been doing this too long again. You need to… reset."

"You think sparring is the way to do that?" I asked, narrowing my eyes at him. In the back of my mind, I acknowledged that I was in a sour mood, but I couldn't stop myself from glaring at him in suspicion.

"You've been stuck inside for days, sitting on a sofa, staring at paper. You need exercise," he argued.

"He's right, you know," Catrin offered without looking up from her book. I sighed, feeling my shoulders slump. I just didn't have the energy to argue, and the idea of going outside did sound nice.

"Fine. Get your sword, soldier," I said as I stood from the sofa, and Rhys grinned at me with infectious brightness.

A few minutes later we stood in the yard, washed in bright afternoon light. White puffy clouds floated through the sky above the pointed treetops, and the air was a perfect warmth of a late spring day. I closed my eyes and inhaled deeply, the fresh air a comforting balm after days spent indoors.

"Are you ready?" Rhys asked from a few feet away. I opened my eyes and saw him standing with his sword at his side, looking at me with a curious smile.

"I think so," I said. I raised my own sword and gave it an experimental swing. I was extremely unskilled with sword fighting, as I had spent all of my energy on archery, and I suddenly grew embarrassed. Would Rhys laugh at my ineptitude? I looked at him, concerned, and he must have noticed my change in emotion, as he frowned.

"What's wrong?" he asked, taking a step towards me.

"Well…" I sighed, knowing that being honest would be the easiest way out of this situation. "I'm actually quite unpracticed."

His frown fell away and was replaced by a grin. "Perhaps this could be a lesson instead, then," he suggested. "I'm not the most skilled, but—"

"I'm sure you are talented," I muttered, and he paused for only a moment.

"I would be happy to teach you what I know," he finished, setting the point of his sword in the earth between us.

I felt a slow smile grow over my face. "Alright. I would appreciate that," I said with a small nod.

"Well, then," he said, clearly pleased, as he lifted his sword from the ground and held it upward. "It all starts with your feet."

The lesson proved to be much more exhausting than I had anticipated. Rhys was a thorough instructor and was also incredibly patient. My movements were slow and inaccurate, but he never berated me, only offered me advice on aspects of the forms that I wasn't quite understanding.

"Your grip has slipped," Rhys said at one point. I was breathing heavily as I had been swinging this rod of metal for over a half hour, and barely comprehended as he carefully placed his hands over mine and readjusted the placement of my fingers. I blinked and looked up at his face, suddenly so close to mine, his warmed fingers overlapping mine, and felt myself take in a sharp breath. His eyes settled on mine, and his gold-brown irises glowed like fire in the warm sunlight. I blinked and felt his hand tighten nearly imperceptibly around mine.

Then we heard the kitchen door open into the yard, and we pulled apart just as quickly as we had come together.

I turned to look at the door, feeling my braids swing over my shoulders with the abrupt movement. I was still breathing heavily, but now I wasn't sure why. My eyes narrowed as Aerona stepped across the yard to us, offering us each an awkward smile.

"Catrin has found something and would like to share it with you immediately," she said, eyeing me with some curiosity. Before either of us could reply, she continued. "Were you practicing?" she asked with a small frown, gesturing at the sword in my hand.

"More like learning," I said, huffing out a dry laugh. "I'm very inexperienced."

"Ah," Aerona nodded, surprisingly amiable. I hadn't really expected her to respond to my explanation, as I had assumed she didn't actually care and usually did whatever she had to do to avoid conversation. "I've never learned how to use a sword, honestly," she added, a bit meekly, looking off into the forest as to avoid eye contact with either of us.

"Would you like to learn?" Rhys asked her, and I barely stopped myself from sending him a sharp look. A slow smile spread over Aerona's face as she appraised him, and then she nodded.

»«

It was decided that I would lend Aerona my sword, while I went inside to find out what Catrin had discovered. The sun was low in the sky at that point, and I knew that Rhys wouldn't have too much time to teach Aerona, but a discomfort grew in my stomach as I handed her the hilt of my sword and turned back towards the house, hearing her excited chatter behind me, and Rhys's jovial responses.

Aerona was awaking something in me deep, unyielding, and ugly. I wasn't so naive that I couldn't recognize jealousy when it coursed through me with aggression. I simply couldn't understand where this feeling was coming from.

Sure, Rhys was nice and good-looking by most standards.

But I didn't feel anything towards him.

I turned back for one more glance as my hand gripped the door handle, and the sight I saw in the yard made my abdomen clench with a sickly feeling. Aerona placed her hand on Rhys's arm and laughed at something he said, her eyes shining up at him, and I felt so much that I could barely handle it. I took a deep, steadying breath, opened the door, and tried to leave the image behind me.

"That bad?" Catrin spoke from the kitchen table. I opened my eyes, having closed them in exhaustion while leaning against the inside of the door, and saw her sitting in the dim light of the kitchen. She was grinning at me, her eyes twinkling in understanding and humor. I blinked, surprised by both her presence and her words.

"What?" I asked dumbly.

"Sparring practice," she elaborated, the humor still there despite the innocuous question.

"Um…yes," I said, moving away from the door and grabbing some flint, beginning to light a few candles. "Why are you sitting in the dark?"

"Why are you denying your feelings?"

I whirled around to look at her, a lit candle now fluttering in my hand. "Excuse me?"

"You have feelings for him," she said.

I rolled my eyes. "No I don't."

"You're worried Aerona is going to form a stronger bond with him than you two already have," she continued.

"I don't feel anything like that for him," I muttered as I set the candle down on the table. "I just…"

"You can sense a change within yourself," Catrin said, leaning forward slightly. "Your feelings are shifting, and you're feeling something you haven't felt before. And it terrifies you."

I stared at her levelly. "I don't find any of this funny, Catrin. Stop trying to mess with me."

"If you deny your true nature, your true feelings, so rare and powerful, you will surely begin to wither."

I sighed. "Okay. Thank you for the warning." Catrin sat back, smiling at me in a smug way. I sat down heavily across from her and stared at her curiously. "So?" I asked after a moment. "Aerona said you found something."

Catrin nodded. "Do you want to wait for Rhys to hear this as well?"

I shook my head. "No. I'll just tell him later. Or you can."

Catrin nodded, with an uncharacteristic frown. "Alright, then. Here is what I found: a poem." She opened a tiny book, perhaps the size of an open hand, and flipped to a specific page, and then turned it around to face it before me on the table.

> "Tales of magic, skills of yore.
> Forgotten legends at their core.
> Weak at two, strong at six.
> The powerless they do transfix.
> Some a light within the dark,
> While others wish to leave a mark.
> A forest silver, a mountain tall,
> In these places they will fall.
> From the heavens they are crowned
> And to the Sky Queen they are bound.
> No one knows all they can do,
> They are the Sacred Twenty-Two."

I frowned down at the words before me, wondering what to make of them.

"The Sacred Twenty-Two," Catrin repeated, leaning over the table towards me. "No one knows all they can do. Bound to the Sky Queen. Some wish to leave a mark. Forgotten legends."

I was silent for a moment, still studying the page before looking up at Catrin. "You think…you think this is about the powerful people I saw?"

She nodded. "More than that. It's a prophecy about them."

I picked up the book and looked at the cover. The title was faded and written in an antique font that I recognized as a popular one used in the Empire over three hundred years before. I squinted, bringing it slightly closer to the light of the candle, and saw that it simply read *The Seer*. I glared at Catrin.

"Who wrote this?" I asked, finding it unlikely that she would know. I couldn't see a name anywhere.

"It is signed on the final page," Catrin said. I blinked, and then flipped to the last page, where an indecipherable signature was scrawled in the top right corner.

"What does it say?" I asked, looking up at her again.

"The Prophet Adelais. He is also mentioned in a clerical roster of the holy temple of Silvania in the second age— about four hundred and fifty years ago." I blinked, suddenly more thankful for Catrin than ever. Still, I wasn't sure what to make of this new information.

"So these people…have legendary powers?" I asked slowly. "And this prophet from hundreds of years ago wrote this prophecy about them?"

"Adelais was a real prophet, Eira," Catrin said lowly, sensing the disbelief in my tone. She frowned slightly. "He is well remembered among the priests and priestesses of the temples in Silvania, for having a special connection to the Sky

Queen. Most of his writings are kept in the great holy temple there, and they would pay a massive sum to get their hands on this little book."

I sat back slowly, still dubious. "Well, does he write more about these Twenty-Two?" I asked, frowning at her.

Catrin sighed and shook her head. "He mentions the Sacreds over and over," she said, clearly irritated. "But nowhere else is there any detail. Except…" She grabbed the book from me and flipped through it again. "Ah, here it is. Here, he mentions these Sacreds and their innate connection with the Himminir. Although he calls them the Inherents."

I blinked. "The Himminir? Of Aornadur?" I questioned, thoroughly surprised. "That you write of in your book on Aorlanda?"

Catrin nodded. "Yes, see right here: 'On a great mountain in the southern reaches of the world live the Inherents, Linra's last real connection to the Sky Queen. The Sacreds are bound to them, and so they await the arrival of the Sacreds.'"

I was silent for a moment, considering this. "Alright, well." I frowned at the table. "Are we sure the Inherents or the Himminir… Are we even sure that they're real?"

Catrin stared at me, clearly affronted. "Of course. You think I would write of people that don't even exist as if they did?"

"Well—" I began, but Catrin continued.

"The Himminir are certainly real. The town of Geirr exists at the base of their mountain, and occasionally zealots trek to their castle to leave offerings. It is well documented."

"Alright," I said, not wanting to anger her any further; and besides, I did believe her. "And you're sure he's speaking of the same people?"

"Read through the book yourself. Perhaps with more context, you'll have less doubt," Catrin said as she handed the book back to me.

"I believe all of this," I said, taking the book from her. "I just don't know what to make of it. This means they're...they're godlike in nature."

"Perhaps that is one way to look at it," Catrin nodded, although her tone suggested that she didn't entirely agree with me. I flipped through the pages, already getting a headache from Adelais's scrawl.

"What else could they be?" I asked her, not looking up from the book. "They're connected to the Himminir and the Sky Queen—"

"That is how Adelais chose to contextualize these powers. I think you're focusing on the less important facts, Eira."

I glanced at her, a bit annoyed. "What are the important facts, then?" I asked as I closed the book. She looked back at me levelly.

"There are twenty-two of these people."

"Yes."

"How many did you meet?" I frowned, considering this.

"I think...only two. But one implied that there were more of them."

"Do you think all twenty-two of these people have banded together to attack your home?" Catrin asked, raising an eyebrow.

"It seems unlikely, considering they come from all over Linra..." I trailed off, thinking of how at least two foreigners had joined forces with Cassia and Varina, who were themselves Remisian. Cassia had mentioned the names of the two people watching Calliten in another room, and I wasn't entirely sure but the names had sounded distinctly Shukorian, people hailing from a continent across the Eastern Sea. If these people could come from that far away, that complicated things quite a bit.

"Exactly. Perhaps the answer to your problem—who these people are, and how to fight them—is to find the others."

I frowned at the table between us. It had grown dark outside, and I wondered why Rhys and Aerona hadn't come back inside yet. "How could I possibly do that?" I groaned after a moment. I shook my head before Catrin could venture a response. "I just need time to think all of this over. I believe it, but it still sounds…mythic to me."

"I think in this case, these people aren't myths, but the legends that myths arise from," Catrin said, and I simply shook my head again, then proceeded to rub my forehead, feeling the beginnings of a headache.

"You didn't know about these…these people before?" I asked her.

She shook her head. "Sometimes you only notice things when you look for them," she said as she gazed at the book still in my hands. Then her eyes met mine, and she smiled warmly. "So I'm thankful you arrived and gave me a reason to find this."

I laughed lightly. "You always see the positive side of things."

Catrin nodded. "It's the best side to see."

»«

Catrin told Rhys and Aerona what she had discovered over dinner. I thought she would be able to explain it better than

I could. We sat around the small kitchen table with plates piled high with roasted potatoes, Rhys and I next to each other facing Catrin and Aerona. Aerona wasn't really interested in what Catrin had to say, as she focused on eating her potatoes with small, careful bites, but Rhys seemed just as confused as I was as he sat upright and tense, studying Catrin with a silent frown as she spoke. It was now pitch-black outside, and the kitchen was lit with the light of a few candles set on the center of the table.

"Why haven't we heard of these people before?" Rhys asked once Catrin had summarized her findings.

"I think you've realized by now that you haven't heard of a lot of things," she said, before shoving a fork full of potatoes in her mouth.

"Yes, but for twenty-two people to exist around Linra, all with different, legendary abilities—"

"Well," Catrin said, setting down her fork, "Adelais notes that while there are twenty-two of these Sacred powers, there aren't necessarily twenty-two people alive that wield them."

"What do you mean?" I asked, curiosity piqued. She turned to look at me, perhaps a bit surprised by my interruption. I had been silent so far.

"The powers come and go on Linra, he says. The right people have to exist to use the power, and if the right sort of person isn't around…well, then the power won't be either."

Rhys looked at me and sighed. "I think we both need to read this book carefully," he said with a tired smile. I nodded, beginning to think that the more we knew, the less we understood.

I looked back at Catrin after a moment of studying my potatoes, a frown on my face. "If it's not for certain that all of these people exist at the same time, how do we know if we'll even be able to find more of them?"

Catrin considered my words calmly as she ate, studying the candle that flickered on the table in between us. "I guess we don't know," she said after a moment. She looked up at me finally, wearing a small smile. "Perhaps you can come up with a better idea after reading this book."

I groaned. "While we're stuck here reading, Lithe is falling apart," I muttered, pushing the potatoes around my plate with my fork. I had completely lost my appetite over the last few minutes.

"We don't really know what's going on, Eira," Rhys said softly from my left. I looked over at him, a bit surprised by his comforting tone. "It's probably not good, but we don't know for sure that all is lost."

"When have you ever heard of invaders making a place better?" I snapped, then immediately regretted it. Before I could apologize, Catrin interrupted.

"Remisia invaded the ancient folks," she commented. When I looked at her blankly, she continued. "Remisia is a nice place, isn't it? A military to be admired, a powerful government, wealth beyond comprehension. I'm sure the ancient folks didn't have those things. Otherwise, they wouldn't have been invaded."

"Remisia created this lie about Eosiaids just to gain more power over commoners," I said, glaring at her. "And what are you suggesting—that Lithe has fallen because we're weaker than whoever these people are?" I couldn't help but be offended by the suggestion.

Catrin raised an eyebrow. "Am I wrong?" My mouth contorted into a tight line as I considered her words and knew that no, she was not wrong. These people were incredibly strong and powerful, and Lithe hadn't stood a chance.

"We don't even know who has control where," Rhys broke in, obviously frustrated. His hands were closed into fists on the surface of the table, his shoulders tense. "We saw Nefyn fall, and we met Hartanians and Varina in Maenynys, yet there's no sign of them here."

"We've talked about this," I sighed. "If Maenynys has fallen, it's only a matter of time."

"They must be incredibly powerful if they were able to cut straight through the country to get to the capital," Aerona said, pausing in her small bites to look at each of us. Her expression was inscrutable, but I thought I saw a bit of uncertainty in her eyes. I wondered if she was uncertain of her words or of speaking up at all.

"Maybe even more powerful than the people you met," Catrin agreed, nodding at Aerona. "I wouldn't be surprised if the ones in charge are, well, especially ferocious."

"I wish I knew what their powers are," I said, rubbing my forehead in frustration. "And how they work."

"We'll figure it out," Rhys said softly, after a moment, and I looked over at him, my hand still resting on my forehead. He smiled softly, and I wanted nothing more than to believe him.

»«

The next day, we decided that I would read *The Seer* first, then Rhys, and then we would discuss it with Catrin. While we read, she would continue searching the few remaining tomes that we hadn't been able to read through thoroughly.

Aerona went off to report for her job at the library, and Catrin, Rhys, and I sat on the sofas around the low wooden table still covered with books, and for most of the day we were silent, with just the noise of the crackling blaze in the fireplace filling the room, and the occasional shuffling of pages.

Reading Adelais's book was more difficult than I had anticipated, due to the antiquated language and cramped handwriting. I was able to make it through slowly, with deep concentration, though I did nearly ask Catrin for help a few times.

And while I read in silence, the words I was reading were confusing me even more than I thought they would.

In this world, forgotten powers roam among us as humans. I am one of them, and it is my sacred duty to learn all I can, and record all I know.

That was how Adelais started his story, and it only grew stranger from there. He described twenty-two powers in the first section, but with only their titles and no explanation. The Seer. The Suppressor. The Helper. The Minder. The Finder. The Planner. The Mer. The Fault. The Verdant. The Feeler. The Feather. The Hammer. The Flame. The Gale. The Corpse. The Peacekeeper. The Advisor. The Interpreter. The Ghost. The Destroyer. The Rememberer. The Fader.

These titles or names were nonsensical to me, save for one, the Seer, as that was what Adelais called himself. Everything else was entirely meaningless, as he provided no context as to what these powers were. Still, I considered every word to be important, and knew it was possible that the people I had seen matched up with some of these names.

Then came a section on the history of the Seers, and how they were somehow connected to the Destroyer. Whenever a Seer came into existence, they could only hope that a Destroyer did not exist at the same time.

Above all, he wrote, the Seer felt a need to learn as much as possible. Adelais felt a constant yearning for some information that he could not find, though he read every single book and scroll he could get his hands on. He was able to synthesize all of his knowledge and create new theories about history, language, religion, physics, and magic, and that was why his writings became so incredibly valuable. Though I was annoyed at having to squint at his cramped writing for hours, I admired him. I wished I had such a passion for learning. And the more I read, the more it became clear to me that Adelais's teachings had had a huge effect on modern knowledge.

And then, near the end of the book, came perhaps the most important section.

When all of the Sacreds exist at once, then will come the end of the Sacreds. They will be reunited with their counterparts, the Inherents. The Inherents are immortal beings that live in the highest reaches of the world, waiting in their ice-frozen abode for the Great Return. I do not believe it will happen in my lifetime, and the teachings of the Sky Queen have forgotten this Sacred Passage. It exists, though, written in the Ancient Tongue of the Queen, on an unremarkable tablet kept in the crypts below the Great Temple of Silvania. None of my peers read it as I do; only I can see the truth etched into its surface. The one true authority that remains on the Sacreds and their Return is the Inherents. The Souls of the Beginning. Someday I will venture to their peak, and attempt to return my soul, though I know even now they will not accept it. Perhaps I wish only to meet them, once in this lifetime.

The book ended soon after, and I shut it softly as I looked up at Catrin. Golden afternoon light filtered in through the window I was facing, and I blinked as I saw the way it made the floorboards glow with fire. Catrin seemed to have been waiting for me to finish reading, as she looked up from the book in her hands as soon as I shut mine.

"And?" she asked eagerly. Rhys, sitting beside me, was also summoned from his reading stupor, and I sensed him looking at me expectantly.

"I believe that these Sacreds are real," I said, still gathering my thoughts on all I had read.

"Of course," she nodded, frowning in impatience. "What else?"

"Is there something you want me to say?" I asked, narrowing my eyes at her. She grinned.

"I only wish to know if we found the same passages important," she replied.

"Well," I said slowly, glancing down at the nondescript cover. "The Seer is a Sacred that searches for knowledge. Adelais became one of the greatest philosophers as a result." Catrin nodded, still smiling, but made no reply. I continued. "I'm especially concerned about the section that mentions the Inherents. It seems they are the same as the Himminir."

"Indeed," Catrin said. "As I said. And do you know what the word 'Himminir' means?" she asked me, her smile growing slightly. I shook my head, frowning at her. "The beginning," she said, her eyes twinkling.

"The Souls of the Beginning," I said, blinking once at the book in my hands.

"Over time, we lost the truth of what they are—not monks, as I had thought, but beings beyond our comprehension," Catrin said. I glanced at Rhys, wondering what he was making of this conversation as he hadn't read the book yet. He was frowning at Catrin, his mouth in a tight line and his eyebrows deeply furrowed.

"And somehow, they're deeply connected to the Sacreds," I said. "But why would he want to return his soul to them? Especially if he already knows they won't take it..." I wondered out loud.

"Adelais was a strange man," Catrin said, waving a hand dismissively. "That is well documented. In any case, it seems this book is just a short manifesto on how he wanted to live the remainder of his life." She looked over at Rhys now, and gave him an apologetic smile. "This must be incredibly confusing for you. It's your turn next—although I would like to read one more section again, before you start." Rhys nodded without comment, still seriously considering all we had said in silence. Catrin turned to me. "Would you pass me the book, dear?" she said, leaning over the table with her hand outstretched. I leaned forward a bit until the book was in her hand, and my index finger barely brushed her thumb. And then there was a rushing sound in my ears, blackness in my eyes.

Catrin stood outside a castle at night, and the first thing I noticed about her was that she was incredibly young, her hair a rich brown that I could see even in the poor light. She wore a heavy black traveling cloak, covering her entirely except for her head. There was no moon, and the stars twinkled brightly overhead. I whirled around, wondering where we were. We stood on a stone bridge just outside the bailey of the castle, and Catrin looked up, over the gray stone battlements and ramparts, where a candle burned in one of the tower windows. The form of a person was silhouetted there, and Catrin seemed to be staring at them, with an intense mix of emotions that I simply couldn't understand.

"Catrin—" I said, but she did not seem to hear me. She turned suddenly, walked right past me, and began running down the road, which soon curved into a forest. I followed her for a moment, stumbling over the stones of the road, before the rushing and blackness returned, momentarily knocking the air from my lungs and divorcing me from my senses.

Then there was bright light on the other side of my eyelids, and Rhys's voice.

"It happened again," he said, tone frustrated with worry. I blinked my eyes open and saw that I was still sitting on the old sofa, the red Conotrian rug beneath my feet and Catrin sitting across from me. Her expression was strange, untrusting, and I felt my stomach sink at the sight. Adelais's book was clutched in her hand, but she continued to stare at me.

Rhys was sitting next to me, tense and staring at me as he had turned his torso to face me. I sat up slightly, as I had slumped against the couch, and felt the fear settle in my bones. It had happened again. I looked at him, my eyes wide.

"I'm okay," I whispered, my voice cracking slightly.

"What happened?" Catrin asked, and I turned to look at her again, not knowing what to say. I knew I had to be honest, but I honestly didn't know what was happening to me.

"It's…hallucinations," I said finally. She blinked, clearly surprised by my use of the word. "Sometimes… It's only happened three—four times now."

"What were the other times?" Catrin asked. There was no judgment in her voice, only curiosity. Still, I knew what had happened was alarming, and I didn't want her to become distrusting of me. I sighed, glanced at Rhys, and he gave me an encouraging nod. Honesty. I hadn't told him about the incident with the dagger, which was still stored underneath the guest bed. I pursed my lips, and knew that I had to tell both of them the whole truth.

"One of the attackers. The Remisian woman, Cassia. And then on the road coming here, with Rhys. And…once while holding a dagger I took from Varina." I glanced at Rhys with caution, and saw that he was frowning at me.

"What? When was this?" he asked, his tone more surprised than anything else.

"The first night we were here. Before I went to sleep. I just…I didn't want to concern you," I said, hoping he could sense my regret. His facial features smoothed slightly, but before he could respond, Catrin was speaking.

"What happens in these hallucinations?" Catrin asked. I closed my eyes for a moment, wondering how to describe it.

"I see the person I'm with. First Cassia, then Rhys, and now you. It's always some moment, in another place, at another time. It's like I'm there, but you couldn't see or hear me. It lasts for a few seconds, and then I'm taken back. And in the case of the dagger…I saw both Cassia and Varina. Cassia was giving Varina the dagger."

Catrin considered this for a moment, and I waited, wondering if she was going to say I was insane. I reminded myself that Catrin was very unlikely to consider anyone insane, as she was quite an odd person herself. But the problem was that I felt insane. And a part of me wanted someone to agree with me.

"What did you see just now?" she asked me, looking at me intently.

I hesitated, but only for a moment. "You. I think you were younger. Your hair was brown. It was nighttime and there was no moon and a clear sky. You were outside a castle wearing a cloak. And you looked up at a window that had a candle in it, and there was a person there. And then you ran off down the road and into a forest."

She blinked at me. Another silence stretched between us, and I began to worry that I really had said something wrong.

Then she let out a shaky breath and said, "I remember that."

I stared at her. "What?" I asked after a moment.

"The night I left. That was the night that I left my home." Her voice was soft and her eyes were distant as she remembered. I waited a few moments, unable to look away from her as her words hit me.

"You're saying that was real?" I asked, my voice sounding odd and weak to my ears.

"You described the moment perfectly. That was the night I abandoned my post as a Benadur. When I ran away. Why I'm in hiding now," she explained. Her eyes looked watery as she appraised me. "How did you…?"

I shook my head quickly. "I don't know. It just happened. I have no control over it."

Catrin simply appraised me for a moment, then smiled slightly. "Seems like you're full of surprises as well."

I blinked, and then it all began to hit me. Like boulders falling on me from a great height, I felt as though I couldn't possibly survive this—not all of this. Not everything I had learned in the past couple of days.

It was simply too much.

My body took over, and I felt like I was moving as a ghost, standing from the couch and running across the room, throwing the door open. They called my name behind me, but it didn't matter to me. Fresh air met my face and hands, golden light filled my eyes, and soft earth was compacted beneath my boots. Then I was immersed in the trees, and all of the quiet noises of the forest crashed onto my ears.

Leaves and branches rustling in the slight breeze. The shuffling of small animals through the understory. The calls and songs of evening birds.

Then I heard my breathing. Harsh and rough. Vaguely, I was thankful that I wasn't hyperventilating. Coming back to myself and catching my breath, I took in my surroundings.

I was on the small path that led to Catrin's cottage, but I wasn't sure how far I had gone along it towards the main road. I inhaled deeply, somewhat comforted by the earthy smell of the forest, and felt the sweat begin to dry on my forehead.

Then I heard heavy footsteps echoing along the trail between me and the cottage, and I held in a sigh. Maybe I just needed a moment to myself. A moment to question everything I thought I had ever known.

But I turned and was unsurprised to see Rhys emerge moments later from behind a large, gnarled oak, a cautious expression on his face as he stepped slowly towards me.

"I'm fine," I bit out before he could say anything. He paused, and smiled slightly, a patch of sunlight lighting up his eyes.

"You don't seem fine."

I blinked at his honesty. "It's just a lot to come to terms with. In such a short amount of time," I said, looking away from him, at the thick layer of leaves and broken twigs on the left side of the path. The varying shades of brown mesmerized me as I studied the patterns hidden among all those different textures. I waited for Rhys to respond, feeling tears begin to form in my eyes.

"It is a lot," he said after a moment, his voice soft and calm. "And I'm sorry. It is more than you should have to deal with."

I looked up at him, surprised by his words even though I shouldn't have been. What else would Rhys have said? The kindest person I had ever known, of course he would only try to make me feel better. I wondered vaguely why I expected criticism, even from him.

"Thank you," I said after a moment, sniffling as the cold air made my nose start to run, and the tears fully filled my eyes. I blinked, allowing them to escape down my cheeks, and then hastily rubbed my face with my sleeve.

"Don't thank me," he said with a small smile, and stepped towards me again, until he was only a few feet away. "It's the truth. You shouldn't have to deal with it. So let's...let's forget all of this tonight. All these new things we've found out— about your parents, the Sacreds, these visions you keep seeing. Let's go back to the house and have dinner, and play games and talk about anything else."

I felt my face break into a smile, but my heart broke in a different way. Both breaks felt good, though I couldn't explain why, even to myself. I supposed his words had made me happier than I had expected, and that emotion shocked my heart a bit. It didn't make sense to me—or I just didn't want to make sense of it.

"Okay," I said quietly, still smiling, and we turned back in the direction of the house, where I was intent to ignore my problems. At least for the night.

11

The Empire's Soldiers

It was easier than I thought it would be. Catrin was perfectly fine with putting aside all of the books we had been searching through for the past few days, and pretending along with me and Rhys that everything was perfectly normal. Aerona arrived home a bit after Rhys and me, and began making dinner soon after. The food was a good distraction, and when we were done eating, Rhys encouraged us all to partake in a card game.

Aerona seemed a little surprised but agreed to play along, and soon the four of us were sitting in the living room, laughing over shenanigans and accusing each other of cheating. The fire burned bright in the grate, warming the whole room, and stars twinkled through the window outside, where faintly, I could hear the sound of the wind whispering through the leaves and branches of the forest. A comforting sound, and a comforting place.

Eventually, Catrin and Aerona decided it was time for them to sleep, and wished both of us goodnight. I was overwhelmed at the realization, as the hallway door shut behind them with a soft clicking sound, that I felt at home in the cottage. That Aerona no longer bothered me, that Catrin was something of a confidant to me. I let out a sigh, as though that could release all of the odd emotions I was feeling. Rhys looked at me as he put the cards back in their small wooden box.

"Did you have fun?" he asked, his voice oddly hushed and a little jarring after the few moments of silence. I looked at him, and thought I saw something odd in his eyes, but couldn't make out what it was. There was simply too much in my head to interpret something like that.

"I did." I smiled.

"I was thinking we could go into town tomorrow," he said, setting down the box on the table between us and sitting up straight. He looked at me expectantly, whatever I had seen in his eyes suddenly gone. Now he was just curious, and perhaps a bit cautious.

"I don't know," I said slowly. "I can't put off all these issues forever. We have to figure out what we're going to do, if we can learn more…"

"One evening is not enough, Eira. At least, I don't think it is. Ultimately, I will leave it up to you, but I think you would benefit from spending at least the morning in the city. We could shop at the market, have a nice midday meal… And then, when we return here, you will feel more prepared and steady to focus on some of these…issues," he said. He and I both knew that "issues" was a weak word to describe what was going on, but clearly neither of us could come up with a better alternative.

I thought over his words for a moment, and decided I didn't even care if he was right or not. I simply wanted to put it off for longer, and maybe that meant I wasn't ready to really think about the Sacreds and my parents and my visions. That they were real. He was offering me a way to escape, just for a few more hours. And I wanted to accept.

"Okay," I agreed with a smile, just like I had in the forest. My gratitude for Rhys slammed into me at that moment, but I refused to express it. Just like everything else, I would put off understanding the nature of my feelings for him. Just like everything else, it was simply too much.

»«

The next morning, Rhys and I arrived at the marketplace within the city just as the sun was becoming high enough in the sky to crest over most of the buildings. The market was a collection of tents and awnings of all different colors, under which merchants sold their wares. They ranged from fruit and fish and bread, to clothing and fabric and shoes, to tools and masonry and lumber. Caergarth was a wealthy city, and that showed as the market was filled to the brim with shoppers, the sounds of laughter, haggling, and general chatting echoed off of the walls of the buildings that bordered the market. These were mostly other businesses, as we were in the merchant district of the city.

I looked through many different tents, happy to just peruse what was for sale with no intention of buying. As Rhys had said the first day we were in the city, we had to be careful with our money, and there wasn't really anything that we needed to buy.

It was simply nice to be in that busy atmosphere, where people were living their lives, and the pleasant normality of it all. After days of searching through ancient texts and making life-changing discoveries, the simplicity of the morning market was a warm respite.

At one point my blood nearly ran cold at the sight of silver-blond hair, wisps blowing in the breeze, but then the crowd of people shifted and the sight disappeared. I let out my breath, then inhaled deeply, and was glad Rhys hadn't noticed how I had so easily been triggered, just by a certain hair color.

While having a meal at a nearby tavern, bustling with patrons and a lutist performing in a corner, I felt a sense of calm come over me. The street outside was bright through the windows, and people passed by frequently. The tavern was dim except for the light coming in from the windows that faced the street, and was filled with the warm and hearty smell of stew. People chattered and laughed as they gathered around tables and a bar that lined the back wall of the room, and Rhys and I ate our stew mostly in silence, sitting at our own small table in the corner beside the door. I ate slowly and allowed my thoughts to return to what I had been avoiding for nearly twenty-four hours.

I set my spoon down, my soup only half eaten, and looked up at Rhys. He was gazing distantly at the lutist, who was now singing rather awkwardly to one of his songs.

"I'm ready to go back to the cottage," I said, and Rhys blinked in surprise as he focused on my face.

"Already?" he asked, clearly surprised. I nodded.

"I've calmed down. I suppose I've come to terms with everything—as much as I'm going to." I believed the words I was saying, and I hoped that he could hear that in my tone.

"Alright," he said with a curt nod, setting down his spoon as well—his bowl was essentially empty anyway. He smiled softly, and my brain momentarily stalled at the sight. That golden hair, those warm eyes, his handsome face… He radiated a comforting kindness that he seemed unaware of. I barely stopped myself from shaking my head in an attempt to get rid of those sorts of thoughts, as he continued speaking. "If you're sure. Perhaps Catrin has found even more while we've been gone."

"Maybe," I said with a small shrug. I was still irritated by the feelings I had just been experiencing, annoyed at myself for allowing them to exist at all. I had no time or emotional capacity to deal with…with whatever that was.

Rhys didn't seem to notice, however, and soon we were riding back down the hill and away from the city.

Catrin and Aerona welcomed us back when we opened the door. Aerona hadn't gone to the city that day as it had been her day off from the library. They sat in the old cushy chairs beside the fireplace, each reading a book in silence. They looked up as we entered, the door shutting with a loud creak behind us.

"How was the city?" Catrin asked with a grin, setting her book down in her lap. Aerona continued reading, a small frown on her face.

"Pleasant," Rhys said, glancing at me for only a moment, before taking a seat on one of the sofas. I sat opposite him, feeling a bit awkward. Before anyone could say anything else, I turned to Catrin, and the words began to pour out.

"I'm sorry for my behavior recently," I said in a rush, and she blinked at me in surprise. "I feel that I have overreacted. But I feel…I feel settled now, and I'm ready to learn as much as I can."

Catrin raised her eyebrows, a small smile appearing on her lips. "About what?" she asked.

"Well…everything," I said, now frowning. "The Sacreds, my visions. Why this is all happening now…" I paused, and felt everyone's eyes on me. My face grew hot but I continued on. "I was overwhelmed. I learned many things in only a few days. But I understand that there is yet more to uncover."

Catrin smiled, her kind eyes twinkling with warmth.

"There is no need for you to apologize or explain yourself, Eira. I have also found out more than I could have expected, and I owe it to your arrival. I never would have so carefully read Adelais's book without the quest you provided me. And of course it is overwhelming. Your visions alone would cause anyone to fall into a self-questioning spiral." She sighed, set the book she was holding on a small wooden table then stood and sat on the sofa across from me, beside Rhys. Aerona had finally put her book down to listen to the conversation, but she didn't move from her place beside the fire.

Catrin gazed at me intently for a moment, and I waited for whatever she would say next. "But the beauty of it all is that you're on your way to discovering the truth."

"It was easier when I didn't know any of it," I mumbled.

Catrin laughed, and I glared at her without meaning to. "Are you sure? Was your life really easy before this?" she asked. I sighed and looked down at the table between us. The smooth wooden surface was clear of books for the first time in many days.

"In some ways," I said after a moment. "I wasn't having these visions until the day I left."

"Perhaps the stress of the attack kindled this latent ability," Catrin said thoughtfully, but with a tone that suggested only a mild curiosity. "But I believe you are focusing on the wrong aspects of all of these events. Having the truth hidden from you doesn't make life easier. It makes it cloudier, with you lost in the haze."

I wasn't sure what to say to that, and managed half of a shrug. She smiled softly and dropped the topic.

»«

Shortly after, Aerona prepared dinner and we ate and chatted, and continued chatting in the sitting room after the meal. It wasn't long before I felt exhaustion settle over me like a weight in my shoulders. I let out a yawn and stretched my arms upward, barely stopping myself from groaning.

"I think I'll sleep now," I mumbled, glancing at Rhys on the sofa beside me. He nodded at me, his eyes looking as tired as I felt. Aerona yawned out an agreement, bid us all goodnight, and slipped down the hallway without another word.

"Eira," Catrin said as I stood from the sofa, with the intent to go to the guest room, as it was my turn to sleep there that night. She stood from the other sofa and seemed to evaluate me for a moment. She smiled slightly, with an unusual hint of discomfort in her eyes. Rhys turned to look at her as well, obviously curious.

"Yes?" I asked, curious myself. Still she paused, fidgeting with her shawl. I had never seen her so unsure of herself.

"I think I know where you can get answers," she said, now frowning slightly, maintaining eye contact with me as if to let me know how serious she was. "About the Sacreds and about your visions."

I blinked. "Have you found something else?" I asked eagerly, but she shook her head.

"I think you know the answer too," she said, that weak smile returning. I frowned at her. I couldn't think of anything that I had read or discussed with her that could provide the answers I sought. "There are those that know all about the Sacreds, because of their bond with them— those that we know exactly where they live, and how to get there—"

"No," I cut her off, realizing what she was saying. I heard Rhys stand up behind me. He understood what Catrin was saying as well. "It's impossible. They're on the other side of Linra!"

"I'm not saying it would be an easy journey," Catrin said calmly, then took a deep breath. "But the Inherents are the only ones on Linra who know all there is to know about the Sacreds. And they will probably be able to tell you about your visions as well."

"We only know this based on one man's account from four hundred years ago," I said, crossing my arms defensively. I didn't like arguing with Catrin, or anyone for that matter, but I couldn't understand how she could so casually make such a suggestion.

"And you also read all of the things he was right about," Catrin countered. "I told you he was a real prophet. And more importantly…why do you think we have so many legends about the Himminir? These mysterious people who live on top of a frozen mountain? That they are connected to the Sky Queen, that they're the authority of Awyrcred… It's because they are those things, and more. More than we can even comprehend."

I let out a heavy sigh, and felt the weight of lethargy settle in my bones. I glanced at Rhys, still standing tensely near the sofa, and he looked back at me. I shook my head, exasperated by the conversation.

"We should get some rest, and consider this in the morning," he said softly. "I'm willing to do what needs to be done to save Nefyn and Lithe."

"But this trip will take months, Rhys," I argued, gesturing with my hands more than I usually did—a sure sign I needed to go to bed, and the entire situation was frustrating me. "By the time we return, everything could be different."

"And what are you going to do here, now, without answers? Without understanding who these people are?" Catrin asked, and I turned and saw her looking at me with a raised eyebrow.

"We'll talk in the morning," I said, rubbing an eye as I gave up. Without another word or waiting for a response, I crossed the dark room and passed the dying, smoldering fire, and approached the guest room.

"Goodnight, Eira," Catrin said, and I turned to look at her, a deep frown on my face. But she was smiling, more in her natural way than before.

"Goodnight," I said with a small sigh. With one last glance at both Catrin and Rhys, I opened the door to the guest room and escaped inside.

»«

I was awoken by loud pounding echoing through the wooden walls. It was so powerful that it seemed to almost be shaking the bed, and I sat up quickly, already alarmed. I was on my feet before I could really even process what was happening, and wasn't even surprised when Rhys threw the door to the room open, just as I was pulling my boots on.

"Who is it?" I whispered before he could speak. His eyes were wide, hair messy from sleep, and I thought that he had been woken by the knocking as well. He shook his head at my question.

"I don't know. Soldiers of some sort. They haven't announced themselves but I caught a glance through the window. They're wearing expensive armor, but I couldn't recognize the make." I nodded, my boots now securely on my feet, and motioned for him to turn back into the sitting room. I followed him, and saw Catrin and Aerona standing near the cold fireplace, looking just as alarmed as Rhys and me.

"What's going on?" Aerona demanded. Her hair was unbraided, cascading over her shoulders, but both she and Catrin were fully dressed.

"Open up!" a harsh voice yelled from outside the front door, before pounding on it once again.

"They've found me," Catrin said calmly. Then she frowned, and looked at each of us in turn. "You all must escape. They'll arrest you too."

"Arrest?" I said, somehow angered by her words. "We can all escape—"

"Can't we negotiate with them?" Rhys suggested. Catrin shook her head in response to both of us.

"The Imperial Eosiaid Guard has been looking for me for twenty-five years. They will not be negotiated with."

Aerona suddenly whirled to face us, her eyes filled with fury. "What did you do in the city?" she hissed. "Who did you talk to?"

I gaped at her, but Catrin put a gentle hand on her arm, and she softened slightly.

"It's fine, Aerona. They were likely going to find me someday." The pounding grew louder, shaking the door, and Catrin continued, ushering the three of us abruptly towards the kitchen.

"What are you—" Aerona said, too surprised to fight back against Catrin's hand on her back. Rhys and I walked ahead of them, not fully understanding what was going on.

"You three have to leave now. Take the horses and ride south into the forest, away from the road," Catrin said.

"No," Aerona said, barely stopping herself from yelling. We reached the door to the kitchen and she turned around to face Catrin. She was a few inches taller than Catrin, and glared down at her with more rage than I had ever seen in a person. "I'm not leaving you."

"We need to leave," Rhys said, moving past them back into the sitting room. "I'll gather our things."

"The dagger is under the bed," I burst out, barely thinking about what I was saying. He glanced at me and nodded as he crossed the room.

"Take Adelais's book," Catrin called to him as he entered the guest room.

"You can escape with us," Aerona said, pleading. Catrin shook her head again.

"No, child. We only have the one horse for the two of us, and we won't ride fast enough. They'll find us before long, and then all of us would be taken in. It only has to be me."

"No—" Aerona was saying as Rhys returned, carrying both of our packs and cloaks piled in his arms. I ignored Aerona and Catrin's argument as the door rattled again, and the voice outside grew more threatening and angered.

"We have to go," Rhys insisted, and it was only then that I noticed how tense he was. And then it fully hit me. If we were captured along with Catrin, it wouldn't be long before they figured out I was also an Eosiaid who had abandoned her position. I nodded, suddenly feeling frantic, and swept through the kitchen blindly. The guards hadn't noticed the side door, and probably hadn't thought to search for one on such a small house. Just then there was a great crash in the sitting room, the sound of splintering wood and thump I could feel in my bones, as the door was broken from its hinges.

"Go," Catrin said somewhere just above a whisper, as heavy boots stomped across the living room floor, and calls for Catrin to surrender herself echoed through the doorway to the kitchen. I stood with one hand on the doorknob that led outside, and felt my body pause as some unfamiliar emotion took hold of me. I stared at Catrin, her kind smile, even now radiating serenity, her knowing eyes, and shimmering silver hair kept in its neat braid—and I felt pain.

Somehow, when she looked at my face, she knew. She once again looked at each of us in turn, the footsteps growing closer. "Go, now. For me."

It was a simple command, but it sent me into action. This was the best thing I could do for her in that moment. I opened the door to the yard and stepped outside into the muddy grass, and heard Rhys and Aerona following behind me. Catrin shut the door to the sitting room, blocking us from view of whoever was inside the cottage, but I came to a sudden stop as another soldier began to round the house, coming towards the yard we were in. He was tall, but all of his other features were obscured by the regal and official armor of Silvania, all shining silver over a red tunic and trousers. I turned around, pushing against both Rhys's and Aerona's shoulders, hoping my urgent movements would let them know we were about to get caught.

"What?" Aerona gasped, but then she saw the soldier as he took in the yard, and we were just able to slip back inside the kitchen before his eyes fell over the open side door. We collapsed inside, crouching below the counters, instinctively staying out of sight of the small glass window situated to the left of the door.

"What do we do?" Rhys asked in a rough whisper, looking between me and Aerona, his eyes wide but somehow calm. He was still thinking rationally, about how we could get out of this situation. I looked at Aerona, and though she was flushed and tense, something had changed in her over the last few moments.

"Don't follow me," she said, her voice low and earnest, and Rhys and I had no time to respond before she was standing up. She looked down at us, as we remained close to the floor and huddled up against the wooden cabinets, still full of pots and pans and flour and sugar, and she smiled slightly. "Go, and get away. Catrin told me you have something you need to do. And I have nothing without Catrin. I'll take care of this."

"Aerona," I whispered, unsure of what I was trying to say. She shook her head, still with that soft smile, her long red hair waving around her shoulders.

"Be safe, you two," she said, then stepped into the yard, shutting the kitchen door behind her. Her muffled voice reverberated through the wood, as she greeted the soldier as though nothing was amiss.

"Can I help you?"

There was a short pause. "Are you a resident of this cottage?"

"Yes, sir. May I ask what this pertains to?"

"We have reason to believe that one Cerys Glynn resides here as well. She is wanted for evading capture and abandoning her province."

"I do not live with a Cerys," Aerona replied evenly.

"And who do you live with?" the soldier asked, his tone growing frustrated. I felt like I couldn't breathe listening to this conversation, and Rhys was so still beside me, I doubted that he was breathing either.

"A Catrin Morgan."

"Come with me," the soldier said without pause. We heard the soft sound of footsteps in the soft earth, then Aerona began speaking louder.

"I have no reason to—let go!"

There was the sound of a slight scuffle, but Aerona didn't put up much of a fight—and it was then, through the haze of shock and confusion, that I realized these soldiers were Eosiaids. The feeling that I had only experienced once before was suddenly clear to me, a strange buzzing of anxiety in my chest and gut. I blinked, then realized that they had to be— only Eosiaids could capture another Eosiaid. Aerona was being forced, with magic, across the yard—the way she was stumbling was a sure sign of that. I looked at Rhys as the sound of her stumbling feet grew fainter, as she was taken back around to the front of the house.

"Now?" I asked. He paused, then nodded and stood slowly from his crouch. I followed suit, and watched with tension as he slowly opened the kitchen door, so slow that it didn't even creak. He poked his head outside, then looked back at me, nodding just slightly. It was then that we heard a commotion in the sitting room, giving us pause.

"Aerona!" Catrin said, surprised and dismayed.

"You said no one lived with you," one of the soldiers bit out—a woman who was clearly angered by Catrin.

"Well, she left this morning," Catrin said easily. "She wasn't living here."

"Catrin," Aerona sighed. "Don't worry about me."

"I've searched the rest of the house," the first soldier said. I frowned at Rhys—had she overlooked the kitchen? "It's just these two."

"Alright, then," the soldier who had apprehended Aerona outside replied. "Let's get them back to the city."

"Come on," Rhys said, knowing that we didn't have a moment to waste. We dashed out the kitchen door, though I tried to shut it carefully behind me, and untied our horses with frenzied movements. If the guards decided to round the outside of the cottage one more time, we would surely be seen. But soon enough we were in our saddles, and urging our horses into the dense forest south of the cottage, away from the main road. We would hide there for a while, and figure out what our next move would be.

As we guided our horses through the maze of trees, shrubs, boulders, and crevices, we were silent. And the disaster I felt inside of me choked any words that I attempted to utter.

What now?

»«

"Let's stop," Rhys said after some amount of time my brain was unable to measure. I knew we had left Catrin's cottage just after dawn, and now the sun was streaming straight down through the trees, casting lovely, dappled patterns on the mulchy forest floor. We had barely spoken for hours, as we individually processed the events of the morning. "Alright," I said, pulling back on Nimue's reins. She huffed as she came to a stop, and I realized both horses were due for a rest. Though we hadn't broken into a gallop at any point, as it would have been nearly impossible through the dense brush of the forest, we had maintained a fast walk for most of the day. I looked around, my senses coming back to me, and saw that Rhys had decided to stop in a small clearing. The land was flat and the trees fairly far apart from one another. "Do you think there's a stream around here?" I asked, squinting into the distance, but not seeing or hearing a trace of any water.

"Probably," Rhys said as he slid from the saddle and landed in the leaves below with a dull thump. I followed his lead, already sore from the ride. I stretched my legs for a moment, content with listening to the sounds of the forest, the birds and the rustling leaves. "We can water the horses soon. I thought it best if we stop now, if just for a moment, and… and talk," he continued after a moment. I turned to look at him and tried to read his expression, but he looked just as exhausted as I felt. There were shadows under his eyes, and his entire face was tense as he glared at the leaves covering the ground between our feet.

"About what to do next," I supplied. He looked up at me, his eyes oddly conflicted, and nodded.

"I got the prophet's book," he said. I paused, a bit surprised by this information, but more surprised that he chose this moment to mention it.

"Alright," I said slowly.

"Catrin seemed to think that…that the Inherents—"

"Rhys," I groaned, and he stopped talking immediately, his mouth quickly snapping shut and his lips forming a thin line. "We don't have time to travel all the way to Aorlanda."

"Then what else can we do?" he asked, a hard edge to his voice. He was frustrated. He was trying to not let it show as he kept his face passive and open, but I could tell.

"We could…we could go home," I said, looking away from him, letting my eyes wander across the forest, studying those dappled splotches of light against the ground and the tree trunks. I heard Rhys sigh, but I knew I couldn't look at him.

"We can't, Eira. We know who they are now. And it's more than we could have expected."

"All we need is a plan," I said, turning back to him suddenly. He blinked, clearly surprised by my words, but I continued speaking before he could reply. "We know who they are— that's all we really set out to do. Now, we just need to narrow down which powers they possess, and then come up with a plan to defeat them."

"And if one of them is inhumanly strong? And one of them can…can read minds?" Rhys asked. I froze, surprised he had read the entire book so thoroughly—the details of the types of powers were hidden amongst rather boring details of Adelais's life as the Seer. "How could we possibly challenge them?"

I blinked at him, noticing a patch of sun catching the gold in his hair. It was a much prettier thing to think about than what Rhys was presently saying to me.

"I don't know," I said, barely above a whisper. I felt my eyes grow hot as tears started to form, and I turned away from him again. "I don't know…but—"

"Why don't we both think about our options as we ride to the closest town," Rhys said with a heavy sigh. I sniffled, and felt the tears that were threatening me die back slowly. "We won't be thinking clearly now, anyway."

Hesitantly, I let my eyes meet his once again, and gave him a soft smile. When he returned it, I was surprised that my exhausted heart was still able to flutter at the sight.

12

The Warrant

The day wore on, and yet my mind only seemed to grow more confused as we rode through the trees. We had consulted a map, and knew that we would reach a main road by nightfall, one which led to the port city of Tan y Mor. If we were to travel all the way to Aorlanda, we would be able to find a ship there. But I simply couldn't imagine traveling so far, and every step we took farther south made me wish more and more to just return home. I couldn't accept it, the gravity of the situation. I couldn't believe that my home was truly lost to these legendary people, and I wanted to run back to Nefyn if only to see the proof once again.

When the sun slipped below the horizon and cold shadows enveloped us, we finally came to the road. It was narrow and unpaved, just hard packed earth from hooves and wheels, but it was a welcomed sight for both of us.

"There should be a town coming up, I think it's called Gruddws. We can stop there for the night," Rhys said, and though his voice was quiet, I could hear the relief in his voice. I didn't respond. I was still trying to sort through all of my thoughts, all of the paths we could take, and which one would be the most helpful for Nefyn.

Stars twinkled in the black expanse above us, and a crescent moon hung just over the treetops to our right. Owls and night birds called out through the chilly air, and the constant rustling through leaves and branches on either side of us began to set me on edge. I glanced at Rhys periodically as he rode beside me, but he seemed unperturbed; although it was quite difficult to read his features in the low light. I could tell Nimue was growing tired, and assumed Cai was as well, and hoped for all of our sakes that we would reach the town soon.

Then lights began to appear from between the distant trees that lined the road before us, and the horses seemed to speed up on their own, understanding what that sight meant. I felt a bit more energized too, knowing that I could soon rest. I registered that I was also quite hungry. We hadn't had time to pack any food before escaping, of course, and I realized we would probably have to eat before finally going to sleep.

The road widened, and we found ourselves in the small town of Gruddws, composed of only a few dozen small wooden buildings. Some had lanterns lit outside their doors, and most windows were still lit with candlelight, as it was still early in the evening. We passed a few residential homes before finding the very small inn that was barely bigger than one of the houses. There was no stable, just a few posts emerging from the dirt to tie reins to, so we secured Cai and Nimue, and entered the inn without a word.

The innkeeper, an elderly man with an impressive mustache and a worn blue tunic, looked up in surprise from his desk beside the door as we entered. "Good evening," he greeted us, unable to keep the surprise out of his tone. He looked at each of us in turn, then continued. "How can I help you?"

"We would like two rooms," I said, pulling out my coin purse.

"Alright," the innkeeper said. "That will be twelve bens."

"And dinner," Rhys added.

"I'm afraid we do not provide meals here," the man said with a small frown. "But the tavern across the way is still serving, I'm sure."

I glanced at Rhys, and he shrugged. "We haven't eaten all day," he said, looking and sounding weary. I handed the innkeeper the coins for our rooms and nodded at Rhys.

"We should eat. Even if we're exhausted," I said. I turned back to the innkeeper, who was counting the coins I had just passed him, and attempted an exhausted smile. "Thank you. We will return soon."

"Your rooms will be those two there," he said, pointing to the opposite wall where we could see two doors. I took a moment to take in the rest of the inn: a small stone fireplace set in the wall across from the front door, the two rooms that we would be occupying, and two more doors on the opposite wall. And there were no other patrons that I could see. It was certainly one of the smallest inns I had ever seen.

"Thank you," Rhys said, and then we both left the inn, emerging back into the cool, fresh air. The tavern was obvious now that we were looking for it, as large windows filled with warm light glowed out onto the street, and people inside could be heard talking and laughing. I also thought I could hear the melody of some instrument beneath all of the chatter, as Rhys and I made our way across the dirt road.

Inside it was as lively as I had expected, with a dozen or so of the local townsfolk gathered around a few small tables. The din of the voices nearly drowned out the lutist in the corner, who was playing an upbeat number, though it seemed no one was paying attention to him.

"This table is empty," Rhys said, gesturing to a small table set just beside the door. We sat down quickly, and were soon being served a dinner of roast chicken and potatoes. We ate in silence for some time, and I allowed myself to continue my study of the room, glad to be able to focus on something other than the future. I could eavesdrop on some of the conversations, mostly town gossip, and in general just numb out some of the panic I was still feeling from the events of the morning. I didn't allow myself to think of Catrin and Aerona. It would only serve to panic me even more.

"It will be alright, Eira," Rhys said softly as he set down his fork, his plate empty. I looked down at mine, and saw I had only nibbled a few bites. I knew I was hungry, but I had no appetite.

"How can you say that?" I asked him. I was too exhausted to convey emotion, or look at him. I continued to stare at my barely touched plate, letting the sounds of the tavern wash over me: the bard beginning a new, slower song, a particularly loud laugh, the clatter of a dish being set down on a table.

"Because we know more than they think we do," he replied easily. I still refused to look at him.

"What do we know? That they're powerful, legendary, nearly forgotten from history. How does any of that help us?" I asked. The words felt numb and mumbled as they left my mouth, and I wondered if he could even hear me.

"We know who we can go to now to learn more about them," Rhys said. I finally looked up at him, beginning to feel my panic mutate into anger.

"And while we're traveling around the world, what do you think will be happening here?" I demanded, unable to stop the glare that covered my face.

"We can't do anything here, Eira," Rhys said, his voice suddenly sharp, the muscles around his face tensed. He was frustrated with me, but I didn't care. "Can't you see that? We can't fight them. But if we found the others—"

"Who is to say that there are others right now? Adelais said that they have never all existed at the same time."

"The Inherents can say if there are others—"

"And why would they help us? The Inherents or the Sacreds? Why would anyone want to help us?"

"Because these people are powerful and a danger to the greatest empire on Linra," Rhys said, perhaps a bit loudly. He paused, glanced around to see if anyone was looking at us after his minor outburst, and then continued speaking in a more subdued tone. "No one in the world would want these people to extend their reign any further, which they are sure to do. If they gain control of the Remisian Empire, there would be no way of stopping them, and they would pose a threat to all of the Four Lands."

I sighed heavily. "That's all conjecture, Rhys. We can't know that for sure. And I feel that it is quite extreme to travel all the way across Linra based on this possibility."

"What about your visions?" Rhys asked suddenly, his voice low as he leaned his elbows on the table. I stared at him, not knowing what to say. "Catrin said that the Inherents—"

"I don't care about the Inherents," I said, barely stopping myself from yelling. I took a deep breath as Rhys stared at me in surprise and tried again, more calmly. "I mean to say, they aren't real to me. They're people, or…or entities, mentioned in a diary from four hundred years ago."

"We know they're real, Eira. Catrin wouldn't lie about that," Rhys said.

"We know the Himminir are real. Is it possible Adelais made up this connection between these Inherents, and the

Himminir, and the Sacreds?" I asked him. I couldn't believe he didn't hold any doubt about any of this.

"But Catrin said Adelais was always correct in his predictions—she said he's a trustworthy source," Rhys argued. I dropped my face into my hands and barely stopped myself from groaning.

"Catrin said a lot of things," I said, the words muffled by my palms.

"And now you don't believe her?" Rhys asked after a moment's pause. I looked up at him, blinking with exhaustion and exasperation.

"I don't know what I believe," I said, and was surprised by the honesty of my own words.

Rhys sighed and leaned back, clearly just as exasperated as I was. For a moment we both sat in silence, and I looked down at my food again, contemplating eating it.

"Let's sleep on it, then," Rhys said. I gave no indication that I heard him, but I was relieved. I wanted nothing more than to stop thinking about these sorts of questions. I was sure that we wouldn't be able to find the answers to them. "Are you going to finish that?" Rhys asked after another short pause. I nodded slowly, once, and picked up my fork.

It was at this moment the door opened beside us with a loud creak, and two people walked in. I dropped my fork as the feeling washed over me—the feeling of a nearby Eosiaid. I froze and didn't dare look up, wondering if the Eosiaid could sense that I was one as well. Rhys noticed my sudden discomfort and frowned at me.

"What?" he asked, voice quiet as though he knew that I didn't want anyone to hear what had just happened. I waited for the two newcomers to make their way to the counter on the other side of the room, and allowed myself to relax only slightly.

"An Eos just walked in," I said quietly, picking my fork back up. Rhys continued to frown, and glanced at the two newcomers, now ordering their food.

"Which one is it?" he asked, looking back down at me.

"I don't know," I said, then risked a glance over my shoulder. One was a young man, elegantly dressed in velvet and gold trim, a long, pristine black traveling cloak, and fine leather boots. The other was a woman with a long brunette braid that trailed all the way down her back, wearing old and well-used leather armor. She had two swords, on one each hip, and a large canvas travel pack slung on her back. I turned back to look at Rhys, pretty sure which one of them was the Eos.

"It must be the man," I said with a small frown. "He's a noble."

Rhys studied the two figures for a moment longer, then shrugged. "He didn't seem to notice you. Walked right past you."

I nodded, glaring at the chicken on my plate. At this point, I knew it was pretty much cold. "I don't think the sensation allows you to pinpoint who it is. Just how I couldn't tell who it was between the two of them. All he knows is that someone in this room is an Eos. I just hope he doesn't try to figure out who it is."

"Well, finish eating, and then we can head back to the inn," Rhys said quietly, periodically eyeing the pair that had walked in. I turned my seat slightly so that I could better see at least part of the dining room, and realized that they weren't together; the noble was sitting alone near a window, with all of his attention directed on his food and drink. I looked away quickly, not wanting to give him reason to notice me. At the same time, the feeling of the nearby Eosiaid was dimming, just as it had done with Catrin. I began to relax, and started eating again. I would only fully relax once we were out of the tavern.

"I'm assuming the noble is staying at the inn as well," Rhys said suddenly. I had just taken a bite of chicken, and I frowned at him as I chewed.

"Probably," I said. "Does it matter?"

"Well, once there he might be able to figure out that it's you."

"The feeling is gone, Rhys. I assume it's the same for him," I replied as I stabbed a small potato.

"Oh," he said with a small frown. "That's that, then. Nothing came of it."

I nodded, thinking the same thing. Minutes later, I was done with my meal. We paid the bartender and left the tavern, relieved to finally be out of that room, and to be on our way to sleep after such a long and horrible day.

Rhys walked before me, but came to a sudden stop in the middle of the dark street. Many of the lanterns that marked the doorways of the businesses along the road had been extinguished as it was now quite late, but the light outside the inn was still burning bright. And in the halo of that light, just outside of the inn's door, stood five soldiers.

They were talking lowly with each other, but noticed us just as Rhys stopped short. I studied them with growing tension as they stared at us, and saw that the type of armor was once again Hartanian—but now they wore a different crest. In the low light I couldn't make out what it was, but it certainly was not the outline of a stallion that had been branded on Hartanian armor for hundreds of years.

"Evening, travelers," one of them, a middle-aged man, said. They weren't wearing helmets, but all I could see of this man was the deep shadows on his face, cast by the lantern above him, and the dark gray streaks through his otherwise brown hair.

"Evening," Rhys said, and I echoed the greeting with a hollow voice.

"Mind telling us where you're traveling from?" he asked. They all wore stony expressions, and I grew more and more uncomfortable by the second.

"Caergarth," I said quickly. It wasn't a lie.

"Caergarth," the man repeated. "That's interesting. We heard the Empire's soldiers were searching for someone in that area earlier today."

I held my breath, and realized that lying would have been a better route.

"Good luck to them," Rhys said evenly.

"You support the Empire, then?" the soldier asked, squinting at us. Rhys and I glanced at each other. The question was unsettling.

"The emperor is our sovereign," Rhys said slowly. The soldier chuckled lightly, and glanced at a couple of his peers.

"Not for long," he said after a moment had passed. "I would advise you not to play the fool tonight. The news has traveled far and wide."

"What news?" I asked. But I feared I already knew the answer.

"Is it not true that the strongest Empire in the Four Lands should be led by the strongest people?" He waited for a response, but we offered none. Somewhere in the woods beyond the town, an owl screeched. "And they have come to lead us."

"Who?" I asked. I already knew.

"Some call them the Syrthiaid—but they will be known as Emperor Age and Empress Riki soon enough," the soldier told us, sounding more and more like a zealot. "And their four acolytes."

"Why should they be rulers over the bloodline that the Empire has seen for over a thousand years?" Rhys demanded. I knew he understood that it wasn't an actual bloodline, now that we had learned the truth about the birth and parents of Eosiaids, but I was sure that it was the only argument he could come up with.

"You will soon hear tales of great things that they have accomplished. The emperor can see the future, and plan around his enemies' moves," the soldier said, all too happy to tell us as his tone bordered on glee. "And the Empress can read minds. And their followers…have their own impressive skills. Do you not, milady?"

I wasn't exactly surprised when Varina came into view, standing right next to the soldier who had just been speaking. She ignored Rhys and I even as we tensed and drew our weapons, and looked at the man. "That's enough now, Brennol. You've made your point." She turned to stare at me and Rhys, frozen in the middle of the street with our swords clenched tightly in our hands, her eyes glittering in the moonlight. A slow smile spread across her face as she appraised us for a moment. "I think you both know better than to fight me this time. I underestimated you before, but I won't again."

I felt nauseous at her words, knowing that she was right. Even if I was able to summon that burst of magic like I had on the bridge, so outside of my control, I wasn't sure it would be enough to incapacitate six people. Plus, Varina knew the full extent of my strength. She would do her best to avoid such an outburst this time.

"I'll go with you if you don't harm him," I said, barely understanding the words coming out of my mouth. Varina's smile only grew.

"Give me back what you took, and maybe I'll meet your demand," she said, narrowing her eyes.

"It's in the inn," I said, a growing sense of dread rising in me.

"Eira—" Rhys started, but I shot him a silencing glare.

"Stop, Rhys. I don't have a choice," I hissed.

"But you can't go with her—"

"It's true. She doesn't have a choice," Varina grinned, and the lead soldier chuckled lowly. "Every soldier under our control has heard your description. The warrant for your arrest has been spread far and wide. Nowhere is safe for you unless you come with me."

"I'm not letting you take her," Rhys said, setting his feet in the dirt and raising his blade above his shoulder, like he was ready to strike at any moment. I floundered for a moment, wondering what would be the best thing to do, what would end this situation as quickly as possible. I dropped my sword and looked at Varina's face as the clang echoed through the still night air. Her eyes met mine, and the malice that glittered in them, the sparkle of glee at my surrender, made anger rise above my fear. I searched for my magic as she stepped toward me slowly, but failed to find the same energy that I had felt on the bridge. I felt numb, empty.

I felt my anger grow even more, though, when Rhys stepped in between Varina and me, facing her with his sword pointed at her. She paused, and smiled at him with her malicious humor.

"Stay back," Rhys said, his voice oddly firm, his sword held before him in steady hands. Guards were trained for confrontations and battle, but he knew well enough that Varina's power made his skills obsolete. Varina opened her mouth to speak, her posture relaxed—she was so self-assured—when a voice spoke up behind us, cutting off whatever she might have said.

"What's going on here?" the person standing behind us in the road asked. I jolted as I turned to look at the source, not knowing what to think when I saw the woman that had entered the tavern just before the Eosiaid standing in the middle of the street, relaxed and calm as she gauged the situation. Rhys didn't remove his focus from Varina and the soldiers behind her, but they stared in surprise at the woman who had suddenly appeared.

"Doesn't concern you," Varina said with a huff. "Don't get caught up in this."

"Seems unfair, doesn't it?" she said, stepping slightly in front of me, literally positioning herself between me and our attackers alongside Rhys. He stared openly at her, clearly surprised by her words and actions. "Six against two."

"This woman is under arrest," Varina said, an edge of impatience entering her voice. "Move aside."

"Why would I do that?" the woman asked, her tone lacking any clue as to whether she was asking seriously or not. I could just see the side of her face, and her expression was passive as she stared at the blond woman with blank eyes.

"This has nothing to do with you," one of the soldiers spoke up from behind Varina, clearly irritated with this new distraction. Varina let out an annoyed sigh, then disappeared all at once.

The next few seconds passed as a blur before my eyes, and my brain had a hard time catching up with what happened. The woman from the tavern didn't even hesitate though a person had seemingly ceased to exist right before her eyes. Her swords were drawn from their sheaths nearly at the same time Varina disappeared, as though she had anticipated this. A sound of metal against metal rang out as the tavern woman raised her swords and they met something solid in the air— Varina's sword, I realized. Then she was moving swiftly, clangs and grunts cutting through the night as the two women fought, one of which I couldn't see at all.

"Make sure she doesn't escape," Varina's voice rang out, from where the tavern woman was swirling and stepping lightly in the road, intuitively knowing where Varina was, and when her blade would come close. I blinked as I understood her words, and watched as the five soldiers shook themselves from their stunned observation of the fight to turn and look at me. Rhys was already charging them, fighting three at once as the other two ran at me. I looked at where my sword lay on the ground a few feet from me, and knew I had no other option. The desperation of the situation allowed me to finally access what I had been looking for. I felt the power rise up in me, weaker this time than the last, and pushed it outward.

The two soldiers stumbled backward, losing their footing and falling to the ground with hefty thumps. Rhys had already disarmed two and injured them. They were now bleeding on the ground and groaning, their swords laying in the road a few yards away from them. I watched as he cut the forearm of the last soldier, leaving a red gash in the wake of the blade. She dropped her sword with a gasp and fell to her knees, leaning over her arm in tense agony.

The two soldiers I had pushed to the ground were attempting to crawl to their feet, and I found the energy again. It was growing easier, I realized. It was similar to how I found my healing magic, but had a different feeling, a darker, stranger space inside of me. The opposite feeling of healing, really. I maintained a level pressure that I levied against them, and they groaned as they were consistently pressed back into the ground. I didn't know how long I could hold it, but I maintained my concentration even as the silver swirl of the tavern woman's lightning-fast blades cut through the dark air in my peripheral vision.

But only a few moments later she paused, breathing deeply through her nose, her body poised and tense. Then we all turned quickly as Varina wavered back into view a few yards down the road, breathing heavily. There was a cut on her upper arm, slowly dripping with dark blood, and I was shocked that this mystery fighter had been able to land a blow on her.

"Who, in Sky Queen's name, are you?" Varina bit out, staring at her adversary with murderous rage, still catching her breath.

"I'm the Valkyrie," she said, and for the first time I thought I heard a hint of a smile in her voice, but I couldn't see her expression to know for sure. Varina barred her teeth, and her image seemed to waver for a moment before becoming solid once again. She let out a frustrated groan.

"My friends are going to retrieve their belongings. And you are going to allow them to do so," the woman from the tavern said. Varina gritted her teeth but didn't move, her eyes darting between our faces, evaluating her options. Three of her soldiers had been incapacitated by Rhys, bleeding on the ground near his feet, and I still maintained my force against the remaining two, though I could feel myself weakening. Varina let out a noise somewhere between a grunt and a growl, and I could feel her anger and frustration reverberating through it. Then she began to back away from us, fading in and out of visibility. After a few yards she turned and sprinted, disappearing into the woods.

The dual-wielding woman turned to me just as I released the two soldiers from my power. She didn't seem to notice what I had done, and I wanted to keep it that way. There was no reason for her to know that I was a runaway Benadur.

"Go," she said, nodding her head towards the inn, insisting that I go get all of mine and Rhys's things so that we could make our escape. My legs began moving on their own accord, and I clumsily ran to the inn's door, still completely in shock. I threw it open and was surprised to see the innkeeper still up, and frowning at me as I appeared in the doorway.

"Everything alright out there?" he asked, angling his head to try and get a glimpse of the street through the open door. I shut it quickly and attempted a smile.

"Of course. Just got to chatting with some townsfolk," I said, before walking quickly to my room where I had left my pack and cloak.

"Pleasant people, aren't they?" the innkeeper commented even as I walked away from him at speed, and I didn't bother to respond. I threw the door open to my room, slung my bag over my shoulders, and donned my cloak, before stepping over to Rhys's room and gathering his belongings in my arms.

"Leaving so soon?" the innkeeper asked, eyebrows furrowed in confusion. "Typically, one spends the night at an inn."

"We apologize," I said quickly, feeling the words rush out with not enough air. "Something has come up and we must continue our travels tonight."

"I must return your money," the man said resolutely, and brought out a box of coins from a drawer in his desk. I flushed and shook my head.

"No, no. Please keep it—for the inconvenience," I said. I turned towards the door and barely managed to open it despite my full hands, and ignored the protestations behind me.

The scene had barely changed, except now, the woman who had come to our aid was keeping an eye on all five soldiers, who were quite clearly scared of her. The two I had held down still lay in the dirt, having barely moved, and I wondered if simply being held down had robbed them of their energy.

Rhys was by the horses, readying them for travel. I approached him without a word and began fastening our bags to the saddles, and soon we were both astride and riding past the woman and the soldiers.

"Thank you," I murmured, frowning down at her. She nodded.

"Don't thank me. Allow me to ride with you," she said. Rhys and I glanced at each other, as he rode on the other side of me. He leaned forward to look around me and stare at her.

"You don't even know where we're going," he said.

"That's fine. I'll make my way where I'm going either way," she said with a small shrug. "Go on. I'll catch up to you within the hour."

Rhys and I exchanged a look, one of suspicion and doubt. But it was hard to not trust this woman, as she had just saved us from being arrested from the new enemies of the Empire—from the people who had stolen my home. I nodded at her, hoping to give nothing away in my expression, that I was as blank as she had been during the encounter, and urged Nimue forward with my heels.

I heard Rhys follow behind me, the walking pace of the horses feeling unbearably slow. I wanted to gallop away from this town and leave that confrontation behind us, and the things that I had just learned as well. We didn't look back as we passed the last building on the edge of the forest, and were once again hidden among the tall oaks.

>‹‹

We didn't speak as we rode, as both of us needed time to process what had just happened. I wasn't surprised as I heard the rhythmic pounding of a trotting horse behind us about a mile down the road, and we both turned to see the shadowy form of a rider approaching. It set me on edge, even though I knew it was the person who had just helped us escape, but I relaxed a little when her features came into view in a patch of moonlight. She came to ride between us and slowed her gray spotted horse to a walk, and Rhys and I both stared at her for a moment, not knowing what to say.

"No need to look at me like that," she said with a small frown. "I did only what I thought was best."

"Why?" Rhys asked, his brows furrowed in confusion. He glared at her, still as untrusting as I was. "You don't know us."

"I know who those people were, though," she said quietly, now staring forward, keeping a rigid and upright posture as we continued riding down the dark road. "They've been ruthless in these parts for a week now. And they've completely destroyed Tennart."

"Tennart," I said, perhaps a bit too eagerly. She glanced at me, blinking in surprise. "That's your accent," I said, a bit more subdued. "I couldn't place it. You're from Tennart?" Tennart, the kingdom south of Hartania, was known for a few things: panpipes, a strong amber liquor called stioch, and their thick and garish accents.

"In a way," she said, and I didn't feel comfortable enough to ask her to elaborate. "I'm Runa. Surprising you haven't asked my name yet," she said, her eyes narrowed slightly. I thought that the expression might be teasing, but I couldn't really tell.

"Sorry," I said. "I'm Eira. That's Rhys. We-we're very thankful for your help tonight."

She shook her head and waved a hand through the air. "I take joy in making fools of people like that. And now I can say that I've fought one of the Syrthiaid themselves, and came out the victor."

"Still," Rhys interjected, leaning slightly towards us as he rode on the right edge of the road, his horse's hooves practically in the shallow ditch that separated the road from the forest. "We owe you for our freedom."

"No, definitely not. You should never owe someone for something that never should have been taken from you in the first place." She didn't look at him, now keeping her eyes straight forward on the road once again, and Rhys and I exchanged a confused glance. He shrugged, and didn't try to thank her again.

"I've never seen anyone fight like that," I said, unable to hide the awe from my voice. "You couldn't even see her, and—"

Runa interrupted me with a laugh. "That was certainly a new challenge," she said with a curt nod. "She may have that extraordinary power, but her sword fighting was ordinary."

"How did you know where she was though?" Rhys asked.

Runa shrugged and kept her eyes on the road ahead. "She was predictable and loud," she said, and Rhys and I waited for her to elaborate, but she never did. Instead she turned to Rhys with a grin. "Five soldiers at once, though— that's quite a feat."

He glanced at me and I shook my head slightly, urging him not to reveal I had been involved in the fight.

"Well, I am a guard," he said awkwardly, looking away from both Runa and me. Runa shot him a curious expression, but didn't push the subject; instead, she changed it.

"So, where are you headed? I'm heading south myself, so I was relieved when you both began riding this way."

I felt fear clutch my stomach. I knew what the answer had to be, but I didn't want to admit it yet.

"Eira," Rhys said, his voice quiet and pleading. I looked at him on the other side of Runa, and saw how his hands were tense around the reins, his eyes fixed on mine. "We can't go back. Not with things like this," he said. I nodded.

"We only have one option if we want to help Nefyn," I said, my voice just as quiet as his. I expected Runa to interject and ask us what we were talking about, but she remained quiet, looking forward as though she was ignoring us.

"We're going to Aornadur," Rhys said through a sigh. This made Runa jolt, and stare at both of us in turn, her braid swinging wildly through the air as she turned her head.

"What?"

13

The Fire of the Sea

"I still think this is insanity," Runa said as we packed up our camp in the cold gray dawn. She rolled up her bedroll with aggressive movements as she periodically glared at Rhys and I, standing nearby and readying the horses. "Do you even know what Aornadur is?"

Rhys paused in his movements to glare at her. "The tallest mountain in Linra? Yes, we're aware."

Runa let out a sigh and a shrug. "Least I can do is get you a ship. I'm not here to tell you what to do, though."

"We would once again be very grateful for your help," I said, tugging on the cinch of the saddle beneath Nimue's belly.

"Like I said, I have to get to Rhea. I need the ship as much as you do." She stood and carried her bag over to her horse, who I had learned was named Freya, and hefted the bag up on the back of the saddle. Soon, all of our preparations were made, and the camp was completely deconstructed, once again just a patch of decomposing brown leaves and twigs beneath the towering branches of the oak forest.

We were only two days away from the port city of Tan y Mor. We rode as quickly as we could without hurting the horses, as we were worried about meeting soldiers on the road.

Despite our conversation from the previous night, Runa remained mostly silent during the first day of riding, as she sat up straight in her saddle for hours on end, riding a few yards before Rhys and me, claiming to keep a keen eye out for any sign of riders coming toward us. We met no one, though, and the first day passed with no encounters.

When the sun fell and the chilly stillness of the night covered us, we all agreed to travel off of the road as we had the night before, and set up another camp. The forest was beginning to thin; the trees were smaller and farther apart, and the mulchy layer that we spread our bedrolls on wasn't quite as springy as the night before. I knew from looking at the map that we were nearing the end of this oak forest, and early the next day we would emerge into the farm-covered hills that surrounded Tan y Mor.

We snacked on some provisions Runa had been kind enough to share with us, and which we fully intended to pay her back for, once we could figure out how to get her to accept the money. We all ate in silence, a small but warm fire glowing and crackling in between us, that Runa had managed to light with ease. She was experienced in battle, survival, riding—yet we knew almost nothing about her. I knew Rhys wouldn't pry, and I felt far too uncomfortable to ask any questions.

I glanced at Rhys, staring blankly at the fire as he chewed on a bite of slightly stale bread, and wondered if he felt as odd about this situation as I did. Traveling with a stranger, one who had just saved us from capture, without knowing anything about her besides her name. I missed the days at Catrin's cottage, but knew that thinking about that would only bring me sadness, as I would wonder what had happened to her and Aerona.

Runa didn't seem to want to know why we wanted to travel to Aornadur, although she warned us against doing so a few times. She had given up trying to convince us, though, and now it seemed as though none of us were willing to start up a conversation.

But there was a question nagging at me, one that would need to be answered before we arrived at the gates of Tan y Mor.

"Runa," I said, pausing in my eating to look at her from across the fire. She looked up at me, still chewing on a bite of dried meat, and swallowed quickly. "How will we get into the city?"

"Tan y Mor?" she asked, frowning at me. She leaned her elbows on her knees as she sat cross-legged on her bedroll, and waited for me to elaborate.

"There's a warrant for my arrest," I said. "They'll surely want to arrest Rhys too. I'm sure Varina is still looking for us… And if the city is under the control of these new soldiers…" I paused, not sure if I needed to continue.

Runa nodded slowly. "I passed through Tan y Mor about five months ago, and everything seemed normal," she said, now frowning at the fire as she thought. "But these people have spread their forces quickly and violently. So quickly, there hasn't even been a response from Silvania… Tan y Mor would certainly be one of the most strategic cities to capture."

"They have taken provinces in the north and Maenynys," Rhys added. She glanced at him, but didn't react to his words.

"And Conotra, Hartania, and Tennart," she murmured.

Her words chilled me.

"What?" I asked. "All of them?"

She frowned at me as she nodded. "Yes. Conotra was weak with civil war, and these Syrthiaid easily took the throne and control of the army. It was easy to then take Hartania, who was distracted with their little battles with Lithe and Ronoa.

With two kingdoms under their control, it was only a matter of time before Tennart and Lithe were taken as well."

"Who are they? I mean, what do you know about these people? The Syrthiaid," I asked, unable to keep the shaking out of my voice entirely. Rhys and I sat with equal tension as Runa appraised us.

"You haven't heard the rumors, then?" she asked, eyes narrowed in suspicion.

"We…we've been a bit isolated for the past couple of weeks," Rhys said.

Runa shrugged, apparently deciding that it didn't matter why we hadn't heard. "They say they have great power. Those soldiers last night mentioned some of their abilities, and obviously we witnessed one of them. I've heard the same story from multiple sources now. Murmurs in the markets, quiet conversations in taverns. It's not affecting the day-to-day yet. But I could tell it's all about to fall apart. That's why I'm heading back to Aorlanda."

I blinked, glanced at Rhys, and tried to figure out what I wanted her to elaborate on the most. "So…you believe that these people…have these powers?" I asked slowly. "Obviously, the woman in Gruddws had her power… But some of those rumors are, well, insane."

She shrugged. "Doesn't matter too much if it's all true or not. They've conquered all of the Southern kingdoms save for Ronoa, but that won't be too far off now."

"Ronoa has their canopy fighters," Rhys argued. "They'll be hard to fight off, even with the armies of all of the other kingdoms."

"We'll see," Runa sighed. "It's not my problem anyway."

"Don't you care about Tennart?" I asked, displeased by her nonchalance.

She frowned at me. "A bit. But it really doesn't concern me. I've lived in Aorlanda for fifteen years."

"Oh," I said, only growing more confused by her past as I learned more about it.

"What brought you back here, then?" Rhys asked, which earned him a stern glare.

"Doesn't matter," she said, her tone short and irritated. Rhys tensed but didn't reply, surely not wanting to upset her further.

"What do we do if these Syrthiaid soldiers are stationed at the gates?" I asked again, wanting to have a plan in place before we needed to think of one.

"I know other ways into the city," she said with a slight smile. When she didn't elaborate, I grew uncomfortable.

"How?" I asked, trying not to show my unease.

"I have an acquaintance in one of the brickyards," she said simply, and I was too tired to get any more answers out of her.

"We're trusting you," Rhys said, but there was an edge to his voice—a threat, a warning. She attempted to smile at him, but it looked odd on her usually composed face.

"I already said I need a ship as much as you do. And after what I did last night, there's probably a warrant for me too. If there are Syrthiaid forces at the city gates, we will find another way in."

Rhys and I nodded in response, and I was ready to let the conversation die, and perhaps restart it in the morning with some of my residual questions, but another one tugged at me, irritating me to the point that I found myself speaking it out loud.

"Why are they called the Syrthiaid?" I asked her, and she looked at me, her slightly widened eyes showing a bit of surprise. The word was familiar to me, but I couldn't remember where I had heard it, and in what context.

"I would have thought everyone in Lithe went to temple every month," she said with a huff and a small smile, and I frowned at her.

"I went," I said, not appreciating the lack of an answer. "What does that—"

"It's in the Awyrlyfr. Near the end…" She paused as she thought, staring at the fire, and my frown deepened at the mention of the holy text of the Awyrcred, which priestesses usually recited from for their sermons. "When the Sky Queen sought to cleanse the world of the darkness that had spread in her absence, those she and her allies fought against were called the Syrthiaid. In the Old Tongue, it meant 'the fallen ones.'"

There was a pause, and then Rhys said, "Why would anyone ever call themselves that?" I was also trying to figure that out, as it was acknowledging that what they were doing was inherently evil.

But Runa shook her head. "I don't think they came up with that title. It came with the rumors, and grew along with the fear of these people. The soldiers from Hartania and Conotra might know, but I believe they worship slightly differently than we do in Tennart and Lithe—they often avoid talking about those dark sections of the Awyrlyfr and focus on the joyful parts. So they also might not fully understand the word." She shrugged again. "Doesn't matter. It seems they've claimed the title, whether they understand the meaning or not."

"Their goal is the Empire," I murmured, not caring if anyone responded. Runa nodded, and looked at me with a grave expression.

"You two are taking a wise course—getting out before everything changes for good," she said. Rhys and I glanced at each other again, and we both shook our heads just slightly; we agreed, then. We would not tell Runa why we were really leaving Remisia.

She wasn't likely to support us in our quest to defeat the Syrthiaid.

>«

It was strange riding through the bright and open hills of the Tan y Mor farmland. The land was fertile, and the hills were divided by rushing streams and rivers, all running to the delta that Tan y Mor was built around. The agrarian region was peaceful and sunny, and we spotted many farmers working the fields, hunched over between the rows of young wheat stalks or hidden among the branches of various flowering fruit trees, all dotted with pink and white blossoms. There were no soldiers to be seen, and despite my better judgment, I felt myself relaxing in the warm sun and pleasant breeze that rolled over the hills.

Once again, our ride was silent. It seemed Runa was only talkative around the fire at night, and was alert and ready for any trouble while on the road. I appreciated her presence as time wore on, slowly beginning to trust her as an ally. I would never forget how she had helped us two nights earlier.

I tried not to think about the road ahead. I knew myself well, and understood that thinking of all we were about to face would overwhelm me. And there simply wasn't time for that.

I couldn't save Nefyn without help. And I couldn't find help without the Inherents. Rhys and Catrin were right— this was the only course left. All I could do was accept it.

As the sun began to settle toward the rolling hills lined with crops in the west, the dim, dark, and imposing outline of a city wall appeared on the hazy southern horizon. A large hill rose up to the east of the city, dark gray against the deep blue of the evening sky. Runa slowed Freya to a stop abruptly, and Rhys and I followed suit, looking back at her in surprise.

"I will approach alone," she said. Her tone was matter of fact and nonnegotiable. "If the Syrthiaid are here, we will go to the brickyard. If they aren't here, we'll go through the city gates. Wait for me until I return. Okay?"

We hesitated for only a moment, and then nodded. We had both resolved to trust her, and knew she was our only way into the city if it was under the control of the Syrthiaid.

"Where shall we wait for you?" Rhys asked. She pointed southeast, where a small copse of oak trees could be seen rising from a small valley between two hills. It was about half a mile from the road, over a flat stretch of land.

"There," she said. "I'll be there before night has fully settled."

We nodded, and she gave us one last, questioning look, before deciding that we would be fine. Then she urged Freya forward, passing us, and breaking into a thundering gallop quickly. The dust rose behind her and passed over us on the breeze, and I fought the urge to sneeze.

Rhys and I reached the little grove before the sun had set and it lit up the grass and trees around us in warm golden light.

"It's a nice sunset," Rhys commented as he stepped down from Cai's back. I nodded as I dismounted as well, and we stood facing west for a moment, just inside the trees, our horses munching on the lush grass behind us.

"Haven't seen one for a while," I commented. "Seems we've been in a forest for a few weeks. Or months. Maybe even years."

Rhys laughed lightly. "Time moves in mysterious ways sometimes."

"Especially when people keep attempting to arrest you," I muttered softly. He was able to hear me, though, and he let out a dry laugh. We stood in silence then, our boots sinking in the grass, the sound of a brook nearby echoing through the small valley, and the sun setting fire to the high wispy clouds, like rivers of flame lighting up the evening sky. As it sank, the colors changed and deepened, with reds and pinks appearing, and later purples and blues. Time was strange and immeasurable, but as the sun touched the rolling horizon so many miles away, I became aware of Rhys standing beside me. It was an odd feeling. He had been beside me most of the time for the past several weeks, but I felt like I hadn't been as aware of him before as I was at that moment. I didn't have to look at him to know how his hair glowed and how his eyes were alight with interest as he studied the colors of the sky.

I became tense, suddenly uncomfortable. What would he think if he knew what I was thinking about? I resolved to never let him know. It would pass eventually, anyway. And there was no room for any of these thoughts or feelings on the journey ahead.

Still, I couldn't help but finally glance over at him, my curiosity getting the better of me. He looked almost exactly as I had expected, but even more dazzling, glowing brighter than I could have imagined. And it was then that he decided to turn his head away from the sunset, and look at me.

I felt my heart freeze, but some instinct told me to not look away—that would seem even more suspicious. And truth be told, I was captivated. The sun caught the sides of his warm brown irises like fire, and there was some expression in his eyes that was hard to understand. Curiosity, concern, a softness that seemed to be its own type of magic.

"Eira?" he said, my name awakening me from whatever stupor I had been caught in, and I turned away quickly, stepping towards the horses as though I wanted to check on them. They were still happily munching on the grass, and didn't even look up as I approached them.

"Sorry," I mumbled, facing away from him as I placed a hand on Nimue's neck. There was something very comforting about her; perhaps just because I had known her for a long time.

"What are you sorry for?" Rhys asked. His voice sounded quiet in the evening air, and I refused to turn.

"I don't know," I replied, my voice surprisingly clear.

"Eira, I—" he began, and something in his tone made me even more tense than I already was. But then we heard the rhythmic beat of a galloping horse through the grass nearby, and then felt it reverberate through the earth beneath our feet. We emerged from between the trees to see Runa approaching, her blank expression giving nothing away as she pulled on the reins, bidding Freya to stop.

"They're here," she said, and her tone was grim, her lips tight and she delivered the news. I didn't respond, but felt frustration and a hint of dread fill my stomach.

"Alright," Rhys breathed out, clearly as upset as I was as he frowned at nothing in particular. Then his eyes focused on Runa, still astride Freya and looking down at us with expectant eyes. "Now what?"

>«

It was completely dark as we approached the brickyard along a stone road that led to many of the brickyards that existed in the area. Built into the base of the large hill to the east of Tan y Mor, it was still alight with activity. I considered calling the hill a mountain instead, especially as we grew closer to it, with it stretching into the sky at this angle. It was covered in the same lush, green grass as much of the delta was, and had a rounded peak, which made it seem much more hill-like from far away. Around the base were at least five different brickyards, all run by different business owners, and the one Runa was leading us to was quite close to the city wall of Tan y Mor.

Encased all around by a seven-foot stone wall, with a large wooden gate marking the entrance to the yard, we were still a few dozen yards away when we were able to see in the low light of the moon, a large cart driven by four horses emerging from the yard and onto the road, laden with stacks and stacks of bricks. As the gates began to shut behind it, Runa sped up, leaving us behind and scrambling to match her pace.

She reached the gates just before they closed, and Rhys and I were still too far away to hear the words she exchanged with someone just inside. We sped up to a gallop without speaking to each other. All I wanted was to be safely inside Tan y Mor, and this entire operation was so unfamiliar and uncertain to me, that I felt as though I could fall into a panic attack at any moment.

"If you could please let him know that I'm here," Runa was saying. She and Freya were positioned at the opening of the partially shut gates, talking to someone inside. We rode up behind her, and I looked past to see a young woman covered in soot, wearing a heavy leather apron. She was glaring at Runa, her arms crossed and lips pursed.

"You sure he knew you were coming?" the woman asked her, glancing at Rhys and I with displeasure in her stern gaze.

Runa sighed. "I don't know. He might have forgotten. We were held up in Caergarth because of…well, you know."

The woman suddenly reached a gloved hand up to rub her temples. "Yes, I know. I'm not surprised." She glanced at each of us once again, and then sighed heavily. "Fine. I'll let him know. Stay outside the gates."

"Thank you," Runa said, backing up a few feet so that the woman could shut the gates all the way. It was only when the gates were shut, and silence fell on us, that I realized the sheer amount of noise that was emanating from the brickyard. I could hear it all even now, though it was slightly muffled: people yelling, the clanging of metal on metal and metal on bricks; the creaking of old wheels and the sudden hissing of steam.

"Busy in there," Rhys commented.

Runa looked at him with a curious expression. "Bricks are what Tan y Mor are known for. All of those kilns have to be kept running almost all of the time to keep up with the demand."

"Do you know what Tan y Mor means?" I asked them, wanting to distract myself by sharing my random knowledge of the Old Tongue. They both looked at me, slightly surprised, with small frowns on their faces. But Rhys decided to humor me.

"What?" he asked, attempting to smooth his confused expression.

"'Fire of the sea,'" I said. "It's a port with a lot of kilns. So…"

"Interesting," Runa said as she turned her attention back to the gates before us, her tone suggesting that she didn't find it interesting at all. I didn't mind; somehow I felt numb to everything. Perhaps my body and mind had finally reached the limit of how many shocks they could endure before simply shutting down.

Runa sat up straight as the wooden gate before us gave a great jolt, and slowly started to creak open. In the gap between the two halves of the gate stood a man, who was in a similar state as the woman who had been standing there only a few minutes before.

"Runa." He grinned, streaks of black ash on his pale cheeks.

His jet-black hair was kept short, appearing somewhat shiny and glossy in the moonlight. "I didn't think you'd be passing through so soon."

Runa shrugged, then dismounted and approached the man. "It's time to leave." She paused, then gave the man a smile. "It's good to see you, Ioan."

"You too," he said, then glanced at me and Rhys. "Who are they?"

Runa looked at us, and indicated by waving a hand for us to join her. I slid from the saddle and onto the stones below, and heard Rhys do the same on the other side of Nimue. We came to stand next to Runa, as she introduced us.

"This is Eira and Rhys. I'm helping them find a ship to Aorlanda," she explained. I attempted a smile, but was so drained I was unsure if I was successful. Ioan seemed a bit surprised by what Runa was saying, but didn't comment on it.

"Why stop by the brickyard?" he asked, his tone purely curious. His eyes flitted from face to face, as Runa took a moment to respond.

"We may have gotten into a spat with some of these new soldiers a couple days ago. I noticed they've taken over Tan y Mor," she said, trailing off as she clearly wanted to know more.

Ioan sighed, then looked around. There was no one near us, but he still seemed uncomfortable with the direction the conversation had gone in. "Let's not talk about this here," he said quietly as he turned. "Tie your horses over there. I'll get some meals for you all."

"Oh, thank you," I said, but Ioan was already turning away.

To the left of the gate were some posts, and we secured our reins there, and listened to the horses as they drank from the adjacent water trough. I was growing used to the banging and clanging sounds of the yard, and took a moment to look around. It was lined with low gray brick buildings, some of which looked like they were used for storage, and others for sleeping quarters. The entire yard was paved with the same gray stones, and every few feet a large, rounded kiln was built into the ground. I counted twenty-four that I could see, stretching across the grounds in two rows. They were in various states of use. Some were actively being loaded with unfired bricks, some were being unloaded by workers wearing thick gloves and armed with massive tongs, and others were in the middle of a firing, completely sealed except for a small hole in the top, where black smoke escaped into the night sky, obscuring the stars. All was well-illuminated by dozens of lanterns mounted on posts, so every inch of the yard could be seen even in the dark of night.

Ioan returned to us suddenly, and I expected him to be holding some sort of food, but his hands were empty. Perhaps I looked confused, because he smiled and gestured to one of the buildings nearby to the left. "I've got your plates ready in there—the refectory. Everyone else has eaten by now, so we can talk further while you eat."

Runa nodded and beckoned for him to lead the way, and set off across the yard, leaving our horses at their posts by the gate, and then climbed some shallow stone steps to reach the door to the refectory. It was slightly ajar, and Ioan held it open for us, allowing us to enter before him. Inside, glowing orange lanterns lined the walls, and tables and chairs were set up around the room. There was a long wooden table against the wall opposite the door, and I assumed that was where people normally dished up. Now all of the tables were empty except for one, which had three plates on it.

We sat down at the table, in the far corner from the door, me and Runa sitting across from each other, and Rhys and

Ioan on either side. I looked down at the plate and saw some type of mash or porridge; I really couldn't tell exactly what the substance was, but I was thankful for a warm meal.

"So you're all going to Aorlanda," Ioan said as Runa shoved a large spoonful into her mouth without hesitation. He spoke softly, even though the room we were in was completely vacant, and there were no other doors leading to rooms in which someone could be eavesdropping. The walls were all solid brick that I was sure sound wouldn't travel through easily.

"Yes," Runa said after her bite. I picked up my spoon and tried the food, still unsure of what it was. After a small taste, I determined that it was extremely bland porridge. Edible, but tasteless. "I'm going back to Rhea, and these two are going to Durnaland," she continued, and Ioan glanced at us with curious eyes. I thought it was a bit strange that Runa decided to only tell him what kingdom we were going to, and not the mountain specifically. I suppose she thought he would react as negatively as she had, or maybe just that it would bring up too many questions.

"And you're leaving now because of…of the Syrthiaid?" he asked, leaning slightly over the table so he could speak even more softly. I noticed he had bright blue eyes then, that contrasted sharply with his black hair and the soot on his face.

Runa gave a small shrug as she pushed some porridge around on her plate with her spoon. "I don't want to be here when things really go sideways," she said, her voice now subdued as well. She looked up at him suddenly, a small frown on her face. "What happened here? Everything was normal five months ago."

Ioan let out a deep sigh and leaned back in his seat. He looked exhausted. "They came in about a month ago. The city garrison was completely destroyed. There were no survivors." He looked at the table, avoiding our eyes, and a silence fell over the table for a moment.

"And civilians?" Runa asked after a few seconds had passed. Ioan looked up at her and blinked, as though he was surprised she had spoken.

"Fine for now. Taxes have gone up, but nothing too drastic…yet. The mines are heavily monitored, as are our shipments. The soldiers visit every morning and inspect everything."

"There's been no talk of a…a revolt?" Runa asked, before taking another bite. Ioan shook his head.

"Not that I've heard. We've all heard the rumors, and we know what the leaders are said to be capable of. Last I heard, they're mostly keeping their center of control in Hartania. We don't want to attract their attention. And anyway, like I said, not too much has changed for most people."

"For now," Runa said.

"For now." Ioan nodded.

A short silence followed, until Runa broke it once again. "I'm guessing you know why we're here."

"You're not just stopping by for a visit?" Ioan joked, and Runa gave him an unamused look. "Ah yes. I supposed you aren't keen on entering the city through the main gates."

"No," Runa agreed, pushing her now-empty plate slightly away from herself. Rhys and I were making much slower progress on ours. "That is not a possibility for us. I remember that you told me one time—"

"It can be dangerous," Ioan said, a warning note in his voice. He was staring at her intently. "And I know they haven't found this end of it, but that doesn't mean they aren't aware on the city's side."

"What are we talking about?" Rhys asked with dying patience, speaking for the first time since we had sat down to eat. Ioan glanced at us, and then at Runa, obviously uncomfortable as he shifted slightly in his seat, and then sat up straighter.

"There's a way into the city from here that the new city guards probably don't know about," he said, running a black-smudged hand through his hair. "It's an old tunnel that's been out of use for decades. It leads to the city, since all of the processing and firing used to happen within the city walls, until it could no longer accommodate the need, and was moved out here…" He trailed off as he realized he was getting off topic. "You can travel through the tunnel. But I cannot guarantee what the exit inside the city will look like at this point."

"What about the horses?" Rhys asked. "Can they fit through the tunnel?"

"Yes, but they won't like it," Ioan replied, brows furrowed. "And I must warn you—the walls of the tunnel may be unstable. It hasn't been maintained for over twenty years."

"We don't have a choice," I said. "There is no way we're getting past the guards at the gates. If this is the only way in, then…"

Runa nodded, her eyes serious, her mouth set in a thin line. "You worry too much, Ioan. It'll be fine."

Ioan let out one more sigh, then smiled at Runa. "Alright. I won't stop you. When do you want to leave?"

Runa stood abruptly, the legs of her chair scraping slightly over the floor. "Now," she said.

»«

Runa, Rhys, and I stood before a large black opening in the side of a cliff, our reins in our hands and our horses beside us. The moon was half-full overhead, casting just enough light to see the jagged and rocky face of the cliff, but nothing could be seen inside the tunnel.

"You're sure about this?" Ioan asked one more time, stepping around the horses to face us, the lantern in his hand lighting his face, which was incredibly anxious. His eyebrows were turned upward, his bright eyes staring intently at Runa. She nodded in one curt movement, and stepped forward.

"We're sure. Don't worry so much." She tried to smile at him, but it looked a little unnatural on her normally serious face.

"Well, take the lantern," he said with a small sigh, holding it out to her. The flame inside flickered as it moved through the air, and stabilized as it was settled in Runa's hand. Ioan glanced at the opening to the tunnel, and then back at us, now with a resolute expression.

"It's hard to get lost in there. There's only one fork, so make sure to stay to the left. You should reach the other side within an hour," he said. Behind me, Nimue snorted with growing unease, and I found myself worrying about the horses more than myself. They weren't trained for cramped, dark spaces, and the smallest noise could spook them.

"Thank you, Ioan. We owe you," Runa said. Rhys and I echoed our thanks, and Ioan gave us a weak smile.

"Just don't get arrested. Or die," he said, with a small, awkward laugh.

Runa nodded, and then stepped forward, Freya following closely. The gray horse was beautiful and shimmery in the moonlight, but she took short, cautious steps, already wary of the direction they were headed in.

I followed next, pulling on Nimue's reins, who snorted again and swung her head but obeyed my pull. I heard Rhys follow along with Cai, and we said one last goodbye to Ioan, before stepping into the tunnel.

Runa was before us with the lantern, and though it still burned bright, it wasn't enough to put me at ease. There was something unnerving about being in the tunnel, and I couldn't tell if it was simply the feeling of being trapped. The ceiling was around seven feet high, so even Rhys didn't have to duck, and I guessed that it was four or five feet wide— plenty of room for us to walk single file. The glow of Runa's lantern barely reached the walls beside me, so Rhys and Cai were walking in near darkness, but neither seemed perturbed. As Runa held the lantern in front of her, both she and Freya cast long shadows back towards me, making it hard for me to see some of the ground directly in front of me.

But the ground was level and fairly smooth, with loose rocks catching under my boots every so often but never putting me off-balance. The walls were coarse, though, and the dim light that we had only made them seem more jagged and rough. I was careful not to brush up against either side, and hoped that Nimue would keep her footing.

We walked on in silence, with the sounds of the horses' breaths and our many steps echoing oddly around us. There was a constant smell of dampness, and I guessed if I looked closely, I would be able to find moss growing in the crevices on the walls. It was cold in the tunnel, but humid. I found it quite unpleasant, and wondered if Rhys and Runa felt the same way.

Runa walked with confidence before me, and all of the horses were calm, if a bit tense. I let out a deep breath I hadn't realized I was holding onto as a few minutes had passed and nothing catastrophic had happened.

After about fifteen minutes or so, the tunnel widened, and Runa slowed down, turning to look behind her, her eyes inquisitive. She stepped around Freya and held up the lantern to look at me and Rhys, and then pointed back, further into the tunnel.

"The fork," she said, and when I squinted, I could barely see the two paths before us, and the darkness of the cavern wall dividing them. The two words echoed around the little area we were in for far longer than I expected.

"Ioan said to go left," Rhys said. Runa nodded and set off again, and the tunnel narrowed back to the same dimensions it had been before the fork.

"Runa," I said, getting her attention as she walked ahead of me, Freya in between us.

"Yes?" she said, not turning back to look at me, but keeping her eyes forward and the lantern held slightly above the height of her shoulder.

"I was wondering how you know Ioan," I said. I inhaled deeply, getting the feeling that I was beginning to panic. I wasn't sure if I was claustrophobic, but I didn't want to find out in a tunnel we were using to sneak into a city. I thought maybe distracting myself with conversation would help, so I had asked the first question I could think of.

"We worked on a ship together. That was a few years ago," she said. She sounded relaxed, but the short answer made me wonder if she would prefer I didn't ask her personal questions.

Still, I was curious, and that answer only brought more questions to my mind. "You worked on a ship?"

"Yes, a merchant ship. Mostly wines and other liquors."

"In Aorlanda?"

"Mostly. Sometimes we would sail to Remisia or Kyonto." She paused, then glanced back at me, but she was too far ahead of me, and too shadowed by the lantern, for me to be able to read her expression. "Why?"

"I was just curious," I said quickly. "We've been traveling together for a couple of days, and, well…"

I saw her shoulders tense and then drop in a shrug as she faced forward again. She stepped over a particularly large and jagged rock, and a few seconds later, I did as well. "I don't talk about myself much. I'm not particularly interesting."

"Working on a ship and living in Aorlanda is interesting," I argued. The smell of the damp, moldy air was beginning to make me feel ill, so I hastened to continue the conversation, internally hoping that we weren't too far from the exit. "You're from Tennart but have lived in Aorlanda. I've never heard of anyone moving away from their hometown to such a distant place before."

"It is odd for someone to leave Remisia, but that's because they make it difficult," Runa said. "The Empire doesn't want things to change. And the more open the borders are, the more other kingdoms could influence the Remisian people."

I was surprised by the political turn the conversation had taken, but I was thankful she was speaking to me more freely. The distraction was working well, as my mind focused on something besides the horrible, constant echoes, and the sickening odor of mold.

"Why did you leave, then?" I asked. "Or how?"

"I was just a kid. I didn't like my home. An Aorlandan ship captain hired me when she stopped in Port Lochayr. I was there just trying to get by. She thought I looked scrappy, I guess."

"How long were you on the ship?" I asked, just as I stepped in a puddle, the splashing sound surprised me. No one else was bothered by the odd noise, even the horses, and I hoped that my boots weren't too worn that the stagnant water could seep through.

"About three years." Back to short answers. I decided I would continue to pry until she asked me not to. Rhys walked in silence behind us; I wasn't sure he could even hear our words clearly enough to understand what we were talking about, with all of the hoofbeats and echoes and periodic snorting of the horses.

"And then what did you do?"

"Travel around Aorlanda mostly." She paused, then let out a dry laugh. "I find it unlikely you're genuinely this interested in my past. Are you alright?"

Not wanting her to know that I was barely holding myself together, I decided to lie. "Yes, I'm fine. And on the contrary, I find your past to be very interesting. Especially as I'm traveling to Aorlanda, and you're clearly very familiar with it."

"Well. I'm not familiar with Aornadur," she said, and something in her tone told me she still thought our goal was insane. She wasn't exactly wrong. "So I won't be of any help to you there."

"Still. It's an entire new continent to us. Maybe on the ship you can teach us some of the languages we might have to use, dangers we might not know to look out for..."

"There are lots of dangers," Runa said, nodding as though she was agreeing with me. I frowned, suddenly finding the conversation distinctly uncomforting.

Then a new smell met my nose—the smell of fresh air, with a hint of smoke and salty sea air. "Do you smell that?" I asked, a bit loudly, so that both Rhys and Runa would be able to hear me.

"Yes," Runa nodded again. "We're almost out of here."

Our pace sped up with the promise of freedom, and soon the hazy outline of moonlit, grass-covered ground beyond the cave could be seen glowing only a few yards ahead of us. And then we were emerging into the fresh and clean night air, and I inhaled deeply as the horses nickered in relief.

Before any of us relaxed, we took a moment to take in our surroundings. The city wall was built up on either side of the opening we had just come from, and before us was a shallow grassy slope, dotted with carved stones.

"Oh." I blinked at the sight. I hadn't expected to be standing in a graveyard.

"Surely Ioan knew this is where we would end up," Runa huffed. Tan y Mor's temple for the Sky Queen rose above the field a hundred yards down the slope, an impressive, rounded sanctuary with a golden dome roof, and even from where I stood I could tell it was twice as large as the temple in Nefyn.

"Alright, well. We'll find an inn for the night, but keep an eye out for soldiers. They probably have all of our descriptions at this point," Runa said, then moved to mount Freya. I had come to stand beside the gray mare, and it was at that moment, with Runa standing beside me, that my vision blurred and my legs gave out as I fainted.

"What—" Runa was barely able to mutter, before I felt her arms catch me beneath my arms, and attempt to help me to my feet again. But as soon as she did, my vision turned to black entirely, and my senses were completely lost.

When the world came back to me, I was almost aware of what was happening. There was a precedent, but that didn't make it any less strange. I found Runa standing before me in the yard of a house. It was sunny but not very warm, and a chill wind cut across the grass. I looked around and saw the house was built at the top of a small hill, and a dirt trail led down to a little town, where I could see smoke rising from chimneys.

I looked back at Runa, and saw that she was agitated. She rocked back and forth from toe to heel, staring at the door to the house with a deep glare. She looked younger, but I couldn't quite place her age—perhaps in her teen years, I thought. When the door opened, a middle-aged man with silver hair and a trim beard emerged, holding two wooden training swords.

Runa let out a huff. "Took you long enough." The man laughed and then tossed her a sword, which she caught without looking, still fixing him with her glare.

"Are good warriors impatient?" he asked her.

"I don't know," she said, rolling her eyes slightly. She held her sword up and set her feet, ready to attack—or be attacked. "Don't waste my time."

"Someday you'll learn." The man grinned, and then raced at her with his wooden blade swinging. And then it all disappeared.

When my eyes opened again, the clear night sky was above me, stars blazing through the darkness. I was still leaning against Runa, who was struggling to support me. Breathing heavily, I jumped to put all my weight back on my own feet, and I whirled around to look at her, scrambling for something to say.

"Are you alright?" she gasped, her eyes wide with concern. Rhys stood just behind her, his entire body tense and mouth open in shock.

I nodded, a bit frantic, still getting my bearings. I knew only seconds had passed. There was no way Runa could have supported me for much longer, as I had turned into an awkward dead weight.

"Yeah…I'm sorry," I said, my voice sounding strange and weak to my own ears. I cleared my throat, but knew that it wouldn't help. I was shaken. "I think the tunnel…the smell and everything…"

Runa nodded, and pulled a waterskin from the bag on Freya's saddle. "Drink this. When you're ready, we'll go find an inn, alright?" I took it from her, grateful for the gesture, and nodded. She turned to mount Freya, and I looked at Rhys, shaking my head slightly.

He nodded, understanding. Runa didn't need to know what actually happened when I fainted in her arms. She didn't need to know about my visions and that I had seen a moment from her past.

14

Setting Sail

We found a rundown inn far from the center of town, and Runa was kind enough to purchase some bread and cheese for me from the innkeeper. If the inn had served dinner to their patrons, it had ended a long time before we arrived. I doubted that they would have bothered, as the inn seemed desolate, with no one else in the common area besides the three of us. I sat in a rickety wooden chair beside an open firepit built into the center of the room, enjoying the warmth of the flames after so long in the cold and dank tunnel.

Rhys sat next to me, in silence, staring at the flames, leaning forward with his elbows on his knees. I didn't want to talk to him about what had just happened, and I was relieved when Runa returned with my food, and any chance for discussion was gone.

"Here," Runa said, handing me a wooden bowl that had a generous amount of bread and cheese inside. She sat down in the old chair to my right with a heaviness I understood well. It was then that I realized I wasn't even sure if I was hungry, but I didn't want to seem ungrateful, and began taking large bites.

"Thanks," I said after I had swallowed my first bite of the bread. It was white and soft, better quality than I had expected.

"How are you feeling?" she asked, looking at me with just an edge of concern. Even though I had only known her for a couple of days, her expressions and mannerisms were becoming familiar to me, and I knew how rare it was for her to express soft emotions.

"I'm fine. The mold got to me, I think," I said, looking down at the food in my hands. She nodded as she frowned, accepting my answer.

"It smelled awful in there," she said, wrinkling her nose at the memory. "I'm sorry that you became ill, though."

"I promise I'm much better now," I said, before taking a large bite of cheese as though that could prove my words.

"It looked like you blacked out for a moment," Runa continued. "I tried to catch you, but—"

"Thank you," I said quickly. She stared at me, her gaze level and intent, and I got the feeling that she knew there was more going on than I was telling her. More than just the mold.

"I think…I've become a bit overwhelmed," I said slowly, meeting her gaze with what I thought was equal intensity. "I've been through a lot in the past couple weeks. And I'm not sure traveling through that tunnel helped. It was…it was too much for me to handle on top of everything else that has occurred recently."

Runa attempted to give me a soft smile, but I wasn't surprised when it looked odd on her serious face. "I'm sorry. I should have assumed you've been through so much at this point. People don't travel to Aorlanda because they want to… At least, that's what I've discovered over the years."

I blinked at her, sensing a miscommunication. She frowned at me. "You two are escaping, aren't you?"

I glanced at Rhys, who wore the blankest expression I had ever seen on him. He simply shrugged at my inquisitive expression, then returned his gaze to the fire. I turned back to Runa, and tried to ignore the growing sense of dismay I felt by Rhys's behavior.

"Yes," I said, blinking at her once again. "Our home was attacked by the Syrthiaid."

She let out a small sigh, gazing at the fire like she didn't want to look at me. "I'm sorry," she said simply. Her tone was warm and honest, and I felt myself relax slightly, despite everything.

"When we left, we found refuge with a woman hidden in the forest outside Caergarth. We thought…we thought she could help us. But the Empire found her." I was surprised by the words spilling out of me, but it felt important to say out loud. Rhys seemed to be mentally somewhere else in that moment, and I wanted to talk. I couldn't tell Runa everything. It was far too complicated to get into with someone I had just met. And there was no telling how she would react to claims of Sacreds and Inherents, and the quest that Rhys and I had taken up. But still. I could tell her everything else.

"The Empire?" Runa asked with a frown. "Not the Syrthiaid?"

I shook my head. "The Empire had a warrant for her. And they still have complete control over Caergarth."

"Not for long, most likely," Runa said, her tone dark. I nodded, pursing my lips.

"Then in Gruddws, those soldiers attacked us. The same day we had escaped the Empire while they arrested our friends." It couldn't be helped; my voice cracked on the words as I finally accepted the weight of all that had happened. I wondered if it was my fault. Aerona's biting words came back to me as the soldier banged on the door: *What did you do in the city? Who did you talk to?* I found myself racking my brain, wondering if Rhys and I had somehow exposed Catrin's location while visiting the city that one morning. I sighed heavily without thinking, and Runa looked at me with a soft and curious glint in her dark brown eyes. The fire jumped in them, making her seem warmer than she was.

"You're here now," she said in a tone to match that soft look. "Everything else is in the past. You can only move forward from here."

"You're right," I nodded. I wanted to feel comfort from her words, because I knew them to be true. But I didn't. I felt hollow and tired and worn down. The bowl of food lay forgotten in my lap, and I urged myself to eat more, if just to show my appreciation to Runa, but my hands did not move from where they lay holding the bowl.

"Perhaps you need sleep more than you need food," Runa suggested in a soft and kind voice, and I looked at her, feeling a wave of exhaustion overtake me. "Rhys also looks like he would benefit from some rest."

"I'm fine," he said, and I turned to look at him, surprised he was even paying attention to the conversation. He remained leaning forward and staring at the fire, an expression of anger on his face. It was unsettling—Rhys, normally good-natured, calm, and thoughtful, now looking as though he was about to go into a rage. I stood, bowl in hand, and looked down at Runa, doing all I could to ignore this sudden behavior from Rhys.

"I'm going to bed," I said, and she nodded.

"Feel better," she said softly.

I nodded and attempted a smile. I turned to Rhys, taking a deep breath as though I was about to do something dangerous. "Goodnight, Rhys."

"Goodnight." He didn't turn to look at me, but remained frozen in place. And the words were cold. I felt my stomach drop, disappointment and fear mixing with the exhaustion to create an intense feeling of sickness in my gut.

»«

When I awoke the next morning, and wandered into the common area still a bit dazed with sleep, I wasn't too surprised to find Runa already sitting around the fire, snacking on what looked like the same bread that I had eaten a slice of the night before. I sat next to her, and tried to smile.

"How are you feeling?" she asked as I took my seat beside her, and I held my hands closer to the flames to warm them. The night had been cold and the inn hadn't warmed up yet, though bright morning light shone in through the windows on either side of the front door. Once again, the only person in the room with us was the innkeeper, who sat behind his desk beside the door, filling out documents of some sort.

"Better," I said, enjoying the warmth of the fire on my chilled hands. "Thank you."

"Don't thank me. I was really concerned when you collapsed," she said.

"I'm sorry I scared you," I sighed, then realized, unlike the night before, I was quite hungry. Runa saw me eyeing her bread, and grinned. "Just go ask him for some. He's happy to provide breakfast at no cost."

Moments later, I had a bowl of bread and cheese just like the night before, but this time it was gone within minutes. Just as I was finishing up, Rhys appeared and sat down next to me. But this time, instead of looking angered, he looked haggard. His eyes were dark and his hair messy and tangled, and overall he looked as though he hadn't slept.

"Are you alright?" I asked without thinking. I hadn't forgotten his behavior from the night before, and still felt as though I must have done something to upset him—perhaps he thought I had said too much to Runa about our travels. But now he looked so appalling, I wasn't even thinking about that.

"Didn't sleep well," he said, his voice gruff and weary.

"Go ask the innkeeper for some food," Runa suggested. "Might help you wake up."

Rhys nodded and stood without a word, and I watched him walk towards the innkeeper with that sick feeling returning to my stomach.

"This sort of mood seems unusual for him," Runa commented. "Am I wrong?"

"No," I murmured, deciding to look at her instead of Rhys. "You're not wrong. Something upset him last night, but I'm not sure what."

"Maybe he also felt sick from the tunnel," Runa said through a mouthful of cheese.

I frowned at her, but shrugged. "Maybe."

When Rhys returned to sit beside me in front of the fire, the three of us fell into a silence while he and Runa ate, and I allowed my gaze to soften over the fire. I was still feeling a bit overwhelmed from all that had happened, especially in the last couple of days, and I was content with silence for the time being.

But once Runa was done eating, she turned to look at us and began talking quickly, surprising me. "I'll find a ship for us today. You two can stay here. It's best if you don't go out."

"Oh," I said, somewhat surprised, but seeing the logic in the suggestion. "I suppose—"

"Thank you," Rhys said, his voice cold and distant. Runa didn't seem to mind, and she left the inn soon after.

"We should probably just stay in our rooms, in case a soldier comes in for some reason," I said, standing from my seat abruptly, my empty bowl still clutched in my hand.

"Eira," Rhys said, standing as well and turning to look at me. I glanced in the direction of the innkeeper, suddenly feeling awkward, but saw that his desk was vacant; he must have gone to a back room. "I'm sorry," Rhys continued, his voice soft and quiet, his tired eyes regretful as he looked at me.

"Why?" I asked, caught off guard.

"For everything that's happened... And I know what happened last night. When you fainted in the graveyard."

I smiled despite everything. "I know you knew," I said. I cleared my throat, feeling like my voice was coming out softer than I intended it to. "I'm sorry if I worried you."

"I was very worried," he said.

I looked down, not knowing what to say. I felt embarrassed, in a way, that I had been the source of his worry. But I knew that I couldn't have done anything differently.

"Are you okay?" Rhys asked before I could come up with a response. I looked back up at him, surprised.

"Yes," I said. "I mean…yes. The tunnel was rough, and then I had that…that vision. But I'm fine now, I promise."

Rhys let out a sigh, and nodded once. He paused before looking at me with an odd, curious expression. He seemed hesitant to say what he wanted to say, as he pursed his lips for a moment. "So you saw…Runa's…?" He trailed off with a frown, obviously not sure what to call it.

"She was there," I said, my voice low even though no one could hear us. "She seemed younger. So…so, yes. It seems I saw another vision. Of someone's…past."

Rhys took a step toward me, surprising me once again, but I didn't move. I studied his face as emotion after emotion passed over it, and he placed a hand on my shoulder. I felt the comforting warmth and weight, but kept my face blank and stony. He didn't need to know.

"We're going to find answers, Eira," he said. The concern in his eyes pleaded for me to believe him.

"I'm not sure we will—about this, anyway," I replied. Still hushed, but I felt like I was yelling. "Finding the Inherents is more important than whatever is happening to me."

"I'm not so sure," he said with a soft smile. And my heart fluttered in equal parts joy and fear.

»«

Spending a day alone in my room at that old inn was not ideal, but it was inarguably the safest thing for both Rhys and I to do. I passed the time reading through Adelais's accounts again, and then again, as though I was on a quest to memorize it. So many sections were vague or the language was archaic, and I wanted nothing more than to understand every single word. I supposed I still hoped that an easier answer could be found within those pages, one that wouldn't require us sailing to a distant land and climbing an infamous mountain.

In the evening, I heard Runa calling for us softly from the hallway outside our rooms, and I cracked the door open just a sliver to make sure it really was her. Rhys did the same, apparently, as Runa let out a huff in annoyance.

"Vigilance is wonderful, but I promise it is really me," she said, her tone flat. A few moments later we were gathered at our now-familiar spot around the firepit, and Runa gave us a surprisingly natural grin.

"I found a ship," she said, then leaned back in her seat with a slightly smug affect. Rhys and I were silent for a moment, surprised by a sudden turn of good news.

"So easily?" I asked, feeling a smile spread across my face as well.

"Suspiciously easily," Runa said, her grin suddenly souring into a frown. "Honestly, things have changed around here. Captains would never take on travelers without the proper documentation, and that documentation was hard to come by. But now…it seems the Syrthiaid aren't enforcing the documents. The borders are open."

I ignored her wonderings as a wave of excitement and anxiety hit me. "A ship?" I pressed, leaning towards her slightly.

"Yes," she said, smiling again. She still wore her black cloak, and I could only assume she was about to overheat as we sat so close to the fire. "We leave tomorrow afternoon."

"So soon," I said. The words came out as a shallow breath, because the air had suddenly left my lungs at Runa's words.

She noticed the change in me and frowned in concern. "Eira? Are you alright?"

"Yes…just…" I took a deep breath, attempting to settle myself. "I hadn't left my province before a couple weeks ago. And now…Lithe, the Empire…"

Runa's eyes were concerned as she seemed to chew on the inside of her cheek. "I understand this may be a huge undertaking—for both of you." She glanced at Rhys, sitting beside me, who hadn't moved or spoken for a while. I didn't risk looking at him, worried he would look as terrified as I felt. It wouldn't help how I felt to see him like that. "But, to be honest…it isn't really Lithe anymore," she said softly.

It shouldn't have been comforting. It should have sent me into another fit of hyperventilation, or another fainting spell. So I was surprised when I felt a wave of acceptance at her words. It wasn't Lithe anymore. It was whatever the Syrthiaid wanted it to be. And judging by how they were burning through city garrisons and taking control for themselves, I doubted very much that they wanted it to be anything that I could accept.

In a very real way, my home was gone. And I was going to do whatever I had to do to get it back.

>«

The next day passed in much the same way, with Rhys and me in our respective rooms, waiting for Runa to return with supplies, and then guide us to the ship we would be traveling aboard for the next two weeks.

She had explained the night before over dinner that our route would not be straightforward at all. "You're going to have to cross a lot of land once you get there," she had said through her mouthful of chicken.

"Why?" I frowned, setting down my own forkful.

"The sea is too dangerous around the northeastern coast of Tamania, and few ships, if any, venture through. Durnaland is east of Tamania. So…we're going to dock in a West Tamanian town called Tremenra. And then we will have to ride for a few weeks for you to reach Aornadur."

"Why is the sea so dangerous?" Rhys asked, sounding as concerned as I felt.

"Pirates," Runa replied, before casually taking another bite of chicken.

"Pirates?" I repeated, staring at her and marveling at her nonchalance.

She sighed and set her fork down, looking at us with her full attention. "Yes," she said, obviously bored by the conversation. "I know you two have been isolated up in your northern province, but it's actually shocking how little you know."

"Excuse me?" I said, rightfully feeling attacked.

"Do you know about the war?" Runa asked, already exhausted, and she hadn't even really begun explaining anything.

"No," Rhys said.

"I think so," I said at the same time. She raised her eyebrows slightly, and I continued. "It's a civil war? It's been going on for decades and decades in Tamania."

"Yes," Runa nodded. "Nearly a hundred years. East Tamania has been trying to split off for that long. Obviously, it hasn't been happening consistently for the last one hundred years… But every time it seems peace is within grasp, another battle breaks out and sets everyone off again." She let out a heavy sigh, one which told me she had little patience for the politics of Tamania. I almost felt bad that we were forcing her to explain it. "East Tamania is always looking for any way to get an upper hand over West Tamania, as the West has the major armies, and if it wasn't for the East's successful use of guerrilla tactics, they would have lost long ago. So…they do quite a bit of pirating and raiding. They're exceptionally good sailors, the East Tamanians." She paused and looked at each of us once again, as though checking to make sure we were now caught up.

"Alright," I said, hoping some of her irritation would dissipate now that the explanation was over. "East Tamanians essentially have a pirate fleet terrorizing the waters around the northern side of Tamania. So we're going to land on the far west side?"

Runa nodded. "Hold on, I'll get the map," she said, before jumping from her seat and stepping lightly to her room. I looked at Rhys and couldn't help but sigh.

"Nothing will ever be perfect," he said with a small smile. I mirrored it. Sometimes seeing the humor was the only way to get through.

"No. But we're going to get there one way or another," I said, and he nodded. Runa returned seconds later with an old, rolled-up map in her hand, which she quickly spread on the table between us.

The map showed only Aorlanda, but I was familiar enough with maps of the Four Lands, and could orient myself to this map quickly. She pointed to a small dot on the northwest coast of Tamania.

"This is Tremenra, where our ship will drop us," she said. Then her finger slid over to the middle of the continent, and landed on a drawing of a mountain range. "And this is where you're going. Aornadur."

"How many miles?" Rhys asked. Runa studied the map for a moment, and then bit her lip. I braced myself for her answer.

"Around a thousand, I think," she said, unusually sheepish. "I'm actually going farther," she said, as though that made it any better. She moved her finger slightly further east. "See?"

"A thousand miles?" Rhys repeated. "That will take weeks and weeks to cover."

"Not to mention…there's a bit of a mountain range in the way," Runa said, cringing slightly. She pointed to a small range noted down the center of Tamania, and I barely stopped myself from groaning. "But there is a pass. It shouldn't be difficult to cross."

Rhys dropped his head into his hands, resting his elbows on the table. I rubbed my eye, and wondered, not for the first time, what we had gotten ourselves into. Runa looked at each of us with a frown, and I thought she looked a bit irritated again. "I'll be there to help guide you, you know. I've traveled all across Aorlanda."

"You've done so much for us already—" I said, my instinct to protest assistance kicking in.

"It would be idiotic for you to set out on your own when we're going the same direction."

"Why are you helping us?" Rhys asked, raising his head from his hands to fix Runa with a serious expression. She paused, and sat back in her seat slightly.

"Well…" she said, clearly unsure what to say. "You needed help. I told you, I found you under attack by Syrthiaid soldiers. And I knew whatever you'd done…you didn't deserve that."

"Why help us now, though?" Rhys asked, not satisfied with that answer.

"I don't need to help you, if you'd rather go it alone," Runa snapped.

"That's not what he means," I said quickly, shooting a glare at Rhys. "We just don't understand. We're still strangers to you."

Runa sighed, letting her shoulders drop as though she had just been defeated in some way. "I'm escaping. I'm heading back to Aorlanda. I thought…I thought I should help you two escape as well." Rhys and I glanced at each other, and I found her explanation oddly sincere. She continued before either of us could reply, the words tumbling out now. "It's bad enough they were trying to arrest you. Before long you won't have anywhere to hide. I suppose I just…didn't think it was right to let that happen to you."

"You're nicer than you look," I joked, and she tensed, before relaxing when she saw my grin.

"I know we've said it before, but we really appreciate your help," Rhys added, now smiling slightly as well.

"I'm happy to," Runa said, returning our smiles with rare softness.

»«

Wisps of white clouds streaked across the sky, the sun hanging just above the roofs of the gray brick buildings that lined the wooden dock. Only a few ships were docked when we arrived, and Runa led us to one at the far left end of the long dock. I hadn't seen many ships in my life, though they were often depicted in paintings. But I hadn't been fully prepared for the sheer size of the structure floating before us. It had two masts soaring into the air, the sails still furled. The length of this ship also surprised me, and I estimated that it was over two hundred feet long.

We led our horses down along the side of the ship, and I continuously looked up at it, occasionally catching a glimpse of a sailor working above on the deck. Runa halted suddenly as an older man turned to look at us, his long white-gray hair tied into a low ponytail. He smiled when his eyes fell on Runa, the crows feet wrinkles around his eyes crinkling.

"You made it, then," he said, his voice both warm and gravelly. He turned to look at me and Rhys, standing beside Runa, and I gripped my reins more tightly without meaning to. It only hit me then that I wasn't just nervous to leave Remisia. I was also nervous to sail.

"And these are the other two you mentioned," he continued and Runa nodded.

"Eira and Rhys," she said, introducing us.

"Afternoon," the man grinned. "I'm Bevyn, the captain of the *Gwynt*. I'll have someone sent out to board your horses, and then another sailor will show you to your quarters."

We thanked him profusely, and then our horses were led away, and a young woman led us up the ramp that led to the deck, and then down a ladder below deck. Down a short passageway, she opened a door on the right and gestured for us to enter, before setting off back down the passageway without a word.

Runa entered first, and Rhys and I followed. It was one of the smallest rooms I had ever seen. It had four beds, two on either side of the room, one built into the wall above the other. After a short inspection, it appeared that each bed was really just a wooden board fixed to the wall, with two thin blankets spread on top. The top bunk on either side was at the same height as my shoulder, and there wasn't too much space between the bottom bunk and the top bunk. I was already imagining sitting up too fast in the morning and hitting my head on the bed above me.

"I call this one," Runa said as she threw her leather bag onto the top bunk on the right side of the room. Rhys turned to me and shrugged.

"Which one do you want?" he asked. Sensing my response already, he added, "I really don't mind any of them."

I paused, debating whether or not to believe him, and then deciding that it probably wasn't a big deal what I chose. "I'll take the other top bunk," I said, tossing my bag on the bed in question as Runa had done. Glancing over at her, I saw she had already climbed up, and was sitting cross-legged and looking down at us with a serene expression.

"I want to go above deck," Rhys said as he deposited his bag on the bed below mine. "Watch us set sail."

"Alright," I said with a grin, liking the idea very much. "I'll go too."

"Stay out of the way," Runa warned us as we opened the door. "Sailors have short tempers."

»«

Rhys and I found a section of the railing that we could lean against that faced Tan y Mor and was seemingly out of the way of the sailors, who were still readying the ship for departure. At least, they didn't seem to need to come near us, and I couldn't see any ropes or rigging nearby that we were blocking.

Tan y Mor was a mass of gray bricks and black rooftops, stretching towards Gray Hill, where we could see the smoke from the brickyards rising into the air in distant plumes. The golden dome of the temple shone against the side of the hill like a jewel, by far the most beautiful part of the city. The din of rattling carts and talking people and whinnying horses could barely be heard over the more immediate sounds of feet thumping over wooden boards and shouting and the lapping of the water against the hull below us. For a few minutes, Rhys and I stood in silence and simply took in the view and the sounds and everything around us, and I tried to keep my sadness at bay.

But somehow Rhys knew. I felt like he always knew, even when I tried to hide my feelings so well. "It's alright to feel grief right now," he said softly, keeping his eyes on the city before us. "Just know that it won't last forever."

I blinked, feeling tears fill my eyes. Blinking didn't make them go away, and I hastily rubbed a sleeve over my eyes, with the unrealistic hope that Rhys hadn't noticed.

"I'm fine," I said after a moment, once I was fairly sure that my voice would come out normal. He turned to me and smiled, pure warmth and kindness. But then the smile fell as he took in my face. I frowned at him, wondering if my tears had really surprised him so.

"Are you alright, Eira?" he asked, still studying my face with a curious expression. I wasn't sure how to respond. I thought it was quite obvious that I was not okay. "You look…ill."

I rubbed my forehead, leaned my elbow on the railing, and sighed. "Now that you mention it, I do have a headache," I said. I hadn't really noticed the pulsing pain in my skull while all of the emotions of leaving my home had been running rampant through me.

"Do you want to—" Rhys started, but then the captain gave out an incredibly loud set of orders, and moments later the ship gave a great lurch as we turned out to the open sea.

This seemed to agitate the headache, as the rocking of the ship suddenly grew more extreme, and I closed my eyes even more tightly.

"Eira?" Rhys pressed as I felt an awful sensation rise out of my stomach. I leaned over the railing, just barely realizing what was happening before it happened. As my guts spilled over the side of the ship, it was painful enough to keep the embarrassment at bay. I vaguely hoped that no sailors were witness to such an uncomfortable moment for me, and forced myself to not think about Rhys standing right beside me.

When it was over, I straightened up just slightly, with my arms still on the railing, and heaved out a huge sigh. I kept my eyes on the water passing below us. I refused to speak first.

"I don't want to make this worse, Eira, but..."

I glanced at him, my neck feeling weak and saw him staring at the dock that we were quickly pulling away from. I turned my gaze in that direction, and felt a different type of nausea grip my stomach.

Varina stood watching our departure, her eyes hard and cold as they met mine. Her hair was loose and fluttered around her face in the sea breeze, and her hand rested on the hilt of her sword. We seemed to stare at each other for a long time, and she didn't smile.

15

Landing in Aorlanda

The voyage was worse than I ever could have imagined, because I had never imagined that I would get so seasick. But the constant rocking of the ship made my stomach clench consistently, and it was impossible for me to keep food down. As I spent much of the day vomiting, Rhys and Runa had asked to sleep in the sailor's quarters, which meant their beds were effectively hammocks—but it was still better than sharing a room with me, and hearing my constant retching.

It was so bad that I only occasionally remembered the sight of Varina on the dock, knowing how close she had been to us, inducing some waver of anxiety. But it was always quickly overcome by the nausea, and pushed from my mind with the more pressing need to vomit.

Rhys checked on me often, usually multiple times a day. Though I protested, he insisted on bringing me broth and water, and emptying my sick bucket, which I kept constantly by my bed. As I rarely got out of bed, my body drained from the effort it went through with every bout of illness, I had changed my mind and decided to sleep on a lower bunk after all. That way, I was closer to the bucket.

I was miserable, but more than that, I was deeply embarrassed. Runa and Rhys had to leave the room because of me, and I was sure the whole ship knew about my weak constitution while at sea. I felt guilty for being such a burden, especially to Rhys, who refused to leave me alone and allow me to deal with my problems on my own.

At times, I attempted to alleviate the discomfort in my stomach using magic, but I knew self-healing was nearly impossible, and the pain I was feeling was too vague, not specified to a certain part of my body, that the energy I tried to direct at myself had no effect. After a few days, I stopped trying, and just waited with dying hope that my body would grow used to the ocean waves.

>«

The temperature was another issue entirely, one which I didn't really have to deal with, as I couldn't get out of my bed anyway. But I could sense the air growing colder in the small room, and began huddling more and more into my blankets. Whenever Rhys returned from dumping my sick bucket over the side of the ship, the evidence of the chill weather outside would show from his flushed cheeks and nose, and the occasional bit of frost on the edges of his cloak.

One day he returned with my bucket, and I was beginning to feel the sense of stability in my body—not enough to trust it, but enough to sit up, and smile at Rhys when he opened the door and came inside, setting the bucket on the ground next to me.

"You look better," Rhys said. "You still looked tired when I was in here a minute ago."

"I'm very tired," I agreed, fidgeting with one of the blankets that still covered my legs. "But I also might be feeling a little better."

"Well, that's wonderful." Rhys grinned. "I'm glad. And we're almost to Tremenra—only two days away."

I stared at him, fully surprised by this information. "What?" I asked after a moment. His smile remained, but I could see a hint of confusion in his eyes.

"We're two days from the port," he said again, a bit more softly. "We'll be on solid land soon enough."

"I-I had no idea. I've been so sick…I guess I lost track of time," I said with a small frown.

"You needed the rest. I'm sorry you had to go through this, though. Next time we're on a ship, let's see if we can find a potion or some medicine that might alleviate the sickness, at least a little bit." I grinned, appreciating his forward thinking.

"That won't be for a while," I said through a sigh. "We have to climb a mountain."

"Someday we're going to come back, Eira," Rhys said, his voice still so soft, and now he was looking at me in a way that I didn't really understand. Maybe I was too tired to understand it. Or maybe I just didn't want to. "I promise, we'll come back and make things right."

I smiled back the warmth I felt from his words, and I hoped that he could feel it.

>‹‹

Tremenra consisted of a small dock and a collection of wooden buildings with steep slanted roofs. All were made out of dark wood planks, nearly black in color, which were striking against the few inches of pure white snow that covered the ground. The main road had been cleared of the snow, and the large gray stones that formed it led right up to the dock that we were finally stepping onto.

It was strange being off of the ship, and the world seemed to wobble underneath me, making me feel a bit sick all over again. My body didn't threaten me with the urge to vomit, though, and I waited alongside Rhys and Runa for our horses to be brought to us with an increasing feeling of relief mixed with anxiety.

The sky was clear and the air was cold, and the fresh air was wonderful after so long in my room aboard the ship. Besides the smell of the sea, salty and omnipresent for the last couple of weeks, I could also smell the smoke of fireplaces coming from the many chimneys protruding above the town, and the light and fresh scent of pine trees, which bordered Tremenra on all sides except for its dock. The massive trees peered above the distant structures, dark green needles contrasting against the icy blue of the sky, shuffling slightly in the light breeze.

"How are you feeling?" Rhys asked me in a soft voice as we took in the sight of the town before us. I turned to look at him, not entirely sure how to answer that question.

"Fine," I said after a moment. "What about you?"

He huffed out a dry laugh. "Fine too, I guess." I opened my mouth to ask what he meant, but three sailors arrived with our horses in tow behind them, guiding them down the dock. I was happy to see Nimue looking well after the trip, and Cai and Freya also seemed healthy. All three were tossing their heads and snorting in excitement, and I assumed it was more to do with getting off of the ship than with seeing their masters again. They were handed off to us and I took a moment to speak to Nimue in a quiet voice, in a vain attempt to calm her. But her hooves repeatedly attempted to paw the wooden boards of the dock, and it was clearly a lost cause.

We thanked Bevyn and the sailors who had cared for our horses while aboard the ship, and then Runa led Rhys and I away into the town, where she promised there was a surprisingly nice inn awaiting us.

»«

Tremena's sole inn was quite impressive for such a small town. We settled in quickly in the dark common area, which I suspected seemed darker than it actually was due to the tone of the boards that formed the walls. They really were nearly black, with just a slight warm tinge of reddish-brown running through. I had never seen trees that color in Lithe, and I couldn't help but find it strange and off-putting.

In the center of the room was a large firepit, at least three feet by three feet around. The smoke rose straight up through the room where the base of a chimney was situated directly above the fire, the stones built into the slanted wood of the ceiling.

After finding our rooms, which lined a hallway that stretched away from the common area through the back wall, Runa, Rhys, and I returned to the fire and attempted to warm up. Runa saw me looking up at the smoke and how it disappeared into the opening of the chimney, and decided to explain the design.

"It's built so that most of the heat stays in the building, but the smoke can escape," she said, pointing unnecessarily at the ceiling.

"Oh," I said, still frowning upward. After a moment I looked back down at the fire, and sighed from the warmth. It snowed every now and then during the winter in Nefyn, but

303

I had rarely felt a cold like I had while walking from the dock to the inn. It had seeped through my cloak and my tunic, and seemed to settle in my very bones. Now, before the fire, I felt myself slowly begin to thaw.

"When will we leave?" Rhys asked, looking over at Runa who was sitting to his right. I looked at her too, across the fire from me, and knew I was still a little tired from the illness I had experienced for the last couple of weeks as I studied the fire flickering on her face, having a hard time concentrating on her words. "There's a chance we're still being followed by Varina."

"I know you saw her on the docks," Runa said with a frown, "but it would be an incredibly desperate move to follow us all the way here." She paused and looked at Rhys who was glaring thoughtfully at the table at her words. She let out a short sigh. "In any case, there's no reason to waste time. We'll leave tomorrow morning," she said, frowning at him slightly. "Are you both alright with that?"

I nodded and repressed a yawn. Somehow Rhys sensed my exhaustion, and smiled at me in a comforting way, almost as warm as the fire. "Maybe you should get some rest now, Eira. The sun will set soon anyway, and you're still recovering."

"Well, I—" I started, but Runa interrupted me.

"It's going to be a hard few weeks of riding, with only a few towns to stop in and rest. You should get all the sleep you can," she said. I would have been annoyed by her decisive tone if I hadn't been so thoroughly tired and ready to admit that they were both right.

Still, I had one more reason to argue. "What about the supplies?" I asked. Runa had worked with Bevyn while we were on the ship to convert all of our bens to tils, the currency used in Tamania. Runa had insisted that Rhys and I use some of our funds for furs to keep warm while on the road, as well as a large supply of food to sustain us between towns.

"Don't worry about that," Runa said with a frown. "I'll take care of that in a few minutes. If it's okay with both of you."

"I can help," Rhys said. I nearly let out a sigh at how predictable he was, but managed to stay silent. The weight of exhaustion weighed on me, and I felt myself giving in.

"Okay," I said, and stood from the rather comfy wooden chair and cushion I had been slowly sinking into. I bid them an early goodnight and made my way across the room and down the hallway. All of the bedrooms had slanted ceilings, as the roof of the building sloped almost all the way to the ground. Runa explained that this was to prevent cave-ins under heavy snowfall. It was apparently a traditional style of structure in most of Aorlanda, as the people of the icy continent had to learn to live with extreme levels of snowfall for most of the year.

The ceiling closest to the door and hallway was well above my head, but it slanted towards the bed on the other side of the small room, where there was ultimately only about a foot of clearance between the bed of the ceiling. It was an odd design, but I understood the necessity of it. I was careful not to hit my head as I gratefully climbed into bed and fell asleep within minutes.

»«

I woke early the next morning, though I didn't know it as there were no windows in my room for me to check the light of the sky. I felt well-rested and more attuned to the solid ground beneath my feet. The fire was still roaring in the center of the inn when I emerged from the hallway, and I was a little surprised to see just how early it was, judging by the dark blue sky that was slowly lightening in the high narrow windows above the room. The innkeeper hadn't risen yet, and I was surprised to see that Rhys and Runa had, and were sitting right where I had left them the evening before.

"Good morning," Runa said as I sat in the same chair, not looking up from the maps she had spread over a small wooden table. The table hadn't been there the night before, and I wondered where she had pulled it from. Rhys was also studying the maps, a deep furrow between his eyebrows.

"Morning," I said. "Are you studying the route we'll be taking?" I asked after a moment.

Runa nodded and finally looked up at me. "The good news is we're traveling before any of the heavy snowstorms should hit. It will be icy, but hopefully not dangerous."

"Hopefully," I repeated, and she grinned at me.

"I hope you know that you didn't choose an easy journey to go on," she said, looking back down at the maps for a moment, before folding them back up, and slipping them back into her bag that was leaning against the legs of her chair. It was then that I noticed the chair next to her, vacant except for a pile of brown and black furs and pelts. Runa saw me look at them and grinned.

"These should be enough to keep us all warm," she said, patting them lightly. The way her hand fell into them showed me how soft they were even without touching them, and I was suddenly very thankful Runa had gone out of her way to do the purchasing the evening before.

"Thank you," I said, smiling at her. "I'm glad we won't freeze to death."

"Hopefully," she said, and the morbid joke actually made me laugh.

》《

The road we found ourselves on just an hour or so later was made of hard-packed and icy dirt, with the tall and ancient trees of a conifer forest rising above us on either side. Many of these trees were three yards in diameter at the base, and the upper branches looked to be over fifty yards from the ground. The pink light of the morning sun filtered through gaps between the trunks and branches, making the patches of snow that dotted the road glow with an icy warmth. The land was fairly flat in this area, and Runa said that it would stay flat, save for the occasional hill or dale, until we reach the mountains in about a week. After only a day of traveling through the forest, we would emerge from it into a marshland. Runa had assured us that the road continued through it, although it did have to wind a bit, as it had been built over the most solid and stable areas.

With every exhale I could see my breath, and I was thankful to be wrapped in one of the warm pelts that Runa had bought. She said mine was made of a large species of wolf that lived in the Tamanian mountains. Russet brown with streaks of gray, and very soft to the touch, it covered my shoulders, back, neck, and arms like a blanket.

There was something awkward about riding along the old dirt road through the forest, as the three of us rode spread out in a line in complete silence. I wasn't sure why I found this so strange. Perhaps the massive volume of thoughts constantly filtering through my mind made it all the more noticeable how quiet we were, but I couldn't bring myself to voice any of the thoughts. Most were simply anxious musings that didn't deserve to be spoken aloud, but I also found myself wondering about Runa's past again. She gave information about herself sparingly, and I didn't want to make her uncomfortable by asking her things she hadn't offered to talk about.

But I was curious where exactly she was going. She had only told us that it was past Aornadur, on the eastern side of Aorlanda, in the kingdom of Rhea. And I wondered why she had been in Tennart so recently when she said she had spent most of the last few years traveling around Aorlanda. She seemed to have a nomadic life, which intrigued me to no end, as a person who hadn't left her home her entire life until a couple of weeks ago.

The silence only served to make me more anxious, so I was very relieved when Rhys slowed Cai slightly, until we were riding parallel to each other, with Runa up ahead of us by a few yards. I smiled at him, feeling how frozen my face felt, and wondered how long we had been on the road.

"How are you feeling?" he asked with a small smile. I could still tell he was concerned, though he tried to hide it.

"Perfect," I said, wanting to assuage any anxiety he felt about my well-being. "I...I need to thank you. I don't remember if I've said this yet, but...I really appreciate your caring for me on the ship. I'm sure that wasn't pleasant for you."

"Don't thank me," he said immediately, his smile turning into a frown in an instant. "I was happy to be there for you."

"It was...quite gross, though," I said, looking away from him, and thankful that my face was so cold that I doubted it was possible for me to blush. "It wasn't something you should've had to deal with."

"Eira," he said, his tone more serious than I thought the conversation warranted. I turned my head to look at him again, wondering what he was thinking. "I promise. I was happy to take care of you. You were delirious most of the time, and there was no possible way you could have taken care of yourself."

"Delirious," I repeated, smiling slightly. He let out a small laugh.

"I doubt you remember a few days there. You were barely conscious. Actually scared me for a bit," he said, cringing slightly. "Your body just needed rest, though."

"I hope I didn't say or do anything strange," I said, meaning for it to be a joke. But the slight pause from Rhys suddenly made my stomach flip. My smile fell as I stared at him, a sense of dread growing in my heart. "Oh no. Did I say something?"

"No," Rhys said quickly. Too quickly. I narrowed my eyes and wondered how bad it could be. I tried to remember anything I could have said that was incriminating, but nothing came to mind—it was all a haze of illness and sleep on repeat.

"Tell me," I said, keeping my tone level as I tried my hardest to keep any hint of panic out of it.

"It doesn't matter," Rhys said, lifting a hand from his reins to wave my demand away. "People can't be expected to make sense while in such a state."

"So I didn't make sense?" I asked.

"Exactly. It was a bunch of gibberish."

I still glared at him, suspicious. "If that's all it was, why didn't you want to tell me?"

"Because it was silly, and you embarrass easily," he said with a small sigh. "Honestly, I can't even remember any details. I just remember laughing."

"You laughed at me?" I said with mock outrage, and his eyes widened in concern before he saw the glint of humor in my eyes, as my lips curled slightly. Then his warm smile returned.

"I apologize, milady. But in my defense, if you had been conscious you would have been laughing too."

I rolled my eyes, and looked forward, over Nimue's relaxed ears. Runa rode on her shimmery gray mare upright and alert as we rounded a slight bend in the road, and more of the forest was revealed to us. It was a picturesque view, those towering trees with the top branches laden with snow, old pine needles covering the ground, little banks of white frost dotting the areas that spent most of the time in the shade, underneath the trees. The sun shone brightly now, and it looked to be midmorning. The crisp forest air filled my lungs, and for the first time since leaving Lithe, I felt a hint of confidence as I looked back at Rhys with a grin.

"Next time I'm delirious with illness, write some of the things I say down, so you have evidence. And so I can have a laugh too."

"Well, I must say I hope you never get that ill again," Rhys said, now a bit grim. He still shook off that negative tone, and smiled at me once again. "We'll find medicine for you before we board a ship again."

"Yes, that's a good idea," I agreed. I smiled as I felt that confidence grow. We would return to Lithe, as Rhys had already said. Next time we were on a ship, we would be going home.

>«

We made camp in a clearing that night, one which luckily didn't have much snow. We passed around some of the dried meat and bread Runa had bought the previous night, and ate in silence around a fire she had been able to start rather easily. Now that I was tired after a full day of riding, the silence didn't bother me as much. I allowed the sounds around us to wash over me as I satisfied my hunger, my eyes unfocused over the fire. The flames flickered up towards the branches high above us, and the small section of the clear night sky that could be seen through the treetops. The screech of an owl, and the tweets of evening birds, and the scuffling of creatures through the snow all echoed through the still air, feeling much more immediate and close than I knew they were. Though it was eerie, being in that dark and cold forest surrounded by nocturnal life and unable to see their forms, I was quite relaxed. We had been traveling through forests for long enough that I was used to those sounds.

"So tomorrow, you said we'll reach a marshland?" Rhys asked after he had taken his last bite of food. Runa had already finished hers, and turned to look at him from where she sat cross-legged to his right. She nodded, her face blank, an expression that I was beginning to recognize as her default.

"Yes. But the road is built well through it," she said. "It might be harder to find a place to camp some nights, but it won't be impossible."

"Will we stay in a town anytime soon?" I asked, absentmindedly picking at the last piece of bread in my hands.

"Unlikely," Runa said with a slight shake of her head. "Not until after the marshes, and that will take a few days to traverse. Soon after that, we'll stay in the capital of West Tamania, Fjall."

We went to sleep soon after this conversation, and even though Runa had explained the route our travels would take, my mind had a hard time imagining marshes that stretched for hundreds of miles, and the mountain range that we would have to cross, or any other part of our journey. I fell asleep to numb wonderings about what was to come.

But in the morning, with the sun bright through the trees and making our little clearing glow with vibrant orange light, I felt refreshed and more open to the road ahead. It didn't truly matter what was going to happen along the way. All that mattered was that we made it to the Inherents.

As we turned onto the road from where we had slept within the forest, I urged Nimue closer to Runa, and hoped that she might start a conversation with me. I still had all of those questions about her, but even if she didn't want to answer those, I thought it would be a good thing if we got to know each other a bit better. And we had a lot of road to cover, and thus a lot of time to talk. Rhys and Cai were not far behind us, and he rode with a calm expression, his shoulders relaxed and covered in his gray fur cloak that Runa had picked out for him.

After what felt like around a half hour of silent riding only a couple of feet to Runa and Freya's left, I took a deep breath and turned to smile at her. "I'm surprised how nice the weather is," I said, knowing full well how awkward it was to start a conversation with a comment about the weather. Runa looked up at the sliver of sky above the road, bright blue and beaming down on us, and nodded, as though she hadn't considered the weather before I had mentioned it.

"It can get bad more quickly than you might think, so don't get used to this," she said, keeping her eyes forward. I nodded, even though she wasn't looking at me. The dark green needles shifted in a slight breeze as we passed below them, and the road wound lazily around large trunks and the occasional boulder or gulch, reducing our visibility. Runa had trained herself to be aware of her surroundings at all times, so I wasn't surprised that she was so unwilling to divert her attention to me.

"I wanted to thank you again, for everything," I said after a short pause. To my surprise, she snorted.

"You two say thank you way too much. What did you expect me to do? Look the other way when I saw two people get bullied in the street? Abandon you even though we're heading the same direction? Especially when I know so much more about Aorlanda than you do," she said, now frowning at the road.

"Well, yes. You don't know us. You had no reason to—"

"We've been over this. I've told you, I only did what I thought was right. And you two are quite kind and good people to be on the road with, so it was clearly a good decision." She sighed slightly, and risked a short glance in my direction, only for a second. "You two also worry a lot, it seems."

"Well, you don't know a lot about us and we're worried you'll change your mind," I said, thinking quickly. "And we don't know a lot about you either."

She smiled at this, the corners of her mouth just barely turned upward. "Ah. Perhaps you're worried about your decision to travel with me, then?"

"No, not at all," I said quickly. Perhaps too quickly, as she let out a small laugh.

"What do you want to know?" she asked, after pausing for just a second. I hesitated, not sure where to start.

"Um…well," I said slowly. "Where are you headed? You said it's past Aornadur."

"A town called Ferning," she said promptly, unbothered by the question. She surprised me even more as she elaborated. "I'm visiting my mentor."

"Mentor?" I repeated.

"Garett. He trained me in sword fighting, and taught me how to live in Aorlanda. It's far different from Remisia. You'll see soon enough."

"I've already noticed it's a good bit colder," I joked, and Runa gave a slight smile again.

"It's more than that too. Remisia is… Well, I suppose the greatest difference is how magic is treated, and those who use it."

This piqued my curiosity, and I spoke without thinking. "Eosiaids?" I said.

"They're called Drekligr here. Or Drek," Runa said. Her voice had an odd tinge, as though she was speaking of something taboo. Like she knew she shouldn't be talking about it at all. "They don't have a place in society here, as they do in Remisia."

"What do you mean?" I asked, frowning at the profile of her face. She was frowning too, and I was glad that that stern expression was not directed at me.

"I thought you would have known by now," she said, her voice soft. She still didn't like the subject we were on, but something kept her talking about it. She glanced at me again, and I was surprised that her eyebrows were now upturned in concern. "People with magic are outcasts. They're hated. So…for your own well-being, don't speak of them in public places."

My stomach dropped at her words, thinking for a moment that she knew I was an Eos, which I had avoided revealing to her for fear that she would be more inclined to turn me into the Empire or the Syrthiaid. Most Remisians believed that an Eos should never abandon their position, as it was their duty to serve the common people. But now I saw another issue entirely.

If what Runa was saying was true, I could not risk revealing myself as an Eosiaids in Aorlanda.

"I didn't know that," I murmured, looking down at Nimue's flicking ears. She snorted, as though sensing my sudden discomfort.

"It's one of the main reasons the war is still being fought," Runa continued. "East Tamanians want to be harsher on Drekligr, even more than banishment. They would have then executed."

"How would they manage that?" I frowned. "Commoners against someone with magic. I don't see that going very well for the commoners."

Runa shrugged. "They've done it before. Enough of them, and even they can overpower someone with magic."

"But surely some would die in the fight—"

"And they have. And they will continue to do so. They consider it an honor."

"Why?" I asked, accidentally raising my voice a little.

"Why do they want to kill them?" Runa asked with a deep frown.

"Why are the Eos so hated here?" I hoped Runa couldn't hear the slight emotion that I couldn't keep from my voice. It was disturbing, and set me on edge, that we would be traveling through the lands of people who would want to kill me if they knew who I was.

"Because of the curse," Runa said as though it was obvious.

"The curse," I repeated.

"The birth curse. You—I'm sorry. I thought you would have known by now... I forget sometimes, how the lie is upheld in Remisia," she said, almost to herself. She looked even more avidly at the road ahead, as though she was now avoiding my eyes. Her lips set and jaw clenched, she was exceptionally tense in that moment.

"I know about the curse," I said softly. "And the lie. Rhys knows as well." She relaxed at this, and smiled at me awkwardly.

"Oh. Well, good. And that is why they're hated here. It's believed that they were cursed by the Sky Queen, not blessed. Being the reason for two peoples' deaths far outweighs any gift of magic they may possess. It is also thought that their true nature is to destroy, since that is how they come into the world."

"But they can also heal," I said.

Runa shrugged. "Herbalists and physicians are common in Aorlanda, because we do not rely on Drekligr to heal us. No one would trust their life in the hands of a Drek."

I was silent for a moment, allowing this information to settle in my mind. It was hard to fully understand; after all, I had lived in Remisia my entire life. I had only learned the truth of my birth recently.

"Well, I won't mention Drekligr to anyone," I said eventually. Runa nodded, pleased that I agreed to this. "Thank you for telling me."

"Of course. Perhaps tonight I can go over some other… differences you and Rhys might need to be aware of. To avoid any trouble."

"That's a good idea," I agreed. "I'd like to tell Rhys what you just told me now, actually. But we can speak more later, around the fire."

Runa nodded in agreement, and I pulled on Nimue's reins, slowing her slightly until Rhys and Cai were beside me. He smiled at me, but there was a curious glint to his eyes, and I could tell that the conversation had not gone unnoticed by him.

"There's a few things you should know," I sighed. In a low voice, I repeated everything Runa had said to me, phrasing it carefully so that he wouldn't remark in a way that revealed I was an Eos. I wasn't sure how good Runa's hearing was, and though she was riding a few yards ahead of us, I didn't trust that she couldn't hear us.

"How odd," Rhys said after I was done talking, but I could see the weight of my words in his eyes. "I'm glad she told you. I would hate to say something unfortunate in an inn."

I nodded. "She realized there's probably quite a bit that we should know, and wants to talk to us more in depth when we stop tonight."

Rhys nodded, and then we rode in silence, a bit more grim than when we had started. Aorlanda was proving to be more complicated than we could have imagined.

16

The Road to Fjall

The evening discussion took some time, but in a way I was glad for it. We were stopped in another clearing, this one with even fewer patches of snow. But the air was colder, and wispy clouds periodically covered the moon and stars. The night sounds echoed around us again, but the conversation diverted my attention from them, eerie or not. The quiet dinner the night before hadn't been unpleasant, but it was quite nice to eat and talk as a group, even if the conversation was really just a list of things Rhys and I shouldn't do while in Aorlanda. Tamania was especially riddled with secret rules, from how to enter a room to how to correctly hand over payment and receive goods. She taught us some key phrases in Tamanian, and it was only then that I realized how useful it would be if I could also learn the language.

"Will you teach me?" I asked Runa, just after she had taught us the word for good morning. Runa glanced at Rhys, as though silently asking if he knew what I was saying. Then she looked back at me with a frown.

"What do you think I'm doing right now?" she asked after a short pause.

"I mean the whole language," I said, fighting the urge to roll my eyes.

"Oh. Well. I'm not sure we have enough time before Fjall for you to really learn it, but...I can continue to teach you important phrases while we're on the road and when we stop for the night."

"That would be lovely," I agreed emphatically, unable to hide my smile. Not only did I like languages, I also picked them up easily. I was fluent in the Old Tongue of Lithe, and knew that I had the ability to learn Tamanian quickly—maybe even more quickly than Runa expected.

"Do you want to learn too?" she asked Rhys, leaning forward to warm her hands over the fire as she sent him a curious glance. He immediately shifted in his cross-legged position, looking uncomfortable.

"I don't know. I've never learned another language. I doubt I'll be any good," he said, his eyes shifting between me and Runa.

"You don't have to be fluent," I said. "Just learn a little bit. If Runa's going to teach me, you might as well learn a bit too."

He sighed, then nodded once. "Fine," he said as he ran a hand through his hair. "I'll try for a little while at least."

"Great," I said, sitting back slightly in satisfaction. "We shouldn't have to rely on Runa for everything." Rhys made a sound that was somewhere between a grunt and a sigh, and didn't respond. His trepidation didn't discourage me, though. We needed something to distract us on the road anyway.

»«

The next morning we reached the marshes, a seemingly endless expanse of mud and puddles and ponds, divided by small hills covered in grass and low shrubs. Sedges and rushes grew in every damp spot, often lining the road. Here the road was paved with large, flat, gray stones of varying tones, and it wound in a haphazard way through the ponds and streams like a snake. Runa explained again how carefully it had been built to traverse the marshland many decades before, and was maintained when needed by Fjall's forces itself.

"Why?" Rhys asked as he rode alongside Runa, with me right behind them.

"There's a port closer to the mountains than Tremenra, a larger one that Fjall relies on for goods from Shukoria. There isn't a lot of trade between Aorlanda and Remisia because Remisia enforces such strict trade rules—or at least, they used to," she added, and though I couldn't see her face I knew she wore a deep frown. "But Shukoria doesn't have the same restrictions, and they provide a few exports that Tamania pays hefty sums for."

"Like what?" Rhys asked, his curiosity piqued.

"Teas and spices mostly," Runa said with a shrug. "You would be surprised how valued those items are here."

"Interesting," Rhys murmured. A few moments later we passed a shallow hill that had stretched along to our left, and a massive white mountain range was revealed in the distance.

"Those are the Windfjall Mountains," Runa said, gesturing at their tall and jagged peaks. They stretched south, into the distance, seemingly growing shorter until they melded into the horizon along with the marshlands. "They're also simply called the Tamanian Mountains, as they mark the border between East and West Tamania."

"I've never seen mountains like that," I murmured, still taking in their sheer mass. Even the base of the range, with snow-capped foothills and dark splotches of forest, were more impressive than any range I had seen in Lithe.

"How will we pass them?" Rhys said, his voice tinged with concern.

"There is a pass. I promise, it's easy enough for the horses to traverse. It's just east of Fjall, called Rodljost Pass."

Rhys looked over at Runa, riding to his left, and I could see the uncertainty in his eyes. But he simply nodded, and chose not to push the subject any further.

>«<

We started our Tamanian lessons not long after that, winding through the marshes as the road curved back and forth, even back-tracking slightly at times. Runa was impressed with my language acquisition skills, and within a few hours I had memorized dozens of important phrases like, "how much does this cost?" And "three rooms, please."

Rhys, however, had a harder time. He did not have a knack for getting the right pronunciations, and Runa had to spend longer with him on each new consonant sound. He also grew frustrated quickly, but was successful in pushing that feeling aside and continuing on with the lessons. To her credit, Runa remained patient with him, and was actually quite nice about his inability to learn.

After a few hours, both Rhys and I had grown tired of practicing Tamanian, and the conversation returned fully to Remisian. The light around us became golden in the evening sun, and only a couple of hours later we were stopping to make camp on a dry bit of land beside the road. It wasn't a particularly large space, but enough for us and the horses without being too cramped. It was flat too, and the earth was hard and frozen clay beneath our feet and bedrolls. A few rushes grew along the edge where this little island met the water surrounding us, swaying slightly in the icy breeze. There was no material nearby good enough to build a fire with, so we huddled in our furs and blankets, and ate while chatting intermittently.

The cold was truly beginning to wear on me. Perhaps it was because it was the first night without a fire, or perhaps the flat expanse of land we were traveling over felt colder as gusts of wind could blow across it uninhibited, while in the forest around Tremenra, the trees provided some relief from the wind. Or I had simply had enough of the freezing temperatures. I suspected this was the true reason.

Though I wore warm knit gloves, my cloak, and all of the furs and layers Runa had thought to pick out, I had slowly been feeling the cold settle in my bones over the previous couple of days, and there was something harsh and cold about the marshland that had suddenly made it so much worse.

>«

The days began to pass with the slow gait of the horses, and my body became attuned to the sway of riding once again after the many days lying down on the ship. My retention of Tamanian only increased as we continued our lessons along the winding and often putrid-smelling road, while Rhys plateaued early on. Eventually, the land became more solid, the ponds and reeds falling away behind us, and the road straightened as the ground became hard, frozen, packed clay beneath the wide stones. The Tamanian Mountains still rose above us to our left, changing slightly day by day. Sometimes I could see forests at the base, and sometimes it seemed like there were only sheer cliffs; most of the time, it seemed that the foothills were gently rolling and covered in snow. Though it was cold enough in the flatlands, I was thankful that we weren't trudging through deep snowbanks—yet.

Fjall appeared before us one day as a spikey block of gray against the pale blue sky, thousands of wisps of smoke disappearing above it like clouds floating up into the sky.

"We'll reach it by nightfall," Runa called to Rhys and me once it was obvious what the odd smudge on the horizon was. Rhys and I rode a few yards behind Runa and Freya, and I wondered when we had fallen behind her so early in the day. We had only been riding for an hour or so, and the morning sun was still shining pale above the Tamanian Mountains, making them glisten like white jewels.

Rhys called back with some words of acknowledgment, but I was no longer paying attention. The cold wind bit my nose as it blew against us from the east, but I was used to it by that point. The cold was something I could tune out with enough effort. It was no effort at all now, as my mind wandered to the future, and all of my anxieties that were wrapped up with it.

"You're overthinking, Eira," a deep voice said to my right, and I blinked at the way it so easily cut through my thoughts. I turned to see Rhys smiling at me softly, as though he knew exactly what I was thinking about, his eyes clear with understanding.

"Am I?" I challenged.

"Yes, I can tell by the way you squint into the distance, but still look like you aren't looking at it."

"I have no idea what you mean," I said, turning to look back at the road, Runa in front of us on her silver mare, the brown grass and small shrubs that dotted the icy landscape.

"Well, you wouldn't. It's something you do without being aware of it," Rhys replied with a casual tone. I frowned, wondering why he was so relaxed.

"What was I thinking about, then?" I asked, still not looking at him. Cai snorted and shook his head, as though annoyed with my question.

"The only thing you ever think about. The future," Rhys said.

"There's a lot to think about," I conceded. "You must be worried as well."

He paused, and I almost glanced over at him. "In a way," he said finally. "But I don't let it control my thoughts."

"Well, that's wonderful for you," I muttered.

"You can do it too, you know."

"You don't think I want to stop worrying?" I asked, turning finally to glare at him. "Of course I want to. But there's too much at risk."

"I'm not trying to offend you, Eira," Rhys said, as calm and collected as usual. It was beginning to infuriate me. "But we've made it this far, haven't we? Runa is guiding us, and we trust her. So we can just take one issue at a time. Can't we?"

I clenched my jaw for a few moments, knowing he was right. I let out a sigh, and my jaw slowly relaxed, my frown smoothed away.

"Sorry," I mumbled. "I'm very tense."

"It's all right," Rhys said easily. "You shouldn't apologize. Just remember that we're doing this together."

"Thank you," I whispered, and looked over at him to see him smiling at the slowly growing shape of Fjall in the distance. And for a moment I couldn't help but let that same smile spread over my face as well.

>‹‹

The sky was pink and gold, full of warmth and the dying flames of the sun, when we reached the large metal gates of Fjall. Runa explained that there were three gates, and we were approaching the North Gates. The sheer size of them awed me, and as we approached I was sure that I was somehow miscalculating their height. The massive stone black-brick wall that stretched out from either side of the gate was also impressive, topped with ramparts and guardhouses overlooking the valley.

We were ordered to halt just outside the gates by three soldiers, all dressed in plate armor and fur-lined black cloaks, the hilts of the swords protruding just slightly from underneath the fabric. While Runa spoke to them in fluent and breezy Tamanian, I looked up at the gates and estimated that they were fifty feet tall. The black metal was shadowed as the sun set behind the city, but I could still see the multitude of rivets that held the panels together. Two doors formed the gates, and upon a call from the soldier that Runa was speaking to, they were split and then we were beckoned to pass through the gap created. Though they had only been opened about halfway, the gap was wide enough for all three of us to pass through side by side on our horses.

And then the city stretched before us, and the doors were shut behind us with a clang that reverberated through my heart.

"There's an inn not too far this way," Runa said, leading us down the wide road to our left. I was still taking in the sights of the city. We seemed to be in a market, with stalls set up selling food and clothing, the peddlers yelling out prices and deals, and customers haggling and putting produce and bread into their rucksacks. It was bustling, reminding me a bit of Caergarth, the last vibrant city I had been in.

The buildings were a mix of black or dark gray stone and wood, and most of the roofs were built in that sharp triangle shape that I had seen at the inn in Tremenra. Though Fjall wasn't covered in snow at that moment, I was sure winter brought blizzards and heavy snowfall. Luckily for us, it was still midsummer, and the ground merely froze with ice at night. No snow would fall from the sky for a few months in the city.

The inn Runa brought us to was three times larger than the one in Tremenra, and boasted two stories of rooms in addition to the tapered roof. There was a common room just inside the front door, which housed the largest firepit I had ever seen in my life. The walls of the inn were all of the same dark stone, but the roof was the dark cedar that was common throughout Aorlanda. About ten people sat in wooden chairs or cushion armchairs around the room, mostly gathered around that central fire. The pit was a long rectangle, about twenty feet long and five feet wide, and a servant that worked at the inn was nearly continuously stoking it and adding more wood in areas where the fire was dying down.

Bedrooms lined the walls, marked by narrow doors, and two staircases led up to a second floor balcony on either side of the room. Looking up as Runa, Rhys, and I found seats together near the firepit, I saw more of those narrow doors on the second floor, all along the outside of the balcony.

"Those rooms are cheaper, so I reserved three of them," Runa said to my right, where she sat warming her hands over the fire.

"Why are they cheaper?" Rhys asked, leaning past me to frown at Runa.

"The roof is slanted. The upstairs rooms have those tapered ceilings like our rooms in Tremenra," Runa said, focusing on the fire.

"Great," Rhys said, somewhere between a huff and a sigh. "I really enjoyed hitting my head when I woke up. Wonderful that I can do it again."

I snorted at his sour tone, but pretended not to notice that he was glaring at me.

"Be more careful," Runa said, not feeling any sympathy.

"That's easy for you to say. What are you, barely five feet?" Rhys jabbed, leaning to glare at her once again.

This did rouse Runa's irritation, and she looked back at him with a deep frown. "I'm five foot, three inches," she snapped. "And I could still take you in a fight."

"Okay," I laughed, beginning to feel a bit of legitimate tension.

"I'll let you think that," Rhys muttered.

"You think just because you're as tall as a tree that you could beat me?"

"No. What—you're the one who brought up fighting, Runa," Rhys said, and I relaxed a bit, as he moved the conversation away from dueling. "I was saying that you have an advantage in these low-ceiling rooms. Although I think I must have struck a nerve," he continued, now with a small, sly smile on his face. "It's not your fault you're short, Runa."

"I'm not short," she muttered, looking away from him with a deadly glare that she decided to fix on the fire instead. "You're just tall."

"Whatever you have to tell yourself," Rhys said, now smiling with obvious satisfaction.

"We've been on the road too long," I muttered mostly to myself, but the comment earned a low laugh from Rhys and a snort from Runa.

"We should spar, though," Runa said to both of us, her features now relaxed as she sank into her seat a bit more.

"When we get back on the road. Less Tamanian and more fighting."

"I like Tamanian," I protested with a frown.

Runa rolled her eyes at me, but smiled slightly as well. "Both, then." She let out a wide yawn then, her eyes shut tight, and then she blinked at me wearily. "I think I'll head off to bed. We'll go to the markets in the morning."

"Alright. Goodnight, Runa," I said, repressing my own yawn. She bid goodnight to Rhys and me, and then we sat in comfortable silence for a while. People chatted, mostly in Tamanian, and the fire crackled, and heavy cartwheels rolled by and crunched over the stones outside the building. Despite all of the noise, I felt a strange sense of peace.

"Excuse me?" someone said to my right, where Runa had been sitting minutes earlier, and something about the tone of the voice alerted me to the fact that they were speaking to me. Rhys and I both turned quickly to see a young woman in leather travel clothing and a fur cloak sitting in Runa's abandoned chair, staring at us with wide blue eyes, her hands fidgeting in her lap. Her light brown hair was pulled back into a ponytail, but small braids framed her narrow face. Something about her told me that she was older than she looked. I paused, caught off guard by her sudden appearance, before responding.

"Yes?" I said, allowing all of the hesitation I felt to color my voice.

"I heard you speaking Remisian, and, well, I thought you might be from Lithe too. If I heard your accent right."

I blinked, turned to frown at Rhys who looked just as surprised as I felt, and then looked back at the girl. "You're from Lithe?" I asked, already knowing the answer. Her accent was undeniably that of a Lithian.

"Yes, Brynffynon," she said. A northern town. She smiled suddenly, her eyes shining with excitement. "I hope you don't mind me coming over. I just haven't seen anyone from Lithe for weeks and weeks."

"Of course," I said, feeling myself smile as well. Though I was tired, I couldn't deny it was a bit energizing to meet a fellow Lithian so far from home. "We don't mind at all."

"I'm Liliwen," she said, then paused, still smiling, but now with a bit more hesitation.

"I'm Eira," I said, then looked at Rhys.

"Rhys," he said with a smile. I could tell he was still unsure of the situation.

"It's nice to meet you both, and so far from Remisia," Liliwen said, tucking one of her braids behind her ear. "May I ask what brought you to Fjall?" she asked, tilting her head slightly with open curiosity.

"We're traveling with a friend to Durnaland," I said.

Liliwen blinked in surprise, her mouth opening slightly. "I'm traveling through Durnaland myself," she said, with an odd, small frown now. "It's quite far, isn't it?"

"Are you traveling alone?" Rhys asked, also frowning, but for a different reason—he was concerned about her.

Her frown melted away as she grinned. "I look weak, but I can handle myself," she said, and Rhys simply smiled in response, clearly not knowing what to say to that.

"Through Durnaland?" I asked.

She nodded. "I have distant relatives in Rhea. I'm hoping they'll be willing to help me, but…" She gazed at the fire for a moment, before looking back at me and Rhys. "You're escaping too, aren't you?"

"Well…" I began, pausing at the concern that I saw in her eyes. "Yes," I said quickly. "We're from Nefyn. We were attacked by the Syrthiaid a couple months ago, and we barely managed to escape the city."

Liliwen sighed heavily, and rested her elbows on her knees, her shoulders rounded as she looked into the fire again. "Brynffynon was taken just after Maenynys. It's the closest major city. They started a draft for their army soon after."

"A draft?" I repeated, feeling a chill at her words.

She looked up at me, her eyes now heavy. She nodded. "They're building an army. Ronoa is next. It won't be easy to take, will it?" she said this on a sigh, the question rhetorical.

"When did you leave?" Rhys asked.

"Over a month ago. It took me a while to find a ship in Aberffin. The voyage took a couple of weeks, and I've been resting here for a few days now."

"What do you think is going to happen?" I asked quietly, looking away from Liliwen, allowing my eyes to unfocus somewhere on the stones of the wall across the room. I heard her take a deep breath, and sensed that she was shaking her head.

"I can't say. Silvania will have to get involved before too long, won't they?" she said, sounding just as uncertain as me.

I hated it—not that she was uncertain, but that our home, and most of Remisia, was in such turmoil that the future was vague and bleak.

"At least…at least we're here, and not there," Rhys murmured. I sensed a sudden movement from Liliwen, and looked at her to see her glaring at Rhys, having just turned sharply in his direction.

"I wish I could do something," she said, her tone low and serious. She frowned at both of us for a moment before consciously relaxing her features. "I'm…I'm sorry," she said quickly. "I suppose…my feelings about being here and not there are complicated."

"I understand," I said without thinking.

She stared at me, a tentative smile on her face. "You do?"

"Well, I…" I wanted to backtrack, but I knew perfectly well why I had claimed agreement. I sighed, looking down at my fur-covered lap for a moment, before back up at Liliwen's open face, determined to be honest with this person. A stranger, but someone more like me than I could ignore.

"I feel guilty for leaving," I said honestly. "It felt wrong—terribly wrong to board that ship. But…we're going to return. And we're going to set things right."

"Eira," Rhys said in a warning tone, but I held up a hand, choosing to ignore the warning.

"What do you mean?" Liliwen asked. "Set things right?"

I looked at her levelly. I searched her face, her open and curious eyes and slight furrowed brows. Perhaps I wasn't thinking clearly. Was it wise to let another person know about our plan, especially when Runa didn't even know? Was it worth it to involve another person?

I didn't care, because Liliwen deserved to know.

"Rhys and I are going to save Lithe from the Syrthiaid," I said, and Liliwen's frown deepened. "That's why we're here. We're going to climb Aornadur."

Her eyes widened, the frown disappeared, and she froze for just a second. And then she let out a loud cackle as she sat up straight in her chair.

"I'm sorry," she said as her laughter died away, with the smile remaining on her face. "I don't see how you two dying on a mountain is going to save Lithe, but…well. I had no idea I was talking to two lunatics. Have a nice night, then," she said, moving to stand up.

"Wait!" I said, trying to hide my anger at being brushed off and called a lunatic.

"Let her go, Eira," Rhys sighed to my left, but I ignored him again.

"No, let us explain," I said, pleaded, and she paused as she stood up, looking down at me with dubious eyes. "We've… We know why they're so powerful. The Syrthiaid. We know why they were able to defeat the Southern Kingdoms so easily. And we know what we need to do to gain the upper hand."

Something I said, or maybe even the desperate way I had said it, caused Liliwen to sit back down in the armchair next to me. She looked at me expectantly, silently bidding me to continue, and I glanced at Rhys. He raised his eyebrows and gestured at Liliwen with an open hand, letting me know I was on my own. He hadn't wanted to tell her in the first place.

"We went to Caergarth before we left, and met with a scholar there. We searched the library for information about the Syrthiaid, about people with extraordinary powers—"

"Those powers are just rumors," Liliwen said with a frown. "Exaggerations."

"No, I met them myself. Some of them anyway. And it's true—they can do extraordinary things, things we've never seen Eosiaids do before."

Liliwen sighed, shook her head slightly. She was still unconvinced. "The library?" she pressed, already weary from this conversation. I resisted the urge to grind my teeth in frustration that she still didn't believe me.

"We found a book by an old Silvanian prophet, Adelais. He writes of twenty-two special Eosiaids he calls the Sacreds. We believe that the Syrthiaid are some of these Sacreds, come together to take as much land and wealth as they can."

"So you don't have proof?" Liliwen said, leaning back in her seat and folding her arms while glaring at me. I stared at her in surprise, not expecting the questions. "This is just a hunch you two have."

"Well—" I stumbled, not knowing what to say to that.

"And what does this have to do with Aornadur?" she asked, her frown deepening.

"Have you heard of the Himminir?" I said, losing all hope that I could convince Liliwen of anything. Rhys had been right. It had been a mistake to try to talk to her about this. Why would anyone believe it?

"Yes," she replied.

"Adelais claims that they are bound to the Sacreds, like some sort of counterparts. He writes that they know more about the Sacreds than anyone else. To the rest of Linra, the Sacreds are mere rumors, like you said. But the Himminir know the truth. He calls them the Inherents."

Liliwen chewed on her lip and looked at the fire as she considered my words. "You know you still sound like a lunatic, right?" she said after a few moments.

I nodded once and looked away from her, resentful at her words.

"We're sorry for bothering you," Rhys said, leaning forward to look at Liliwen. "Our quest is our own. We don't mean to involve you."

Liliwen shook her head slowly, still not looking at us but frowning deeply at the fire. "It would be nice to know…how to stop it," she murmured. "It sounds too good to be true… that you two have found this information. That it might actually help Lithe."

My ears perked up at the slight hesitation in her voice. She wasn't throwing away what I said outright. She was still considering my words.

She turned to look at me and gave a small shrug, the gray fur hood of her cloak rising to brush her ears. Then she smiled softly.

"You might not have realized this," she said slowly, the smile growing into an open warmth, "but I'm a lunatic too. So…tell me more about your plan."

I glanced at Rhys, unable to hide the surprise from my face—eyes wide and mouth slightly open. He grinned at me.

"Go ahead," he said, and I turned back to Liliwen, mirroring her smile once again.

»«

The conversation with Liliwen lasted late into the night, but the innkeeper kept the fire burning even as other patrons made their way to bed. The street outside grew quiet with the passing hours, and soon it felt like we were the only people awake in the city. Our words grew quieter as the only other sounds around us became the crackling and popping of the fire before us, and even the innkeeper retired.

"Here's the book," Rhys said, pulling it from the leather pack that was positioned under his chair. As he did, the Syrthiaid's dagger fell out and clattered on the wooden floor between our two chairs, and I didn't think as I reached down and grabbed the hilt, intending to put it away. I wasn't sure why, but I felt a deep need to keep it hidden, perhaps because I knew I wasn't supposed to have it in the first place.

I realized my mistake just as my vision darkened, my fingers tightening around the gold. My mind scrambled to stop the memory, desperately attempting to stay in the present, but the vision overtook me despite my efforts, and I saw Varina in the great room of my Benaty, kneeling before two people I had never seen before, and Cassia beside them. They were assembled at the base of the wide staircase, and I stood only a few feet away with my feet planted on the tiled floor, looking around me completely disoriented. The two people standing before Varina emanated an energy that made me uncomfortable, and as I studied them I saw how intimidating they really were. One was a tall man, about forty years old with sandy hair and deep lines around his mouth and eyes. His eyes were a cold blue, nearly gray, and he looked down at Varina with a coldness that would have scared me if it had been directed at me.

The person next to him was a much shorter woman, perhaps a bit younger, with straight black hair and narrow eyes. She looked Shukorian, but I couldn't tell for sure. Unlike the man next to her, her brown eyes were filled with fiery anger, and she glared at Varina's kneeling form, her jaw tense and lips thin.

"You think you can accomplish this?" the man asked, his voice soft, but somehow still harsh. His tone was as cold as his gaze, cutting to my heart even though he wasn't speaking to me. Varina kept her eyes cast downward as she nodded.

"I am sure. She is weak and untrained. Calliten made sure she would not be able to fight him. So she certainly is no match for me." Varina said this plainly, and I listened with growing dread.

The two people looked at each other, and the man nodded. "Stand, Varina," he commanded, and she did so instantly, rising to her feet and clasping her hands behind her back.

"If we give you this task, you understand what it means, correct?" the dark-haired woman said. It sounded like a threat, but I didn't know what it meant.

"I understand," Varina said with a curt nod. I glanced at Cassia, still standing to the side and clutching the dagger, and was almost surprised to see anger in her deeply set brows. I remembered her appearing calm, even when holding me captive.

"The Reclaimed Kingdoms are relying on you to bring this girl home," the man said.

"I understand, Emperor Age, Empress Riki," Varina said, raising her voice just slightly. Then she bowed, dropping her gaze to the floor. "I will stop at nothing to capture Aneira Elfyn and bring her back to you."

A slow smile spread on Age's face, still void of any warmth. Then he looked at Cassia. "You know what must be done, Lady Cassia," he said. She stepped up to Varina and together they walked to the massive front doors of the Benaty, opening them together and allowing the afternoon sunlight to rush in and fill the great room with blinding white light.

I blinked furiously, willed myself back to the inn in Fjall, and when I fully opened my eyes again I was there, gasping for air. I dropped the dagger back on the ground as I slowed my breathing back to a normal pace and sat up straight in my seat.

"Eira," Rhys said, and I met his eyes as I sat up straight again, and the concern there sent guilt running through my veins.

"Are you alright?" Liliwen asked from my other side. It was difficult for me to look away from the expression on Rhys's face, but I managed it after a moment and turned to look at her while forcing a smile.

"Yes, I pulled a muscle, I think. Too much riding lately. I'm quite sore," I lied quickly. I heard Rhys finally pick up the dagger and put it back in the pack, as Liliwen's confused concern faded into an accepting nod.

"Some sleep will do you good," she said with confidence and a small, comforting smile.

Rhys chose to ignore what had just happened, which I was thankful for. He reached across me to hand the book to Liliwen, who took it with delicate fingers. She glared down at it in her hands for a moment, before flipping through the pages. "You can borrow it for a day, if you like. When you read the words yourself, it's hard to come to any other conclusion."

Liliwen nodded slowly. "Thanks. I'll read it tomorrow. You'll still be here in the evening?" I began to relax fully, leaving the memory of the dagger behind, and refocusing on the issue of whether or not we could convince Liliwen of the validity of our quest.

I nodded. "We're leaving in two mornings."

"And the person you're traveling with? She knows about all this, doesn't she?"

"Uh." I shifted in my seat, as I had been hoping that this subject wouldn't come up. "Not exactly. She's more of a guide than an accomplice."

"Accomplice," Liliwen repeated with a grin. Then the smile fell away as she considered the other words I had said. "Why haven't you told her?"

"We told her we're going to Aornadur, but she never asked us why," Rhys said with a shrug. "She's a private person, and respects when others don't want to share."

"I see," Liliwen frowned. "How far will she travel with you?"

"She'll take us at least part of the way into Durnaland," I said with a frown. "We haven't discussed all of the details. We simply know she's going to Rhea too, to a town called Ferning."

"I see," Liliwen murmured. Then she yawned and rubbed an eye, the other hand still holding onto Adelais's book. "I think I must sleep now," she said, blinking at us. She smiled softly. "I've enjoyed speaking to both of you, and I will see you tomorrow, at least to return this book."

She stood and we wished her goodnight. As she climbed the stairs on the left side of the room, heading to her second floor room, I leaned back in my chair and sighed heavily.

"Are you alright?" Rhys asked quietly, turning to look at me. I ignored his gaze and looked at the fire instead as I nodded.

"I am now. But I…I saw…Varina," I said. I frowned as I felt him staring at me, but didn't look up. "And Cassia. There were two others with them. Varina called them…the emperor and empress."

"Emperor and empress?" Rhys murmured. "Of what?"

I shook my head, still putting together the memory. "They called it the Reclaimed Kingdoms."

Rhys was silent for a moment, and I let out a deep sigh. "What were they doing?" he asked eventually.

"Varina was asking their permission to do something," I frowned as it came back to me, and then my eyes widened as I remembered fully. "To hunt me, and bring me back."

"What?" Rhys said, suddenly loud and very tense. I finally turned to stare at him. "What else did they say?" he leaned toward me, and I continued to look at him, biting the inside of my cheek as I thought over all that had been said.

"She said that she would stop at nothing…that Calliten hadn't trained me properly in order to keep me weak." The words were coming out quieter and quieter until I was whispering. But Rhys heard everything I said clearly, and the tension in his body only grew, and he looked like he was ready to jump up at a moment's notice.

"So she really is hunting you," he said, barely managing to speak above a whisper himself. "If that's true, then—"

"Then she's still following us," I said, finishing his thought.

"Maybe she wasn't able to find a ship," he said, trying to sound hopeful.

"She has access to armies. She'll find a ship," I said, shaking my head. "The best we can hope for is that she was delayed, and that she's lost our trail."

A heavy silence hung between us, and then Rhys let out a deep sigh, allowing his shoulders to relax as he leaned back in his chair, suddenly exhausted. "Don't touch that dagger anymore," he said with a weak huff of a laugh, turning his head to look at me again. "It scares me when you go into that trance." I sent him a slight smile at this.

"I won't," I promised, choosing not to point out that by touching the dagger I had just found out quite a bit about our enemy. He nodded again and leaned back in his chair, now turning his gaze to the fire with an expression of thorough exhaustion.

"You must always make things more complicated than they need to be," Rhys said, but I could hear the teasing note in his tired voice even without looking at him. "The visions, and now bringing someone else into all of this."

"It seemed the right thing to do," I mumbled. The fire danced before me, and I watched the flames lick towards the high ceiling, realizing only then how stressful the conversation had been. It had been overshadowed by the stress of the memory, but had taken a toll on my energy as well.

"Because she's from Lithe?" Rhys asked.

"Yes. Because it's her home too. And she should have hope, like we do."

Rhys was silent, and I closed my eyes as I leaned my head back against the wooden back of my chair, attempting to relax. I knew I should just go to bed, but something kept me from standing up and climbing the stairs.

"You have hope, then?" Rhys asked, surprising me. I sat up slowly and opened my eyes to look at him, and I saw him looking at me with an odd expression, one that I was too tired to try to understand.

"Yes," I said after a moment. "I wouldn't be here if I didn't."

"Where would you be?" he asked me softly. My stomach fluttered—maybe I did know his expression after all.

"I don't know. Hiding in a forest somewhere in Lithe, probably," I said. "Maybe I would try to save Catrin and Aerona." The thought came out as spoken words without me really thinking about it, and I was surprised by the sudden stab of guilt I felt. I turned away from Rhys, hoping he hadn't seen that expression on my face.

Of course, he had, though. "It's not your fault, Eira. Catrin was—she was at peace with being found."

"That's what she told us to get us to leave," I muttered, leaning my elbows on my knees and looking at the toes of my boots, peeking out from under my dark cloak.

"Even Catrin isn't that good of an actress," Rhys tried to assure me, but I was in no mood to be convinced. I found the guilt and sadness strangely comforting.

"We just left them, Rhys. And Aerona surrendered herself just for us. She was supposed to escape with us—"

"Aerona will be fine," Rhys said firmly. I bristled at his words, but I didn't know why. Some feelings that had been numbed were awakening, and I ignored them as best I could. "Catrin will be too."

"Probably," I said. "It still doesn't change what happened. After all they did for us—housed us and helped us search those books, and provided us with food…We just left them."

"We had to, Eira. Catrin wanted that—even Aerona did too—"

"Even Aerona," I echoed with a scoff. I regretted it immediately, freezing and hoping that Rhys wouldn't take note of the mocking tone of my voice.

"Why did you say it like that?" he asked. I refused to look at him, still gazing at the fire like it was who I was talking to.

"I don't know. I'm very tired."

"I know Aerona wasn't very kind to you at times, but—"

"It's not that, Rhys. I shouldn't have said anything. Of course I'm very thankful for everything Aerona did for us."

"Then what is it?"

"Nothing. I'm just tired. Not thinking straight," I snapped. I looked at him then, showing him my face so that he could see the evidence of my sleepiness in the way my eyelids were drooping. But from the way he was glaring at me, I could tell that he wasn't going to back down.

"I feel like you're lying," he said softly. It was then that I realized he was offended, not because I was potentially insulting Aerona, but because I wasn't being honest with him. I sighed, too tired to argue with him anymore.

"I like Aerona," I said honestly. "She was helpful and sacrificed so much for us. But she was also… I felt, sometimes… quite rude to me, and quite nice to you."

Rhys nodded as he gazed down at his hands folded in his lap, and I studied him for a moment, waiting for him to respond. I didn't want to tell him the whole truth—that I was jealous of Aerona and how she had been obvious about her feelings for him.

"Aerona didn't like me any more than she liked you," Rhys said after a moment, and I snorted as the words hit me. He turned to glare at me, but I could tell he was mostly surprised by the reaction.

"I'm sorry," I said, suppressing my laughter. "It's only… you're quite obtuse, Rhys."

"What?" he said, still frowning at me, turning to face me even more.

"Never mind," I sighed suddenly, realizing how little I wanted to explain to him that Aerona had feelings for him.

"No, not never mind," Rhys insisted, and I was surprised by the strength in his voice and the tension in his shoulders as he faced me, turned in his seat. I blinked, and then shook my head slightly to myself, knowing that I was too tired to lie convincingly.

"Aerona was much more fond of you than she was of me," I said, feeling my cheeks begin to heat up. "She was quite fond of you."

Rhys frowned at me, now confused by my words. "Sure, I think we became good friends before we had to leave," Rhys said slowly. I shook my head, frustrated by how blind he was.

"She fancied you," I blurted out before he could continue. His eyes widened for a moment, and he let out a short laugh.

"No," he said, now with a confused grin, like his face couldn't decide which emotion to portray. "No, I think I would have known."

"Would you?" I said, raising my eyebrows. "It was obvious to me. To Catrin as well."

"You talked to Catrin about this?" Rhys asked, the humor gone from his voice and face.

"It came up," I said. "In any case, it doesn't matter does it? We had to leave. I'm sorry that sometimes I still have bitter feelings about Aerona, but—"

"So you didn't like Aerona because she was kinder to me than she was to you?" Rhys asked slowly.

"Yes," I said. I decided not to elaborate, lest he figure out the whole truth buried in that sentence: I didn't like Aerona because she liked Rhys. It had nothing to do with the way she treated me, and everything to do with the way she treated Rhys. But there was no way he was going to get me to admit this, so I stood suddenly, momentarily overcome with a head rush. Blinking it away, I grabbed my bag from under my chair and turned back to Rhys.

"I'm going to sleep. We've been up far too late," I said. Rhys nodded slowly, and as I turned away I heard him stand up behind me.

"I still feel like you're lying about something," he said, once again in that soft voice. It felt manipulative somehow— welcoming and warm, like he knew exactly how to speak to make me want to spill my secrets to him. But I wanted nothing more than to forget my feelings for him, as much as I wanted to hide the embarrassing fact that I had been jealous because of him. I turned back to look at him, his hair almost red in the firelight, and forced a smile.

"If I am, I'll tell you the truth in the morning," I said. "I'm too tired now to say another word."

He smiled slightly, like he was too tired to use his whole face. "Fine," he said, then came to stand beside me.

"Did Runa show you where the rooms are?" I asked, blinking up at his face. Still with that slight smile, he nodded, and led the way up the stairs.

17

An Exchanging of Truths

Early the next morning, Runa, Rhys, and I emerged from the inn, into a busy street filled with people, carts, oxen, and horses. The smells of the city were nearly overwhelming then, animals and spoiled food, mixed with the scent of fresh baked bread and crisp morning air. Runa led us through the chaotic roads, winding through crowds of people with ease, and Rhys and I struggled to keep up. Eventually, we arrived at a different marketplace than the one we had seen near the gate the day before. I couldn't quite tell where I was after so many turns down different roads, but it felt much closer to the center of the city.

We allowed Runa to make most of the decisions regarding food supplies, as she knew much better than us how often we would be able to stop in towns on the rest of our journey. Dried meats, some cheeses, and a bit of bread were loaded into our leather bags, and Runa was satisfied with our supply before noon.

One thing caught my eye in the marketplace that was not on the list. I paused at the booth that housed parchment, quills, ink, and other items necessary for writing, as a certain quill shimmered in the sunlight in a way I had never seen before. The feather was a beautiful iridescent green, and the pen was a shining silver. The owner of the stand, an old man with wispy white hair and deep wrinkles, greeted me with a cheerful hello. I barely managed a hello in response as I continued to appraise the quill, knowing that it wasn't necessary, but wanting it nonetheless.

"It's beautiful," Rhys said from over my shoulder.

"It's a waste of money," I said, turning away and attempting to immerse myself back in the crowd. But Rhys didn't budge when I turned to face him, his eyes looked at the quill with thoughtful seriousness. "Come on," I insisted.

"You have quite a bit of money on you still," Rhys said. "Just ask the shopkeeper how much it is."

"It doesn't matter how much it is," I said as I folded my arms and frowned up at him. He met my eyes and smiled, apparently finding something humorous in my countenance. "I refuse to be stupid with my money."

"Fine," Rhys said with a shrug before sidestepping me, and asking the old man how much the quill cost in rough Tamanian. Before I knew what was happening, Rhys was pulling coins from his own pouch, handing them to the shopkeeper, and picking up the quill, some paper, and a small bottle of ink. My mouth hung open when he turned back to face me, holding these items out to me like an offering.

"If you don't want to be stupid with your money, then I'll be stupid with mine," he said with a grin.

"Rhys," I said, shaking my head. "I don't need…"

"Sometimes it's okay to get the things you want, not just the things you need," he said gently.

I took the items from him after another moment of hesitation, and turned the quill in my hands, watching how the filaments danced with color in the light. The base color was an emerald green, but other flashes of blue, yellow, and purple would appear at the right angles.

"You know," I said as I continued to twist it between my fingers. "Your money used to be my money."

Rhys laughed and ran a hand through his hair. "And I hope that you know…that this was not a stupid use of that money. Not to me," he said. Something in his voice forced me to look at him, and I felt my face heat up when I saw the softness in his eyes as he looked at me. He held my gaze even as he continued. "Besides, it's meant to be yours. It's green. Like your eyes."

I huffed, something between a scoff and a laugh. "That's ridiculous. This feather has a million colors in it. My eyes are just green."

Rhys shook his head, suddenly serious. "No, definitely not 'just green,'" he insisted.

We studied each other for a few moments, the quill forgotten in my hand, when Runa appeared beside us, nearly making me jump with her sudden appearance.

"What are you doing? I thought I lost you," she huffed, looking between us. Whatever had kept us staring at each other was gone, and I placed my new items in my bag while Rhys tried to explain.

"We got distracted by these quills," Rhys said, gesturing to the stall behind us. Runa glanced at the quills on display and then shrugged, turning her attention back to me and Rhys.

"Well. Do you want to walk around a bit more or head back to the inn?" Runa asked as she adjusted one of the straps of the heavy bags on her shoulders. She didn't seem too uncomfortable, though. I considered the question. The weather was fairly nice. It was cold but the sun was out and the sky was clear save for some wispy clouds being pulled by the wind high above us. This part of the town seemed nicer than the part we were staying in, with fewer offensive smells meeting my nose. As we had made our way to the market, I had caught glimpses of the castle, the capital building of West Tamania, between the slanted roofs. The narrow gray spires topped with gold figures reaching for the sky, and glittering windows on the towers—I was intrigued by the architecture.

"How far away is the castle?" I asked Runa. She stared at me blankly for a moment, before frowning.

"Grundar's Keep?" she asked. I returned her question with a blank stare, and she smiled. "The monarch's home. It's less than a mile from here, actually. The closer you get to it, the nicer the streets are."

"I'd like to see it up close," I said.

Runa shrugged, like it was an odd request. "Okay. We can't go inside, though."

"I wouldn't think so," I frowned. She laughed.

"I didn't want to mislead you if that's what you were thinking. Come on, it's this way," she said, leading us back through the marketplace, the colorful tents passing us on either side. Runa walking swiftly, dodging people with quick agile movements.

Once we were out of the market and walking down a residential street, with small but well-built stone houses and angled roofs, Runa slowed slightly, and fell in step beside me, our feet hitting the stone-paved ground in unison. Rhys was slightly behind us.

"Why do you want to see the keep?" she asked me, eyeing me with curiosity. I smiled and hoped the request wasn't truly strange.

"I thought it looked beautiful from far away," I said.

"It is," she agreed. "But most castles are, aren't they? The nobles like to show their wealth."

"The castle in my province wasn't so grand," I murmured.

"This is the home of the king, not a Benadur," Runa said, making a face as she turned right abruptly down a smaller side street, and I ran a few steps to catch up with her. "Of course this is more grand."

I shrugged. "Still. It's nice to enjoy beautiful things, isn't it?"

Runa didn't seem to have a response to that, and I got the feeling that she wanted to argue a bit. Rhys walked silently behind us, close enough to hear what we were saying but he didn't interject.

We reached the outer gates of the keep a few minutes later, tall iron bars keeping us from entering the grounds. Still, it was enough to peek through them, at the wide brick road that led to a massive set of stairs. At the top of the stairs were large silver-plated double doors, and Runa told us they were the main doors to the keep. Guards lined the fence that kept us out, and ignored us as we simply took in the sight of the keep. At least Rhys and I did; Runa stood slightly behind us, her arms folding with impatience.

I thought it had been worth the short walk. The pale gray walls rose high above us, ending in pointed spires and towers, the gold figures at the top now clearly feminine—the Sky Queen, most likely. They glowed in the bright sunlight, shining against the vibrant blue backdrop of the sky. The keep must have been ten times the size of the Benaty, and four times as tall.

"Are you satisfied?" Runa asked after a couple of minutes, clearly bored. I turned to her with a smile, not at all put off by her attitude, and she blinked at me, clearly surprised by this reaction.

"Yes, thank you," I said. Rhys turned as well, and nodded. Runa smiled at us with an odd look in her eyes.

"You two are strange," she said, leading us back onto a main road that led away from the keep. It was busier than the area around the fence, and seemed to be another merchant district, this one with many stores selling rare and valuable goods, like glass sculptures, paintings, and musical instruments. The people were well dressed, with bright colors and rich fabrics. The gowns were more ornate with lace and embroidery, the suits all seemed to be cut with shimmery trims of silver or gold. Runa continued talking as we passed these shoppers and sellers, ignoring their expressions at our more ratty and worn travel clothes. "I don't see how the keep is all that interesting. Impressive, I guess. But I feel like you could have stared at it for another twenty minutes," she grumbled as she walked with long strides beside me.

"While I'm escaping my home, I might as well enjoy the scenery," I said. I meant for it to be a joke, but it came out in a fairly serious tone. She glanced at me, before looking back at the street in front of her, moving swiftly to her left to avoid a pair of shoppers chatting in the middle of the road. I followed her as she replied.

"I just don't know how to have fun," she said, flashing me a grin, and I smiled back. "I don't mean to be so negative. Perhaps I should try to enjoy the scenery as well."

I laughed, a quiet, subdued noise. Then I shrugged, even though she wasn't looking at me. "It wouldn't hurt," I said eventually.

»«

We returned to the inn a bit after noon, and as soon as we were in the door, Liliwen bounded up to Rhys and me, Adelais's book held in her hands. She blinked when saw Runa come in through the door behind us, and quickly put the book down, clearly remembering that Runa didn't know about the Sacreds or Adelais.

"Hello," Liliwen said, grinning widely as Runa came to stand next to us, wearing a suspicious frown at her appearance. "I'm Liliwen," she said directly to Runa. "I spoke to Eira and Rhys last night."

"Oh. You're from Lithe, aren't you?" Runa said, her frown smoothing away to blankness. "Pleasure to meet you."

"You as well. They said you're guiding them through to Durnaland."

"Yes. I'll be going all the way to Rhea, but Aornadur is nearly on the way, so…" She tilted her head as she appraised Liliwen, who was still smiling despite Runa's chilly persona. "Did you escape the Syrthiaid as well?" she asked, before stepping out of the way of the door; we all followed suit, in case someone needed to get past us, and we ended up against the wall, beside one of the windows that looked out onto the street.

"Yes," Liliwen said quickly. "My city was one of the first ones attacked after Maenynys. I was lucky to get out."

"My condolences," Runa said with a small, formal bow. I frowned at the gesture, which seemed oddly sentimental coming from her. Liliwen smiled once again.

"Thank you," she said.

"Are you staying in Fjall, then?" Runa asked, shifting one of the bags on her shoulders slightly. She had been carrying them for a while, and at this point she was probably dying to set them down.

"No. I have distant relatives in Rhea. I'm hoping they'll take me in. I won't know until I get there, though."

"Do you want to travel with us?" Runa asked with a frown. An awkward silence fell over us, and I felt my mouth open in surprise. Of course, the thought had crossed my mind. Liliwen was nice enough, and was traveling the same way as us. There was safety in numbers, wasn't there? But I hadn't expected Runa to need no convincing, and to actually suggest the idea herself.

"Oh, well, I—" Liliwen stuttered, blinking at Runa in surprise. "I'll have to think about it," she said after a moment, glancing at Rhys and I for just a second. She was tense, feeling uncomfortable, and I wished Runa hadn't put her on the spot.

But Runa only shrugged again. "Let us know. We'll leave tomorrow morning. Listen, these bags are getting heavy. I'm going to go set them in my room," she said, and without waiting for a response, she hefted them by their straps further up her shoulders, and set off across the room to the staircase.

As her footsteps fell away, Liliwen turned to us, looking conflicted. "I…I read this book. As well as I could, anyway," she said, holding Adelais's book out to Rhys. He took it as I asked the first question that came to my mind.

"And? Do you believe us?"

She gazed at me levelly for a moment before smiling, giving nothing away. "Let's sit down by the fire again. It's too drafty here by the door," she said, and Rhys and I agreed, quickly finding a group of three cushioned chairs on one end of the firepit, far away from the other patrons lounging around the room. The fire was a relief. I was growing so used to the chilly weather that I didn't even know when I was cold anymore, until the warmth of the flames hit me.

"So?" Rhys asked as we settled into our seats, formed into a little, huddled triangle.

"Yes, I think you're right. At least, it isn't a bad idea to seek out the Himminir," she said with a small nod.

"What an endorsement," I said, and she laughed lightly.

"You don't need my endorsement, do you?"

"Is that why you don't want to travel with us?" Rhys asked, frowning slightly. I wondered if he was offended that she hadn't seemed interested in joining us and Runa.

But she shook her head, the two small braids on either side of her face swinging delicately. "No. It's just—you two are on a mission, and Runa doesn't even know about it—"

"Why should that matter?" I asked.

She shrugged one shoulder, looking away from me for a moment as she decided how to respond. "It doesn't, I suppose. I just find it strange you won't tell her."

"I mean no offense," Rhys said slowly, "but we just met you last night."

"I know." She frowned. "You two were the ones who brought all of this stuff up in the first place. I just wanted a nice conversation with fellow Remisians."

"I'm sorry if we made you uncomfortable," I said. I thought it best to distance ourselves from Liliwen before the conversation turned any more awkward. "I wanted you to know, since it's your home too. But…well, it wasn't prudent of me to try and pull you into this."

Liliwen sighed, a bit heavily, and looked at the floorboards between us, her eyebrows deeply furrowed. "I'm glad you told me," she said after a moment, still not looking at me. "It's nice to have hope."

I smiled slightly, glad at her words but still concerned about her heavy manner. "It's hard for all of us right now, to see Lithe the way it is, knowing it's just going to get worse. If you want to join us…you wouldn't have to climb Aornadur with us, but at least you wouldn't be alone. And we…we care about the same things, don't we?" she looked up at me, her blue eyes wide with a complexity of emotions.

Just as she opened her mouth to speak, someone appeared next to me, and pulled a chair to sit with us, legs scraping along the floor. I looked to my right to see Runa sitting heavily in the chair she had just brought over, looking at each of us with her inscrutable expression.

"What are we talking about?" she asked, leaning forward slightly. I glanced at Liliwen, and then Rhys, and sighed. I turned to Rhys and studied him for a moment, wondering if he could read my thoughts.

He frowned at me. "You want to tell her," he said. I sat back a bit in surprise. He could read my thoughts, after all.

"Yes," I nodded.

"Tell who what?" Runa asked, tone impatient. "Fine," Rhys sighed. "It has to happen sometime anyway."

"What does?" Runa said, glaring at us.

"You never asked us why we're going to Aornadur," I said as I turned to look at her.

She frowned at me, a bit of suspicion in her eyes. "It's none of my business," she said.

"We think you should know, anyway," Rhys said, and I was glad for his help. Liliwen simply sat and watched the exchange, and it felt a bit odd to have her present for this.

"We're going to speak with the Himminir, because they can help us stop the Syrthiaid," I said. Then I let out a deep breath, emptying my lungs. Runa stared at me for a few moments, and then Rhys, her face blank as usual, her frown gone.

"Why do you think that?" she asked eventually.

"Think what?" I asked, frowning.

"That they can help with the Syrthiaid." A small frown was beginning to form on her face as my words sank in.

"We have this book," Rhys said as he pulled Adelais's writings from his bag, so recently returned to him. He passed it to Runa who frowned at the little book as she held it in her hands, not bothering to open up the cover. "It's by a prophet. He predicted this rising of people with special powers and their coming together, and notes that the Himminir are deeply connected to them. He calls them the Sacreds."

"Sacreds," Runa repeated, still looking down at the book. "So you two... You weren't just escaping?" she said, now openly frowning at us.

"No," I said after a moment. "Ever since we had to leave Caergarth, this was our only option. We decided shortly after we met you that we had to try to reach Aornadur."

"And you told Liliwen because...?" She stopped talking abruptly, looking at the girl in question with a confused expression.

"Because it's her home too. And I was very tired last night, and I thought she deserved to know. I don't know if I was thinking clearly, but..." I trailed off, rubbing one of my temples. I wasn't sure how this conversation was going.

"I'm glad they told me," Liliwen said, speaking for the first time since Runa sat down. "I read the book, and I agree with them. This is the only glimmer of hope I've seen since the Syrthiaid invaded Lithe."

Runa swung her head to glare and Rhys and I suddenly. "Well, why didn't you tell me?" she demanded, taking me aback.

"What?" I said.

"Why weren't you honest about your reasons? Did you think I would tell you not to?" she asked. I realized she was offended, which I really hadn't expected at all.

"No, it's just... When you heard we were going to Aornadur, you told us we were insane. We thought you would just think we were even more insane if we told you why," Rhys said, using his most calming tone. It didn't seem to work on Runa, though, as she continued to glare at us.

"So why now? You told a stranger and you felt guilty?" she asked. I was beginning to get a bit offended, especially by that accusation, but I was careful to hide it.

"We're setting off into the mountains, into the rebel side of Tamania. We know it's more dangerous," I said. "We want to be open with you. And we want you to be able to trust us."

Runa shrugged again. "I didn't know there was any reason to not trust you until now," she said, pursing her lips slightly. Then she sighed. "It's fine. I'm not going to get in the way, if that's what you're worried about."

"Well...thank you," I said, glancing at Rhys. An uncomfortable silence followed, and Liliwen cleared her throat, but didn't speak.

"So this book," Runa said, finally breaking the silence and holding up Adelais's book slightly. "You want me to read it?" She looked between me and Rhys, ignoring Liliwen.

"You don't have to," I said, unable to hide my frown. "We only wanted to show you the reason we're doing this."

"I'll read it," she said, looking down at the book like she hadn't heard what I had just said. "I'm curious now. I would think I know you two well enough at this point to know that you're not entirely insane."

"Thank you," Rhys said in a flat tone. She grinned at him, but it was a tired smile and didn't quite reach her eyes. "I'm sorry. It's a bit hard for me to understand."

"What is?" he asked.

"Wanting to…to fight. There are a lot of places you could call home, you know. You could settle anywhere in Aorlanda. I wouldn't recommend Tamania, but the eastern countries are nice enough," she said. There was something in her voice— a bit of hopefulness.

"Lithe is our home," I said, leaning past Rhys to fix her with an honest look. "We have information that could help save it. It's our duty."

"Duty for a country that lied to you your entire life?" Runa said, an edge in her voice.

"Regardless, all of our loved ones are there. If not for the country itself, then for them, we have to try," Rhys said.

"Lied about what?" Liliwen asked, and I felt my stomach sink. Runa stared at her, mouth open slightly as she had been about to reply to Rhys, and she shut it tightly, realizing the situation she had just created.

"You…you haven't heard, then," I said, already exhausted. How many things would we have to tell Liliwen that would sound unbelievable to her? I wasn't going to back down from explaining the truth about Eosiaids and their birth to her, but it was going to take the rest of my energy.

"Well, I don't know if I have, since I don't know what we're talking about," Liliwen responded with a tense, irritated smile.

"About Eosiaids and their parents," I continued.

"I've gathered they have different roles here than in Remisia, but I haven't figured out what they do yet," she said with a frown. "I'm still working on my Tamanian. To be honest, I've only had a few conversations since I've gotten here, mostly with other Remisians."

"I'll understand if you don't want to believe us," I said, closing my eyes for a moment, trying to approach the subject as carefully as possible—if one more person said or implied that I was insane that day, I really would lose my mind. "The Remisian Empire has been covering up the truth about Eosiaids for a thousand years at least. When one is born, their parents die. The bodies are disposed of, and the child is given to an Eosiaid couple of childbearing age. There is usually enough time to fake a pregnancy, and, well…create the illusion of magical blood."

Liliwen stared at me, giving away no emotion. Her brows began to furrow slightly, but then she shook her head, and her brow was smooth again. "That doesn't make any sense, and you know it," she said.

"It's the truth," Runa broke in with a harsh glare. "And everyone knows it here. All of Linra knows it to be true, outside of Remisia. Why do you think there are so few foreigners in Remisia? If they were allowed in, they would bring the truth with them."

Liliwen stared at each of us in turn, her mouth open slightly. "This is…absurd," she said, barely above a whisper. "What possible reason would they have to do this?" she asked, her tone now demanding.

"The illusion of unity. Of divine right," Runa said, as though the answer was obvious. "Someone born to a couple already in power is more deserving of that power than a person with dead parents. Especially a person who caused the death of their parents just by existing."

"What?" Liliwen said, but it was obvious that she wasn't asking for clarification.

"Magic is a blessing and a curse—at least, that's how most people see it," I said quietly. "A long time ago, one of the first Emperors wanted the people to forget about the curse. The system was put in place to hide the deaths, to create these fake bloodlines, and over the generations, the truth became less obvious, invisible, and then forgotten."

"Eosiaids are born so rarely, it isn't too difficult to prepare for their births," Runa added.

Liliwen shook her head, leaned back in her chair and folded her arms, glaring at us with defiance. "I have no reason to believe this. There is no evidence."

My jaw clenched as I thought of my mother's journal, the evidence clear in her later entries. The last thing I wanted to do was reveal myself to be an Eosiaid, so I had no plans to speak of the journal to Liliwen. The evidence was just so obvious to me, and it angered me that I couldn't share it with her.

But Runa snorted, and gestured at the inn around us. "Look around. Who is in power here? Commoners. The kings and queens and nobles and magistrates—all commoners. And where are the mages, the Drekligr? Hidden in the forests and the cheap towns, pushed from society. As soon as one is discovered, some helpless baby—well, oftentimes relatives feel guilt and take them in, only to reject them once their magic emerges as a child. Others leave them in the snow to die."

Liliwen stared at her, and even Rhys and I were shocked by these morbid details. "Those who live to adulthood have to find creative ways to support themselves. It comes down to a choice: hide the magic, suppress that part of themselves, or leave civilization. Those who hide themselves often go mad eventually, and they are called shadows. Those who leave the cities and towns and roam the forests, often becoming robbers or corrupt tinkers, they're called wanderers." She told us this like it wasn't ghastly to hear. It was then that I realized how Runa felt about Drekligr—she hated them just as much as everyone else did in Aorlanda.

Liliwen leaned forward and rubbed her temples, clearly overwhelmed by all of this information. "I need some time to think over all of this," she sighed, staring off into space, somewhere beyond us.

"We understand," I said with a nod. "If you didn't hear it from us, you would have found out soon enough."

She nodded absently, like she wasn't really hearing me. "I think I need to rest for a bit. Will you be here for dinner?" she asked, looking at me with weary eyes.

"Yes, we'll eat here," I said.

"I'll join you for dinner, then," she said, before standing, giving us a small, limp wave, and stepping quickly to the staircase.

I let out a heavy sigh, and Rhys nodded like I had said something he agreed with. Runa frowned at us.

"What?" she said.

"That was a bit of an exhausting conversation," I said.

"At least she knows now," Runa said, shifting in her seat slightly to lean back. She tilted her head back against the chair and took a deep breath. "Everyone deserves to know the truth, don't they?"

»«

That night we sat around a small square table with bowls of stew provided by the inn, and I looked up from my bowl when Liliwen appeared and sat down on the opposite side from me with her own meal, between Runa and Rhys.

"Alright. I believe you," she said, stirring her stew once. Then she dropped the spoon and looked up at us with a serious expression. "And I want to join you on your travels."

I was surprised at the relief I felt at her words. I hadn't realized how strongly I had wanted her to come with us. I grinned.

"Great. It will be safer for you. Like I said, Runa is going all the way to Rhea, so—" But Liliwen cut me off with a shake of her head, those little braids waving in front of her face again.

"No. I'm going with you. To the Himminir. The Inherents," she said, her voice so strong and aggressive, it took me aback for a moment.

"What—really?" Rhys said.

"Yes. If it's alright with you two," she said with a curt nod. Runa stared at her with an open mouth.

"You're all mad," she said. Then she shrugged slightly, and took a large spoonful of soup. I glared at her, but was still caught on Liliwen's surprising decision.

361

"Are you sure?" I asked her, leaning towards her slightly, the steam of my soup warming my face. Even the delicious smell and my own hunger couldn't distract me.

"Yes. We're the only three Lithians who know about this, and I want to help any way I can. I won't be able to live with myself if I don't," she said. Though I had known her less than a day, her face was unusually stern, absent of the humor I had often seen in her.

"You might not live if you do, though," Runa muttered over her stew, and I shushed her.

"You're welcome to join us," I said after a moment, grinning despite Liliwen's serious manner. "But I hope you know that...that this wasn't our goal. I really just wanted you to know the truth. To have some hope."

Her glare melted and she smiled softly as she nodded. "I know. And I'm grateful for that. But I'm here now, and I want nothing more than to do what I can to help our home. If this is all I can do...then I'll do it."

Even Runa didn't have a quip for that, and Rhys and I simply nodded. There was a short silence, and then Liliwen laughed lightly, back to her humorous self.

"Let's not dwell on the sad parts for too long. We can enjoy our dinner, can't we? And then tomorrow, the road stretches before us."

"Into cold, harsh mountains," Runa added, pointing her spoon at Liliwen. "So enjoy this hot meal while you can."

Runa's words had an effect on me, and I savored every bite.

18

The Windfjall Mountains

Though the sun was bright and warm the next morning, it did little against the harsh and cold wind that whipped through the city streets, and as we rode to the eastern gate, we all pulled our furs and cloaks tightly around our faces and necks, in vain attempts to protect us.

We rode in a line, Runa in the front, then Liliwen behind her, followed by me, with Rhys in the back. Liliwen's horse was a beautiful black gelding with large white markings on his flank—very striking. He was also the mellowest of the horses, the only one who wasn't protesting the early ride into the cold morning with annoyed snorts and flicking ears.

Outside the gates, the ubiquitous stone road stretched across the gently rolling icy land, straight towards the Windfjall Mountains. Runa assured us that the road through it consisted of gentle switchbacks and an easy pass through the peaks, but the jagged, snow-covered formation was intimidating nonetheless. The first day, at least, would just be crossing the last bit of valley, and we would reach the foothills just before nightfall.

The ride was oddly silent, even as I rode side by side with Liliwen once outside the city, the dull brown and pale green landscape passing us on either side. The wind had died down only slightly, and we were still huddled in our cloaks. I wished for conversation as a distraction, but I wasn't sure what to say to her. She seemed more outgoing than me in general, and I wished she would look over at me, riding beside her, and say something—anything.

Eventually, I decided to break the silence by saying the first thing that came to mind. "Your horse is beautiful," I blurted out, and she looked at me in surprise before smiling.

"Thank you. I bought him in Fjall just a few days before I met you. A hefty purchase, but...I knew I would need him. His name is Sindri."

"He seems of good stock," I said. I really knew very little about horses, but Sindri was obviously calm, strong, and obedient, all wonderful qualities in a horse. Liliwen nodded, leaning forward to pet his neck once before sitting back up.

"I'm very impressed with him so far. I was going to set out soon anyway for Rhea, even though I was quite liking Fjall," she said, looking ahead, where Runa and Freya were riding a few yards ahead of us.

"You did?" I asked, a bit surprised.

She nodded. "I hadn't been in such a busy city before. I've been to Maenynys, of course, but...Fjall must be twice as big, at least."

"Hmm," I said. "I visited Maenynys when I was very young, and I don't remember it well. It felt massive, though—I remember that much."

"And how did you like Fjall?" she asked me, sounding genuinely curious.

I smiled and gave a small shrug. "I liked it well enough. But I wouldn't want to stay there for too long." Liliwen nodded, as though she understood what I was saying.

I frowned at her, wondering what she was thinking. "I thought you liked it there—that you would have stayed longer."

"I would have," she agreed with a small nod. "But that doesn't mean it's where I want to be."

I knew what she was saying then. "I want to go back too," I said softly. "But it's not the same right now."

"I know. I saw the soldiers invade my town," she said. She was subdued too; like neither of us wanted to be having this conversation, but neither of us could stop. "Riding with you—it feels like this is impossible. But it's also the only thing I can think of doing. I don't want to just…run away."

I glanced at her, riding with a tall posture and serious forward gaze, and admired her. "You came around to the idea much faster than I did," I admitted. She turned to look at me in surprise, and then frowned at me.

"What do you mean?" she asked. "I thought this was your idea."

"No. I didn't want to do this initially. I thought it was insane and I just wanted to go home. To Nefyn." My voice was soft, too emotional. I cleared my throat and continued, trying to be more casual. "But the Syrthiaid had put out a warrant for my arrest, and we were almost captured by a member of the Syrthiaid herself in Gruddws. Runa saved us—that's how we met her."

"Oh," Liliwen said quietly. "I had no idea. A warrant?" she said, frowning at Runa's back with thoughtful eyes. "Why?"

I chewed on my lip for a moment, feeling that I had made a mistake by mentioning that. "I had escaped after meeting some of the Syrthiaid when they invaded Nefyn. I met two of them—I suppose that made me dangerous. One of them followed me all the way to Tan y Mor and nearly captured me twice."

"Do you think there's a warrant for me too?" she mused, sounding slightly entertained by the idea. I felt relief that she accepted my little lie, and that I had avoided making her suspicious of the truth—that I was an Eosiaid, and they hadn't wanted me to escape for that reason.

"Maybe," I said, sounding more cheerful than I should have, but Liliwen didn't seem to mind or notice.

The silence that fell between us was much more comfortable to me this time, but Liliwen interrupted it soon enough.

"This does seem rather insane, doesn't it?" she said. I knew she wasn't looking at me, and it wasn't too serious of a question. I kept looking forward at the ever-growing mountains glowing in the late morning sun, and nodded.

"It might be. But so is the existence of the Syrthiaid. The further we travel, the more I realize how…inevitable this is."

"Inevitable?" Her tone was doubtful, but I didn't mind.

"Yes, it…it seems fitting. Some mythical beings are destroying Remisia, and we want to stop them. Where else can we go, but…one of the most mythical places on Linra? To meet these people that no living person has met?" I shook my head at my own words, glad that I had said them out loud. "Sometimes I think I can feel destiny."

To my surprise, she laughed. I looked over at her, not offended by the little outburst, but she immediately looked guilty, and smiled at me sheepishly. "I'm sorry," she said, shaking her head slightly, as though trying to shake away the laughter. "Every few minutes I realize what we're doing, and my body doesn't know how to react to it. This time it laughed." She let out a sigh, a tired one, even though the day wasn't yet half over. "I'm glad I'm here," she said after a moment. And I smiled.

"I'm glad you're here too."

»«

Just as the sun set behind us, the snow turning pink and gold in the fading light still barely peeking over the shallow mountains in the west, Runa led us off the road to a rocky outcrop. We had been riding through the foothills for about an hour, winding through little valleys and gulches, and patches of snow were becoming more and more common. No snow stuck to the large stones and outcrops that dotted the land, slightly warmed in the sun, and Runa found the perfect one to set up a camp on. I knew the rock would cool into the night, but we were able to find enough branches from the nearby shrubs to light a fire, and I allowed myself to be pleased with the warmth for as long as I had it. I was also thankful to not have to sleep in the snow or on the mostly muddy ground that surrounded the rock. The gray surface was flat and smooth, and though it wasn't a bed in an inn, I was happy to settle for it.

Runa passed around dried meat, bread, and cheese, and we chatted about the ride thus far, and Runa detailed how the next couple days would go as we scaled the mountain. She reiterated that it wasn't terribly difficult, and the horses would be able to navigate the road just fine.

"It will get colder, though," she said with a grim-set mouth as she glared at the fire. "You can try to mentally prepare, but soon enough we'll be sleeping in the snow whether or not you want to."

I sighed. "For how many nights?" I asked.

Runa thought for a moment, now frowning up at the star-speckled sky, shining with an intense brightness on us. "Maybe five, maybe more. I don't know how far the snow line goes down the other side of the range. It's summer, though. So probably not too far."

"Well, that's not bad," Rhys said with a weak smile, trying his hardest to be positive.

"It really isn't, but I know you all aren't used to the snow," Runa huffed, stoking the fire absentmindedly with an extra branch. Embers flew into the sky, dancing into the dark expanse above us.

"We get snow in Lithe," I muttered, taking another bite of bread.

Runa shot me a look. "For a week or so in January, right? It's not the same and you know it."

"You're acting like we've never seen it before," I said. I laughed a little, hoping she knew I was just messing with her. I realized she might have been taking me completely seriously when she relaxed at my laugh. "I know it's much worse here, but we can deal with it," I said.

She nodded with a small smile. "Just want you to be prepared. I'm not attempting to insult your survival skills."

We went to sleep soon after, our bedrolls provided insulation from the now cold rock beneath us, all wrapped in our cloaks and all of the furs and blankets we were carrying. The horses dozed a few feet away, tied to a small but sturdy bush, and the stars moved across the sky with their slow and steady pace. I stayed awake for a while after the others were asleep, and watched the stars, and the gibbous moon, and felt a light wind brush chilly fingers against my face, the only part of my body exposed to the air.

I knew it would get worse, but I knew that I could handle it. Just like the stars continued on their path with inevitability, so I would continue on mine.

»«

The snow began to cover the road the next day, though it had already fallen days before. Even though the sun was out, the layer of glittery ice didn't melt, as the air temperature was well below freezing. It was uncomfortable, but Runa had picked out enough furs and blankets of good quality that the bitter cold was bearable at least.

The road did become a bit steep as the switchbacks climbed up the cliffs and edges of the mountains, but the horses handled it just fine as we traveled in mostly a single file line. And while I was surviving the cold conditions, I was a bit on edge and had no energy to speak. The icy road wound before us and I concentrated on its passing, wanting nothing more than for the next few days to pass quickly.

By the end of that day, the snow was ubiquitous and thick, and we spread our bedrolls over a flat expanse beside the road with a sense of resignation. Runa was able to find enough dry branches to light a fire in a ring of stones, and we huddled around it as we ate silently.

"I know I can be quiet myself, but you three are unusually mute," Runa said suddenly, once we had finished eating and were laying out our cloaks to sleep under. I frowned at her, surprised by the irritation in her voice. She was sitting on her bedroll across the fire from me, looking at us with an odd, questioning look.

"What?" I said, only then realizing how tense my jaw was.

"You haven't spoken all day," she said.

I glanced at Rhys and Liliwen, surprised that Runa was upset by this.

"There hasn't been much to talk about," Rhys said after a short pause.

"That's ridiculous," Runa snapped. "We're climbing a mountain range so you three can try to find some magical monks—"

"That's a bit reductive," I muttered, finally sitting cross-legged on my bedroll and pulling my cloak over my legs.

"—who are supposed to help you defeat some magical despots. And you say you have nothing to talk about?"

"Okay, you're right," Liliwen sighed, before glaring at Runa. "But we're cold. Right?" She glanced at me and Rhys for confirmation.

I nodded. "I don't have energy, Runa. It's freezing. All I can think about is getting out of the mountains." Runa huffed, but Rhys began talking before she could argue with me.

"It's true. We're not used to this," he said, his cloak and blanket wrapped tightly around his shoulders, concealing everything but his face, his nose bright red from the cold wind.

"We're still in the mountains for at least four more days," Runa said, glaring at each of us in turn, the fire flickering in her stern eyes. "You're all going to be miserable until then?" she asked.

I sighed as I lay down, burrowing under the furs and searching for warmth. "Yes," I said. "Goodnight, Runa."

She muttered something in response, but I easily ignored her as sleep overtook me.

»«

The next day was much the same, and the day after that. Runa grew used to our silence, which I was still surprised had bothered her for some reason.

On the third day of the climb, the sun still shining brightly and illuminating the banks of snow that piled high on either side of the road, she turned round to look at the three of us following her, and slowed Freya until we were all riding quite close together.

"The pass is controlled by the West Tamanian army. There's a small chance I'll know someone stationed there right now. Either way, we'll find out from them the safest way through East Tamania."

"Safest way?" I repeated.

"Well, the war is slowed a bit right now—the East Tamanian forces took a hit last year that they haven't fully recovered from, and they're attacking infrequently and with caution. Still, the soldiers at the pass will know if there are any areas to avoid."

"Right," Rhys said, looking as cold and downtrodden as I felt. It was like some of his life force had left him, and though I knew I looked the same way, I couldn't help but feel dismayed at the sight. "And when will we reach the pass?"

"Within hours," Runa said, and that had me perking up a bit.

"And then we'll start downhill?" I asked, with the most emotion I had heard in my voice for days.

"Yes," Runa said with a small, rare smile. "Come on, then."

Though I still didn't feel like talking, as I was concentrating on not feeling the cold make my bones ache, I watched the road as it twisted before us with suspense, wondering what turn would bring us to the pass.

It wasn't the sight of the pass that alerted me to its presence first, but the sound. High boulders stood to our right, and above and past them I heard the low murmur of voices in the distance. Runa said nothing but urged Freya slightly, and we followed at that quicker pace. When we rounded the next switchback, we saw the road had been cleared of snow and the hard, light brown icy soil was exposed to the sun. It led straight up a shallow incline, at the top of which we could see the undefined distant figures of soldiers and makeshift tents, collected under a few towering pine trees. The land was flat up there, and relief coursed through me at the sight. We had finally reached Rodljost Pass.

The soldiers noticed us only a second after we turned onto that last stretch of road, and quickly formed a wall six people wide across the road. When we were a couple hundred feet away, Runa dismounted and we did the same, leading our horses by the reins to meet the people standing in our way.

"Halt," one said in Tamanian, once we were close enough to hear her clearly. Two long golden braids descended from underneath her silver helmet. All six of these soldiers wore the same style helmet, rounded with a short visor, and the same armor: metal plates with thick wool and fur underneath for warmth. And each person's right hand rested on the hilt of a sword at their side, a casual threat. "State your—" the golden-haired woman was saying, but then I saw her blink at Runa, her stern and bored expression turning into one of surprise. Her eyebrows raised and mouth open slightly, she blinked again. "Runa?"

Runa grinned. "I was hoping you would be here," she said with a small laugh. "It's been a while, Einarra."

"Indeed," Einarra said, clearly not recovered from Runa's appearance. Then she looked at me, Rhys, and Liliwen, and a slight frown returned to her face. "And they are?"

"Friends," Runa said. "I'm guiding them to Rhea." I was surprised she had decided to lie about our destination, but I knew better than to let that show in my expression. I kept a blank face, the same one I had been wearing for most of the ride up to the pass.

"I see. Well, please rest for a moment before you continue on your way," Einarra said, gesturing at the collection of low canvas tents behind her, and the other soldiers moved to the side of the road, allowing us to pass. I realized Einarra must have been a leader or captain of some sort.

"Thank you. If it's not too much trouble, we would actually like to rest here for the night." I frowned at this, but saw that the sun was beginning to lower to the western horizon, and I found myself agreeing with Runa that some shelter— even just tents—for one night would be welcomed, and it wouldn't set us back too much time.

"Of course. We'll have tents set up for you right away," Einarra said, before nodding at two of her soldiers, who immediately set off back towards the tents. "Davar, Raegar, and Astrid will care for your horses." The last three soldiers stepped forward, and a young woman with red hair tied into a ponytail below her helmet took Nimue's reins from me, leading her off down the road, along with Cai, Freya, and Sindri. Einarra smiled at us, a genuine and warm grin, her emerald eyes glowing a bit in the afternoon sun. "Follow me. Would you like some stew? We have it left over from the midday meal."

"We would be grateful," Runa said with a nod, and Einarra led us up the rest of the road and into the camp. We began passing between the tents, eyed by the occasional soldier with curiosity as they paused in whatever activity they were doing, until we arrived at a tent that was large enough for a person to stand up in, in line with the other ones. Einarra held back the flap and beckoned for us to enter. Inside we saw a low table in the center of the space, with a collection of pillows on the ground around it. In the corner was a bedroll piled with blankets and furs, and besides those few pieces of furniture, the tent was empty.

"Please take a seat," Einarra said, gesturing at the cushions arranged around the table. I chose a round, deep blue one, and sat on it without any more encouragement, happy to sit on something soft after days in the saddle. Rhys sat next to me, and Runa and Liliwen sat on the other side of the table from us—all of us looked exhausted, even Runa.

Einarra excused herself, saying she would find someone to bring us the bowls of stew, and Rhys asked what I had been thinking as well.

"How do you know this person?" he asked, looking directly at Runa, sitting across from him.

"I used to…I used to be a mercenary," she said with a small, misplaced shrug.

"What?" I blurted out without thinking. She glanced at me with an odd expression, and then looked down at the table.

"I used to get paid to fight. You know what a mercenary is, don't you?" she said with an edge to her voice.

I repressed a sigh. "But why didn't you tell us?" I asked.

"Why should I?" she countered. "I don't do it anymore. The war died down and my services are no longer worth as much as they used to be."

"So you fought for Einarra's unit?" Rhys asked. Runa nodded, looking back at him with a blank expression.

"Up until about a year ago," she said. "I was very good, by the way," she said, suddenly smug as she folded her arms across her chest. "That's how I got the name Valkyrie."

"Oh," I frowned, remembering her saying that word to Varina. I had never thought to ask her about it, with everything else that had happened that night.

"Don't pass judgment on me," she said, glaring at me, completely misunderstanding my *oh*. "I was essentially homeless and my only skill is sword fighting—"

"I'm not judging you, Runa," I said, as quickly as I could despite my exhaustion. "I remembered you saying that to Varina, but I forgot to ask you."

"Oh," Runa said, looking sheepishly at the table for only a moment, her eyebrows furrowed. Then she looked back up at me with a slight grin. "In Tamania, that title has meaning. It didn't have the same effect that night."

"The stories of your feats might have yet to reach Remisia," Rhys said, smiling just slightly. Runa smiled back and relaxed, her shoulders slumping with relief.

Einarra appeared in the opening of the tent with two bowls of steaming stew in her hands, followed by a young soldier, her hands also full. They set them on the table in front of us along with a collection of wooden spoons, and then the soldier left. Einarra sat at the head of the table, and grinned at us. "Please, eat," she said, gesturing at the bowls. She removed her helmet as we picked up our spoons.

"What brings you back to Tamania?" Einarra asked Runa, sitting to her left. Runa stirred her stew and shrugged slightly.

"Remisia is…not the best place to be right now. They're all Remisian," she said, pointing her spoon at me, Rhys, and Liliwen.

"Oh. Do you all speak Tamanian?" Einarra asked us with a frown.

"I can understand enough," I said. Rhys and Liliwen understood Einarra's question but shook their heads, already frustrated at not being able to understand the conversation. "I can translate for you later," Runa said to them in Remisian, then shoveled a large spoonful of stew into her mouth. I took my first bite as well, and was thankful for the warmth and the rich flavors. I was growing tired of stale bread and dried meats.

"What's happening in Remisia?" Einarra asked, brows furrowed as she turned her attention back to Runa.

"The kings and queens are being overthrown in the south," Runa said, her tone annoyingly casual. I took another bite of stew, chewing on a bit of beef and forcing myself to allow Runa to tell the story. "We got out right before it really got chaotic."

"The Southern Kingdoms are falling?" Einarra asked, now concerned, her shoulders tense.

"In a way. They've got new leaders that want to take control of the Empire. There were rumors of a draft going around, higher taxes… And so far, the emperor isn't taking it seriously. Considering they're said to have powers nobody has ever witnessed before, like mindreading and seeing the future, I'm not sure why."

"How odd," Einarra said, frowning down at the surface of the table in front of her.

"What is?" I couldn't help but ask, setting my spoon down without thinking. She looked up at me with wide eyes and raised eyebrows, but she shook her head with a slight smile, regaining her composure.

"Nothing. It's only—there are rumors here too," she said, too cryptic for my liking. We waited in silence for her to continue, and she let out a heavy sigh before she finally did. "Well, I'm not sure it's related. But some travelers passed through here a couple of weeks ago—a family from East Tamania looking to get away from the chaos there. They paused for a few hours here, and the mother struck up a conversation with me. She said she had heard a large unit of the East Tamanian army had been annihilated a few months ago, in the forests outside of Lagey. There were rumors… that the people who had done it were so powerful, they were unlike normal Drekligr. So much more powerful, so much healthier and stronger. At the same time, this woman said, stories were traveling from town to town about a Drekligr army rising up. But nothing ever came of it…"

"You think the people in Remisia are from Aorlanda?" I asked, leaning forward slightly without thinking, my whole body tense. I felt Rhys looking at me, but I couldn't look away from Einarra.

"It seems to match, doesn't it?" she said with a small shrug. "We can't know for sure, can we? But they certainly didn't come from nowhere."

"No, they didn't," I agreed, stirring my stew again as I thought.

Runa waved a hand in the air and frowned. "It's not our concern anymore. We got out in time," she said, giving me a pointed look. I nodded, and refocused on the stew, feeling my stomach clench in hunger.

"Well, I'm glad," Einarra said with a smile. "I don't think I know your names," she said with a surprised blink. "I'm Einarra, the captain of the troop stationed here at Rodljost Pass."

"I'm Eira," I said, forcing a smile. Rhys and Liliwen gave their names as well, and Einarra welcomed us to the pass.

"I'm glad you'll be staying the night. I'm sure you all need the rest. It's not the easiest ride up here," she said with a small frown.

"Thank you for allowing us," I said.

She laughed, a short and light sound. "No need to be so formal. Runa is a friend—I'm sure she's told you," she said, glancing at Runa with an uncertain smile.

"I told them," she said with a curt nod, eyes on her bowl of stew still—it was nearly gone. "I'm assuming my skills are not needed at this time?"

Einarra shook her head, her long braids falling behind her shoulders. "They launched a small attack for the pass two weeks ago, but nothing we couldn't easily handle. I expect them to try again soon, and it will be much the same."

"No lost souls?" Runa asked with raised eyebrows. Einarra frowned.

"No. The East is not well prepared. I don't know for sure if we were able to take down any of them, they retreated so fast."

"How many do you have stationed here?"

"Over a hundred," Einarra said promptly. As their conversation descended further into numbers and tactics, I recognized fewer and fewer words, and soon I had completely lost any interest in what they were saying. Once everyone was done eating, now satisfied and feeling the warmth of the broth flow through my veins, Einarra decided to show us to our tents.

The breeze had picked up and chilled my face as I pulled my cloak tightly around me, but it seemed less bothersome after that warm reprieve. Einarra walked us through the camp, to a couple of tents that had been set up near the cliff that led down to the switchback below. The snow had been cleared from underneath them, and, glancing inside, I saw that a couple of extra wool blankets had been provided.

"There's enough room for two people in each tent, so split up however you see fit," Einarra said with nonchalance. "Dinner will be served about an hour after sunset, so please feel free to help yourselves. It will be stew again," she said laughing slightly. "Let me know if you require anything else."

"Thank you," we all said in Tamanian, and she walked away, back into the heart of the camp. But I felt like my stomach was sinking due to the problem I was now facing.

"So who is with who?" Runa asked, folding her arms and looking at each of us with a frown.

"I don't care," I said quickly, in the most relaxed tone I could muster. I worried that Rhys could see through me, but I remembered how dense he had been about Aerona's feelings, and I found it unlikely to be any different in this case.

"I don't care either," Liliwen offered.

"Since Eira and I have been traveling together for so long, perhaps it would make sense for us to share a tent," Rhys said, his tone suggesting he was trying to solve a puzzle. I barely managed to stop myself from whirling on my feet to stare at him, and I remained rigid and staring at Runa.

"That's fine," I said after a moment.

"Alright. Liliwen, you're stuck with me," Runa said, pulling aside the flap of the tent on the right and entering without another word.

"I'm not sure about stuck," Liliwen muttered as she followed. I turned to stare at Rhys, already dreading what I was about to say.

"Are you sure?"

"Of course. It makes the most sense, doesn't it?" he said with a small frown. I blinked, and realized something I hadn't wanted to consider, something even worse than him knowing I had feelings for him.

He didn't have any feelings for me.

It should have been obvious; he had never given any indication, and even just learning to say my name instead of milady had taken an uncalled-for amount of effort on his part. Had I been holding out some hope that he was hiding, just like me?

I couldn't look at his face as I nodded, opened the flap to the other tent and threw my pack in without looking. Runa and Liliwen were emerging from their tent, having put their stuff down more carefully, but I was already walking away, not able to bear standing there like an idiot any longer.

"Eira? Where are you going?" I heard Rhys call behind me.

"Just want to go for a walk. Maybe check on the horses," I said, pausing to turn and look at him for just a moment.

"Would you like me to go with—" he started, but I shook my head, turning away again.

"No. If it's alright, I'd like some time to myself," I said, and walked away without waiting for his response, to where I could see the pointed ears and dark manes of many horses rising above the low tents of the camp.

It was strange, but for the first time in a long time, I wanted nothing to do with Rhys.

19

The Battle of Rodljost Pass

No one spoke of my odd behavior when we sat around one of the campfires at dinner, and I was very thankful for that. Runa was eating elsewhere, talking over recent events with Einarra and some other soldiers she had met before, so it was just me, Liliwen, and Rhys sitting on short wooden stools around a small fire just outside of our tents. I could sense Rhys glancing at me every now and then from where he sat to my right, but I refused to look at him. Instead, I chatted with Liliwen throughout the meal, entertained by her stories of home, and for some reason, Rhys never broke into the conversation, choosing to eat his stew in silence.

"My brother tried to make sweet rolls one time, and they were such a disaster," she laughed, her eyes shining with the memory. "Sugar and flour all over the kitchen. I didn't know one person could make such a mess."

"Sweet rolls aren't even that complicated," I laughed. "How did he manage that?"

She shook her head, still grinning. "I don't know. It was a mystery then, and it remains one now."

She glanced over at me as I took a bite of stew, this one made with chicken, still with some humor in her eyes. "What about you? Any siblings?"

I set the spoon down in my bowl carefully, for some reason uncomfortable by her words. The question was innocent enough, but I wondered at what point I would have to start lying to her about my background. "No," I said, smiling at her. "I'm an only child."

"Oh," she said, looking a bit surprised, but unbothered by my short pause. "More attention for you then."

I let out a dry laugh. "I suppose. But more attention isn't always good attention, is it?"

She tilted her head, and I realized I had probably said too much. "What do you mean?"

I gave a slight shrug. "I don't know. Parents can be a bit overbearing, can't they?"

Liliwen nodded as she chewed on a bite of chicken. "True," she said eventually. "Even my parents could focus on me too much sometimes. But maybe that's because I'm the youngest. I don't think they were as concerned with my brother."

"Are you close in age?" I asked, eager to turn the conversation away from me.

"He's five years older than me, so not really," she replied. I saw something wistful enter her eyes then, as she looked at the fire before us with a sudden intensity.

I thought I knew what she was thinking about, the wellbeing of her brother, and I hastened to distract her.

"And Brynffynon? How was growing up there?" I asked. "I've never visited."

"Oh, it's lovely," she said, snapping her eyes back to mine. "Green hills and cliffs over the sea. And only a day of riding from Maenynys, so we would visit the city often enough."

"That does sound lovely," I said, and couldn't stop the little sigh that left my mouth at the end of the sentence. She looked at me curiously again, this time with a softness in her eyes.

"Don't worry about me," she said, her smile a bit sad now, almost turning down at the corners. Her eyes were downcast, avoiding me for a moment.

"I didn't mean to—" I started, feeling my eyebrows turn up in concern. She shook her head with a smile.

"It's fine. I think about home all the time. It's good to talk about it," she said. Then she sighed, and set her empty bowl on the ground beside her. She leaned her elbows on her knees, and looked at me curiously for a moment, still smiling softly. "If I wasn't sad to leave, there wouldn't be much of a reason to fight for it."

>«<

I was both looking forward to and dreading going to sleep. I was so tired from traveling and the events of the day that I knew I would fall asleep quickly, but first I had to consciously share the tent with Rhys, and I wasn't sure it was possible for me to feel more uncomfortable than I already did about that. I allowed Rhys to enter the tent first, waiting awkwardly in the freezing air outside while he spread out his bedroll. Then I ducked in as well, and doggedly ignored him as I set up my side of the tent. Rhys had lit a small candle provided by the soldiers, and it was more than enough to light the entire space.

I was under my blankets in record time, rolling onto my side to face the wall of the tent, and wrapping the furs tightly around my shoulders. "Goodnight," I mumbled, my voice sounding strange to my own ears.

"Goodnight," Rhys said, his tone unreadable, but I relaxed as I heard him stop shuffling around under his blankets, and as he finally blew out the candle. For a few peaceful moments I thought that nothing awkward would come out of the situation after all, until I heard him clear his throat behind me.

"Eira?" he said so quietly, I realized he was probably wondering if I had magically fallen asleep in only a few seconds.

I barely stopped myself from letting out a sigh. "Yes?"

"Were you upset earlier?" he asked. I knew he was frowning even without looking at him, how his jaw would be tensed slightly, and his lips would be pulled thin.

"No," I said. Knowing that alone was not very convincing, I decided to play dumb. "Why do you ask?"

"You went for that walk. You seemed…stressed. If it's this tent situation, I—"

"No, it's not," I said, quick to interrupt him as I didn't want to hear how that sentence ended. "I just needed some time to myself is all. It seemed like a good time."

"I got the feeling that I had upset you," Rhys continued, his voice quietly meeting my ears in the darkness. A part of me wished I could see his face for this conversation, and another part was grateful for the distance.

"Well, I wasn't upset," I lied. "Maybe I was a bit irritable, I don't know. It wasn't anything you did, though."

There was an odd beat of silence, and I frowned as it took him a while to reply. "Alright," he said finally, sighing slightly as though he was giving up on something. "You know you can always talk to me, though…right?"

My heart ached, wishing that was true.

"I know," I lied.

>«<

The next morning I was woken up by the sounds of chaos. Voices yelling, swords clanging, and footsteps thumping outside the tent overwhelmed my eardrums as I blinked awake, sleep still clinging to me. But soon I was alert and sitting up, and Rhys was already halfway out of the tent. I followed him without a word after pulling on my boots with hasty, jerky movements, and saw Runa standing in the snow just outside, clearly waiting for us as she stepped forward, urgent in her movements.

"I was just about to wake you," she said, sounding breathless. Liliwen appeared behind her, having just come out of their tent, and was looking at the camp, alarm evident on her face. For a second, I took in the state of the camp, and felt my stomach drop at the sight of soldiers in full armor running toward the east side of the pass, bows and swords at the ready.

"What's happening?" I asked just as Runa was taking a deep breath.

"The rebels are attacking now," she said, urgent but calm. Her features were tensed but there was no fear in her as her hands gripped the hilts of her sword. "Einarra is sure there won't be many of them. It's some kind of last-ditch effort on their part."

"What should we do?" Rhys asked, looking past Runa, just as I was, at the receding figures as they disappeared around the tall and dense grove of pine trees as the road curved to the right.

"It's up to you. Extra hands are always welcome, but you don't have to put yourself in harm's way if you don't need to," she said, shifting from foot to foot. I knew she wanted to join the fight, and the conversation was holding her back. I hadn't even begun to think about what I wanted to do when Rhys spoke.

"I'll fight," he said, and Runa nodded curtly, at most slightly pleased by his help.

"What?" I said without thinking, turning to my right and tilting my head up slightly to stare at his face; he was standing so close to me. He smiled softly, trying to comfort me.

"Don't worry. This is my job, remember?"

"When was the last time you were in a battle, Rhys?" I demanded, glaring at him. He blinked, perhaps surprised by my tenacity.

"You know we're training constantly," he said, now frowning at me. "I can handle myself, Eira. And I want to help with this."

I shook my head and stared at the ground, where a clump of dirty ice held my attention—I would focus on anything else to not think about what Rhys was saying.

"And you, Liliwen?" Runa said. There was a pause, and I looked up at the girl in question, looking back at Runa with a grim frown.

"I'm not well trained," she said slowly, as though she regretted speaking the words.

"You have no obligation. Stay back here or even fall further back down the road if you feel the need," Runa said easily. Liliwen relaxed slightly as she nodded, and then Runa turned back to me. "You should stay with Liliwen," she said.

"What?" I said, once again outraged.

"She shouldn't be alone. I'm sure you can fight alright, but Rhys and I are trained, and you two are not. And if for some reason the rebels are able to break through, you should be together to protect each other."

"But I…" I said weakly, not having a decent argument against that.

"It's fine, Eira," Rhys said, then turned his torso toward me, until he was standing right in front of me. I stopped breathing as he gripped one of my hands, his own cold and strong, holding onto me for a moment as he spoke. "Runa and I will be fine, and Liliwen deserves company. We'll be back soon, so just…stay safe. Okay?"

I stared up at him, his eyes imploring me to listen to him, so warm, but still full of the cold sky as the sun had not hit us yet, hidden as it was still low behind the trees. There was an odd bit of sadness hidden in his irises, but I knew he was trying to hide it, his brow smooth and his lips slightly quirked in a small smile. His hand tightened almost imperceptibly around mine, and I found myself nodding.

"Okay," I whispered, and then his hand fell away, leaving mine grasping nothing in the frozen air. Then the pair of them left, stepping through the icy snow with fading crunches, breaking into a run side by side and eventually disappearing behind the trees along with the rest of the soldiers. As their footsteps faded away, I listened for the cacophony of battle, the yelling and screaming, but the only sound that met my ears was that of the wind whispering in the pines.

"I'm sorry," Liliwen said after countless moments, and I turned to stare at her in surprise. I had somehow forgotten she was there.

"What?" I said, knowing that I had already said that word too many times in the past few minutes.

"I'm sorry," she said again, taking a few timid steps toward me. She clutched the fur shawl that was wrapped around her shoulders tightly in front of her chest, her knuckles pale white. I noticed the shadows under her eyes, and the tired line her lips formed.

"What are you sorry for?" I asked, my voice loud in the quiet air.

"That your friends are… That they left you here with me."

"They didn't leave me here. I could have argued if I wanted to," I said, looking away from her, back to the trees. "It's smarter for me to stay here. I don't know how to fight. I would just get in the way."

"You're worried, though," she said. I paused before I nodded once, still looking and listening for any sign of the battle, hoping the rebels would be defeated quickly.

"Of course. They both mean a lot to me, and neither of them had to… They didn't have to fight today. Put themselves in harm's way… But that's who they are." I felt like my whispers were yelling, but there was no way to speak any more quietly.

"Maybe we should sit down, or"—Liliwen sighed, looking around at the two tents— "pack up. So that we're ready to go when they come back."

I paused for only another moment before nodding and turning back to her. I tried to smile, but it felt like some weird contortion for my face. "Alright. That's a good idea."

I ducked inside my tent to see my and Rhys's bedrolls still rolled out, haphazardly covered with furs and blankets, our bags in between. How simple my worries had been the night before…that he might realize my feelings for him, that he didn't have feelings for me. None of that mattered then, as I folded the blankets and threw my cloak over my shoulders, packing up our beds with meticulous slowness. None of it mattered any longer, because all I could think about was Rhys getting injured or even…

I couldn't finish the thought, and instead I focused on pushing the bags and bedrolls outside of the tent, into the icy dirt beyond. Liliwen was already outside when I emerged, and was standing beside her and Runa's belongings, looking with an anxious gaze towards the trees.

"Anything?" I asked her. She turned to stare at me, a bit of surprise in her eyes, as though she had forgotten my presence. Then she relaxed slightly, and shook her head.

"No," she said softly. I came to stand next to her, and we both looked silently out at the road and where it curved around the trees, the distant snow-covered boulders and cliffs, an irregular mess and dark gray and white below the blue sky. I shifted from foot to foot as the minutes passed in pressing silence, feeling something akin to anger boiling inside of me.

"I could help them," I whispered, feeling my magic flow through me, vibrating in my veins like it needed to explode from me somehow. It was something I had rarely felt, this agitation. I remembered when I had trouble finding this magic before, when Runa had fought Varina and Rhys and I had to take down the soldiers. It had been difficult to find, like searching for a doorknob in a dark room.

This was the opposite of that.

"Are you alright?" Liliwen said, frowning at me suddenly.

I realized my arms were shaking and I worked to soothe myself. I nodded.

"Fine," I said, taking a deep breath. "Just worried."

"It'll be fine," Liliwen said, still sounding concerned. I didn't want to tell her how badly I wanted to run past the grove of pines and find the fight, and hurt anyone who dared try to hurt Runa or Rhys. I couldn't begin to explain the feelings coursing through me.

And then it was just too much. "I have to do something," I said at full volume. I turned my gaze to Liliwen. "Will you be alright here by yourself?"

Her mouth opened in surprise, and for a few moments no sound came out as she stared at me. "Yes," she said finally. "But—"

"Stay here, and don't worry. We'll be back soon," I said, before breaking into a run down the road, feeling the ice cracking beneath my feet.

"Eira!" Liliwen called after me, but my limbs kept me moving, relieved to no longer be standing still.

I followed the road as I rounded the pine trees, inhaling the fresh, sharp scent, passing the snowy boulders on my left. The road curved downward and to the left, around the boulders, and as I passed the trees I heard the clanging and yelling of battle, sword on sword echoing up the hill.

Turning left with the road, feeling my lungs ache as I continued the full sprint, I saw the battle stretch across the pass, and my immediate thought was one of slight relief. It was a much smaller battle than I had anticipated, and the West Tamanian soldiers held the high ground. The road stretched wide at this point, as it began the descent down the east side of the mountains. We were in a slight valley between boulders and cliffs on either side, which stretched up to the sky. It was easy enough to spot Runa and Rhys, as they were the only ones not wearing full plate armor. If not for the silver helmets apparently leant to them by the West, they would have looked more similar to the rebels, who wore leather armor and chainmail. There had to be over a hundred people fighting in total, but I couldn't tell how equal the sides were. A few bodies dotted the ground and I forced my mind to ignore them with a determined numbness.

I focused on Rhys and Runa as I came to a sudden stop, even as I was still a few yards behind the closest soldiers locked in battle, where both of my friends fought near the center of the horde. Runa swirled with a deadly elegance as her two blades cut through weak points in the rebels' armor, bringing two at a time to the ground with splashes of red blood. Rhys, a few yards to Runa's right, moved with less elegance and more anger, his great sword falling on his enemies with cracking blows, moving quickly onto the next adversary with precision.

I watched as they fought with growing tension. It took one misstep, one miscalculation, for a rebel sword to meet them in a deadly way. I breathed in deep and felt my magic still running through me, waiting to get out, but I held it in, until I needed it.

Keeping my attention on both Rhys and Runa was difficult as they swayed through the throng, finding any rebel to attack, turning quickly to swing at another. Certain angles showed me the concentration in each of their eyes, constantly scanning the people standing around them for an opening or a threat. Still, I didn't relax. Disaster could happen at any time, but I could save them.

My concentration was broken, though, as a rebel broke through the soldiers and ran straight for me. There was a determination in his eyes as his heavy boots pounded over the ground, and if my magic hadn't been ready, maybe things would have ended differently in that moment.

I reached out a hand without meaning to, all conscious thought leaving my mind, and let the force flow from me. It hit him as an invisible wall, throwing him backward, where he hit the frozen ground with a great thump, rolling a few yards further down the road away from me. I breathed heavily, but not from the effort. It really hadn't taken much work for me to summon that magic. I gasped from the adrenaline, the success. The rebel did not get back up, and I knew even without checking his vitals that he was unconscious, having hit his head in the fall. And I felt no remorse.

When my surroundings came back to me, I scanned the mass of bodies, searching for Rhys and Runa and finding them quickly once again. They had moved further down the hill, as the West forced the rebels back step by step. I studied Rhys first, seeing how his footsteps were careful and exact, his movements strong and determined as his sword repeatedly met his enemies.

But when my eyes shifted to Runa, something I saw made my stomach clench, and at first I wasn't immediately sure what. Then with incredulous realization, I recognized what I was seeing.

It was blood, appearing from thin air, and dripping into the snow just a few yards past Runa, out of her view as she fought two rebel soldiers at the same time. I blinked, focusing my eyes on the small droplets and how they melted into the snow, how their source was invisible.

My heart stopped when I realized the implication of that observation, and my reaction was innate and intuitive. I focused all of my energy on that one spot and pushed, even as Runa suddenly jolted forward, as though something had hit her from behind. I knew I had been just moments too late, and Varina had accomplished her goal. I couldn't consider the fact that she was attacking Runa when I was standing only yards away, or that she had chosen to physically assault her as opposed to using the Eos from afar, as I had just done. I could think of nothing but Runa's safety, and how Varina's attack would affect her. In the seconds that followed our mirrored attacks, my eyes focused on Runa's form as she barely regained her footing, as she barely missed an incapacitating blow to her arm from one of her adversaries. I winced as the end of the blade still met her forearm, and watched as she bared her teeth even as her blood began to run down her wrist. In less than a second she had regained her composure, whirling her blades with renewed focus.

Even as I watched her, I noticed Varina's flickering form as she retreated, the blood from the wound near her shoulder becoming vivid as it left her body and fell to the ground.

I was torn for a moment, frozen in place by warring desires; I didn't want to lose track of Varina, but Runa was now injured, and therefore weakened while the battle still raged on.

But my decision was made for me when I saw what would easily lead to Runa's defeat—a trio of soldiers slowly making their way to Runa from behind, while she was still locked in battle with the two rebels. Though they seemed fatigued with slower and slower movements, neither gave any indication of backing down. Runa herself was growing tired even as her slashing blades still met their marks, repeatedly making contact with her opponents' swords, blocking their attacks and attempting her own. But it was obvious the pain of her new wound was affecting her as the rotation and range of the arm was diminished, and her other blade was working even harder. Her expression was growing frustrated, and I stopped breathing as the three rebels behind her slowly approached her back. She didn't have the time to check her blind spots as the fight she was in took all of her concentration and energy.

And I couldn't call out to warn her, as that could have distracted her from the two people in front of her.

There was only one thing I could do, the same thing I had done to Varina just moments before.

I focused that wall of energy inside of me on the three that had so stealthily rounded their way through the crowd, now close enough to Runa that she was in immediate danger. My force was unfocused and vague, but strong enough. I reached out a hand again, still so unnecessary, and pushed one of the rebels into the person next to them, with enough force that they flew into the third one, all falling in a heap three yards right of where they had been standing moments before.

They were not unconscious, and they slowly began to stir, but in those few seconds, Runa had been able to finally disarm and cut down the two rebels she had been locked in battle with. Sensing the danger she had just been in she whirled around, and frowned when she saw the three rebels slowly getting to their feet and picking up their fallen swords, completely disoriented.

I looked away as Runa approached them with a grim expression, her bloodied swords at the ready.

The battle was dying down as I turned my attention to Rhys, relieved to see that he was still handling his opponents just fine, if a bit tired in his movements. But the rebels still alive and fighting were growing few and far between. I took a moment to look around, back up the hill and the trees that stood wavering in the wind at the top there, and blinked in surprise when I saw Liliwen, staring at me with her mouth open and eyes wide.

At first I wondered why she was there at all, and then it hit me, why she was looking at me like that. Only a few yards away, she would have heard me if I asked her what she was doing, but no words came out.

I turned back to look once again at Runa and Rhys, and saw they had no more rebels to fight. Einarra was shouting orders to search the dead, and only a few flailing rebels still stood with sword in hand. Most were dropping them and surrendering, or trying to run back down the hill without being captured.

Runa and Rhys were safe, though, so I turned back to Liliwen, and walked up the hill slowly to stand before her. She was still staring at me with her mouth closed now, but her eyes still open wide with shock.

"What are you—"

"What did you just do?" she whispered, cutting me off. My hands opened and clenched into fists at my side, still feeling my magic in my blood, alive and powerful. I thought of denying what she had seen, lying and saying that I had just been watching the battle, trying to summon the courage to join the fight with my sword or my bow, but I didn't want to.

I didn't want to lie to her.

"I'm an Eosiaid," I whispered, partially because I just didn't have the strength to speak at full volume, and partially because I was scared of someone overhearing, though no one was nearby, still finishing up the battle on the road below us.

"What..." Liliwen stuttered, blinking at me in confusion for a moment. "Why are you here?"

"Everything I told you was true," I said quickly. "We're from Nefyn, we had to leave when the Syrthiaid attacked—"

"But you...you must have been a Benadur," she stammered. I wondered at the concern in her eyes for a moment, before I realized what she was truly concerned about—she didn't know how to talk to me, how to treat me.

"Here I'm the same as you," I murmured softly, hoping to put her at ease. "Actually, I'm lesser than you. It's not safe for me to be here. You heard what Runa said. Even she hates Eosiaids. I can't let it be revealed…" I paused, now growing scared that Liliwen would want Runa to know the truth about me. "Please don't tell her. She'll want nothing to do with me if she knew."

Liliwen gaped for a moment again, surprised by everything I was saying. Then she shut her mouth and nodded, meeting my eyes with a determined gaze. "Yes. Of course. I promise."

I let out a heavy sigh, now thoroughly relieved and exhausted. "Thank you," I said with a small smile. It fell away as she continued to regard me with an odd look, as though I had suddenly grown a horn out of my forehead. "Please don't treat me any differently," I said. She blinked again and smoothed her features.

"I'm sorry. I… Well, you would know, wouldn't you? How you're supposed to be addressed. Commoners are not meant to be friendly with Benadur," she said, looking away from me to frown at the ground to the left of my feet.

"Well. I ask that you try. Because I thought we were getting along quite well up until now," I said. This earned a small smile from her, which fell away quickly as something caught her eye over my shoulder. I turned and looked as I saw West Tamanian soldiers lifting their dead and carrying them up the hill toward us. Four bodies were being carried from what I could see, but even that few made my chest tighten.

"Eira! Liliwen!" Rhys yelled suddenly, sounding shocked with a hint of anger. I saw him appear from behind one of the groups carrying a body, an outraged expression on his face, which was splattered with tiny drops of blood, now mostly dried. He approached us with quick footsteps, urgent in his movements to get to us.

"What are you doing here?" he demanded as he glared at us. This behavior was so unlike Rhys, I almost laughed.

"I wanted to help," I said, stretching my fingers at my sides as I thought about the magic that had left me. "I did help, and Liliwen saw me."

He stared at me for a moment, still breathing heavily from the fight. "Saw you?" he repeated, not understanding. I nodded.

"I used the Eos, Rhys. Runa was going to get hurt, so I—"

"Oh," he said, then surprised me by pulling me in for a tight embrace. His arms wrapped around me, squeezing around my ribs, his head leaning down onto my shoulder. His hands spread over my shoulder blades for a moment, before he seemed to remember himself, and pulled away just as quickly as he had pulled me in. His hands fell on my shoulders as he held me at arms distance, and I stared at him, unable to hide my surprise at the sudden warmth he had displayed. "I'm…I'm glad you weren't hurt," he said, his face red even underneath the blood. "You could have been injured—"

"I know, but I wasn't. I was ready to use the Eos to protect you and Runa," I said, keeping my voice strong. I wasn't going to argue with him about something that I had known was the right choice. He sighed, and ran a bloodied hand over his face once, wiping his forehead of residual sweat. "More importantly, Liliwen knows I'm an Eosiaid now. She saw me use the Eos." Rhys blinked at me, then turned his surprised gaze to Liliwen.

"It's true," she said. "But I promised to not let anyone else know, including Runa."

Rhys nodded slowly. "Alright. Well, good. Thank you. Ah—" He turned back to look at the remains of the battle, his right hand coming to the back of his neck in an oddly uncertain gesture. "I should…I should help," he mumbled. He looked back at us with a deep frown. "You can help too but you don't have to. I would prefer that you return to the tents. We'll leave soon, I'm sure."

I looked at Liliwen, and she nodded. "We'll return to the tents," I said with a nod at Rhys. He gave me one last odd look, before nodding once and turning back down the hill, taking quick strides until I saw him meet back up with Runa.

"Come on," I sighed to Liliwen, turning to ascend back up the hill, following a few dozen yards behind the first group carrying a fallen soldier that had passed during our conversation. Only a few seconds into the climb, Liliwen let out a short laugh.

"What?" I asked without looking at her, finding the climb up the hill much harder than the run down it.

"Oh, I'm sorry," she said quickly. Then she remembered her promise and sighed. "It's just… Well, Rhys is odd, isn't he?"

"He's just been nearly murdered a few dozen times in the last half hour," I muttered. "I think that warrants some odd behavior."

"Perhaps. It was like he saw a ghost when he saw you, though. Truly terrified."

"He's sworn to protect me," I said, shaking my head. "He was a guard at my Benaty."

"Guards aren't supposed to pull their Benadurs into a hug," Liliwen said in a cautious murmur, and I chose to ignore whatever she was implying. We finished the rest of the walk back to our tents and belongings in silence, though in my mind I was reliving that embrace, and the relief that my friends were okay.

>«

The fallout from the battle was dealt with swiftly, and Runa and Rhys soon joined Liliwen and I outside of our tents.

Runa, still looking a bit haggard, picked up her leather bag and slung it over the shoulder of her uninjured arm with a small grunt. There was a freshly wrapped bandage over her forearm where she had been cut, and though she was clearly aching, she carried that arm as though there wasn't really anything wrong with it. "I've spoken to Einarra," she said. The camp bustled with activity behind us, and I barely kept my focus on Runa's words as she continued. "She says once we get to the next fork in the road, we should take the right path. The rebels are likely at their own camp down to the left."

"Are we leaving now?" Liliwen asked. I couldn't tell if she was more worried or nervous. Runa nodded.

"If you three are ready. We have no time to waste, do we?" she said through a huff, picking up her bedroll and hefting it under her good arm.

"Do you need to rest first?" I asked her, feeling my eyebrows turn up in concern. She glared at me.

"I'm fine. I want to get out of here, anyway," she grumbled. "Come on," she said before turning in the direction of the horses. I picked up my bedroll, pack, and blankets, as did Rhys and Liliwen, and we followed only a few yards behind her. As we passed between the tents, a few soldiers waved at us in farewell, some still bloodied from the battle, but most ignored us as they cleaned their swords or wrapped their wounds in sterile cloth. I wished I could heal them, but also knew that they wouldn't appreciate it.

We loaded up the horses in silence, and Nimue was more than ready to get back on the road, snorting and pawing consistently as I readied her saddle. I shushed her occasionally, not really thinking about it, and just wanting to comfort her.

Once ready, I heaved myself into the saddle, somehow relieved to be riding again, so far above the ground and ready to be back on the road. I followed Runa as she took off first, leaving the area beneath the pine trees and merging back onto the road.

Soon enough, we were passing through the site of the battle, and the pools of black dried blood in the soil beneath us churned my stomach slightly. Knowing that Varina's blood was among the splotches sent a deep wave of fear through my body. I hadn't found a suitable time to tell the other three about her presence during the battle. Perhaps I just hadn't wanted to. I wondered if I was putting off informing them of what had happened, how she had targeted Runa, because I didn't want to acknowledge the truth of it.

At least all of the bodies had been cleared away. I hadn't had any desire to know just how many people had been lost that morning.

The road began to pass by again, and I sat stiff and silent in my saddle, replaying the battle in my mind, analyzing what I had seen and hadn't seen. At the same time, I observed the landscape around us with a sense of distance. On this side of the Windfjall Mountains there were expansive pine forests, and within a few miles of the descent we were fully emerged in them, as they towered and swayed above us. There was less snow as well, and it was slightly warmer.

We reached the fork Runa had spoken about an hour or so after midday, and turned right without a word. There was something odd and stiff about both Rhys and Runa. They sat in their saddles with unyielding spines, as though they were both frozen in place. Liliwen, riding beside me most of the way, kept stealing little glances at me, and I could only assume that she thought I wasn't noticing. It wasn't enough to bother me, although I was slightly worried that her opinion of me had changed permanently.

When it was nearly dark around us, Runa led us off the road, where we found a dry, snow-less clearing covered in pine needles and dotted with a few boulders.

"Is it safe here?" Rhys asked Runa, looking up at her as he spread out his bedroll, quite close to where I had already placed mine. I frowned, but pretended I hadn't noticed.

Runa didn't look up from where she was coaxing a fire into existence with some needles, branches, and flint, choosing to glare at the kindling in her hands instead. "Nowhere is safe," she muttered, striking the stones twice in rapid movements. Sparks jumped from her hands, but none caught. "But rebels don't patrol this area very often, if that's what you're worried about."

"Why not?" Liliwen asked as she sat heavily on her bedroll and pulled a wool blanket tightly around her shoulders.

"No towns on this road for miles. Nothing to control. Just forests and cliffs," Runa said, hitting the stones again. With this sharp click, the needles below her hand suddenly lit up like a candle, and then a torch as the fire began to grow. She held her hands around the flame for a few seconds, protecting it from the wind, until she was satisfied it could sustain itself. Sitting back, she maneuvered onto her bedroll and pulled out some fresh bread that Einarra had gifted us. She passed it around, and I was still thinking over her explanation of the area we were in as we ate it, along with some dry cheese and meat. The fire began to warm the air between us, but even the warmth could not take away my anxiety over the events of the day, still chilling me to my bones.

"Why are there no towns around here?" Liliwen asked after what felt like many minutes, when she was done with her portion of food. Runa looked surprised at the question, seemingly having forgotten what they had been talking about, just as I had.

"Oh, the land is too mountainous, really. This road is fine enough, but if we had gone left, we would be leaving the mountains by noon tomorrow."

"Is this side shorter than the west side?" I asked with a frown. She nodded, chewing slowly on a bite of bread while staring at the fire.

"Yes," she said after a few moments. "And if we had gone further north, it levels out faster than the route we're on. But still, we'll leave this area and enter into the flat forestland within the next two days or so."

"So there aren't rebels in this area," Rhys said, looking for confirmation as he fought the frown that threatened to cover his face. Runa looked up at him, sensing the disbelief in his tone.

"No, there shouldn't be," she said, narrowing her eyes. "Why?"

"Because if there were, I would suggest we take shifts at keeping a watch," he said, turning over his last bite of bread in his hands absentmindedly. Runa shook her head.

"Not necessary. They have little interest in travelers anyway," she said, almost sounding bored at this point. I could tell she was still drained from the morning battle. "I triple checked with Einarra. We're safe on this side."

Fear once again fluttered through my veins at these words, since I knew they weren't exactly true. I couldn't waste any more time, withholding information that they needed to know.

"Something happened during the fight," I spoke up with hesitation, and all three looked at me with curious eyes. I took a deep breath and continued, the words coming out in a rush. "I saw Varina. She was there."

There was a heavy pause before anyone spoke. "What?" Rhys barely managed to grit out, while Runa frowned at me in confusion. Liliwen was also confused, her eyebrows knitted together.

"Why did you see her, but we didn't?" Runa asked, breaking the momentary silence.

"She was using her power, but she was injured. I saw her blood dripping to the ground, but couldn't see her body. She was…she was following you, Runa," I said, looking at her with what I knew were wide and concerned eyes. "She was targeting you. She pushed you, and that's when you lost your footing and got that cut." I pointed to the gray bandage still wrapped around her arm without meaning to, as if that gesture could make the whole situation make sense. I neglected to explain that I had used my power against Varina, of course. This certainly wasn't the time to reveal that I was an Eos in addition to everything else I was saying.

"Why didn't you tell us until now?" Rhys asked, his voice oddly fatigued. I looked over at him, grimacing slightly.

"I don't know. I wanted a few hours of peace, I guess."

"But she's probably following us," Runa said, an edge of anger in her voice as she glared at me.

"She's injured," I said weakly, knowing it wasn't enough.

"If Varina is hunting Eira, why did she attack Runa?" Liliwen asked, now cutting Runa off. This question silenced us for a few moments. I had been considering it all day, and still hadn't come up with an answer.

"Maybe she wants revenge," Rhys suggested eventually. He was frowning thoughtfully at Runa, who stared back at him.

"Because I defeated her? In Lithe?" she asked as a frown grew on her face.

"She knew what to expect from Eira and me; that's why she brought soldiers with her. We wouldn't have been able to beat all six of them. But you showed up, matched her skill with your own, and allowed us to escape." His eyes flicked down to the fire before him, and then back to Runa's face. "She blames you for her failure."

I stiffened as that last word brought a memory to mind. *You must not fail*, Cassia had said as she handed Varina the dagger. Varina's quest to capture me was most important to her. I knew that from the other memory I had seen, when her emperor and empress had told her that she had to find me.

"I don't know," I spoke up. "She has to capture me; that's her only goal."

"You were standing right there, on the edge, watching everything." Runa glared at me. "She could have taken you then and no one would have noticed."

"I would have," Rhys snapped at her. There was an awkward beat where Runa simply stared at him with a raised eyebrow.

"But you didn't know I was there until the battle was over, Rhys," I said quietly. "I think…I think she thought she would be able to do both. Get her revenge and capture me. But she didn't expect to get injured and had to retreat."

"This is all conjecture," Liliwen broke in. "All we know for sure is that she tried to attack Runa, and she wants to capture Eira."

Runa was silent for a moment while she considered all that had been said, and then she looked back at me with her eyebrows set in a determined glare. "You're sure you saw her?"

"Yes," I said forcefully. I couldn't leave any doubt in their minds. "She…she was injured, and that drained her of her energy. She retreated as she started to…waver back into visibility."

"Then we do need to take watch shifts tonight," Runa said, seemingly repressing a sigh. The suggestion surprised me but I wasn't sure why. "I'll take one of the middle ones."

"I will as well," Rhys said, rubbing his face in exhaustion.

I looked at Liliwen who just shrugged, disheartened. "I'll go first," I sighed, not feeling particularly tired after that conversation anyway. If anything, it had made me more anxious and alert.

Liliwen agreed to take the last shift, and soon the three of them were drifting off into what I could only assume was uneasy sleep, as the night wore on around us and I was left with just the sounds of the forest and my own chaotic thoughts.

>«

A few hours into my shift, not long before I planned to wake Rhys up to take over, I heard a strange noise that alerted me to the fact that I was drifting into a half-awake, half-asleep stupor. I sat up straight and blinked at the darkness around me, already forgetting what the noise had sounded like. The fire was nearly dead before me and I considered throwing more tinder and branches on it, but chose to stay still, waiting for the sound.

The noise occurred again, and I turned to my left, realizing with a sinking feeling that it was coming from Rhys. It sounded like a sob, a quiet, restrained cry. My eyes were accustomed to the low light by then, and I could see the outline of his pale face as he lay on his back, everything but his head covered with blankets. His brows were turned up as though he was in pain, and a tear glistened on his temple as it slipped slowly down the side of his face toward his ear. I stared at him for a moment, too surprised to know what to do, when he grunted again, jolting suddenly as though he had just been cut by something.

I glanced at Liliwen and Runa, but both seemed to be sound asleep, unaware of the noises Rhys was making. I was glad for that, as I assumed he wouldn't want to make a scene.

"Rhys," I whispered as his body gave a jolt again. I didn't want to speak any louder in fear that I would be the one to wake up Runa and Liliwen.

I pulled my blankets off of me and left my bedroll where I had been sitting for my watch, kneeling in the pine needles beside Rhys. I laid a hand gently on his shoulder, and he immediately jerked awake, his eyes flying open before I could whisper his name again.

"What—" he gasped, and I shushed him.

"Don't wake up the others," I whispered, and his ragged breathing began to slow as he lay his head back down, closing his eyes for a moment.

"Why did you...?" He trailed off, glancing at where my hand still rested on the wool fabric of his tunic. I pulled it away as if I had been burned, and his eyes met mine, both of us confused and disoriented. "Is it time for my watch?" he whispered, blinking as he tried to gain some composure.

"You were crying," I said after a few moments of silence. "I was...I was worried."

"Crying," Rhys repeated, sitting up slowly. The blankets fell from his chest to pile in his lap, and he raised a hand to run through his hair. A tear still clung to his skin on his temple, and he brushed it away as soon as he felt it. He looked at me, clearly uncomfortable as he slowly lowered his hand to rest on the blankets.

"I'm sorry...for disturbing you," he murmured.

"Are you alright?" I didn't want to deal with his apologies and his excuses. None of that mattered to me, and he had to know that by now.

"I'm..." I glared at him, narrowing my eyes, and he could tell even in the low light of the stars what that expression meant. "You won't believe me if I say I'm fine," he sighed. I shook my head, and he smiled slightly. "It was just a dream. It wasn't real."

"What...?" I started, thought better of it, and then decided to press on anyway. "What happened in the dream?"

"Well, I…" He paused, and I guessed he was hoping that I would change my mind, and tell him that he didn't have to tell me, but I waited patiently. I felt I had the right to know for some reason. "It was a war, and…I couldn't…"

"You died?" I whispered, surprised when he shook his head slowly.

"No. Not me. My parents. Mari." He stared at those dying embers before us, flickering less and less as time moved forward through the night. "You."

He turned to me then, and I thought maybe his eyes were a bit wet again, but I couldn't tell for sure. "I couldn't save you. I couldn't save any of you."

"It was just a dream," I said, trying to be soothing, sensing the anguish that still filled him from his nightmare. I knew well enough how those feelings, though false and concocted by the subconscious, could last well past their creation. Not knowing what else to do, I shifted toward him just a bit more, and threw my arms around his shoulders, so my chest met his right shoulder, and my hands clasped each other around his left. I felt him take a deep breath, lifting me up slightly as he filled his lungs, and a shaking breath left him as he exhaled.

"You don't have to—" he mumbled, but I shushed him again.

"Everything is going to be okay," I murmured. He was still for a moment, and then he nodded. He twisted toward me slightly so that he could hug me back, his arms wrapping underneath mine and pulling me against him. If I hadn't been tired, drained, just woken from a half sleep, and stressed beyond belief, the feeling of his body next to mine, the warmth of his hands on my back, the beat of his heart against mine—well, maybe it would have overwhelmed me. But there was too much pain between us, and so I held onto the basic comfort his embrace gave me, the same comfort that I could give him.

Maybe if I had been prepared for it, I could have stopped it from happening. But when his hand shifted just slightly on my back, I felt the falling sensation of the start of a memory, and when I tried to open my eyes all I saw was black. I was too drained to even try to fight it, and I waited for vision to return to me.

When it did, I saw that I was in the large dining room of the Benaty, and the long table was fully occupied by people chatting and eating an elaborate dinner; in just a short glance at the dishes I could see steak and seasonal vegetables, and some kind of creamy soup. I frowned when I looked at the faces of the people present, not recognizing most of them. I stood behind a family with two small children, and blinked when I did suddenly recognize them.

Mari was only five years old, and was squirming in her seat as her mother Deryn, sitting to her right, spoke to her in hushed, soothing tones. Rhys, a few years older, sat to Mari's left, and pushed the remaining food around on his plate in boredom. I moved slightly to see their faces better, coming to stand at the end of the table. Rhys's father, Owain, looked down at him and raised an eyebrow.

"It's rude to not finish your food, you know. We were invited by the Benadur himself," he chastised, though his tone was relaxed.

"I'm full," Rhys said. It was strange to hear his voice so young and childish, before he had become the person I knew.

Before Owain replied something on the opposite end of the table caught my eye. Calliten sat at the head of the table, almost twenty years younger, his face smoother than I remembered it ever being. But there was something in his gaze as he looked down the table at his guests, some pain I had forgotten he had ever felt. Next to him sat the four-year-old version of me, and I recognized the blankness in my eyes as I stared at my plate, the stillness with which I sat, the way the world seemed to pass over me, even at such a young age.

I remembered this night, only vaguely. It was a dinner we always held at the Benaty to celebrate the coming of spring, always right before my birthday. In a few weeks, I would turn five. Which meant my mother had just been taken by the Wood Death. The incurable disease, the only one known to withstand healing magic. Calliten and I had been banned from seeing her once the wood had spread to a certain point, and she had died alone, in pain, as her body transformed into lifeless bark.

"Why does she look like that?" A small voice broke me out of my own memories. Rhys had leaned closer to Owain to ask him the question, as Mari continued to fuss next to him, whining something about not liking carrots as Deryn continued to attempt to quiet her. Owain looked around to see if anyone had heard what Rhys had just asked him, and then turned to him with a frown.

"It's not right to ask questions like that, Rhys. She'll be your Benadur someday."

"I know that," Rhys said, a bit sheepish as he looked down at his hands folded in his lap. "She just…looks so sad."

"She is sad," Owain murmured, looking down the table at my young self, who still hadn't moved a muscle. "As is Benadur Calliten. And that's why it's a great honor they asked us to be here, even in such a difficult time for them."

"Why couldn't they save Lady Lara?" Rhys asked, frowning up at his father.

Owain hushed him immediately. "Stop asking questions like that, Rhys. We can discuss it more at home."

"But—"

"Some people can't be saved, Rhys. Sometimes it's too late or it just isn't possible. Now…now what happened to Lady Lara was rare and tragic. But this isn't the place to tell you about it. Do you understand?"

Rhys opened his mouth, but thought better of it at the sight of Owain's unusually stern expression. He nodded and looked away, back at the child on the other end of the table.

"Mum could be her mum too," Rhys said with a determined frown. I watched as Owain carefully hid a sad smile, and shook his head as Rhys turned back to look at him.

"It's a nice thought, Rhys. But that's not how things work. Don't worry about Lady Aneira—she'll heal with time."

Rhys said nothing as he looked back at the small version of me, who was now taking the smallest bite of a potato possible, and chewing it with blind slowness. Then the image faded and all at once I found myself back in the forest, propped up in Rhys's arms.

I sat up quickly and pushed myself away from him, until no part of us was touching at all.

"Another memory?" he asked softly once I had stilled. I glanced at him and nodded, a thousand feelings warring inside of me. "One of mine?" he continued.

"Yes," I said, still a bit breathless. "An old one. You were just a child."

"Do you…do you want to talk about it?" He regarded me with wary eyes, as though worried about what I had seen. I thought it was ridiculous—I had just seen proof that Rhys had always been kind, that he had always thought of my well-being. It made me want to do a thousand things at once: yell at him, run away, run to him, kiss him, push him away.

I stayed still and silent, unable to choose.

"It's okay. You don't have to share, Eira," he whispered, reaching out a hand toward me, but I flinched away. He immediately dropped his hand as though I had slapped him.

"I'm sorry," I said. "My nerves are frayed. I—you were at the Benaty for Spring's Giving. With your family. And you asked your da—Lara had just died. You asked him if I was okay. You wanted…you wanted to share your own parents with me." Once I had started talking about it, I couldn't stop. "You've always cared, haven't you?"

"Cared?" Rhys said, frowning at me.

"About me," I said.

He nodded slowly, still confused. "Of course. Of course I have."

"Why?" I whispered.

Rhys let out a heavy sigh. "I think it's best you get some sleep, alright?" he said. I wondered why he was avoiding my question, but at the mention of sleep I realized how tired I was.

"But it's not quite your turn yet," I argued. He smiled.

"It's fine. I can't go back to sleep after that. But you're clearly about to pass out." He nodded toward my bedroll, insisting.

I crawled into it without thinking, feeling tears prick at my eyes. I didn't know why I was crying, but I hid my tears from Rhys as I whispered goodnight to him. And as I drifted off, I felt the fallout of our moment together settle over me like a heavy blanket. It was a panic, a fear I felt deep in my bones. As long as I was with them, Varina would keep hunting me, and trying to kill them. I had realized two things about her from our conversation earlier in the night: she wanted to get revenge against Runa, but I was her ultimate goal, and capturing me was her only way not to fail. Her true objective. I knew this from the memories I had seen of her, and I couldn't escape that fact. I could only hope that if I went my own way, Runa, Rhys, and Liliwen would be left unharmed. So my plan began to form, even as complete exhaustion stole consciousness from me.

20

Aornadur

We packed up the camp in the cold morning light, the forest around us still gray and flat as the sun hadn't quite risen yet. Rhys refused to look at me, which I didn't find too strange, considering the odd conversation we had had in the middle of the night. I could tell he was still tired, the moments of sleep he had been able to get having been marred with nightmare after nightmare. I hadn't slept well either, for many different reasons.

But Runa and Liliwen didn't seem to notice our silence, as they worked quietly as well. Once the camp was cleared and the saddles loaded, Runa stood up straight and glanced at each of us for a moment. "Ready?" she asked. We nodded, and that word was the only word spoken for hours.

The switchbacks continued down through the trees, which rose up from the steep hills on either side of us, the road itself covered in a thick, mulchy layer of pine needles. At certain places, it was hard to even see where the road was, as it blended in with the rest of the forest floor. Once again, I grew used to the jolting and swaying of being on Nimue's back for hours at a time, and the day passed with a painful slowness.

I was surprisingly calm considering what I had resolved to do. I was conscious of the small bundle of parchment, quill, and tiny bottle of ink that Rhys had bought for me in Fjall in my bag, with which I would write a note when I once again volunteered for the first shift that night. I would leave it where they would easily find it in the morning. And by then I would be long gone, leading Varina away from them.

I only began to feel nervous about my plan when night fell, and Runa once again lit a fire. I couldn't look any of them in the eye, especially Rhys, and avoided entering the conversation, focusing on my food and eating with slow precision. I could sense their concern, the shifting glances they sent my way, but I doubted they had any idea what I was planning to do—they wouldn't think I was capable of it. But they didn't understand how it was the only option left before me. The only one that had any chance of keeping them safe.

I shifted in anticipation when everyone was done eating and Runa and Liliwen burrowed under their blankets without hesitation, murmuring tired goodnights. I looked at Rhys from the corner of my eye, sitting only a few feet away from me, and felt a wave of anxiety as he remained sitting on top of his blankets, looking at the fire.

I took a deep breath before turning to him. "I'm taking the first shift again," I said, forcing a soft smile. "You should get some sleep while you can."

He looked up at me while I spoke, his expression remaining serious despite my smile. "I wanted to thank you," he said quietly. He moved slightly closer to me, and I resisted the urge to back away. "For talking to me last night."

"You don't have to thank me," I murmured, not wanting to think about the night before at all. "You were…distraught."

"I appreciate how you were there for me," he continued, ignoring my dismissal. He stared at me and I realized his eyes were pleading with me to understand. For a moment, I felt like I was planning to do the wrong thing. Rhys had been with me from the start, and the comfort his presence gave me was alluring; my heart ached at the thought of not having him near me. I found myself considering asking him to come with me, but I pushed the idea away as quickly as it had appeared, looking away from his pleading expression, trying with a deep feeling of pain to harden my heart to everything that he was. Varina was hunting me, and anyone who came with me was in danger of being hurt. Rhys couldn't protect me from her, and having him come with me was simply selfish. No, this was something I had to do alone.

"It was nothing, Rhys," I said, and I felt how he hesitated at the coldness in my voice.

"Nothing, then," he repeated. I heard him shifting, and felt relief when I realized he was lying down to sleep. I still avoided looking in his direction, even when he murmured a soft, "Goodnight."

"Goodnight," I whispered back. And when his shifting movements stilled, I knew it was only a matter of time before I would leave, traversing the darkened forest on my own.

»«

After all three people around me had been breathing softly and slowly for some time, I opened my bag and removed the green quill and paper and ink with careful movements, trying to make as little noise as possible. I didn't think about the day they had been purchased, that moment with Rhys in the marketplace. I refused to remember what I knew would only hurt me.

I then sat there for what felt like an eternity, staring at the blank page, orange in the light of the dying fire. I grew frustrated, and forced the words to come out, and then they began to flow, every reason I could give for my departure landing on the page, and an outline for what I hoped they would do next: get somewhere safe and stay there.

When I was done, I placed the parchment on dry ground far enough away from the fire that an ember wouldn't land on it, but close enough to where the three of them were sleeping that they would certainly find it.

Not long after, I found myself loading my pack and bedroll onto Nimue's saddle, then leading her into the forest a few yards, until I was far enough away that the sounds of me climbing into the saddle wouldn't wake anyone. I did all of this with a numbness that spread through my bones and my heart, not allowing myself to think about the consequences. The only thing that mattered was that Varina would follow me; and just in case she was watching from somewhere hidden in the trees around me, I took the dagger from my bag before urging Nimue forward, and strapped it to my hip.

I hoped she was watching me, and I hoped she saw how it was shining in the moonlight.

>«

The night dragged on as I made my way through the forest, keeping to the road but wishing I could cut through the trees just to make the journey go faster. The land leveled out after a few hours of silent riding, and soon a faint pink light was shining through the eastern trees. I had resolved not to stop until sunset, intent on riding through both the night and the following day. I was numb enough that I didn't think it would be too difficult.

It was when the pink began to turn into a vibrant orange that I became aware of a consistent sound echoing through the trees behind me. Hoofbeats, and they weren't Nimue's.

I tensed and resisted the urge to look behind me. I wasn't exactly surprised that Varina had decided to close in on me so quickly. I wasn't really capable of being surprised in that moment, numb as I was. The hoofbeats began to draw closer as she broke into a trot and then a canter, gaining on me quickly with rhythmic thumping.

I had two choices, and I already knew which I was going to choose. I would turn Nimue around when the time felt right, and face her. I had no desire to run from her any longer. I began to summon my magic, gathering all the force inside of me that I could, and imagined it exploding out of me at the right moment. But it couldn't be a vague sort of wall as it had been in the past. This time, I would try to control it.

When it sounded like she was right behind me, the beating hooves hurting my eardrums, I pulled tight on Nimue's reins and turned her around. She snorted in surprise, but obeyed, and the sight of a girl mounted on a black gelding in the middle of the road left me momentarily speechless.

"Why did you do that?" Liliwen yelled at me, still a few yards away as she pulled back on Sindri's reins. She glared at me with an accusation in her eyes and betrayal in her voice. I gaped at her, still completely shocked that it wasn't Varina in front of me.

"What…what are you doing here?" I managed to ask eventually, still staring at her with wide eyes. I blinked, and though the light of the morning was still cold and pale, it was undeniably Liliwen.

"I'm coming to stop you," she said, now still and sitting stiffly in her saddle. "I read your note. What is wrong with you?"

"What?" was all I could manage.

"Why would you treat us like this?" she asked. She opened her mouth to keep yelling at me, but I found that my mind and my emotions were waking up, and I needed to defend myself.

"Runa was almost killed because of me," I snapped.

"You also saved her life," Liliwen shot back. "We are all with you because we want to be, Eira. You don't get to make those decisions for us—"

"If you're going to get killed because of me, then I have to do what I can to stop it," I said, only growing more frustrated by her words.

"How are you going to face her alone? What if she goes after Runa instead?"

I shook my head as she spoke. "You don't understand, and I don't need to explain to you," I replied. I tried to keep my voice strong but there was a slight waver in it, and I felt my throat tighten as tears threatened my eyes. "Go back to the others. You can go straight to Rhea and be safe there."

Her eyes narrowed at me and for a moment she didn't speak, and I wondered if I had somehow convinced her.

"You know that wasn't the right way to leave, Eira," she said softly.

"It was the only way."

"But if…if you come back now—"

"I'm not going back," I said firmly, and felt my hand clench around the reins. "You should, though."

"I'm already here," she said, her jaw set and her voice as determined as mine.

"She could attack me at any moment—"

"I already knew that."

"You're putting yourself in danger, and for what—"

"For Lithe!" She cut me off, raising her voice once again. Her usual timid nature was completely gone, replaced with determination and anger. "I deserve to do what I can. I've lost my home and I have nowhere to go. I don't want to be safe in Rhea. I want to fight for Lithe. With you, Eira." With that last sentence her voice softened and her eyes lost some of the anger. She was pleading with me.

This was why I had told her about the Sacreds and the Himminir in the first place—because it was her home too. My shoulders slumped as I lost the fight, knowing I couldn't deny her request. She deserved to fight as much as I did.

"If anything happens to you, I won't forgive myself," I told her, and she sat up straight at my words.

"If she attacks us, we will fight," she said with confidence. I thought it might be unearned, but I chose not to comment on it.

"Let's keep moving. If the other two catch up with us, then my escape really was for nothing," I said on a sigh, turning Nimue back down the road, listening as Liliwen hastened to catch up and ride alongside me.

"Do you think your note will work?" she asked quietly, barely loud enough for me to hear over the noise of the horses. I felt my lips turn into a thin line as her question sent a wave of anxiety through me.

I had asked for them to go to Rhea and stay safe. I had told them that it wasn't their fight, and if they were hurt because of me I wouldn't be able to live with it. I told them I had to do it alone.

"I don't know," I said honestly. "It didn't work for you."

She shot me a look out of the corner of her eye before returning her eyes to the quickly brightening road ahead.

"No. But I don't think I love you the way they do."

My body couldn't decide between a snort and a scoff; I ended up choking for a second. "What do you mean?" I asked once I could breathe properly, my eyes watering a bit.

"I'm here for Lithe, Eira," Liliwen said, refusing to look at me. "But they were here for you."

"Rhys is from Lithe too," I argued.

I watched as a small smile appeared on the corners of her mouth. "And I think he would let our country burn if that was the only way to save you."

I had nothing to say in response to that. I only wished she hadn't said it at all.

>«

As the first few days of travel with Liliwen passed, I grew less worried that Runa and Rhys would catch up with us. Liliwen didn't bring them up again, and I forced myself to focus on the road ahead, and not what we had left behind.

Liliwen and I didn't speak much at all. I sensed a divide between us. Though she had insisted on joining me and dedicated herself to the same cause, the truth remained that I had wanted to travel alone. I was still uncomfortable that she was there, and she seemed to sense that.

We would light a fire at night and share rations of food, but rarely spoke. We would take turns keeping watch, never knowing when Varina might choose to attack. The fact that she hadn't, even after a week of riding away from Runa and Rhys, made me feel sick with worry.

>«

After a week of riding with Liliwen, the shadowy silhouettes of the Aorna mountain range appeared in the distance in the morning haze. Like a jagged gray-blue wall against the sky, it rose from the horizon as an ominous mass. I located the tallest peak, quite close to the center of the formation, and knew from reading descriptions and speaking with Runa that it was Aornadur. As we traveled throughout the day, and the one after that, the mountains seemed to grow taller, and the haze of the atmosphere fell away to reveal splotches of white snow and glaciers, slate expanses of boulders and jagged cliff faces, and near the base, the gray-green dots of small forests. The peaks crossed over each other and confused my eye occasionally like some massive geologic illusion, but Aornadur always rose above them all, growing more and more intimidating as we drew closer.

Finally, as we neared its base, meeting some of those forests of cedars and firs and traveling underneath their boughs, the road led us to the town of Geirr. Geirr was a collection of small, wooden triangular buildings, arranged in two straight lines on either side of the road. There were so few inhabitants that I could only count a few houses; the other buildings included a stable, an inn, and a tiny and understocked general store. As we rode past the first few residential homes, their chimneys coughing smoke into the air, filling it with the smell of burning cedar, I remembered that Runa had explained the odd town a few days before I had gone my separate way from her.

"There's a larger town called Thrune only a few miles down the road," she had said, pointing on the map laid out over the snow beside the fire one night. "The people who live in Geirr usually feel some sort of obligation to live as close to Aornadur as possible."

As I remembered her words, I glanced up at the towering mountains behind us, like a wall of rock and ice disappearing into the clouds high above. Behind it, the rest of the range extended to the east and west, but it wasn't nearly as impressive as the highest peak.

We found the small inn and managed to communicate with the innkeeper well enough to rent two rooms. The people of Geirr didn't speak Tamanian, but a much older language called Thronsurian. I could hear some similarities to Tamanian, but it was different enough that I wouldn't even attempt to speak it.

The innkeeper was a kind, elderly man who didn't seem to mind the language barrier, and was more than happy to show us to our rooms. After we had dropped our bags in our rooms we met back in the common room, drawn to the large fireplace set into the wall opposite from the door.

"Are you tired?" Liliwen asked me, her voice hushed as she held out her hands to the flames. I took a seat in one of the old, creaky chairs set by the fire as I shook my head.

"Not any more than usual," I said. The sound of the fire crackling filled the silence between us for a moment before I looked up at her, still standing in front of the fire. "Are you?"

She shrugged slightly. "Probably. I feel more cold than tired right now, though."

I didn't have anything to say to that, and I relaxed into the chair as much as I could, slowly allowing the tension of riding for weeks to leave my muscles. A few minutes later Liliwen sat down across from me, but she sat with a rigid spine and a serious expression set on the fireplace and the dancing flames.

"Are you nervous?" I asked without thinking. She turned to meet my gaze, and forced a small smile.

"Of course," she said with a short laugh. "Aren't you?"

"I…I don't know," I said. I felt myself frown as I tried to assess my own feelings. "I don't feel much of anything right now."

Liliwen's forced smile fell away. "I know you wanted to be alone, Eira."

I stared at her, unsure why she had said that. "I'm not upset that you're here," I said after a moment.

"I think it would be easier for you if I wasn't."

"There's no version of this journey that ever could have been considered easy," I said, frowning at her once again. "You deserve to be here, like you said. You deserve to get answers, same as me."

She stared at me levelly for a moment, before nodding once. "I appreciate that. Even if you don't really believe it yourself."

"I mean it, Liliwen," I said sharply, beginning to grow frustrated.

"Forgive me for not believing you, then," she snapped. "But you've barely spoken to me this entire time. You've barely even looked at me. So I'm sure you're able to understand why I feel like you don't want me here."

"My behavior—it isn't because of you," I stumbled through the words, caught off guard by the entire conversation. "I don't…I can't feel anything." That came out as a whisper, as though I was admitting something terrible. Liliwen's expression remained angered, but I saw something shift in her eyes. Some uncertainty.

"What do you mean?" she asked, the anger slowly leaving her voice.

I shook my head. "It doesn't matter how or what I feel. I made my decisions and I can't go back."

"What…?" she began to ask again, and now I only saw concern in her eyes as her brows knit together.

"It doesn't matter," I said again, shaking my head. I found myself looking down at my hands clasped in my lap, and a sudden movement to my left made me look up in surprise. Liliwen had moved to sit in the chair right beside me, and she was staring at me with wide, honest eyes, imploring me to understand whatever it was she was going to say.

"You can talk to me, Eira," she said. "We're about to…to do something incredibly dangerous, and we need to be open with each other. We need to trust each other." She leaned towards me just slightly, and I studied her face as her words hit me.

"Yes," I said softly, nodding. "I'm sorry. I'm sorry for leaving."

"For leaving…Runa and Rhys?" she clarified. I nodded. "You're trying to protect them."

"Does it matter what I was trying to do? I hurt them. I…I lost them. I'll probably never see them again," I whispered the last sentence. It was a thought I had been trying to avoid over the last few days.

"Eira, listen to me," Liliwen said, and the strength in her voice made me refocus on her face. Once again, her determination surprised me. "I left my family. After my brother was drafted, I left."

"Your brother was drafted?" I asked, blinking in surprise.

She nodded, her lips thin. "I know I'm never going to see him again. I left my parents, not knowing if I'll ever see them either. But you know why it's okay, right?"

I shook my head, frowning at her. A slow smile spread over her face. "Because sometimes we have to do hard things so that we can do the right thing." She paused and studied my face, and when I didn't respond she continued. "I knew I had to leave, but my parents refused, hoping my brother would come back. So I left them, drawn to Aorlanda since I have family here. I thought maybe they could help, somehow. But you know what else?" She didn't wait for me to respond this time, consumed as she was by telling her own story. "Something else drew me here too. And I didn't know what it was; I just followed blindly. I hoped I would figure it out, that I could find something at the end of it all. And then I met you." She blinked at me, as though mystified by her own words. "You told me the truth, showed me the book. And I knew. I was brought here to join you."

I shook my head slowly; not a dismissal, but because I was overwhelmed. "Maybe that's true, but—"

"I want you to listen to me, Eira," she said, her voice low, her eyes serious. I shut my mouth. "We've both made sacrifices. We've left people behind. But as long as we remember why we did these things, then we can be at peace with the past."

I stared at her, and she stared back. "Why we did these things?" I said after a moment, and she nodded. "Why…" I repeated again, looking away from her, at some spot on the floor. "Because what we're trying to do is bigger than us," I murmured after a moment. I looked back at her, suddenly feeling awake like I hadn't in days, maybe weeks. "We made sacrifices because we had to—for Lithe."

Liliwen smiled at me. She nodded slightly, the tension and seriousness leaving her. She reached out a hand and let it fall gently onto my shoulder, and in my raw state I felt the weight pull me down. My eyes closed and I fell through time, knowing what was happening perfectly well. I just hoped that it wouldn't last too long.

I was suddenly surrounded by bright light, and I blinked, trying to discern my surroundings. Before me was a small house, and I stood on the road outside. The road extended to the left and right, cutting through vibrant green grass that stretched to the horizons. I looked around for Liliwen, and found her when the door opened with aggression, slamming against the outside wall. Liliwen strode from the house with a set expression on her face. She was wearing travel clothes— brown trousers and a green tunic, and a billowing black cloak. As she descended the porch stairs, two other people emerged from the house, calling after her. They were middle-aged and looked like her in some ways; I was sure they were her parents.

"Lili!" her mother called, following her along with the father as she rounded the house and made her way to a small shed. I followed the three of them, curious as to what was happening.

"Where are you going?" her father asked her, his voice weak. Liliwen ducked into the shed and returned a moment later, a sheathed sword in hand.

"I'm going to your cousins," she said, looking at him with a closed expression. I knew she must have been hurting in that moment, because that expression was so unusual for her; she was normally very open about her emotions. I could tell she was hiding how she really felt, and her parents could too.

"You don't have to go, Lili," her mother said, pleading with her.

"We need money, and I know the Aorlanda cousins have it," she said, strapping the sword to her waist. When she was done she let out a deep breath, and looked at each of her parents steadily. "You two need to escape too. I'll get the money, and meet you wherever you are."

Her parents looked at each other, aghast, and then back to Liliwen. "What about Lewys?"

Liliwen's expression turned stony once again. "He's not coming back. You have to accept that."

"No…he—"

"Mum, listen to me," Liliwen said. She looked up at her father. "Da, please, both of you. Get somewhere safe. Get far from Maenynys."

"Lili," her mother begged, but she could tell it was no use. "Be safe," she said in a whisper.

Liliwen nodded. "I will," she said. And then the sight before me faded, and the present Liliwen sat in front of me, cringing as I slowly returned to the present.

"Are you alright?" she asked, realizing when I was aware of my surroundings. I had slumped in my seat during the vision and I forced myself to sit up straight, slowly shaking off the memory.

"Yes," I said, forcing a smile. "Just—"

"What was that?" Liliwen asked, eyebrows furrowed in concern.

"I…" I scrambled for something to say, not sure if I should lie. Then I let out a deep sigh, knowing that lying wouldn't help. There was nothing I could say that would put Liliwen at ease about what had just happened to me. "Sometimes…I have these visions."

"Visions?" Liliwen repeated.

I nodded. "Yes. Visions about people. Pieces of their past."

Liliwen was silent, her lips thin as she considered what I was saying. "You saw…a part of my past?" she said hesitantly.

I nodded again. "It was when you left your home to come here. Talking to your parents."

Liliwen sat back in her seat, in a similar position to how I had been slouching moments before. "How long has this been happening?" she asked after a moment.

"Since…since my home was attacked," I said. "It usually happens when someone touches me. But also…when I touch certain items."

Liliwen blinked, then frowned. "The dagger. At the inn in Fjall. You touched it and did the same thing you did just now."

"Yes," I agreed. "I touched it and saw memories of the person who had it before me. The woman who is hunting me, Varina."

"You can see her memories?" Liliwen asked, sitting upright.

"Yes," I said, frowning at her reaction. "Some of them. Just the ones when she had the dagger near her."

"Have you…touched the dagger to do this on purpose? Find out more about her?" Liliwen pressed.

"No, it's not controllable like that," I said, shaking my head at the idea. "It just…happens."

"Maybe you just haven't tried to control it," Liliwen said.

I paused, not wanting to disagree with her outright. "Maybe," I said finally. "But we don't have time for that right now. We have to get ready for the climb."

Liliwen let out a sigh, then nodded as she smiled. "Alright," she said. "We have some errands to take care of then."

21

The Sacrifice

That evening we bought supplies from the general store and replenished our stock of food and water, our packs now bursting and heavy with all that we needed for the long journey up the mountain. The most important item we had to buy were snowshoes, flat wooden contraptions strapped to our boots that would prevent us from sinking into the snowbanks. The horses would not be able to make the climb as some of the terrain was treacherously steep, so we boarded them at the stable, tipping the stablehand in advance in the hopes that they would be well cared for.

While having a hearty soup for dinner by the fireplace in the inn, Liliwen asked as many questions as she could think of about the climb, and I answered as best I could.

"Is the trail up the mountain well marked?" she asked with furrowed brows.

I nodded, setting down my spoon. "The path is said to be marked by large stone cairns. As long as we keep seeing them, we're going the right way."

Liliwen nodded as she took another bite, staring thoughtfully at the fire. "Good. I think it would be all too easy to get lost on such a large mountain." I didn't disagree with that statement.

We went to sleep as early as we could that night, hoping to get an early start in the morning. And when the sun rose and woke us with its brightness through our windows, we got up, packed, and left in the silent, still morning.

After our serious conversation the day before, I decided to make more of an effort to chat with Liliwen. I quickly found that our conversations made the day move faster, and helped me feel more grounded. It also distracted me from the heavy weight of my pack on my shoulders, and the fact that we were walking on foot, something my legs were well aware of after a few hours.

The road led us into the cedar forest at the base of the mountain, and we spent hours beneath the branches, many laden with snow, and the understory dotted here and there with patches of snow and ice. The road was mostly straight but climbed steadily upward, leading us out of the foothills and into the snow-covered, mountainous landscape proper. In the afternoon it became quite steep, and I heard Liliwen huffing as much as I was.

"This is quite tough after riding for so long," she said with a breathy laugh. I tried to smile at her as I nodded in agreement, but had to concentrate all of my energy on just continuing the climb.

When we emerged from the forest just as the sun was setting, a field of snow that stretched into the distance lay before us. It inclined sharply upward, stretching toward the sky and blocking the peak of Aornadur from our view.

"The first cairn," Liliwen said, her voice hushed in the gentle breeze that blew across the snow. I looked at her and saw that she was pointing to a nearby tree just a few yards away, and then saw the tall stack of stones sitting beneath it. It was at least six feet tall, and made up of a multitude of flat slate stones stacked on top of each other. The base stone was at least two feet in diameter, and they got progressively smaller the higher up the cairn they were placed. We paused and appraised it for a moment, before glancing at each other and nodding. The real climb had begun.

»«

An hour and two cairns later, the sun had just set below the jagged peaks in the west, and everything around us was fiery and orange, but growing duller by the second.

"Let's stop for the night," I said as we reached a slight plateau on the hill, flat enough that I hoped we would be able to sleep comfortably. Liliwen nodded and dropped her pack with a groan, and we got to work setting up our bedrolls. There was nothing nearby to light a fire with, so we wrapped ourselves in blankets and furs, and ate slowly, hoping to make our small meal for the day last.

"How far do you think we walked today?" Liliwen asked as she wrapped her arms around her folded knees, having just finished eating. I took my last bite and shrugged.

"Hard to say. The cairns are supposed to be three miles apart. I would guess…at least fifteen miles."

Liliwen let out an abrupt laugh, and I looked over at her to see her smiling down at the way we had come, our footprints distinct lines in the snow leading into the distance.

"What's funny?" I asked, feeling a smile on my frozen face.

She shook her head slightly, but her grin remained. "Nothing. I just…I never could have imagined doing something like this a year ago."

"There was no need a year ago," I said.

She rolled her eyes as she turned to look at me. "Of course. But even just this physical labor—it would have sounded absurd to me. I would have said I couldn't do it." In the low light of the moon and stars, I could see her uncertainty again as she chewed on the inside of her lip, still trying to keep her smile.

"Never underestimate motivation," I said after a moment.

She let out her short, unsure laugh again, but didn't reply immediately. She was looking out over the slope again, and I turned to study it too. Far below us was the dark expanse of the forest, but everything beyond the trees was obscured in an atmospheric haze. The haze melted into the horizon, which blended into the sky; I couldn't quite tell where the land ended and the sky began.

I was surprised when Liliwen began speaking again, lost in the view as I was. "What about Varina?" she asked, her tone uncertain. She wasn't looking at me, so I didn't look at her. But I felt my mouth set in a grim line.

"I don't know. I'm relieved she hasn't shown herself, but...I can't help but wonder if she..." I trailed off, not wanting to say what I was thinking out loud.

"If she followed Runa and Rhys," Liliwen finished in a soft voice. I nodded, glaring out at the darkness of the night. "I doubt it, Eira. She was sent to find you, not Runa."

"Maybe she lost our trail," I said with a small shrug, pushing the idea of Varina attacking Runa and Rhys from my mind. "Or maybe she's still following us, wondering where we're going."

"We can see everything behind us for miles," Liliwen gestured down the slope before us.

"And she can become invisible," I reminded her. I heard her let out a sigh, and then shift slightly on her bedroll. "But in one of the memories I saw from the dagger..." She stopped shifting as she listened closely. "It was clear that I'm her real target. I believe she was momentarily distracted at the battle of the pass."

"What happened in that memory?" Liliwen asked eagerly.

"Varina promised to hunt me down and bring me back to them—these people she called the emperor and empress. The leaders of the Syrthiaid. I don't know why they want me to come back, but…" I trailed off, thinking about the memory, how she had mentioned Calliten. "They had been talking to my mentor. She said he had told her that he had kept me weak and untrained so that I wouldn't be able to fight him."

"That's awful," Liliwen said softly. "Eos are supposed to be strong, to protect the commoners."

"He only taught me how to heal," I said, shaking my head slightly.

"Maybe…" Liliwen began, but seemed unwilling to finish the sentence. I looked at her in annoyance.

"What?" I asked.

"Maybe you can find out more about what he said to her," she suggested. I knew exactly what she was saying, but I wasn't sure why she was saying it.

"Why do I care what he said to her?" I asked, looking out over the silvery moonlit snowfield.

"We might get a better idea of why they want you returned to them," Liliwen said. "All they know about you must be from your mentor."

I shrugged. "I don't see how it matters, though."

"Aren't you at least curious?" Liliwen pressed.

I sighed. "I suppose…a little bit," I admitted. "But memories take a lot of energy. And I don't know how to control it. The memories are always random. I have no idea why I see what I see."

"It's worth a shot," Liliwen insisted, then pointed to my bag. "Go on, give it a try. I'll make sure nothing bad happens to you."

I let out another sigh, this one more shaky, but found myself reaching for my bag, overcome with morbid curiosity. What had Calliten told them about me? Why did they want me to come home so badly?

I pulled the sheathed dagger from the bag and held it in my lap, looking down at the shining hilt warily.

"Go on," Liliwen said softly. "You'll be safe, don't worry." I took a deep breath and nodded, already formulating a plan to try and get this to work.

I needed to see a memory attached to the dagger that involved Calliten. Varina wasn't in possession of the dagger until they already had the information from Calliten about me, so someone else was wearing it. It must have been Cassia, who had given the dagger to Varina just before she left in search of me.

As I gripped the hilt of the dagger with both hands, I thought about both Cassia and Calliten, their faces, their voices, remembering as much as I could about the former as I had only met her briefly. I tried to encapsulate their whole persons in my mind, and hold them there as I felt the cool metal beneath my fingers. For a few long seconds, all I did was think about those two people, feel the metal, and breathe deeply. And then—

I fell so quickly I almost tried to stop it, but I held on. My reality had changed, and I was in a well-decorated room full of bookshelves. A plush carpet covered the floor beneath my feet, and in front of me, five people sat on sofas. I realized where I was almost instantly. It was Calliten's personal library.

I felt my pulse increase at the sight of the people on the couches, all of whom I recognized. Cassia and Varina sat beside each other on one sofa, Age and Riki, the pretender emperor and empress, on another, and Calliten on a third across from them. Cassia had the dagger on her hip, sitting with it obviously visible.

I had expected Calliten to look like a prisoner, perhaps even being kept in a cell, but he was perfectly at ease, obviously free in his own quarters. I felt like my blood was going to boil when I realized he must have cut some kind of deal with them.

"So you understand, then," Age was saying, a thin smile on his face. He leaned back against the cushions, while Riki sat upright next to him. "We don't have time to find your…protégé."

"I'm afraid that you might not understand," Calliten said calmly, leaning forward just a bit. "She would be a great asset to your cause."

Age's smile grew, cold and menacing. "Of course, we value every magical life. However—"

"She is no ordinary mage," Calliten said. Age's smile fell, and Cassia and Varina glanced at each other, Cassia's eyes wide.

"You mean—" Riki said, somewhere between a whisper and a hiss.

"Oh yes." Calliten nodded. "You lose her, and you lose a weapon."

I felt the memory start to fade even as I tried desperately to cling to it, to hear more. But it faded to black, my energy for the memory used up, and I found myself gasping, lying back on my bedroll in the cold wind of Aornadur.

"Eira! Are you alright? What did you see?" Liliwen asked as she tried to help me sit up with an arm around my shoulders. I leaned over my knees, still catching my breath. Still processing what I had seen.

I looked up at her, unable to keep the confusion out of my expression. "I don't understand," I murmured, already growing frustrated. Liliwen tried to wait patiently, but I could see her dying to ask me what happened again. I rubbed my forehead, thinking over the few things I had heard said.

"Calliten—my mentor… He told them that they needed me. That I wasn't a normal Eos," I said, shaking my head. "He was lying to them. He—"

"But you aren't normal," Liliwen said, frowning at me. "Look at this power you have."

"It is not a power," I snapped, and she glared at me. I took a deep breath, and tried to speak more calmly. "It's…some kind of curse, maybe. A disorder. And it never happened until right before I left the Benaty, so there's no way Calliten knew about it. No, he was lying to them. Because he never wanted me to leave." My eyes focused on a random clump of snow as I pieced it together. "He told them to find me, that they wanted me, because he hates that I escaped, and he didn't."

I could feel Liliwen staring at me, but I couldn't raise my head to look back at her. All I felt was anger, disgust. How could he be so selfish? Why was I surprised?

"I'm sorry, Eira," Liliwen said softly. I shrugged, not having anything to say. "But you know they're not going to get you. If Varina attacks, we'll be ready. Okay?"

I huffed out a laugh and turned to look at her. "You really believe that?"

She nodded, serious, and I searched her face for any hints of doubt; there was none. I felt a weak smile take over my face, and I nodded back, comforted by her steadfastness.

A comfortable silence fell between us, and as the moon continued to climb higher in the starry sky, I considered turning in for the night. "I might go to sleep soon," I said softly, the hush of nighttime making me not want to speak too loudly. We had already agreed that she would keep watch the first half of the night, and I would watch the second half.

Liliwen nodded. "The earlier, the better," she smiled. "Don't worry about me. I'm still wide awake."

I nodded and crawled into my bedroll, pulling furs and blankets over me until I felt like the cold was kept at bay, and settled into the softness that surrounded me. But even when I kept my eyes closed for many minutes, I couldn't shake the desire to say one more thing.

I turned onto my side to face Liliwen, and saw her sitting as she had all evening, her legs folded and knees to her chest, her inquisitive eyes peering into the darkened landscape around us. But she wasn't looking around as Runa did, with suspicion and eyes searching for danger, but with curiosity, appreciation, contentment. I felt myself smile slightly. She was an interesting person, and a comforting presence.

"Liliwen," I said quietly, and she turned to look at me, clearly surprised.

"Are you okay?" she asked, her brows furrowed in concern.

I nodded with a smile, trying to put her at ease.

"Yes. I just wanted to say something. I was feeling awful when we got to Geirr. I'd been feeling awful for days, really. And I...I feel like I didn't thank you properly for talking to me about all of that. You really...helped me. So I want to thank you." It was hard to translate what I was feeling into words, and that was as good as I could do.

Liliwen grinned at me, her eyes sparkling with moonlight. "You don't have to thank me, Eira," she said. "What you've gone through is unimaginable, and when you explained it, how you were feeling…well, I enjoyed talking to you about it. Maybe enjoyed isn't the right word." She frowned as she thought. "But I was glad you opened up to me."

I propped myself up on an elbow as I felt the urge to disagree with her. "You've gone through more," I said.

"It isn't a competition," she said, then snorted softly. "Look, Eira. We're climbing the tallest mountain to try and save our home. When you think about it like that…doesn't it feel like we've gone through all of this for a reason?"

"What do you mean?" I blinked at her.

"All the fighting and Varina hunting you, the traveling for days on end—this was the goal the whole time, wasn't it? And maybe we're so willing to do this climb because we know, from the past couple months, that we can overcome great difficulty." She was frowning softly as she spoke, unusually philosophical.

"I feel like we're doing this because we don't have a choice," I argued.

"You always have a choice," Liliwen said. And then she was smiling at me again, her face soft and gentle, and I found myself smiling back.

"You're right," I conceded. "I'm happy you're here, Liliwen."

"I'm happy I'm here too," she said, and I could tell as I lay back down, finally ready to sleep, that she really meant it.

»«

It was the middle of the night when I awoke and knew something was wrong. Crashing bangs echoed through my ears as my mind jumped to consciousness. I was on my feet before I knew what I was doing, drawing my sword from its sheath and taking in my surroundings. My heart dropped when I saw Liliwen locked in close battle with a slim figure, their blades whirling through the cold night air, lit up in the moonlight.

They fought only a dozen or so yards down the slope, a trail of deep footprints in the snow leading to them. I followed the trail without thought, knowing it was made by Liliwen. And I knew, even before I could see her features, whom she was fighting. The figure faded in and out of sight, like a ghost stuck between realms.

Varina didn't spare me a glance as I neared them, focusing all of her energy on Liliwen. There was something unrefined about her movements, which gave me pause. She had always seemed so agile in her fighting during our encounters before. But Liliwen, with much less fighting experience, was easily holding her own against Varina. And Varina's advantage of being able to turn invisible was gone; every few seconds the image of her would waver, as though considering becoming invisible, but every time Liliwen's sword swung toward her, Varina lost her concentration and returned to clear visibility.

She was weakened. Perhaps it was the fighting in the pass, or traversing harsh snow-covered forests, but she was not herself.

I rushed to stand by Liliwen's side after only a moment of hesitation, and Varina's eyes flashed to mine, a flare of anger lighting them up. And then I saw the exhaustion in her face, the desperation as she grit her teeth and grunted with every movement. I swung my blade to block her attacks when Liliwen seemed to be too slow, and watched as her eyes flashed both with anger and a hint of fear.

Despite my shock and the chaos I found myself in, a question came out of my mouth when my blade locked with Varina's yet again. "Why did you wait?" I asked, grunting with the force of holding her back.

"Return what you stole," she hissed, ignoring my question. The dagger, secured to my waist, glittered and caught her eye for a second, but she knew that any lapse in her focus would result in her losing the fight.

"If I do," I panted, slashing out at her even as she jumped back, still nimble, "you'll leave us alone." I tried to make a demand, but it sounded weak and hopeless even to my ears. She bared her teeth, pausing ten feet away from me, having backed away as she caught her breath.

"I can't," she gasped, the anger in her eyes mixing evenly with fear. I knew what she feared, at least vaguely. I heard Liliwen's feet crunch softly through the snow as she came to stand beside me, heard her labored breathing loud in the still night air.

"You can. You don't have to serve them," I said, feeling that cold air make my lungs ache. Varina's eyes flashed in the moonlight as she blinked at me.

"I do not serve them," she hissed. "We work together."

"I have seen your memories," I said, the words leaving my mouth plain and matter-of-factly. "And I know they see you only as a servant."

Varina stared at me evenly, not showing any hint of my surprise at my words. "How?" she asked after a moment. "How did you see my memories?"

I paused, surprised by the question. There was some current of understanding running between us that I hadn't anticipated. Like we were saying so much with so few words. "The dagger," I answered honestly, just above the whisper.

"Return it," Varina snapped immediately. Without thinking, I unsheathed it and held it in my hand at my side, my sword still clutched in the other.

"Leave," I said.

"If you have seen what you claim to have seen," she said, her silvery eyes piercing mine through the darkness, "then you know that I cannot. I cannot fail."

"I think you want to fail," I challenged.

"Eira," Liliwen whispered, her voice wavering with exhaustion and fear. I ignored her.

"I think," I continued, "that if you wanted to capture me, you would have done so ages ago. At Rodljost Pass. The evening after—"

"I was injured," Varina hissed, as though angry she had to admit it.

"You attacked Runa instead of me."

"I was blinded to you once I saw her," Varina spat. "She humiliated me—"

"You don't like to admit just how weak you are, do you?" I said. I hardly knew what I was saying. All I knew was that I was getting closer to her truth, I was leading her towards honesty whether she knew it or not. "You know the truth. You're already a failure. And your empress and emperor are well aware of that. They sent you on this chase because they see you as expendable and me as worthless. They knew Calliten was lying about me being special…but it was a perfect opportunity to get rid of you."

Rage burned in her eyes as Varina stared at me, mute and unblinking. I could feel how she was thinking through her options, her eyes flashing from the dagger to my face to Liliwen beside me. She was calculating her odds against us, and she didn't like what she saw. Then, her shoulders slumped.

"Give me the dagger and I will leave," she whispered, her eyes dropping to the ground between us. Her face became smooth and blank, her eyes dull in the low light. I glanced at Liliwen who nodded at me slowly, still stiff with fear. I took a few steps toward Varina with hesitation, and still she didn't look up at me, a picture of defeat standing in the barren snow.

I held out the dagger's hilt to her when I was only three feet away from her. Liliwen followed until she stood just behind me, and I could still feel her tension emanating from her. Being that close to Varina made me incredibly uncomfortable, my system still identifying her as a threat. She looked up at me then, and as she reached out to take the dagger from me I saw my mistake.

She was weak in body, but not in mind.

Her eyes flashed with anger and spirit renewed, her lips twisting into a humorless smile. She closed the distance between our hands with magic, ripping the blade from mine and into hers, then immediately swung out at me with a fiery slash. I jumped back, stumbling through the snow and losing my footing. The blade had only just missed my abdomen, and a thin cut appeared in my outermost tunic. As I fell backwards I saw Liliwen rush past me in a blur, her sword raised as she grunted with exertion.

My back met the icy ground with a thump, my heart racing with the fear of the close call, and I rushed to get back on my feet, knowing that Liliwen needed my help, that Varina's strength was renewed, that she had found some new source of energy inside of her as I had antagonized her—

But before I was fully standing I heard a gasp and some soft, wet noise, a haunting sound that turned my stomach. I scrambled to my feet, whirling around and feeling numb at the sight before me. Varina stood close to Liliwen, too close, and the point of the Syrthiaid's dagger glittered with black blood where it protruded from Liliwen's back.

For a few moments everything was still, slowed down in my mind. How Varina panted with shallow breaths, her limbs shaking, but her fingers still gripped tightly around the hilt of the dagger. How Liliwen stared at her in shock, unmoving, her mouth slightly open, her body perfectly still. Then Liliwen collapsed and the blade fell with her, and Varina stood over her, the twisted smile still on her lips as she looked down at Liliwen's gasping form, bleeding into the snow.

I was frozen, time slowed to a stop as my mind refused to understand what I saw before me. Then Varina turned her grin to me, and took a step towards me, her sword hanging limply from her right hand, the point dragging through the snow.

"With us, you will never know weakness," she said, her voice soft but it felt like screams in my mind. "With us, you will meet true power. Find your destiny, Aneira. It is time. Time to leave the common world behind, and greet the new world we envision."

Liliwen's gasps filled the air as her words fell away on the wind, and I gave no reply. I looked at the girl lying in the snow, the dagger's hilt glowing in moonlight from where it protruded from her stomach. She was convulsing slightly, shifting in the snow as the pain coursed through her body.

When I didn't reply, didn't meet her eyes, Varina grew angry again and I felt her force on me, pushing me towards her. My feet shifted in the snow and for a moment I considered letting it happen. After all, what was the point in fighting anymore? But then Liliwen cried out, nearly a scream, and I snapped out of my desire for apathy. She was alive, she was in pain, but I could save her. I had to. I closed my eyes and pushed back against Varina's force, stopping her all at once. I felt a glimmer of surprise echo through her magic into mine, and I felt my own glimmer of satisfaction in response. For a moment all was quiet and still, and I could feel curiosity mix with her anger as she pushed once again with her magic, her dismay when it hit my wall. She had never known me to be this strong. Neither had I. I was somewhere else, blind to her and the world around me, but suddenly a truth became clear.

Emotion was the key to the Eosiaid. Intent, feeling, truth; it all added up to power when used correctly. It fell into place inside of me, and I felt it all. I felt how the blood roared through my ears, and how the magic of the Eosiaid coursed through my veins. I didn't try to stop the magic from moving and gathering within me. Instead, I let it take hold, fueled by my own truth, by my own heart.

The power welled up in me and exploded out with careful precision as I directed it in a narrow spike right at Varina. It cut through her own wall of energy like an arrow through parchment, the remains blowing away like tatters between us. I felt as my magic hit her body like a lightning bolt, as her ribs were cracked and organs were lacerated. I opened my eyes and watched as she was thrown off of her feet and through the air, before landing in the snowbank yards away from me down the hill, already unconscious. The momentum of her body pushed her further until she was rolling downward, and the snow rolled with her. Soon I couldn't see her anymore lost as she was in the avalanche my explosive power had triggered. The roaring of the snow falling further and further away from us filled my ears and shook the ice beneath my feet like an earthquake, but I barely noticed as I struggled through the snow to Liliwen, whose convulsions had diminished as she still lay on her back on the icy ground.

I collapsed onto my knees beside her and heard her rattling breath, and her eyes met mine as she looked up at me with a hazy gaze. The dagger still protruded from her stomach, and I immediately assessed the wound before I attempted to pull it out. I needed to know what needed to be healed and how quickly before removing the blade, as her blood would begin to flow as soon as I did.

"Eira, I'm sorry," she mumbled as I checked the wound, and felt my body clutched in fear as I felt the extent of it. Her heart, her lungs—so many things had been cut and were already in the process of shutting down. One of her lungs was already filling up with fluid, and it took me a few moments to realize what I was feeling.

I had heard of the limitations of healing magic, that sometimes the body would be too ill or injured to respond to healing power. The Wood Death was the most resilient disease against magic, hardly responding to it at all. Physical injuries like cuts and broken bones were usually the easiest wounds to heal, but at some point, even magic was useless against the worst severities. I had never known I would experience this limit myself, and as I sat there with Liliwen gasping in front of me, I didn't want to accept it. I couldn't.

I threw my magic at the wound as I pulled the dagger out and threw it in the snow beside us. She tried to scream but was unable to make much noise, and instead let out a horrible gurgling sound. I pulled my cloak off and pressed the thick wool fabric over the wound, pressing down hard with my hands and letting my magic flow into her body, energy of healing and rebirth.

But it flowed around the wound, like a river over a boulder, not having any effect at all. Still, I didn't accept it. I had no choice. I pressed harder with my hands, concentrated harder on the wound in my mind, feeling the different parts of her abdomen and how they had been damaged. I felt for any give, any sign that my efforts were working, and I kept my eyes shut tight, focusing on my mental image of the wound and what needed to be done to save her.

But when I felt her cold hand fold over mine, when I heard how her breath was soft and shallow, when my eyes opened and saw her staring at me with a lucid gentleness, acceptance came to me.

I knew it was over, but my words still wanted to fight.

"I told you," I rasped, "if anything happens to you, I can't forgive myself."

I felt a glimmer of surprise when her lips quirked up in a smile. "I chose this. Don't blame yourself," she whispered. She couldn't speak at volume any longer. "You have to keep going, though," she said, the little smile disappearing all at once, replaced with a little frown.

I shook my head without thinking. "I don't want—"

"It's…not about…what you want," she whispered slowly, taking long pauses to summon the energy. Her eyes started to flutter shut, but she forced them back open, struggling to focus on my face. I kept pushing energy into her, and it kept flowing around her, aimless and absorbed into nothingness. I grit my teeth when I felt her organs begin to stall from the lack of blood and oxygen.

"I can't do it," I whispered, and I wasn't even sure what I was talking about. Save her? Finish the climb? Fight the Syrthiaid? I couldn't do any of it.

"Eira," she whispered, and I felt her hand grip mine, just for a moment, just the last bit of her strength. She looked me in the eyes, and I saw that her own were dimming. But she summoned the air and strength she needed.

"You have to."

>×<

There was an exact moment when she left the realm of the living, but I had withdrawn my mind from the wound, withdrawing all the way into myself, wrapped in a shroud of numbness. I didn't really return to my surroundings until the sun's light began to slip over the horizon, bathing the snow around me in pale pink. I blinked and looked down at Liliwen, her eyes shut and mouth just slightly open, her skin white and icy. I realized I was cold too, dangerously cold. My cloak was still draped over her torso, and I wondered how much of her blood it had absorbed. I tried not to think about that any further as I took the cloak back and pulled it around my shoulders. I felt frozen in more ways than one, the temperature on the mountain only one of my problems.

As the pink sky became gold and the sun itself emerged from the eastern peaks, I remembered what Liliwen had said, her words echoing through my mind. I had to keep going. I had to.

So I stood with stiff legs, looking down at the body in front of me and knowing that I had to put her to rest, somehow. It was part of the Awyrcred that people must be buried as soon as possible after their death, as it was believed that the soul would continue to feel the pain of death until the body was allowed to rest.

Though I wasn't sure I believed in souls and pain after death, I thought that Liliwen might, and it was only her opinion that mattered. I used magic to push the snow away in a wide area, hoping to find soil in which I could dig a grave, but all I found was hard-packed ice a few feet underneath the snow.

So I summoned more magic, and cracked the ice, shards flying into the air and glittering like flames in the morning sun. I noticed and thought it was probably beautiful, but couldn't manage to feel anything.

It took a while, but eventually I was able to lay Liliwen to rest in her icy tomb. I pushed the ice and snow back over her, compacting it until she was invisible, hidden many yards below the surface. Only then, standing above her, did I feel the tears on my face as they quickly turned cold in the frosty air.

»«

The last coherent thing I remember doing was picking up the dagger and cleaning it of Liliwen's blood with my already bloodied cloak. I sheathed it once again and put it in my pack. I couldn't understand why I was keeping it, but I felt that I needed to.

It feels strange for me to admit, but I don't remember much of the next two weeks. The days passed in a blur as I pushed up the mountain, following the cairns and ignoring the increasingly poor conditions. I numbed myself to everything—what I was doing, why I was doing it, and everything that had happened in the few weeks before. If I had thought of all of the people I had left and lost, I intuitively knew that I wouldn't have the strength to keep going.

So the landscapes around me passed with the days, and I trekked up hills, cliffs, ravines, and icy slopes mindlessly. I passed through dense, dark fog banks, and days so bright that everything was blinding. I moved forward like I wasn't aware of my body, and avoided thinking like I didn't have a mind. Internally, I felt only a numb peace. Externally, all I knew was that I was tired and cold, but nothing more.

Near the end of the second week of climbing, though, I was no longer able to ignore my body. I was freezing, covered in bruises from the climb, and painfully exhausted. Though my mind remained numb, I couldn't help but acknowledge the fact that my body was beginning to give up. I still chose to push on, as though the pain was something my mind could override.

It wasn't.

It was a bright and sunny day, though luckily not too blinding. The sun was behind me as I carefully stepped up a steep hill, forcing my snowshoes into the soft powder and compacting it, creating small shelves for my feet to wedge into. The slope seemed to extend upward forever, and I had to go straight up with it, as gray, jagged boulders lined either side of it. I had just passed a cairn so I knew I was going the right way.

And then one of my feet slipped from the shelf I had made as it hadn't been compacted enough, and I forced my body to relax as I fell forward into the snow, and then began to slide at speed back down the hill. I shut my eyes tightly as snow and wind rushed past my ears, hoping that I wouldn't hit a boulder.

I let out a breath I had been holding when I came to a stop on the relatively flat expanse of snow at the base of the hill, but didn't move. I searched for the strength to move my arms and push myself up, but no energy came to me. Now that I had relaxed, my body had finally given out.

Then I felt pain in my left forearm, like a deep, throbbing cut. I lifted my head slowly, and blinked when I saw blood seeping into the snow underneath my arm. That sight was enough to get me to lift my arm, energy summoned all at once, and I grit my teeth when I saw a deep gash through the many sleeves I was wearing, cutting all the way through to my skin. I lifted my head further and squinted back up the hill, and saw a large, sharp rock protruding from the snow a few yards above me.

If I had had the energy to curse I would have, but all I could manage to do was sit up with slow care, until I was cross-legged in the snow. Then I set to work dressing the wound, and internally lamenting the state of my clothes. There was nothing I could do about the cuts made to them. But I was able to tear a length of fabric from one of my sleeves and tie it tightly around the cut, which, I realized, wasn't all that deep. The many layers of cloth the rock had cut through had protected my arm from even worse damage.

I knew the pain was getting worse as I tied the cloth around my arm, but my mind was separated from it, unimpressed.

Still, the shock had woken me up a bit, more than I had been in days, and I found myself wondering a vague question.

What was I doing?

There was a simple answer that came easily: climbing Aornadur. And I knew why too. I had to see the Himminir. I had to. She and I had agreed that it was what we had to do.

I frowned and shook my head, not wanting to think about her. If I thought about her, I would want to turn back. Even though she wanted me to keep going, I would want to turn back.

I wondered if turning back was such a bad idea.

I was tired. My whole body ached and it was becoming harder and harder to ignore the pain. I was cold, painfully cold. I had been for weeks, and I was tired of it. I wanted to be near a fire, I wanted to be inside a building. I wanted to sleep in a bed and eat a hot meal.

A part of my brain reminded me that I was closer to my destination than my starting point, and if I kept going it was likely that I would be rewarded with all of those things. And still, I wanted to go back. I wanted to undo the last few weeks, the last few months. I wanted it all to not have happened the way it did.

I shook my head as the pain in my arm began to numb, and I pulled the pack off of my back, intent on eating a small portion of dried meat, in the hopes that I could immediately derive some energy from it. But when I reached into the bag and my hand met something delicate and soft, I paused, wondering what it was. I couldn't remember owning anything that felt like that. And when I pulled the item out, I blinked at what lay in my hand, feeling a glimmer of surprise: a green-feathered quill.

Like your eyes, he had said. The metal pen and nib were cold against my palm, but the feather almost felt warm, and comfortingly soft. The same quill I had used to write that note so many weeks before. The quill I had said goodbye with. I blinked again and barely stopped my hand from wrapping around the feather, feeling strength enter my hand and threatening to crush the delicate item held in it. I could see his expression so clearly when he handed it to me, the incredible warmth that he held, that steadfast kindness. His eyes were so vivid, his face so clear in my mind, I couldn't tell if it was a vision or a memory.

But my icy, windswept surroundings returned to me, and I put the quill back in the bag carefully, and then pulled out the meat instead. I took a couple of mindless bites as Rhys's words turned over in my mind in chaotic whirls. The quill hadn't been necessary, but he had insisted on buying it. It was a poor use of money, and he knew that, and still he had bought it, had told me it was the perfect color, the same color as my eyes.

And then I used it to explain why I had to leave him.

Before I knew what I was doing, I was packing everything up, standing with protesting muscles and joints, and slinging the pack onto my back once again. I hadn't left him for no reason. I hadn't left everything behind just to give up.

I glared at the hill above me, at the point where it met the sky, and I set my mind to it. I wasn't going to fall again.

22

The Inherents

A few days later I became aware that the cairns were appearing closer and closer together, until they were only half a mile apart. The ground was less steep but more rocky, interspersed with patches of permanent ice, easy to slip on. The sky was always clear there, shining with crystal clarity, and the air was thin. Sometimes when I wasn't careful, I would push myself too hard and become dizzy.

But the knowledge that I was close to the end was enough to keep me going at that point. And when the land became completely flat, the ground beneath me all ice and flat granite stone, I knew I was moments away from finding them.

The plateau I stood on wasn't just a bit of flat land. It was the summit of the mountain, and a sharp wind howled and pulled at my braids and cloaks. Before me were towering boulders, as tall and wide as buildings. I began making my way around them, looking for any sign of the Himminir. I didn't know what I was looking for exactly, but was sure that it would be obvious once I came to it.

And it certainly was. As I passed one of the boulders I saw it there before me, a great stone manor that looked like it was carved right from the mountain. I stood just a few meters from the door centered in its facade, and the building stretched out far to either side. I couldn't tell for sure, but it looked like the land fell away on the other side of the manor. It was built on the edge of a cliff. Balconies, railings, and windows were all carved from the same substrate, creating an imposing look that stopped me in my tracks for a few moments.

But then the elation hit me, the pure joy that I had reached the destination, and I began stumbling forward, until my shaking hand was gripping the great handle protruding from the front of the stone door. I pulled, barely breathing, and the door opened easily.

When I stepped inside, I found myself in a dark room, lit only by two torches. Compared to the bright sun outside, it was incredibly dim to my eyes, and it took a few moments for them to adjust. The torches were mounted on either side of a large door on the opposite wall, and on either side of the room were a set of double doors. It was a small foyer, and not at all what I had been expecting.

Before I really had time to react, the door opposite me opened and hooded figures emerged and lined up across the room before me. I froze, suddenly scared of the people I had come to meet, and waited for them to stop appearing. All I heard for a few moments were the sounds of their soft shoes moving across the stone floor, and the shuffling of their cloaks as they walked.

One stepped forward as I was trying to count how many there were—there were supposed to be twenty-two—and when he lowered his hood I saw a calm, smiling face. He had short brown hair and brown eyes, eyes that seemed to be evaluating me as much as they were twinkling with kindness.

"Welcome," he said in a soft voice that he was somehow able to project. "You have traveled far."

"Do you know why I'm here?" I managed to ask, hiding my shaking hands in the long sleeves of my cloak.

He tilted his head slightly as he continued to smile. "There are only a few reasons one could come all the way here. I have my suspicions." I opened my mouth to reply, to start demanding answers from him, but he held up a hand. "You must rest first, before we speak. You are in no state to meet with us yet."

"I'm fine," I said, narrowing my eyes at him. At the same time, I felt how my head was swimming, and how I shivered from exhaustion and cold.

"If you go down this hall," he said, gesturing with an open hand to my left, "the first room you will find has a lit fire and a freshly made bed, as well as an assortment of food laid out. Rest there for as long as you need, and when you feel ready, you may find us at the end of this hallway." He turned and then gestured at the door they had just appeared from. I pursed my lips, split between my desire for warmth, food, and sleep, and my desire for answers. But my human needs won out, and I nodded in agreement.

"Thank you," I said, before bending down and removing my snowshoes, then standing up straight with them clutched in my hands. He was still smiling at me, but somehow it wasn't off-putting.

"Rest well. We will see you soon," he said, bowing his head slightly before turning and disappearing through the doorway. The rest followed him, their hoods still covering their faces, and I turned away from them and opened the door on the left side of the room.

Moments later, I was inside the first room as he had indicated, melting in the warmth of the fire that was roaring and bursting from the fireplace beside the bed. In the middle of the room was a small wooden table and chair, out of place with everything else stone, and the table was laden with bread, cheese, and dried fruits and meats. I hadn't seen fresh foods for weeks, and I mindlessly dug in, relieved to feel my limbs thaw from the warm temperature of the room.

Now warm and fed, the last thing my body called for was sleep, and I was more than willing to take off my boots and cloak, pull back the thick blankets and furs that covered the bed, and crawl in.

I knew it wasn't the softest bed I had ever slept on, but it was still a perfectly wonderful feeling to finally fully relax. And I was drifting off to sleep within seconds of closing my eyes.

»«

When I awoke, pink sunlight was streaming through the narrow latticed window above the bed I was in, and I couldn't tell if it was a sunrise or a sunset. I groaned as I stretched and pushed the blankets off of me, feeling pain course through my muscles. I would have liked to stay in bed longer, but the thought of the Inherents had me opening my eyes wide and pushing myself from the bed, avidly ignoring how sore I was.

I pulled my boots on and made my way back through the foyer, then through the door opposite from the front of the building, finding it hard to pull open. I wasn't sure if it was particularly heavy, or if I was just weak from the climb—it was probably a mix of both. A long hallway extended in front of me, but at the end I could see another set of double doors, already ajar.

I blindly walked towards them and was soon standing on the threshold. I was surprised to see only the man who had greeted me and one other cloaked figure sitting at a large stone table. It was clear that the table was hewn from the same stone as the building, as if it had been carved from the mountain itself. The man smiled at me when I appeared in the doorway, while the blond woman next to him kept her narrow features blank. They sat on the other side of the table from where I stood, in simple wooden chairs, and the man beckoned for me to sit in a similar chair, waving an open palm towards the one across the table from them.

"Please sit," he said, and it was only then I noticed he had an odd accent, the words clipped and unnatural. I did as he asked, moving with slightly tense and unsure movements as I tried to settle into the seat. Behind the two people across from me were tall glass windows stretching the height of the wall, letting in the dying pink light of what I thought looked more like a sunrise than a sunset. The warm light spread over the table and made the dark stones of the walls almost glow with pleasant warmth. In between the windows was another set of double doors, which was odd to me. I wondered where they led.

"Thank you for joining us here. I trust you rested well," the man said, still with his soft smile.

"Very well, thank you," I said, nodding slightly. I cleared my throat without thinking. "Ah…do you…have names?" I wasn't sure what to call the people I was meeting with and it made me uncomfortable.

"You may call me Bem," he said, his voice soft and pleasant. "And this is El. She will be important for you to understand why you are really here," Bem said, gesturing at the woman sitting to his left. She forced a small smile and nodded slightly. I looked at her closely for the first time, and I felt the world shift.

When my eyes met her icy blue ones, I felt my stomach drop and I knew somehow that whatever she said or did would change everything I knew—because when I looked at her, though she was so different from me, I saw myself.

I couldn't speak, and Bem only nodded while El held my gaze. I waited for clarity, for understanding to come from within me, but it didn't. Finally, I tore my eyes away from the woman, and stared at Bem instead, aghast. He smiled softly once again.

"You are made of the same substrate, and that is why it is wonderful that you've come all this way," he said. "The last time one climbed the mountain was over four hundred years ago. And how joyous it was for me to meet him."

His words sunk into me with the coldness of permafrost, and I was appropriately frozen.

Bem looked at me with patient eyes and a compassionate smile. I blinked at him, and thought I understood, but knew that I didn't—not completely.

"What just happened?" I asked, my throat dry. "Who is she?" I pointed at El.

"You don't know who you are yet?" Bem asked as he tilted his head slightly. I felt like he was trying to encourage me to find the answer myself, but I shook my head.

"Is this about…is this about the visions…?" I asked.

"Visions," Bem repeated with a soft smile. "Yes. Eira, you know the answer, don't you? And you know who El is too. You saw in her a part of your soul, and she saw in you a part of hers. You understand now."

I nodded, and felt tears prick my eyes. Not because I was sad, or scared, but because it finally was clear to me. It didn't even occur to me that I had never told them my name. It seemed natural that they knew exactly who I was.

"I'm one of them." I spoke the words myself, knowing somehow that it was important that I say them. Knowing that that was the only explanation for how I felt in that moment.

El smiled at me, a real smile, and her shoulders relaxed. "You have my power," she said in a soft voice, like a cool breeze on a warm day.

"I do," I agreed. The visions of the past that I had seen flashed before my mind, and for the first time I saw them as a gift, a strength, rather than an illness. I smiled back at her, wondering if I looked insane. The words still wouldn't fully come to my lips, but they echoed in my mind. I was a Sacred; seeing the past through memories was a power, not a weakness.

"You are still new to it, but you keep it safe for me, until I must have it returned to me," El continued. I nodded, feeling my expression fall into solemnity. I only vaguely understood, but it didn't feel important to me to clarify her words. Nothing felt important then, except for the truth that had just been revealed to me.

"But that isn't the only reason why you're here. You wanted to understand who you are, I'm sure, but there's another reason you came to meet with us," Bem said, looking at me intently. I nodded once, but wondered if I could focus on what he wanted to tell me. "You want to know about the Sacreds as a whole. Specifically, how to combat the ones who are waging war in your homeland."

"Yes. They're being called the…the Syrthiaid," I said, pulling my mind away from my own personal problems, back to the initial reason I had traveled all this way. "I don't even know what all of their powers are, or if there are others—"

"There are others," Bem said. "Many others. This is the only time in the history of Linra that all twenty-two Sacreds have existed at the same time."

I let that sink in. A line from Adelais's book echoed on the edge of my mind, but I couldn't recall it completely. I shook my head, and tried again to focus on what Bem was saying. "Where are they? Can they help us?" I asked.

Bem, in a surprising move, shrugged. "They are spread throughout the Four Lands. They are all distinct human beings with their own pasts and motivations and hopes. Whether they will help you is for them to decide."

"But how do I find them?" I asked.

Bem let out a sigh and leaned forward. I glanced at El, but she was no longer looking at me. Instead she had let her gaze soften on the table. I felt an energy coming from her that went straight into my heart, as though our hearts were timed to each other. It was an odd feeling, and not one I particularly liked. I refocused on Bem as he finally responded. "You will need the Seer to find them."

"Adelais?" I asked, unable to hide my confusion.

"Adelais is dead," Bem blinked. "No, his…current incarnation, shall we say."

"Where are they?" I asked. "The current Seer?"

Bem closed his eyes, frowning only slightly, a wrinkle appearing between his eyebrows. "She is at the College of Isa. In the northern mountains of the Island of Isa. Her name is Tsukina. She is there, awaiting this." He reached down towards the chair next to him, and produced a small, black leather book. He pushed it across the table towards me, and I took it in both of mine. The cover was cold, smooth, and blank, as was the back. I opened it, and saw only pristine blank pages; I flipped through, the pages sliding through my fingers, but found no words or drawings among them. I looked up at Bem, unable to hide my frown.

"What is this?" I asked after a moment.

"It is what Adelais wanted from me. And it is what I refused to give him," Bem said. "What every Seer wants. The answers to everything."

"It's blank," I said as I set it down on the table in front of me.

"Not to the Seer," Bem said with a cryptic smile. I sighed, and decided it wasn't worth my remaining energy to try and understand.

"Isa?" I repeated.

Bem nodded. "Once the Seer has this, the future will begin to fall into place."

"How do you know she's there?" I asked. "How do you know who she is?"

"I am the Seer too, in a way," he said.

"Then…then wouldn't El always know where I am?" I asked. "There's one of you for every Sacred, right? Couldn't each of you tell me where your counterpart is?"

Bem shook his head, still smiling slightly. "No. Unfortunately, I am the only one who can sense my counterpart. So that, when the time is right, I can return this to the Seer's human soul." He paused, looking at the book with an oddness I couldn't understand. "The time is now."

"For what? What is happening?" I asked, frowning deeply.

"When all the Sacreds exist on Linra at the same time, it is time for us to depart this land, and return to our true home," Bem said, looking not at me but at the wall behind me. I got the sense from his soft voice and distant expression, that he didn't want to discuss this further.

"I don't know if I want to go to Isa," I said honestly. "I've been away from my home for so long."

"You came here to ask how to save your home, to stop these Sacreds called the Syrthiaid. You cannot stop them without the help of the Seer. Now I've told you where to find her. I know it is hard to accept, but your quest is far from over." He returned his gaze to meet mine, and his gentle eyes and calm face placated me, and I found myself nodding in understanding.

Bem smiled, and stood up, and El followed his lead, her expression unreadable. I avoided her eyes, as the feeling of meeting only minutes before was still wearing off, leaving a lasting shock on my system.

"This conversation is concluded for now," Bem said, now with a wide and genuine smile. "In the next room over, you will find food prepared. I'm guessing you are hungry once again. Please, I insist that you eat." Bem gestured to the doors behind us, and I was more than happy to oblige, standing quickly.

"Please don't forget this," Bem said behind me, and I turned around with a frown, only a couple feet away from the door. He had picked up the black book and was holding it out to me. I took it despite not wanting to, accidentally brushing Bem's index finger with my own, and I was actually surprised this time when the blackness overtook me, the roaring of time filling my ears.

But this time the roaring didn't stop even when sight returned to me. I tried to blink but I wasn't able to as both bright light and deep darkness surrounded me. The lights I realized were stars, and the darkness the space between them.

I was so close to them, massive fiery orbs and not the pinpricks I was used to.

I felt like I was moving at a great speed, as something like the wind of time rushed past my face while I passed star after star, moving further into the darkness between. A sense of fear filled me each time I neared one of those great orbs, like I would fall into it and burn within its depths. But I was on a straight track, never wavering.

And when I looked straight ahead, a duller, blue and green disk glowed in the distance. The closer I came to it, the more I understood that it too was an orb, floating quite close to a bright yellow star. And when I was finally close enough, when it filled my horizon and I could see the stretches of storm clouds and the blue sea crashing on cliffs and the emerald grass of rolling hills, only then did I really understand.

Before I could come all the way down to Linra, the vision was cut off like a rope being severed, and my return to reality was jarring. My breathing was heavy and I was sitting in my chair once again. I wondered how I had been lucky enough to fall right into it. When my eyes refocused on the room, Bem and El were still standing across from me. El's blue eyes were round in surprise, her small mouth open slightly, but Bem was smiling, eyes shining.

"The Rememberer, indeed," he said.

»«

I couldn't keep track of the thoughts that whirled through my mind while I ate, and when I was done eating I just sat in the small room, empty plates in front of me. My head hurt from how much I had been thinking, and I didn't even remember eating. One of the few coherent thoughts that entered my mind was that more sleep would do me well, so I stood and exited the room into the main hallway, intent on returning to my room.

But the bright golden light of early morning was now pouring in through the high windows in the room where I had met Bem and El, and I felt drawn to the warmth. I wandered back inside and went straight to the left window, and found myself looking out over a wide half-circle balcony. Without thinking, I opened the large stone door next to me and stepped out onto the balcony, immediately shivering at the icy wind. I ignored the cold as best I could, pulling my cloak tightly around me and crossing my arms over my waist, feeling a glimmer of surprise as I looked around at my surroundings. It wasn't something I had expected to find protruding from the back of the Himminir's home on top of a frigid mountain—there wasn't much of a reason to go outside.

It was a half-circle of stone, with radial lines carved into it, that all met in one point at the center of the doorway. Along the edge of the balcony was a low stone railing, and I walked straight to the center of the edge, placing my hands on the cold stone and leaning over. Below was empty air, as the balcony hung off the edge of a cliff. The ground seemed impossibly far away, and too difficult to accurately gauge. I straightened my back and took a step away, feeling slightly dizzy after seeing how high up I was.

"A little frightening, isn't it?"

I whirled around to see El standing by the doors, a slight smile on her face. Her golden hair was covered by her black hood, and her cloak completely covered the rest of her body, even her feet. It swept along the ground silently as she stepped toward me, and I looked away from her as she came to stand next to me, not wanting to experience that odd feeling when we made eye contact.

"Yes, it is," I said after a moment of simply standing there.

"I know you're…upset," she said softly.

"I'm not." It was a lie, and I could sense the smile in her voice when she replied.

"It would be strange if you weren't," she said. "But I'm here in the hopes that I might help you see your gift."

"It's not my gift," I said, my voice oddly hushed. In the distance, the wind howled through cracks in the rocks, but around the balcony the air was still and quiet.

"Why do you say that?"

"Because it's yours, isn't it?" I glanced at her for a second, but she was looking slightly up in the direction of the sun in the eastern sky, her expression peaceful.

"In a way," she said after a moment. "But it hasn't been mine to use for a long time."

"Why?" I asked.

"Humanity needed these powers more than we did." She didn't elaborate, and I was beginning to grow annoyed.

"Who are you?" I asked, finally turning to glare at her. She turned to look at me as well, her peacefulness at odds with everything I was feeling.

"You mean who are we?" she said, gesturing back at the building behind us. I nodded. "We are the stars and we are the sun. We brought life here and it took its course. And now we have taken ours."

"I'm not in the mood for riddles," I sighed. As was happening quite frequently, I came to the conclusion that I didn't care, and that it didn't matter. "Why are you really here, talking to me right now?"

"I feel that you need to understand the importance of what is happening right now. You came here to save your home, and you have a way to do that now."

"I'm not so sure," I replied. "You told me to go to Isa. That's farther away from home than I've ever been. I'm further from saving my home than I ever have been."

"We told you how to find other Sacreds, others who may join your cause. Is that not what you wanted?"

"I want to know how to stop them, as soon as possible. If I go to Isa, everything I loved about my home could be gone—"

"And what did you love about your home?" El asked. I froze, silently wondering why she would ask me that. Her silence was expectant.

"The people," I said after a moment. "My friends."

"But you weren't satisfied when you were there. You were not satisfied with your life," she said.

"Well, I didn't like...my duties...or how some people treated me. But it was still my home. I still cared about it—"

"Then won't you do whatever you have to do?" El asked. I sensed her looking at me, and I knew with the intensity she held at that moment, I couldn't risk looking at her. "This isn't just about your home, Eira. Sacreds bound together can do more than you can imagine. And right now, with that book Bem gave you, you are the only person with more power than them."

"But I... The book is blank," I said. Even though I wasn't looking at her, a strange feeling was coming over me, like destiny had already been decided, and I was simply floating along as though it was a gentle river. It was peace and excitement and deep, deep fear. I looked at El, and saw her smiling, saw how it reached her eyes and how they crinkled around the edges.

"To you. But to the Seer, it contains all of the world's truths. And you are the one who can unite the Seer and the Prophecy. You just have to realize that one truth, and then the rest are yours to find."

All at once, I relaxed as what she was saying hit me as the truth. The Prophecy, safe in one of the large pockets of my cloak, now settled there with a comfortable weight.

I found myself nodding at her. "Yes," I said. She continued smiling, and for a moment I saw myself in her expression. I blinked, and she was another person to me once again.

"I will go to Isa."

23

Fever

After speaking to El, I was more than ready to start the descent down Aornadur, but I knew that my body needed more rest. I also assumed that more questions would come to mind, and that I would want to speak with either El or Bem again, but I felt surprisingly sure about all I had learned and what I had to do. The journey called to me even as I slept deeply in my room, dreams of the trip down the mountain and past Geirr filling my unconscious mind.

After two more days of rest and substantial food, I felt strong enough to leave. I left my room and found Bem in the foyer, as though he was waiting for me. His hands were folded in front of him, and he stood looking towards the large front double doors. When my footsteps echoed through the small room, he turned to look at me, his calm eyes lucid and sparkling.

He smiled at me in his typical patient way. "You're ready now, aren't you?"

I nodded, feeling my lips quirk just slightly, attempting to return his smile without success. "I am."

"We will provide as much food as you wish to carry with you," he said, bowing his head slightly. "Do you require anything else?"

I hesitated, feeling as though I should be barraging him with questions. But still, none came to mind, only a vague wondering that I was sure he wouldn't be able to answer.

"I'm here to help," he said, encouraging me. And then the words began spilling out.

"Why me?" I blurted. "Why am I…a Sacred?"

He blinked at me, almost surprised. "Because your soul is the same as El's. Have you heard of soulmates?"

I glared at him at that question. "Only in the romantic sense," I replied, ready to argue if he claimed that El and I were destined to be in love with each other.

"That isn't what I'm talking about," he said, a light laugh echoing through his voice. "A mate isn't always romantic, is it? Sometimes they are friends or comrades. Haven't you ever been incredibly close to someone without being in love with them?"

"Of course," I replied, thinking about Mari first, and then Liliwen and Runa. The thought of all three sent pain through my heart, but I tried to not let it show.

"Because souls intertwine with others on many different levels, souls are called to each other for many different reasons," Bem continued. I nodded, relaxing a bit as I understood what he was saying.

"But El…isn't my friend," I said after a short pause.

"No, but she is a true soulmate to you. You felt your similarity when you met a couple days ago, and you intrinsically understood who she was. So similar to you. Because your power belongs to her, and her power belongs to you."

"So she and I are Eosiaid soulmates," I said.

Bem laughed lightly again. "That's one way to put it. But always remember that magic is at the core of this world, and using terms like Eosiaid and Drekligr can water down the true meaning of what it is to be one of them."

"I…think I understand," I said, rubbing the side of my neck as though that would assuage my confusion.

"It's alright. You will learn with time and experience," Bem said. "Now, let's get you your food."

"But I still don't understand," I said, feeling a rush of anxiety. "Why are El and I the same?"

Bem smiled at me and I sensed true compassion in his eyes. "There are some questions, Eira, that don't have answers. You were born with this quality connecting you to El. Why you? Even I cannot say. And it is unlikely you'll ever truly know the answer. It's something you will have to make your peace with."

The anxiety fluttered and then died, replaced with a sense of low resignation in my stomach. I nodded. "Alright," I said.

Bem grinned. "Now, let's get you prepared for your journey."

»«

An hour later my bags were filled with food, I was given extra blankets and furs, and Bem and El were both standing in the foyer as I fastened my snowshoes to my boots once again. When I stood up straight I met El's eyes and this time did not shy away from the odd feeling of knowing a person. Her hood was down, her straight blond hair shining in the fire of the torches. She gave me a soft smile, and if I hadn't known her I would have thought that it was a shy smile.

"Thank you," I said, not really sure what I was thanking her for exactly.

"No need to thank me," she said, shaking her head slightly. "I'm doing my part, as are you."

I turned to Bem, unsure of what to say to him. "Be safe, Eira," he said. "And give my regards to Tsukina."

I blinked. "Does she know you?"

He grinned. "She knows of me."

I paused, debated asking him more questions, but deciding that it wasn't worth it. "I will," I said with a curt nod.

El brushed past me and pushed open the door, flooding the foyer with blinding white light. I blinked repeatedly until my eyes adjusted to the light. Then I turned back to the mysterious pair, and summoned a genuine smile. "I'll do my best," I said, and they nodded, smiling back at me. They stood perfectly still like they were made of stone themselves, but their faces were warm and dynamic, comforting. I wondered if I would miss them or if I would be happy to be away from them and all of their mysteries.

Then I stepped out onto the icy stones, and heard the doors shut behind me. I looked forward to the towering boulders and patches of snow, the bright sun at its peak, and set off, feeling the future pull me forward.

>«

The climb down the mountain went much faster than the ascension, but also felt more treacherous at certain points. My downhill momentum caused me to slip a few times, leading me closer than I would have liked to the edge of a cliff or down a snowbank in the wrong direction from the cairn I was trying to reach in the distance. Still, certain landmarks like oddly shaped boulders or particularly deep ravines told me I was making good time compared to when I had passed them on the way up, and I maintained this pace for over a week.

Well into the second week, when I estimated I was only a few days from reaching Geirr, I began to slow down. Even the climb down was physically taxing, and my arms and shoulders felt heavy and sore from carrying the pack that was still quite laden with food. Still, I pushed on, the thought of seeing Nimue again giving me enough motivation. It was even more motivating than my new quest, which, if I thought about for too long, filled me with anxiety that was difficult to combat.

When I saw the tree line at the bottom of the wide hill where we had slept that first night, I felt an odd mix of emotions. The sun was setting as it had been when we emerged from the forest, and I decided to spend the night in the same spot Liliwen and I had, that flat little area so close to where I had laid her to rest.

The sky was a deep red and the snow was glowing like fire when I finished eating on my bedroll. I looked out over the view before me, remembering how it had looked on that day, how Liliwen had studied everything with curiosity.

Her grave was only a dozen yards or so from me, and I remembered exactly where it was even though the snow had been smoothed over by the wind, and everything was uniformly flat around me. I knew that I could find her again, if I wanted to. But I stayed on my bedroll and looked at everything else around me, trying to find the horizon in the hazy fade from distant land to distant sky.

I fell asleep without realizing it, and in the blinding light of the morning I felt a little more healed than I had been the night before.

>«

I arrived in Geirr that evening, the shadows of the trees and buildings stretching over the road. Nimue nearly jumped out of her stall when she saw me, while Sindri pawed the dusty earth under his feet in anxious confusion. After comforting Nimue and hushing her, I turned to Sindri, and I was surprised to find tears in my eyes. I could see the concern in his, his snorting and tossing of his head showing his emotions with obvious clarity.

"I'm sorry," I said, my voice cracking. I hadn't spoken for weeks, but that wasn't why I had trouble speaking. Sindri was a reminder of what I lost, and my pain was mirrored in his anxious eyes. I stroked his neck and eventually he dropped his head, understanding. Liliwen would not return. When I got to the inn, my mind turned to practicality. Sindri was a strong, beautiful gelding, and though I wasn't in danger of running out of funds, I knew the best course of action would be to sell him. But I also knew that I wouldn't get a good price in Geirr. It was a small town, and not particularly affluent. I resolved to see what I could get for him when I passed through Thrune, and would use him as a pack horse in the meantime. I was thankful that it wasn't the right time or place to sell him, as I knew I derived comfort from his presence, like he carried Liliwen's memory with him. I dreaded selling him when the time was right, though, and I hoped I would be ready when that time came.

After resting at the inn that night, I woke up feeling dizzy and mildly sick. I wondered if I had a fever as I groaned and hunched over my lap as I tried to get out of bed, feeling my forehead with the back of my hand. It was hot and damp with sweat, and I realized I was shivering slightly. It was then that I felt the fiery pain licking up my arm, and with sickening dread I pulled my sleeve up and saw the last thing I wanted to see.

I had forgotten all about that rock that had cut me on the way up the mountain. In the time that I had rested up there, I had checked on the wound once and hadn't seen any signs of infection. But clearly things had changed in the weeks since then, as the cut was now bright red and oozing, feeling as though it was on fire. I grit my teeth as I cut a strip of cloth from one of the sheets I had been sleeping on, hoping that the innkeeper wouldn't notice until I was long gone. Perhaps it was stupid, but I didn't want to bother him with my injury. I just wanted to get on the road, and hopefully find a good physician in Thrune. I wrapped the wound again, hissing at the pain. I knew there was nothing I could do but push on and get to Thrune.

Within an hour I had the horses saddled and loaded, and with much more effort than usual, I was on Nimue's back and riding through Geirr, into the forest south of it. I blinked away the black spots that had appeared in my eyes when I hoisted myself into the saddle and focused on the road ahead, hearing my own breathing echoing inside my head. Sindri's lead was tied to Nimue's saddle and he followed behind us, his head still low. I didn't turn around to look at him very often, put off as I was at the sight.

The day passed slowly, and I found that I was feeling worse and worse as we passed through the pines, snowbanks occasionally piled up on either side. I could hear my heartbeat in my ears and the sounds of the forest were dulled to me. In the evening I felt my whole body begin to throb, and I oscillated between freezing and sweating from sudden heat. Nimue seemed to sense that something was wrong with me as she occasionally tossed her head or let out an anxious snort. I didn't have enough energy to do anything more than pat her neck. But soon I felt my eyes drooping and knew my vision was blurring. I tried to hold onto reality, tried to feel the leather of the reins in my hands and the cold air on my skin, but my senses were fading, and there was nothing I could do about it.

The last thing I felt before everything went dark was the slow sensation of falling.

»«

When my eyes opened next, I immediately registered two things.

One: I was lying on my back on the cold earth, and I was looking up at the stars twinkling between the black branches of the pines above me.

Two: Someone was calling my name.

I felt my face contort into a frown when I realized I recognized the voice. But then I remembered that I was sick and it wasn't possible. He was gone, left far in the past.

I let my eyes flutter shut once again as I allowed myself to imagine warm arms lifting my numb body from the ground, until even that was impossible to feel. Everything was gone, all I could feel was emptiness and all I could see was blackness.

»«

The next thing I registered was the feeling of being comfortably warm, wrapped in softness. Then I felt light on my eyelids, and I became aware of the rest of my body.

478

My eyes blinked open slowly, and I saw that I was in a bed, in a small bedroom. Bright sunlight streamed in through the window to my right, and I vaguely wondered where I was. All I knew was that I had no idea how I had gotten there, but I didn't have the presence of mind to be worried. At that moment I was warm and comfortable in a bed, and seemingly safe; that was enough for me.

I slept off and on as the sun set outside the window, sometimes trying to summon the energy to get out of bed and figure out where I was, but never with any success. My muscles felt spent, and ghostly aches trembled through my body whenever I tried to move.

I was asleep when the door to the room opened suddenly, and I jerked awake. My eyes met those of the last person I expected to see, and I blinked in silence at the man looking back at me, both of us equally surprised by the other.

"You're awake," Rhys said, his surprise evident in his voice.

"Am I dead?" I asked with a hoarse voice, even though I was fairly sure I wasn't. But Rhys's sudden appearance had thrown me off, and I felt less sure as the seconds passed.

His lips twitched, like he was trying not to smile. "No, you're not dead," he said after a moment. He was still standing in the doorway. "You almost were, though."

"What happened?" I asked, looking away from him. I felt distinctly uncomfortable but I wasn't sure why.

"I found you on the road a few miles outside of Thrune. You had collapsed. Nimue didn't leave your side," he said. "I brought you back here. The fever had almost…run its course."

"I had a fever," I said as I frowned out the window, remembering. I had been trying to make it to Thrune to get care, but hadn't made it.

"Yes, you had a wound that was infected—"

I turned my head to stare at him, confused by his words. "A wound?" I repeated. I couldn't remember getting injured.

"On your forearm. A jagged cut. There was a bloody cloth around it, but it hadn't been cleaned properly…"

I pulled up the sleeve of my tunic, remembering the fall and the rock, and wondering how I could have been so stupid. I looked for the scar but saw just a faint silver line, barely visible.

Rhys ran a hand through his hair, a sign that he was flustered. "You were healed. We were able to get rid of the fever and the wound."

"We?"

At that moment, Runa appeared from behind Rhys and stepped into the room with aggression. She didn't stop until she was standing right beside me, blocking the window and staring down at me.

"If you weren't almost dead, I would punch you," she said, venom in her tone. I glanced at Rhys who was obviously cringing as his shoulders tensed and he crossed his arms, but he offered me no help.

"I'm sorry," I said, not really knowing what I was apologizing for. I stared up at Runa, thinking that she looked much the same as the last time I had seen her, her hair long and braided, her face stern with sharp angles and high cheekbones. But there was something in her eyes as she looked down at me that I hadn't seen directed at me before— distrust.

"Apologies won't get you anywhere," she said, now speaking more softly. "We thought you were going to die."

"Well, I didn't —"

"Not just from the fever, you know. You told us to go our own way, and we…we decided if that's what you wanted, then fine. We would do what you want. But we were still scared you were going to die on that mountain," she said. I realized she was barely holding back a complicated show of emotions.

"I shouldn't have… I thought it was right, but I…" I mumbled, looking down at my hands folded over the blankets.

"Never mind," Runa said, waving a hand as she retreated towards the door. Rhys was looking down at his boots with a deep frown, clearly uncomfortable. "I'm glad you're not dead," Runa muttered as she left the room as quickly as she had arrived. A heavy silence fell over Rhys and I as we avoided looking at each other, and I expected him to leave as Runa had, but he didn't budge. Finally, I looked up at him, determined to be honest.

"I really thought it was the right thing to do," I said, and he slowly raised his head to look at me. His face was oddly blank, but I wasn't discouraged. "I thought that Varina would kill both of you. And now I know it was wrong and—" I thought of Liliwen as I almost said the word "pointless," but that was one story I didn't want to tell him.

"It was painful. It hurt us both," Rhys said, his voice low and soft. "I know why you did it. Maybe I would have done the same thing. But she might take some time…to understand."

"And you?" I asked, my voice cracking.

"What about me?" he asked, avoiding the question.

"Will you forgive me?" I waited with a sinking feeling in my stomach as he looked back at me, his eyes soft, his golden hair shining in the evening light.

Then he smiled, and even though it wasn't exactly how I remembered—a bit thinner, a bit unsure—I felt myself relax at the sight.

"I already have," he said. And somehow I knew it was true.

24

The Next Journey

The next morning I was strong enough to get out of bed. Rhys had informed me that he had taken me to Runa's adoptive father's house in Ferning. He had been staying there while trying to figure out what to do next.

"And it became obvious to me, after a few weeks, why I couldn't figure out where to go," he had said. I listened silently, enthralled with the sound of his voice, just the fact that he was existing near me. "I had to go back. I had to find you."

"What were the chances of that?" I said, suppressing an odd smile.

"Apparently, one hundred percent," he replied.

"You were meant to find me then," I said without thought.

"But you don't believe in fate or destiny," he said, smiling at me, but I could see a hint of true surprise in his eyes at my words.

I shrugged, feeling how my shoulders still ached from carrying my pack. "I don't know what I believe anymore," I said honestly.

He wanted to allow me to rest more, and left soon after, promising that we would talk at length the next day, or whenever my strength returned. I didn't want him to leave but I could feel the exhaustion playing at the edges of my consciousness, and I agreed that more rest was a good idea.

So the next morning, I was happy to feel a glimmer of strength in my body. I stood and slowly walked across the room, opening the door despite the pinpricks I felt tingling through my feet and up my legs. The door creaked as I pushed it open, finding myself in a short, sparse hallway. All the walls were made of wood paneling, and the floorboards creaked underneath my feet as I walked slowly towards a staircase that led down to the first floor. I could smell breakfast cooking and it pulled me forward.

I was halfway down when Rhys appeared in front of me at the base of the stairs, looking up at me with mild apprehension. "Are you okay? We can bring the food to you," he said, eyebrows upturned with worry.

I grinned. "I'm fine. I need to figure out how to walk again sometime, don't I?"

He nodded absently as I slowly made it down the last couple steps. He took a couple steps away from me, looking towards an open doorway. "Come on, kitchen's through here," he said, leading the way.

I found myself in a warm kitchen lit with the morning sun, and two people staring at me from the table set in the center of the room. Runa couldn't stop the small frown that spread over her face at the sight of me, but the man sitting across from her immediately broke into a wide grin.

"I heard you'd woken up," he said, gray eyes shining. Everything about him was gray—his hair, eyes, and clothes. His hair was grown to his ears and streaked through with silver, and he had a trimmed gray beard that partially hid his slight wrinkles. But the thing about him that stuck out to me the most was how his eyes sparkled, as though he was always thinking of something funny.

"You must be Garett," I said, feeling my shoulders relax. "Thank you for…" I trailed off, suddenly embarrassed about the situation I was in. He just continued to smile and waved a hand towards the table inviting me to sit. I sat down next to Runa, who remained sitting stiffly chewing her food without looking at me, and Rhys took the chair across from me.

"Don't thank me. Just eat," Garett said, turning his attention back to his own plate. Rhys handed me a dish and a fork, and I loaded it up with eggs, toast, and roasted potatoes. It felt a bit strange to be sitting at a table and eating with Rhys and Runa again, but Garett kept my mind off of it as he chattered to Runa about the local gossip. I wasn't sure she cared as she only occasionally responded to his stories with low humming noises.

I spent all of breakfast looking down at my plate as I slowly worked through the food I had put on it. I wasn't sure what was going to happen when I was done eating, but I knew many difficult conversations would need to happen that day, and I wasn't looking forward to it. I ignored whenever I sensed Rhys looking at me, and felt tension radiating from Runa beside me. Neither one of them was happy with me, and I wasn't convinced that I would ever be able to repair our relationships.

But soon enough my food was gone, and Garett stood up, having finished his meal as well. With his chattering ceased, a tense silence fell over the kitchen table. I finally looked up at Rhys, who seemed to be lost in thought while staring blankly at the table. But when he sensed my gaze his eyes snapped up to mine, and a glimmer of confusion entered his expression, his eyebrows pulling together just slightly.

"Do you...want to talk?" I asked quietly. I wasn't sure where I summoned the courage, but I knew it had to be done sometime; and it would be best to just get it over with.

"Sure," he said with a curt nod, and pushed his chair back from the table. As he stood I glanced at Runa once again, but she was finishing off the eggs and seemingly not paying attention to us.

I followed Rhys from the room and he turned around with a small, unsure smile. "Do you want to go outside? Fresh air would be good for you," he said. We stopped walking in the sitting room at the base of the stairs, and I glanced around at the old furniture, the large stone fireplace with a fire burning brightly. It looked warm and comfortable, but Rhys was right, fresh air sounded like a better idea.

I nodded, and he turned and led me to the front door, opening it with a loud creak. I blinked in the sudden bright light of late morning as I followed him through to a front yard. It was small and enclosed by a worn wooden fence, falling apart in places and missing a few beams. But it smelled of sun-warmed grass even though the air was chilly, and I breathed in deeply.

"So," Rhys said. "Did you want to walk? The town is down that way," he said, pointing toward a collection of buildings about a mile away, smoke rising from the many chimneys as small wisps.

"I think I'm still a bit weak," I said honestly, looking over the town with disinterest.

"Well, there's a bench out back. We could sit there," he suggested. I sensed a persistent cautiousness in his tone and words and it sent a pang through me, but I wasn't quite sure what it meant. It felt like I hardly knew him anymore, like he was far away from me.

"Okay," I nodded, my voice catching on the single word; I hoped he didn't notice.

We walked around to the back of the house, and as Rhys had said there was a wooden bench set against the back wall.

I sat heavily on it, the short walk around the house already leaving me winded.

"Are you alright?" Rhys asked with a soft smile as he sat on the other end of the bench, about a foot away from me. I forced a smile and nodded.

"Still weak," I said, looking away from him and at the green hills and pine trees before us. The hill that the house was built on continued upward, and on either side the land continued to rise and fall, dotted with trees and covered in grass shining in the morning sun. A gentle breeze blew from down the hill and soothed me as I breathed in deeply again.

"You probably will be for a while. Luckily, you can rest here for as long as you want," Rhys said, looking in the same direction as me.

I thought about telling him how I had to go to Isa, but it didn't feel right. We sat in silence for a few moments, until the pressure grew too much for me to tolerate.

"Will you really forgive me?" I asked, turning swiftly on my seat to look at him. I felt my whole body angle towards him, both compelled to be near him and fearful of his response.

"I can forgive you and still feel slighted, can't I?" he said, meeting my eyes with slow deliberateness. I could sense the conflict he felt inside.

"Yes," I agreed. "Will you... Can you ever trust me again?"

He was silent for a while, allowing his gaze to turn to the hills again. His brow was set and serious, his jaw tense as he thought over my question.

"I don't know," he said eventually, refusing to look at me.

I didn't want to respond to that, as it was the exact, painful answer I expected. Maybe it was because I expected it that it didn't hurt that much; it was easier to accept. I had lost his trust, and I deserved that.

"I'll always be scared of you leaving again," he said, his voice soft. I stared at the profile of his face, feeling a stab of regret run through my chest. Somehow, that sentence hurt me more than him admitting he couldn't trust me.

"I won't," I said without thinking. It was an instinctive reaction, the need to let him know that that wasn't what he should be concerned about, that I never wanted to leave again. He turned to look at me, his eyes wary as he studied my face. "I won't," I repeated, more forceful. He blinked. "I don't ever want to leave you again. If that's why you don't trust me—"

"I didn't think you would leave before. But you did," he murmured.

I shut my mouth, not wanting to argue with that. I realized again that he had every right to feel what he was feeling.

He let out a deep sigh, and I let the silence fall between us, sitting stiffly on the bench with my hands folded in my lap, watching the streaks of clouds stretch across the sky. I nearly jumped when he began speaking again.

"I have questions, Eira. I want to know what happened," he said, his voice still soft. He spoke like he was scared of upsetting me, but I was more than ready to talk about everything that had transpired since we had separated.

"I climbed Aornadur," I said, and I felt him staring at me.

"What happened?" he asked. "Where is…?" he trailed off, not saying her name.

I stared at the treetops wavering in the breeze, brushing against each other, dark against the bright sky. "Varina found us. Near the base of the mountain. Liliwen… She didn't…"

I felt my voice crack again, but it was more permanent this time. I barely stopped a sob from coming out, and I took a few moments to compose myself.

"I'm sorry," Rhys whispered after a few moments. I shook my head, only then feeling how matted my ponytail was as it brushed over my neck.

"It was my fault. I shouldn't have let her come with me," I whispered.

"Let her?" Rhys repeated.

"She followed me. I wanted her to go with you and Runa, but she refused. And I believed that…that maybe she deserved to come and find the answers with me. But she didn't deserve…what happened." Now I was looking at the ground, the downtrodden grass and damp earth beneath my boots.

"It wasn't your fault, Eira," Rhys said. I felt as he shifted on the bench, facing towards me. He held out a hand to me, and I looked up to frown at him, wondering what he was doing. "Listen to me. You cannot blame yourself." His eyes were open and unguarded, warm and asking me to understand his words. I placed my hand in his without much thinking, wanting nothing more than to feel the warmth he was offering me. His fingers clasped around mine with strength that I didn't have, and he let our hands drop to rest on my leg.

"I don't know how to not blame myself," I said, feeling the tears finally escape from my eyes. His fingers squeezed around mine for a second, like he was trying to keep me grounded.

"What happened to Varina?" he asked.

"She…fell. I pushed her. She was lost in the snow… It was an avalanche. She didn't survive." I remembered watching her tumble, how I felt nothing, how I could only think of Liliwen.

"Then you avenged Liliwen's death," Rhys said. I sensed him looking at me, but I couldn't raise my head. The memories of that night were nearly overwhelming.

"I suppose," I whispered. "That isn't worth much to me."

"I'm sorry, Eira," he sighed.

"It's my fault," I repeated.

"You shouldn't have had to go through that alone," he said. I looked up at him at that, suddenly indignant. My eyes met his, and I nearly faltered at the kindness there, but my emotions couldn't be stopped.

"I chose my path, and I got what I deserved for it," I said. "I was selfish and got my friend killed because of it."

"Eira, listen to me," Rhys said, leaning towards me and gripping my hand—not hard, but comforting and compelling. "I really need you to hear me. If you blame yourself for this, you won't ever move on. You kept going without her, didn't you? What kept you going?"

I blinked at him, sniffling once. "I knew she wanted me to," I said after a moment's pause.

"And would she want you to blame yourself?"

I glared at him, hating the question because I so clearly knew the answer. "No," I mumbled.

Rhys nodded, smiling gently at me. I felt shame fill me, the feeling that he was being far too kind to me after all I had done. "Can you tell me what happened when you got to the top?"

I felt my stomach flip as I considered this. I wanted to tell him everything, so that someone else would know what I had been carrying with me since those conversations with Bem and El. I nodded slowly, organizing my thoughts.

"They told me how to find more Sacreds. Ones that might help us." Rhys nodded, brows set as he listened intently. "I have to go to Isa. They gave me a book. I have to deliver it to the current Seer. A woman named Tsukina." He frowned at me as he processed this, then nodded once again, slowly.

"The island. Isa," he said.

I nodded, feeling how my face was blank. "They said that all the Sacreds exist right now, for the first time. There are many more spread through the Four Lands. Tsukina can help us find them."

A hint of a smile played at the corner of his mouth. "Us?" he said. My stomach flipped again, but I held my ground.

"Come with me," I said, this time trying to squeeze his hand. His smile grew, but I could see the sadness in it.

"How do I know you mean that?" he whispered.

"Being without you was the worst pain I've ever been in," I responded, breathless, the honesty hurting my chest. "As much as I hurt you, I hurt myself too."

My breathing stopped entirely when his hand let go of mine, and I thought for just a moment that he would stand up and leave. But then his arm wrapped around my shoulders and pulled me against him, his other hand running over my hair. I felt him take a deep breath as I slowly returned the embrace, putting my arms around his waist.

"Then let's go to Isa," he murmured, and I nodded against his shoulder, as both swirling feelings of fear and surety rushed through my abdomen.

A sudden bang to our right had us jumping apart from each other, and when I turned to find the source of the noise, I saw Runa standing with her arms folded, glaring at us. The door swung on its hinges from the back of the house just behind her, but she didn't seem to notice as she glared at both of us.

"I'm going with you."

"You were listening to us?" Rhys asked, clearly surprised by her behavior as he glared back at her.

"Yes, and you're not leaving me again," she said, looking directly at me. I stared back at her, trying to keep my face neutral.

"I want you to come with us, Runa," I said evenly.

"Really?" she said, raising an eyebrow in disbelief. She took a step towards us, tension in her voice and body.

"Yes, really. If you were listening to our conversation, then you know that I regret leaving you."

"I know you regret leaving Rhys," she said, now turning her gaze away from me. I resisted the urge to sigh, and then turned to Rhys.

"Do you mind allowing Runa and me to speak in private?" I asked him. He gave me a faint smile and nodded, standing up quickly.

"Be nice, Runa," he said as he walked past her and disappeared through the back door to the house. I looked at Runa but she was still avoiding my gaze.

"Would you like to sit?" I asked, gesturing to the space on the bench next to me.

"No," she said, glaring at the hills beyond the yard.

"What can I do to make it up to you?" I asked.

Runa scoffed, before finally turning back to me. "You can't. What you did was—"

"It hurt," I said, nodding. "I know."

"How did you know that Varina wouldn't attack me again?" she asked. It was a good question. I could tell from her tone that she had never been worried about that happening. She was looking for a gap in my logic.

I shook my head. "Two reasons, but I'm not sure you'll accept them." She rolled her eyes, and I began to feel anger rising in me, but I managed to control it. "I had something of hers that I knew she wanted back. And I also knew that I was the person she had been sent to find. That day in the pass— she probably saw you first and couldn't help herself, wanting revenge. But that was a mistake, and I didn't think she would let herself get so distracted again."

Runa pursed her lips. "You were guessing."

"It was an educated guess."

"It was stupid. You leaving was stupid."

"You think I don't know that?" I yelled. Her eyes widened at the sudden outburst, but I stood up from the bench to face her, feeling my anger energize me. "You think I haven't regretted leaving you every moment since? Everything went wrong because of my choices. You don't have to forgive me, but at least understand that I already know I made a mistake."

I was breathing heavily, from the anger and the effort it had taken to stand up and yell, but Runa was perfectly calm and still. Her expression had softened, her shoulders had relaxed, and her hands were at her side.

"I believe you," she said, her voice still strong but subdued, all of the anger gone from it. She stepped slowly over to the bench and sat down beside me, and I hesitantly sat down as well, studying her closely.

"Thank you," I said after a moment. She nodded but didn't reply, and we sat in silence for a few moments, the breeze blowing between us.

"So you're going to Isa," she said after a while, regarding me from the corner of her eyes.

"Yes. And I want you to come too. You said you wanted to," I replied.

"The adventure isn't over yet, and I don't want to be left out again," she said. "There is much I have to learn."

"Learn?" I asked, turning to frown at her. "What do you mean?"

She smiled at me, slightly lopsided. "I guess you haven't figured it out yet."

"Figured what out?"

Instead of replying, she grabbed my arm and pulled up my sleeve with jerky movements; I was too surprised to really react. She leaned forward and looked closely at the jagged scar, faint against my skin, and frowned deeply.

"Whoever stitched this did a good job," I said, uncertainly. "You can barely see the scar."

Runa raised her eyes to mine, her eyebrows knit together in an odd look of confusion. "There were no stitches, Eira. Can't you tell by looking?"

I stared at the scar, now feeling just as confused as Runa looked. Then I saw how the scar was silver, how it was thin and smooth. It wasn't just healed well—it was healed with magic.

"An Eos did this?" I murmured. "But..." I trailed off as I considered the logistics of finding an Eos in a kingdom that was hostile towards them. Runa nodded, her expression serious and her eyes concerned, asking me to understand.

"Lucky for you," she said, her voice uncharacteristically soft as she forced a weak smile, "there's one quite close by."

I paused, knowing she could mean one of two things, and not knowing which was more likely. Either she knew that I was an Eos, or she had somehow found another Eos and gotten them to heal me. She noticed that I was frozen, stuck between two thoughts, and her words began to spill out. "I'm not talking about you...but Rhys did tell me who you really are. He had to, to make your departure make any kind of sense to me." I felt my mouth open in surprise, but I couldn't think of any response. I was confused as to why she had let me stay at her house, why she had made sure I had been taken care of, if I was one of the people she hated most in the world. "Obviously, you didn't heal your own wound, Eira..." She held my gaze with a softness she rarely showed. "I did."

It was then I felt an energy that hadn't been there before, a gentle flow of healing that wound around my arm. The scar was set but the energy soothed some of the residual pain I had been ignoring. I blinked as I looked at my arm, and then my head snapped up to stare at Runa.

"I've been...hiding parts of myself for some time," she said. She was worried, I realized. Worried that I would reject this part of her the same way all of Aorlanda had. But my mind was still processing what had just been revealed, and I couldn't come up with the words to comfort her. "I've been hiding for years," she continued, starting to find strength in her voice once again. "But when Rhys returned with you...and you were barely holding on, I knew I had to try."

"Why have you been hiding?" I asked.

"You remember I'm from Tennart, right?" she said. I nodded. "I was training to be a magistrate there. Like how you were a Benadur." She paused, took a deep breath, and continued. "I didn't want that life. So I ran away, started working on ships. Eventually, I made my way to Aorlanda and Garett took me in. He told me that if I wanted to survive, I would have to hide who I am—hide that I'm a Drekligr. And the thing is—he was right. I wouldn't have made it this far…and I'm lucky that he worked through his hatred of Drek and saw who I was beyond that."

I thought she was giving him far too much credit, but I chose not to comment on it. "I hadn't used my powers in ten years when I saw you last week. You were shivering violently, unconscious and burning up. This cut was so infected, it was swollen and…" She shook her head, clearly disgusted just at the memory. I knew it must have looked pretty awful for even Runa to be affected by it. "Rhys brought you straight here because I had told him the truth about me, and he knew the only way to save you was to use magic."

"That must have been difficult for you," I managed when she paused. She nodded, appearing lost in her memories.

"I didn't think I could do it. I had barely learned to heal even before I ran away… But I couldn't leave you like that." She studied the ground, turning her face away from me.

"Even after I left you?" I said.

"Of course," she replied immediately. She was frowning at a small rock half buried in the dirt. "I'm not a monster. Plus," she sighed, finally sitting back up to look at me, "if I didn't save you, I was concerned how Rhys would react."

I grimaced. "That's a fair point," I conceded. I looked down at the scar, shimmering in the sunlight, then back up at Runa. "Thank you."

She smiled but shook her head. "You don't have to thank me. It's enough to just journey with you once again, on this next adventure. So…tell me why exactly we must go to Isa. And who is Tsukina?"

I couldn't help it—I laughed, a short, huffing laugh, when she asked those questions and looked so genuinely confused. "We still have much to discuss," I said with a nod before she could ask me why I was laughing.

She grinned.

>«<

Runa and I talked for a long time on the bench, and I told her everything that had happened, just as I had told Rhys. I told her everything Bem and El had told me to do and tried to explain the Prophecy as best I could. And when I told her about Liliwen, she attempted to comfort me and told me that it wasn't my fault, just as Rhys had. I appreciated how they tried to help, but knew that there was nothing they could do to ease my guilt.

When the sun was in the middle of the sky, she suggested that we return inside the house and eat a midday meal, which I readily agreed with. Discussions of magic, Sacreds, and Isa ceased while we ate with Garett in the kitchen again. Runa had told me before going inside that she wasn't quite yet ready to tell Garett that she would be leaving again so soon after returning home, so not to talk about any of it in front of him for the time being. I agreed, but also wondered how long it would take for her to be ready.

After our meal, I sat with Runa and Rhys by the fire in the sitting room, and Garett announced that he would be going into town for the afternoon.

"Does anyone need anything?" he asked us as he shrugged on his dark gray woolen cloak.

"No," I said, as Runa and Rhys shook their heads.

"I'll be back soon, then," he said with a small wave and a grin, then disappeared through the front door, closing it behind him.

"So you two have sorted it out?" Rhys asked immediately, looking between me and Runa. I grinned at Runa, who wore much the same expression and we both nodded.

"I'm not mad anymore at least," she said.

"And we know the truth about each other," I added.

"Ah," Rhys said, eyeing us with uncertainty. "That you both are—"

"Eos," I said.

"Drek," Runa said at the same time. We glanced at each other, both of us frowning slightly.

"Right," Rhys said, nodding. "And we're going to Isa?"

"Yes," I nodded. "All three of us."

Rhys grinned. "To find Tsukina."

"The Seer," I said, nodding again.

"She'll help us find the other Sacreds," Runa said, attempting to recap the conversation I had had with her.

"Exactly," I said. "Bem made it very clear that she can use the Prophecy to help us."

"Which is a blank book," Runa said, not hiding her doubt as she raised an eyebrow at me.

"It is to us, but not to Tsukina," I insisted. Runa didn't argue with me but I could still sense that she was unsure.

"So the journey continues," Rhys sighed, gazing at the dancing fire, an odd smile playing at his lips.

"We're closer to stopping the Syrthiaid," I said, hoping to add some positivity.

"And one of them is dead already," Runa said with a humorless grin.

"Yes," I agreed with a weak voice, once again seeing Varina get swept up the snow, hurtling down the mountain. I mourned the fact that I did not get to cut her down the way she had Liliwen. But still, I felt relief knowing that she was gone from this world.

Another thought played on the edges of my mind, something vitally important that I hadn't told Rhys and Runa. I would have to work up the courage to say the words out loud, and I found myself worrying over this as the conversation turned away from our goals to what we would have to do to prepare for the journey. I hadn't told them another truth about me, one that I had barely accepted myself.

"And your weapons?" Runa asked, running down her checklist of items required. "What arms do you have?" She looked at me, tilting her head slightly as she frowned.

"A greatsword," I said. "A bow and some arrows. Perhaps I should get more," I said, having a hard time thinking of anything else besides what I needed to tell them, but didn't know how. "And a dagger," I added before she could move on. "Varina's dagger."

Runa glanced at Rhys, then back at me, her eyebrows pinched in worry. "Rhys told me…about your visions. That the dagger made one happen," she said slowly. I looked at Rhys who was obviously uncomfortable, but I didn't mind at all that he had told her that. It saved me from having to explain a few things.

"Yes," I agreed, then took a deep breath. "I have visions of the past. The dagger was a catalyst for a couple of the visions I have seen. It showed me moments from Varina's past."

"Have you had any more of them?" Rhys asked, unable to hide his concern.

"Yes." I nodded. He frowned, perhaps put off by how casually I was responding to their questions. My visions had been a point of stress for me before, but back then I hadn't known what they were. Now that I knew why it was happening to me, it was both more frightening, and comforting.

"Eira?" Rhys said, his eyes darting over my face as he studied my expression. "What happened?"

"I found out the cause," I said, looking from his face to Runa's. Both stared at me, Runa leaning forward slightly. "I'm…a Sacred. I'm called the Rememberer." The words were out, hanging in the air between us, and for a few long moments neither of them moved or blinked.

"What?" Rhys asked finally. "The…the what?"

"The Rememberer. I have the power to see the past through memories. All of those memories—they were all real, just as they had actually happened." I waited for one of them to interrupt me, but they both seemed to be frozen, caught in their surprise. "I'm a Sacred." I felt that it needed to be said again, as though repeating it would help them understand. Silence followed for only a moment, then Runa let out a low chuckle.

I glared at her. "This isn't a joke," I snapped.

She grinned at me, then shook her head. "I know—that's why I laughed," she said, then rubbed an eye wearily. "I feel I should be shocked, but I'm not."

I turned to Rhys, still trying to gauge his reaction. He looked back at me with a calm levelness, now making me feel a bit of surprise. Then his face broke into a warm smile, love in his eyes that made me even more surprised.

"That makes more sense than everything else you've said today," Rhys said.

"What?" was all I managed to say in response.

"You're at the center of it all, Eira. You're a part of this. And that's why…that's why it's you," he said, voice soft and expression distant. "That's why you're going to be the one to save Lithe."

>‹‹

When Garett returned as the sun was setting, Runa told him that we would be leaving in two mornings. I could tell that he wasn't pleased, but he seemed to understand that Runa would never stay in one place, and didn't put up any sort of opposition. He agreed to help us prepare for the journey, and we spent most of the next day doing exactly that.

Runa explained that we would most likely find a ship to Isa from the Cartanian port of Fregskye, which would take a week of traveling to get to. Nothing felt too great an obstacle to me after everything I had gone through; a week of traveling and weeks spent on a ship were inconsequential compared to all that had happened, and all that still needed to happen.

After dinner the night before we were set to leave, I excused myself to get some fresh air. I went to the front yard and sat on one of the beams of the old fence, the sturdiest one, and faced the town, watching the lights flicker in the windows from so far away. Crickets chirped all around me, hidden in the tall grass, and the air smelled of burning cedar as the wind blew the smoke from Ferning's fireplaces up the hill. I breathed in deeply; perhaps it wasn't entirely fresh air, but it still smelled good. When I looked up I saw millions of stars, and I felt like I knew them better somehow. They twinkled and glowed, and I felt like they were speaking to me.

I heard the front door open and shut behind me, and knew who it was even before he spoke. "I just wanted to make sure you're okay," Rhys said in a hushed voice, as though trying not to wake someone sleeping nearby. He came to stand beside me, leaning his forearms on the beam that I was sitting on.

I turned to grin at him. "Making sure I'm not running away again?"

He flushed, which I could just barely see from the light of the lantern I had brought into the yard with me, but then he smiled when he heard how playful my tone was, how the joke glittered in my eyes. "Maybe," he said, continuing the game. "But it seems you weren't even considering running this time."

I shook my head. "I wasn't," I agreed, suddenly serious. "I'm not leaving you."

He stood up straight, and I turned to face him. He was much taller than me, as the fence I was sitting on was low to the ground, but I enjoyed looking up at him, I enjoyed how close he stood to me. Maybe he saw that in my eyes, or maybe he didn't want to wait anymore. All I knew was that we moved at the same time, my hands reaching up to grab his cloak to pull him to me, and his hands cupping my face, tilting me towards him.

The kiss was just like him, soft but firm, warm and comforting, like a fire had just been lit in my soul. His arms wrapped around me and pulled me impossibly closer and I simply allowed myself to feel, for the first time in a long time, feel without thinking. His lips moved against mine with insistence and I answered him and mimicked him, and nothing else mattered but how we moved and the warmth that we created.

I felt the stars dance overhead as I breathed in cedar and Rhys and dewey grass, my arms wrapping around his shoulders, grounding me as I felt my heart settle in calming joy.

>‹‹

When the morning of our departure arrived, I was more than ready. Garett walked with us to the small stables he had beside his house, and we were all quiet in the foggy morning, our boots sinking in the wet grass.

Inside the stable, Garett approached Sindri, then turned to look at us with a quizzical expression. "Are you sure you don't want to keep him?"

Runa shook her head. "You need a good horse. And we have no use for him."

Garett considered this as he reached out a hand and patted Sindri's neck. The gelding let out a low huff, but remained relaxed, regarding Garett with curious eyes.

"Well, I thank you," Garett said, smiling at Runa, and then Rhys and me. "I haven't had a horse for a few years. Perhaps I'll get out of Ferning more often now."

"And perhaps you'll finally have a friend," Runa muttered as she led Freya from her stall. Garett laughed, not offended by the jab. He stepped outside with Runa to help her saddle Freya, while Rhys and I retrieved Nimue and Cai. I followed Rhys and Cai from the stable, smiling despite myself; it felt like things were returning to the way they were meant to be.

A few minutes later all of the horses were saddled and ready to go. Runa turned away from Freya slowly, facing Garett with hesitation.

"Come on," Garett said, a soft smile on his face. "Don't be getting doubts now."

"I'm not," Runa said quickly. "But you know I don't like leaving anyway."

"Yet you continue to do exactly that," he replied. He wasn't upset; perhaps a bit sad, but he also understood Runa well. And I could tell that he was proud of her.

"Maybe you shouldn't have settled down, old man," Runa said as she folded her arms and glared at him. "Then you could come with us."

"Old man," Garett laughed. "Exactly. I'm too old for adventures. I'll just have to live vicariously through you."

He held out his arms, and she hesitated for only a moment. Then she closed the distance between them and returned his hug, squeezing him and causing him to let out a low "oof" in response.

When they stepped apart and Runa returned to Freya's side, checking the straps for the fifth time, Garett turned to Rhys and me. "I know she doesn't need it, but try to keep her safe," he said. I nodded, not able to stop a smile from spreading across my face.

"I won't let anything happen to her," I promised, and Garett seemed to study me for a moment, hesitating, then nodded with his easy smile only growing.

We said our goodbyes to Garett, got in our saddles, and then urged our horses onward. They were more than ready to get back on the road, setting off at a quick walk with barely any pressure from us. We descended the hill that Garett's house was built on, making our way to the main road and then passing through the small town of Ferning in the gray dawn. It was early enough that most of the town was still asleep, and we remained quiet, as though scared of making too much noise.

Then, when we got to the forest, and the sounds of birds and squirrels and the wind rustling the branches met my ears, I turned and looked at my friends, riding on either side of me. And I couldn't help it—I let out a small laugh.

"What's funny?" Runa asked as she frowned at me. I sensed Rhys looking at me too, and when I turned to him I saw his eyebrows furrowed in confusion.

"Nothing. I'm just…happy," I said, not understanding it either.

"Happy?" Runa repeated. She snorted and shook her head. "Nearly dying changed you."

"Maybe," I agreed, turning back to Rhys. His expression had smoothed back to a small smile, and I felt my heart flutter at the sight. Happy. Maybe that word didn't really capture how I felt.

In that moment, I saw how everything had changed. How time had moved and shaped me, pushed me and cut me until

I bled. How it had healed me and comforted me. How time and change were inevitably the same. The only constants in our lives, catalysts for the most wonderful joy and the deepest pain.

It was in that moment that I felt like I could sense the future. I felt how it twisted and turned in front of us, like a winding road meant to make us disoriented. Humans naturally resist confusion and search for the path that makes the most sense; the route that feels most familiar.

But I knew that wasn't for me. I knew I would follow those twists and turns until it brought me to the end, wherever and whatever that happened to be.

The truth settled over me with a surprising amount of comfort, like a warm cloak in an icy forest. My journey had just begun, and I would continue on until the end.

Pronunciation Guide

Adelais- Ah-dell-ays
Aerona- Air-oh-nah
Age- Ah-jj
Aneira- An-eye-rah
Aorlanda- Ay-or-long-ah
Aornadur- Ay-or-nah-durr
Awyrcred- Aw-er-crehd
Awyrlyfr- Aw-er-lee-fur
Benadur- Ben-ah-door
Benaty- Ben-ah-tee
Bevyn- Beh-vin
Brynffynon- Brin-fin-non
Caergarth- Care-garth
Calliten- Kahl-it-in
Cartania- Cart-an-ee-ah
Ceridwen- Care-edd-when
Cerys- Care-is
Conotra- Koh-no-trah
Dafyd- David
Dennu- Deh-new

Deryn- Dare-in

Drekligr- Dreck-lee-grr

Durnaland- Durr-nah-land

Einarra- Eye-nah-rah

Elfyn- Ell-feen

Eosiaid- Ey-oh-see-aid

Fethwen- Feth-when

Fjall- F-yall

Fynnonbach- Fin-non-bock

Geirr- Gare

Gruddws- Grith-us

Grundar- Gren-dar

Gwanwynn- Gwahn-win

Gwynt- Gwint

Gwythllan- Gwith-lahn

Gywenn- Guh-when

Hanien- Han-ee-ehn

Hartania- Heart-ayne-ee-ah

Himminir- Him-in-near

Ioan- Yo-inn

Isa- Ee-sah

Kyonto- Ki-yawn-toe

Lagey- Lay-ghee

Liliwen- Lil-ee-when

Linra- Lean-rah

Llanwenyth- Lahn-when-ith

Llewellyn- Lew-ell-in

Maenynys- Main-in-is

Mariwen- Mah-ree-when

Myneth- Min-eth

Mynyddpen- Min-eth-pen

Naani- Nah-knee
Nefyn- Neh-feen
Nimue- Nim-way
Owain- Oh-wayne
Regilisia- Reh-gill-ee-see-ah
Remisia- Reh-mee-zee-ah
Rhea- Rey-ah Rhys- Reese
Riki- Ree-kee
Rodljost- Rode-ill-ohst
Ronoa- Roh-no-ah
Runa- Roo-nah
Seren- Seh-ren
Shukoria- Shoe-core-ee-ah
Silvania- Sil-vahn-ee-ah
Sindri- Seen-dree
Syrthiaid- Sirth-ee-aid
Tamania- Tah-main-ee-ah
Tan y Mor- Tahn-ee-more
Tennart- Ten-art
Thronsurian- Thron-sir-ee-an
Toryth- Tore-ith
Tremenra- Treh-men-rah
Tsukina- Tsu-key-nah

About the Author

Hello! I'm Carly, a lifelong lover of fantasy. I'm proud to finally share my novel, "The Eosiaid," with the world. Besides writing, I enjoy practicing archery, collecting pretty art prints, and exploring the beautiful nature in my home state of California.

www.carlyfeldmanwrites.com
@carlyfeldman_writes

www.ingramcontent.com/pod-product-compliance
Lightning Source LLC
Chambersburg PA
CBHW031512010826
48973CB00013B/942